LOVE IN T

He could do this for he
could run her ragged until she didn't remember her own
name, squeeze every last drop of passion and pain from
her body, leave her languid as sea kelp washed upon the
shore.

He wanted to.

He wanted to be the white knight that swept her off her capable feet, the man she turned to when the storm thundered.

She ground herself against him. Her hands tangled in his hair. Her teeth clamped down on his lip hard enough to draw blood. It would heal her, and she took it as her right. The darkness raged up inside him, all semblance of control thrown over for a moment as his primitive self demanded he take what was offered and drive himself into her sweet bliss.

She sucked his tongue into her mouth. He saw stars.

But his civilized part heard the sorrow behind her moans. And his civilized part felt the shaking of her limbs and tasted the desperation in her kiss. No man was a saint, him least of all, but civilization depended on man controlling his instincts. Without that fierce self-restraint he was no better than Kingu.

Leif waited a beat for his blood to heal her wounds, and then he softly disengaged. He pressed his forehead to hers. Her heavy breathing bordered on sobs. His forearms supported her weight, while his fingers swept small, soothing circles acros

"It will b

The tens

ghost. She sl

ground. She

the top of he

Books by Kira Brady

Hearts of Fire: A Deadglass Novella

Hearts of Darkness

Hearts of Shadow

Hearts of Chaos
(coming February 2014)

Published by Kensington Publishing Corporation

Hearts of Shadow

A Deadglass Novel

KIRA
BRADY

ZEBRA BOOKS
KENSINGTON PUBLISHING CORP.
http://www.kensingtonbooks.com

ZEBRA BOOKS are published by

Kensington Publishing Corp.
119 West 40th Street
New York, NY 10018

All Kensington titles, imprints and distributed lines are available at special quantity discounts for bulk purchases for sales promotion, premiums, fund-raising, educational or institutional use.

Special book excerpts or customized printings can also be created to fit specific needs. For details, write or phone the office of the Kensington Special Sales Manager. Attn: Special Sales Department. Kensington Publishing Corp., 119 West 40th Street, New York, NY 10018. Phone: 1-800-221-2647.

ISBN-13: 978-1-4201-2457-6
ISBN-10: 1-4201-2457-9

First Printing: May 2013

ISBN-13: 978-1-4201-3197-0
ISBN-10: 1-4201-3197-4

First Electronic Edition: May 2013

10 9 8 7 6 5 4 3 2 1

Printed in the United States of America

To Ryan and J,
who put the "happy" in "happily ever after"

and

to Joy,
who is a ray of California sunshine in my grey Seattle skies

ACKNOWLEDGMENTS

This book was made possible by all the wonderful people who helped watch my new baby so that I could write. Thanks to Prince Charming, aka Mr. Kira, for being a constant source of support and inspiration. Thanks to Joy for being a kickass critique partner and friend. Thanks to the Cherry Plotters for their plotting assistance, and to Joy and Marni for talking me through the tangles. Thank you to Teresa Grasseschi, whose beautiful illustrations brought Deadglass Seattle to life.

This book is a work of fiction. It was inspired by my beloved Seattle, but the names, characters, places, and incidents are the product of my imagination or used fictitiously. There are no cliffs in Ballard. Last time I checked, there were no dragons either. But wouldn't it be fun if there were?

I will knock down the Gates of the Netherworld,
I will smash the door posts, and leave the doors flat down,
and will let the dead go up to eat the living!
And the dead will outnumber the living!

—The goddess Ishtar, from the *Epic of Gilgamesh*: Tablet VI

Chapter 1

Leif Asgard looked up when the blood slave slipped into the crowded council chamber. Hidden in the back of the mob, the slight figure blended with the shadows in a black sweatshirt. A few blue bangs stuck out from beneath the hood. Leif could pinpoint the kid with his eyes closed. No one else noticed. But Leif did, because he felt the ring on his finger softly thrum. It was his brother's ring, and Leif couldn't figure out how to get the damned thing off.

One more thing to curse Sven for. Worse, his brother had the balls to die and leave Leif to this madness. Six months since the Unraveling. Six months since the world turned upside down. Six months since all hell had broken loose, literally, and brought down the civilization he had come to depend on.

Six months since Sven had died and left Leif shackled at the reins of this runaway circus train.

From his seat at the defendant's gate, Leif watched Admiral Jameson ranting across the room. In his mind he turned the sound off like an old silent movie. He was tired of listening, tired of having to defend himself and his kind, tired of having to prove his right to exist when some moments he didn't even know if he believed it himself.

Admiral Jameson wore his navy uniform like a shield. Frayed about the collar and threadbare in some places, it was a nostalgic symbol of authority in the once great United States of America. The fallen government had few spokesmen left. Those who chose to fill the void were frightened, bullheaded, and incredibly paranoid. Jameson pointed his gavel at Leif, and Leif tuned back in. "—let me remind you, sir, that you are under oath. Do you mean to say you have never killed?"

Leif didn't think anyone could survive two hundred years without shedding blood, but the human admiral was having difficulty wrapping his head around the idea of immortality. There was any number of honorable reasons for killing in the course of his two centuries. There had been revolutions, riots, duels. Insults that couldn't be borne. Revenge. Justice. But Leif refused to be tried for past deeds in this laughable shoestring mockery of a court, judged by a mob of terrified mortals.

He wouldn't die for his brother's sins either.

"Dragons are not killers," Leif said, "any more than the lion on the Serengeti is a killer. A predator, yes, but man is also at the top of the food chain."

"Humans don't harvest souls!" Jameson shouted, and the mob in the council audience murmured its agreement. Leif could almost imagine them with pitchforks, right out of Shelley's tale. Time might progress, but humans stayed as ignorant and xenophobic as ever. Zetian had promised him this would be an easy council meeting, but it had turned into a trial.

"But you kill to eat," Leif said. "The imbibing of souls doesn't require the death of the donor. Think of it as a blood transfusion."

"You steal—"

"Our donors are willing." At least his were. "And this really isn't the point of contention, is it? Humans could choose to be vegetarians, but most of you don't. For a Dreki to choose not to eat souls would be suicide."

Tiamat blight him. He'd told Zetian this was a mistake. She sat on one side of the long council bench separated from the Kivati by Jameson and his fellow human representatives. It made a pretty tableau: two shape-shifting races forced to play nice beneath the terrified watch of the humans. Everyone had pulled together to help put the world back to rights after the Unraveling. Leif had left the political wrangling to Zetian, because she was experienced in this bullshit. Astrid Zetian had served Sven's interests on the Seattle City Council for four decades, right here in this room beneath the blithely ignorant noses of the humans. Since the Unraveling, she'd stopped dying her hair grey. She wasn't pretending to be human anymore. None of them were.

Leif didn't have Sven's silver tongue or Zetian's slippery morals. He shouldn't be here debating his people's right to live when he could be doing real work in his laboratory. He was a scientist, not a politician, and he was a damned good one. The Unraveling had unleashed a massive electromagnetic pulse from the Land of the Dead, which had fried the Aether. The Aether could no longer hold an electric charge. There were people dying in the streets. People cold and hungry without jobs, without the skills needed to live in a world without electricity, without shelter from the wraiths. Leif could help those people, but not *here*. He needed to get back to work inventing tools that could make a difference.

"Your kind put us into this situation," Jameson accused.

"Not *my* kind. Not the Drekar." Sven might have set up the fall of the Gate, but a Kivati man pulled the trigger. "Please stop lumping all supernatural races into the same group—"

"You are all killers!" Jameson shouted.

"Please." Emory Corbette, the leader of the Kivati, was elegant in a coal-black three-piece suit, silver rings in his ears. His ebony hair brushed his straight shoulders. A thin circle of violet—the tell of all Kivati shape-shifters—ringed his jet-black eyes. A vein ticked in his temple. His people were an ancient race who could shift into a totem animal: Thunderbird, Crow, Wolf, Bear, Fox, and the like. Corbette's totem was the Raven, and his sharp beak of a nose gave him away. He raised his hand, and a silent wave of Aether licked through the room, quieting tempers, easing the rabid murmurs of the crowd. "This is unproductive. We are all here to help rebuild civilization. We have the same goal. The new Regent is not his brother."

Thank Tiamat for that, Leif thought. But what if he was? He'd felt the darkness swirling in the empty space where his soul should have been. He could easily follow it down and get lost somewhere between despair and madness. It happened to all Drekar eventually. But Sven had always seemed so sane.

Corbette rapped his silver-tipped cane on the banister. Since the Unraveling, everything about the Kivati leader was sharper, crueler. "As a scientist, Leif Asgard was building steam and coal-powered technology in its heyday. He is an invaluable resource for reviving our technological capabilities and building a new world. Even if the Drekar deserve to be exterminated"—and his tone said they did—"we can't afford to lose his skills."

Leif granted Corbette a tight smile. After more than a century of bloodshed between their two races, he was hesitant to trust Corbette. Leif didn't want to be the Regent, and he had good reason. His people still needed a wartime leader, and it would never be him. Dragons might have survived the apocalypse better than most, given their thick hides and imperviousness to fire, but how many would want to live on in this barren new world? Their treasure hoards lay beneath miles of collapsed rubble and dirt. Their once-clear skies were constantly grey with thick volcanic ash. They needed someone to rally behind. A Machiavellian leader who could wield fear to keep them in line.

Not Leif.

Zetian finally decided to intervene. About damned time. She rose. With her black hair undyed, she didn't look a day over twenty-five, though she'd seen the fall of Genghis Khan.

Act charming and a little clueless, the elder Dreki had coached him. *Humans don't trust anyone smarter than them.*

She should be the one standing behind the defendant's gate answering questions, not Leif.

"Admiral, Lord Raven, gracious members of the council." Her smile caught their attention. Gorgeous like all dragonkind, she had the cat eyes of her Mongol father and the fair skin of her Norse mother. Few could resist her charm, even before she opened her mouth. "The Drekar bring many invaluable resources to the council. The Regent, in particular, is almost finished restoring the Seattle Gas Works so that we may have functioning gas to light our city."

Drekar and Kivati burned low on their stores of luminous gas. The humans had none. This was a project to aid all three races.

Out of the spotlight for a moment, Leif spared a glance for the blood slave. The invisible tether burned across the room like a live wire.

"Regent?" Zetian called his attention back to the damned meeting. "Why don't you share your progress on this project with the council. I'm sure they will understand how generously we put our resources toward the good of the whole."

"Right." He shuffled his notes. This was why Zetian had insisted he come. She wanted him to be the face of the Drekar. She needed him to explain the technical details of his project, not that Jameson would care. Leif could smell a ruse as good as the next fellow. But she wore him down until he agreed. She could be as bad as Sven. "The Gas

Works is an old coal gasification plant built in 1906 to create luminous gas for houses and streetlights. Though it was decommissioned in the 1950s, I've spent the last six months restoring it. Corbette has reopened his coal mine at Ravensdale." He nodded to Corbette, who acknowledged the fragile partnership with an answering nod. This was where the project got sticky. The city needed light. The Kivati had the coal; Leif had the factory. Both sides expected a knife in the back at any moment.

Another human on the council, the charismatic and fanatical prophet-minister Edmund Marks, raised his hand. Marks had uncannily predicted the Unraveling one day before it happened and had since then developed a fierce following of those who believed the destruction was heaven's wrath. A fire-and-brimstone preacher, he'd earned a seat on the council because his flock was as violent as it was numerous. His militant arm, the Mark of Cain, was made up of nothing more than organized thugs, but in a city without a police force, they had quickly become celebrated as justice dealers. They would protect anyone as long as he was human. "And where do you expect to put this gas? Who gets it first?"

"The old Victorian mansions on Capitol Hill and Queen Anne make the most sense. Many of them were wired for both gas and electric, as the victor in the gas/electric battle had yet to emerge at the time they were built. I've placed those houses at the top of the list for renovation."

"And how many humans live in those mansions?" Marks asked.

"Ah." Leif hesitated. He'd walked right into that trap. "Retrofitting regular houses for gas will take time."

The mob, who was mostly made up of Marks's rabid followers, hissed.

"Resources for mankind first!" someone yelled.

"Send Satan's minions back to hell!" another shouted.

Leif did his best not to roll his eyes. He sent Zetian a pleading glare. She raised her eyebrows a fraction. She wasn't going to take over and save this thing. Damn the woman. "First we need to get the Gas Works back into commission, then we can identify the most suitable buildings." He raised his voice to be heard over the crowd. "I need resources and man power to finish the job."

"What about wraiths?" a woman called.

"I don't think a few ghosts should be an insurmountable obstacle to retrofitting the—"

The mob started throwing things. More anger. More anti-supernatural hatemongering. The tide had definitely turned. After six months of working together, the survivors needed someone to blame. Leif made a convenient scapegoat.

"What about Kingu?" the woman shouted over the crowd.

"Please," Leif said. "Please hear me out. Light will help. Secure shelter out of the darkness—"

"Resources should be used for training human civilians," the woman called.

"We don't need more armed civilians," Jameson growled. He banged his gavel, but no one minded. "And if you're worried about demons, talk to Marks here." He jerked his gavel at the reverend. "We've got more important things to discuss. Moving on!"

Marks zeroed in on the speaker, and his handsome face broke into a sympathetic smile. He bent to whisper something to the grizzled admiral. Leif turned in his seat to locate the woman. It was the blood slave. She was still half hidden in the crowd, still hiding behind her black hood and hunched posture. He wouldn't let a coward derail his project. "Show yourself," he ordered. The bond between them cracked like a whip.

She jerked forward and threw back her hood. He was startled to find such a delicate face: a heart-shaped chin framed by long, blue-black hair. Coral lips, a slash of anger across her smooth skin. Short, sooty lashes above almond eyes. Those eyes sparked with hatred.

Interesting. In black jeans and a baggy sweatshirt, hunched shoulders and a scowl, she looked like a skinny punk kid. Leif would never have given her a second glance on the street. Perhaps that was her intent.

On his finger, Sven's ring hummed. Leif wondered what his brother had used her for. She looked too small to be trained as a fighter. Perhaps an assassin or thief? He tried to keep his mind from exploring other possibilities. The words "pleasure slave" rose unbidden to his brain.

"What do you want?" he demanded.

"Safety," she said and clapped her hand over her mouth.

Admiral Jameson rose. "What do you think we're doing? We need to control the real, flesh-and-blood threats, not ghosts or devils or spiritual woo-hoo. You got questions about King Whatever-his-name-is? Take it up with Marks on Sunday. He's in charge of the spiritual side of this endeavor."

"Kingu is real!" Her face flushed scarlet. "We must train citizen soldiers to recognize the aptrgangr and take them out. Establish a tougher curfew—"

"She's right, Jameson." Marks's smile widened in her direction. Leif's stomach tightened. The girl was pretty, and Marks could charm the panties off a nun. Leif might not want Sven's blood slaves, but he'd shoot Marks before he'd let any woman in his protection fall under the reverend's spell.

"Quiet, please!" Jameson ordered.

"Gas lighting is a waste of time until we address the direct threat," she continued. Her lips clamped around each word, but they slipped out anyway. "Wraith attacks have tripled in the last week. Hungry, weakened humans are easy prey for possession. And also to prevent weakened humans, the soul-suckers should be ki—"

"Stop," Leif ordered before she could rally the mob in a

direction he most firmly did not want to return to. "Stop. Thank you. You're correct. Safety is more important than power, but wraiths fear the light. The two tasks go hand in hand."

She glared at him with both parts hate and fear. Ye gods, it cut him. This hatred borne of prejudice he had little control over, but he never wanted to inspire fear in his dependents. He would never be a leader like his father or brother. Fear was not something he would seek out. She made him want to jump out of his chair and apologize, but he didn't know what for. For not being able to solve all the world's problems? For "sucking souls," as she so unflatteringly put it? For existing?

Her dark eyes flashed silver.

Leif caught his breath. It might have been a trick of the light.

But the mob swallowed her up in the next instant, and Marks reclaimed his attention. "The girl has a point. What we really need is protection against your kind."

"Yes!" Admiral Jameson sat back in his chair. "Finally. What can we do to protect our people from creatures like you? I don't know about this soul stuff, but I've seen what happens to a man after you do your kiss-of-death thing. It isn't right, it isn't safe, and, damn it, you should be stopped!"

Leif ran a hand through his disheveled hair. "And if I designed something like that, then could we stop this blasted waste of time?" He heard Zetian suck in a breath, but he was too tired to care. He'd botched this meeting, and he might as well continue.

Corbette, who'd been quiet all this time, gave a slippery smile. "It would be a show of goodwill."

"Fine." Forget wraiths, aptrgangr, and demon men—*Leif* was the monster here. The world might have turned upside down, but some things never changed. "Are we done?"

"Go." Admiral Jameson dismissed him. "But the council will be watching you."

Leif stood. "Good day, gentlemen, ladies." He strode to the council doors, and the crowd parted to get out of his way. The hall was empty. He concentrated on the malachite ring and reached out along the invisible tether that connected him to the blood slave. It pointed toward the stairwell. "Mademoiselle?" he called out. His unnatural hearing caught the slight sound of a door closing, and he ran to the stairwell, following the faint scent of rose petals. The need to find her drove him. He told himself it was because her eyes had flashed silver, and he had questions. A purely scientific inquiry. Except his pursuit of science burned with a cold flame.

This need burned hotter.

Leif opened the door onto a wide, circular staircase that was open in the middle. He peered over the banister and caught a glimpse of a dark hooded figure five floors below. Nothing else moved in the stairwell, so he threw his legs over and jumped.

Air swooshed past him. One flight passed. Two. Three more in close succession.

Bone and sinew shot out of his back, sending the sound of ripping fabric echoing in the tower. His membranous wings unfurled and caught the air, halting his free fall. He beat them once, twice, before dropping to his feet on the stairs below the woman.

Who scrambled backward like her feet were on fire. She pressed her back against the wall as if she could tumble through it to escape. The whites of her eyes showed, reminding him of a little black mouse in the paws of a cat.

She was terrified.

"Excuse me." He pulled his wings back into himself. He couldn't do much to repair the ripped suit. "I was under the impression you were familiar with my kind."

She said nothing, but he caught the glint of light off the knife in her hand.

"I need to ask you some questions. Tell me—" He stopped himself. "Please. Please tell me what you know about aptrgangr. About wraiths. Did you know your eyes flash silver?"

"*Pah-lease*," she mocked. Spinning, she would have run back up the stairs if he hadn't caught her by the hood of her jacket. She tried to knife him. He was faster. Defending himself, he grabbed her and pinned her arms so she couldn't move. So small compared to him, but surprisingly strong. Her loose black clothes hid muscle. The top of her head barely hit his sternum. He remembered the spark he had seen in her eyes in the council chamber. Her spirit called to him, heady and filling. He barely felt her struggle in his arms.

Leif hardly knew where he was, or what his body was doing, before he felt her lips beneath his. They were soft and so very sweet. She tasted of cardamom, like glögg at Yuletide, reminding him of warm fires and happier times.

He couldn't help himself. He dipped his tongue between those lips, seeking more, seeking deeper penetration and a fuller taste of her spirit.

Pain lanced through his tongue. He swore and pulled back. The metallic taste of blood spread through his mouth. The minx had bit him.

She scuttled back out of his reach. "Stay the fuck away from me." The knife shook as she wiped her mouth with the back of her hand, hard. She spit on the stairs. The bit of blood and saliva sizzled when it hit the worn wood.

With effort, he reined in the baser part of his being. What was wrong with him? He'd practically raped her soul in a stairwell. If he wanted to prove her fears correct, there was no better way to go about it. "Forgive me. I don't know what came over me—"

She laughed. It was a grim sound. "I know your kind. You're all the same."

"That is patently untrue." Though his actions a moment ago hardly supported that statement. He knew perfectly well that his brethren weren't in accord on the need for consent, but he had always held himself to a higher standard. This caveman routine was beneath him. "But I suddenly understand the need for chaperones. Instinct, in the face of a beautiful woman, turns a man into a flaming idiot."

"Fuck off."

"I only wanted to talk to you."

She snorted. "I know what you wanted."

"No, really. I—"

"Save your lies for the council."

Wasn't that a damning indictment of his honor and professional conduct? "Please. Let's start over. I'll introduce myself properly, will that do?"

"I don't give a—"

"Leif," he said over her. "Leif Asgard. Younger brother to your former—ah." He scrambled to find something reassuring. Announcing he now held her slave bond wasn't the correct way of going about it. "I'm a scientist. With your silver eyes, you could be a Shadow Walker. Am I right?"

"I don't know what you're talking about." She tried to inch past him in the stairwell without touching him. Stubborn woman. He admired her spirit. She might be scared, but she wouldn't be cowed.

Still, he needed her to cooperate. She'd sabotaged his session in the council, and he was still mad. Whether he liked it or not, they were tied together. He had stayed out of her way for the last six months—he'd avoided all the blood slaves since he'd inherited that blasted ring—and things had been going swimmingly. Now was not the time for her to muck things up.

The dragon in him disagreed. He growled at the thought

of letting her go now that he'd had a taste of her. But that was his baser self talking, and Leif ruthlessly tamped it down. The girl seemed to want to bite any hand that reached for her, even one given in aid or kindness. Tiamat damn him, but he wanted to reach for her anyway. He could still feel the heat of her lips, still taste her sweetness on his tongue.

She caught sight of his face and took a hasty step back.

Bloody hell. He shut his eyes quickly and prayed for self-restraint. Why would this skinny, pugnacious girl have such an effect on him? It must have been too long since he had last fed. He would have to resolve that issue immediately. This poor woman seemed to have enough on her plate without being ravaged by his demonic hunger. "I'm really not a bad sort," he said softly.

"Look, if you're so good, why don't you donate your blood to ward houses? Runes could keep those"—she swallowed—"*things* outside. People would be able to tell if their friends and loved ones had been taken. Possessed bodies wouldn't be able to pass over the threshold."

"You know runes?" he asked. "What kind of runes? Old Norse or Druidic? Who taught you? Which would you—"

She scowled. "Forget it."

"Would a human be able to conjure enough magic to use a rune? Perhaps a Shadow Walker could . . ." The puzzle hovered in front of him, so striking in his mind that he barely noticed his informant slipping away.

Until she tried to stab him in the balls on the way past.

He caught her arm a hairbreadth away from turning him into a eunuch. Her wrist twisted in his grip, and she dropped the knife. It clattered to the side. He overbalanced, and they fell, locked together, crashing down the oak stairs. He tried, despite the fact that this woman had attempted to castrate him, to protect her delicate skull from cracking on the hard ground. His large body curled around her so that he took the brunt of the impact.

Pain blossomed along his back and arms, shooting up his spine and along his limbs with red florets of blood beneath the skin. In a human those flowers would metamorphose into ugly purple bruises, but his Drekar blood sparked into action, healing the broken blood vessels and reinforcing the torn skin.

The woman moaned when they hit the ground. Leif lay still, praying the world would stop spinning sometime soon. He didn't let go of her. He couldn't. His muscles refused to work. His brain was foggy from being hit, repeatedly, on each step on the way down.

Beneath the fog, his body knew, instinctively, that she belonged there in his embrace. She felt good in his arms. She felt right. Her lithe body was soft and warm. He buried his face in her blue-black hair and breathed in her fragrance hungrily. She must use a rose-petal shampoo. He wanted to run his tongue over her skin.

His heart drummed loudly in his ears, drowning out all logic, all self-control.

Forget all pretense of civilization. Throw out all notions of decency. At this moment he wanted to spirit her away to a mountain cave where he could hoard her as treasure all for himself, like the dragons of old had done.

If he chose to do so, no one and nothing would stand in his way. He was a creature of power. Might made right. Besides, she had fought him and lost. By the ancient laws, she owed him forfeit.

She belonged to him.

Slowly, his head cleared and he realized she was whimpering in his arms.

Devil take him. This attraction was one-sided.

"Who hurt you?" It was obvious someone had. Someone like him, apparently. Leif wanted to cut out the bastard's heart and skewer his head on a pike.

"*You're* hurting me."

He was indeed. "I apologize." Again.

Leif grasped the banister and pulled both of them from the ground. He set her gently away from him. Digging in his pocket, he pulled out a card. "I truly would like to ask you a few questions in the name of scientific research. I also have information about the Shadow Walkers, should you be interested." He watched her face, but it was carefully blank. He couldn't tell if she knew who or what she was, or might be willing to answer some questions for answers of her own.

She didn't take the card.

"Please?"

"You could order me," she whispered. "I have no choice."

"But I won't," Leif said. So she knew he now held her slave bond. How could he assure her that he wouldn't abuse it? She would never believe that he sought a way to free them both.

"So polite now, huh?" She laughed darkly.

"I . . . ah . . ." Last time he checked accosting a woman twice in a public stairwell wasn't considered polite. He reached out, and she flinched. He carefully tucked his card in the pocket of her sweatshirt, and brushed a strand of sleek hair back behind her ear.

He wanted to cup her smooth cheek and pull her close for another taste of those luscious sweet lips.

But it was not to be.

"Take care of yourself, Walker." Leif stepped away slowly, not giving her his back in case she had another knife, but not moving as if he worried for his own physical safety.

He didn't. His emotional safety was another matter entirely. This young woman had much too strong a pull on his baser instincts. Like the moon's call to a werewolf, she brought out in him something he didn't recognize. Something monstrous.

Leif couldn't afford to become a raving lunatic. His experiments were too close to breakthrough. His people needed him. It was the only value of his damned soul. To betray his people would be unforgivable, for any reason.

"My name is Grace," she said softly, before he stepped through the door.

"Grace," he repeated.

The irony was not lost on him.

Chapter 2

Grace wiped volcanic ash off the thighbone with her sleeve and raised her hammer again. “Shine that closer, would you?”

Elsie obliged, moving the lantern so that it illuminated the cool ivory bone and Grace’s silver needles. The little bells around her wrist jingled with the motion, warning off spirits. Above them, the sky was black with fifteen thousand crows returning to their roost on Queen Anne.

Grace concentrated on carving the rune—Eihwaz for protection, Thurisaz for defense—and not on the debacle of that morning. Her outburst in the council chamber in front of her new owner. He had forced her to speak. Even Norgard—the bastard—hadn’t shamed her so publicly. She’d tried to stab Asgard. Antagonized him. Called him a liar. Was she trying to get herself killed? She was usually so much smarter than that, but the new Regent had thrown her off. It wasn’t his looks; they were just as unbearably handsome as all Drekar. Maybe it was his ridiculous manner, like she’d insulted his honor. Ha. Drekar didn’t have honor.

The cold seeped into her exposed fingers, and she tightened her grip on the silver needle and hammer. She had a reputation for solid spell work, and she didn’t want to mess this up. A whole house load of Ishtar's Maidens, including the one chattering over her shoulder, was counting on her.

"So then I says to him, 'That position will cost you double,' and he pays it!" Elsie said. "How a miner scrounged up silver like that, well, something isn't right. Not in the mine, he didn't. And him with the coal dust still lining his nails. Then he leaves me with a pamphlet from that new church they're building out at sea. You know, the white one with the huge watchtower?"

"Uh-huh," Grace said. She swore as her hand slipped. After three hours carving in the cold, they were starting to shake.

Elsie swung the light. "Like I want to be preached at by the likes of him!" She had once been a good girl from a good family, but even a good girl had to eat. The Houses of Ishtar paid well, and most girls stayed on past their indenture. Protection. Shelter. Food. A little luxury in the better Houses. It was more than most had in Seattle's post-Unraveling economy. It was a good life, if you didn't mind the work.

Grace didn't judge Elsie, but she'd rather risk the mines herself. Luckily, she didn't have to make that choice. She'd been a killer long before the Gates that separated the Land of the Living and the Land of the Dead had fallen. During the Unraveling, cities had crumbled into the sea, Mount Rainier had erupted, countless people had died, and an army of wraiths had escaped into the living world. The wraiths preyed on the survivors and animated the dead. People would pay good money for protection. She'd already cut her blood debt in half. Only five hundred dollars remained between her and freedom.

The golden bands around her upper arms burned slightly, a reminder of the cost of her skills. Sven Norgard could have tossed her in a brothel instead of teaching her to fight. She supposed she had been lucky.

She hoped he rotted in hell.

"Grace? Reaper, are you listening to me?" Elsie moved the parasol so that the ash fell on Grace's work.

"Not if you call me that, I'm not." Grace rose from her crouch and rubbed the kink out of her neck. Even standing, she was a good deal shorter than Elsie, especially with the Maiden's platform slippers. Grace almost wished her boots had a heel, but then she couldn't run. Running was key. "Look, do you think if I—"

A yell from the street corner interrupted her. A moment later, a man ran into the illumination of the torches. Young and strong, he was limping, clutching his left arm with his right hand, and bleeding heavily from a gash across his skull. "Sam's dead!" Panic laced his voice. "They got . . . they got him. I couldn't, God!" He grabbed the bone fence and collapsed, half turning so he could see what was coming after him.

"It's Shelton. Nancy's best patron." Elsie shifted her weight from slipper to slipper, nervously glancing down the street, torn between her duty to the customer and fear of leaving the shelter of the wards. She stayed inside—smart girl. "I should get the Priestess."

"Sure." Grace tucked her tools into the pockets of her leather corset and zipped her hoodie back up. She pulled her bone knife from its sheath strapped to her thigh. "That's my cue."

The problem with wraiths was that they adapted. Unlike ghosts, which haunted their former territory wishing they could touch and taste and smell again, wraiths aggressively sought to regain their living senses. That meant acquiring a body, preferably a still mostly living body. Wraiths sought out weak or injured individuals, pushed their souls aside, and climbed in the driver's seat. Wraiths became aptrgangr, and aptrgangr crushed their victims with their superhuman strength and ate their flesh.

She was lucky the SOBs were too selfish to team up, because that would be a clusterfuck.

"Tell her to have my payment waiting in the kitchen when I get back," Grace said. "And no skimping, not like last time. Otherwise, I won't finish the fence or protect her patrons, and damned if she can find someone better to replace me."

"But you always come back," Elsie said. "You'd miss me."

Whatever. She couldn't do this for free. She needed the money, and her jobs since Norgard's death had been more dangerous and less lucrative. If the Regent sent her on a mission, she got to keep the cash. If she found a job on the side, she owed him a seventy percent take. That meant the fifty dollars she would make warding this fence would net her a lousy fifteen bucks, and she still had to eat. She was too desperate, and Ishtar's Priestesses could smell it a mile away.

Still, she was glad the new Regent had made himself scarce. No games to play, no tolls to pay. Even if it meant she had to live with her bruised ribs and collection of cuts. A little pain she could handle.

A year of training and four years of servitude might have been a lifetime. One step forward, two steps back, she would eventually win her freedom. It couldn't come soon enough.

One job at a time. First up: slay the two aptrgangr that were preying on the House's patrons.

Grace eyed the injured man. He was able to touch the rune-carved bone, so he was probably not possessed, but she didn't leave things like that up to chance.

"Get out of here," she told Elsie. Elsie turned, long skirt swishing out behind her, and walked back into the House as fast as her platform slippers allowed. The light from her lantern bobbed behind her, casting long, eerie shadows in the quiet street. Grace flipped up her hood and gave a low whistle. On the other side of the fence, the man whimpered.

A large cat materialized out of the shadows. Bear, furry and ferocious as his namesake. His long, black and white fur was clean of ash. A little brown mustache twitched on his upper lip. He regarded her steadily, blinking once.

Grace stepped through the gate, beneath the hanging bells that scared the ghosts huddled on the other side of the fence. Grace couldn't see them without Hart's Deadglass, but she knew they were there. The city was full of them. Spirits from all the ages man had walked this spit of earth still dressed in the clothes they had died in. They flocked to establishments where people congregated, hungrily searching for a whiff of passion. Sometimes they forgot they were dead. Ghosts were fairly harmless in this state, but after a while they all turned, twisting into something capricious and mean, hating the living for every breath they took.

Grace ignored them. She watched the cat and tipped her head in the injured man's direction. Bear lifted his paw and gave a lick. Not possessed then. Didn't mean the man was safe. She kept her knife at the ready. Beneath her palm, she felt the runes that ran up and down the bone handle. They tingled lightly as Aether settled in the deep grooves.

Bear stood and led the way down the brick-lined street. He cut a wide path around the injured man.

"Don't go down there, kid." The man's voice was hoarse. "Don't—"

Grace bared her teeth at him. She wasn't a kid.

His eyes widened. "Hey, I know you."

"No, you don't."

He pointed to her knife. "Norgard's blade. They say you ain't afraid of them—"

"Everyone's afraid."

"Thought you'd be bigger."

Grace scowled. She gave his head wound a cursory appraisal. Scalp wounds bled like a bitch, and this one was no different. Still, he'd probably live. "If you can make it to the front door, the madam will stitch you up." For a price.

"I can't—"

"Choose quickly," she said. "They're coming."

He shot a fearful glance down the block and started pulling himself into a standing position using a femur and pelvic bone in the fence. He left a trail of red fingerprints in his wake. She would help him, but she didn't like being touched.

Bear indicated the mouth of an alley. The brick fronts on either side were boarded up. At one time there had been a lively art shop and bakery fronting the alley, with flower baskets beneath the windows and a sunny outdoor seating area in the sheltered nook between the two buildings. Most importantly, there used to be a wide back entrance to the alley. She didn't know if it still existed. Well, fuck it. They'd find her sooner or later. Aptrgangr always did.

The man was wrong. She was afraid. Afraid of the wraiths. Afraid of becoming one of them, trapped within her own body. But she kept her fear like a lucky acorn in her pocket. It hung there with its reassuring weight. Fear kept her sharp. She'd curl herself around it every now and then, letting it cut her, letting it hone her senses. Enjoying the secret thrill of pain that told her she was still alive.

An alley opened onto the street, but the lamplight didn't reach past the mouth, leaving the interior in inky blackness. Bear weaved his way through her legs, the fur on his spine raised in warning. They waited down the alley of brick and charred wood: two young men with torn jeans and the smear of the coal mine in the lines of their skin. One was shorter, stockier, with unkempt black hair that hung over his eyes. The other was tall and skinny, with a receding hairline and a long nose that covered most of his face. Reminded her of Ernie and Bert from that old children's television show, back when there was still electricity, before the Unraveling.

The aptrgangr's movements were uncoordinated, their limbs jerky like marionettes. Classic symptoms of the newly possessed. Given time, a wraith would integrate seamlessly into its host, until even family and friends couldn't tell the soul within wasn't the same. They welcomed the aptrgangr within their sanctuary and were slaughtered. Next to Bert and Ernie lay the pulpy remains of what must have been poor Sam.

"Look, Bear. Beef—it's what's for dinner." Grace tossed her dagger in the air and caught it. The aptrgangr watched her with a hungry, desperate look, mouths hanging open like they could already taste her bloody flesh. Dream on.

The stockier aptrgangr—Ernie—seemed to be in charge. Lunging forward, he swiped out broadly with his muscled fist. It was almost too easy. Grace sidestepped and knocked him on the back of the head with the hilt of her dagger. He stumbled against the brick wall.

He was fresh enough that there was still a chance she could exorcise the wraith and save the human. No use getting more blood on her hands than she had to.

Bert paused a moment, head tilted to the sky to sniff the air. His eyes filmed white. Oh, shit. This one wasn't worth saving. He came at her fast, but she turned his height and weight advantage back on him by slipping beneath his arms and slicing her dagger at the soft spot behind his knees. He screamed, and she knew she'd hit. Score one for her.

Ernie had shaken off the head blow and came back for another. Grace grabbed one of his lurching hands and swung him like a human shot put into the wall. He bounced off and fell on his ass.

She spun just in time to avoid another lunge by Bert. Dropping to the ground, she kicked out and took his legs out from under him. She palmed one of the sharpened iron railroad spikes sewn into her jacket. Like many magical creatures, aptrgangr avoided iron because it leeched their strength. Before Bert could rise again, she drove the iron spike into his shoulder. He roared. She stabbed him again. Debris from fallen trees had collected in the alley, and she grabbed a thick branch and clocked him upside the head. Blood splattered the concrete, but still he struggled to rise, the wraith within giving the damaged body unnatural strength. It could get a new body if this one gave out; it just had to jump before she banished it beyond the Gate.

Straddling the aptrgangr, she checked her belt for the tools of her trade: Thor's hammer, a small copper-handled mallet about the size of her fist with Old Norse runes criss-crossing the iron head; hollow silver needles that held the blood ink; matches and a running iron for branding. She only needed the matches and brand for this job.

After checking to make sure Ernie was still down—he was struggling to roll over, his leg bent at an odd angle, blood matting the long hair to his forehead—she lit a match and set fire to the end of the branch she had used on Bert. The damp wood smoked a bit before it caught. She heated the end of the short running iron in the fire until the dark grey metal warmed to the color of ashes.

Bert bucked beneath her.

"Down, boy," she ordered, grabbing a fistful of shirt and slamming his head back against the concrete. She would be more careful with Ernie—still hopeful he could be saved—but Bert was a lost cause. Completing the ritual before the wraith fled was the hardest part of her job. It helped to knock the aptrgangr out first, as the loss of consciousness would confuse the dark spirit long enough to draw the brands.

Behind her, the cat hissed.

"Give me a minute," she said. The first line of the brand drew red across Bert's forehead. The smoke of burning meat sizzled off his pasty skin. Quickly she drew the other lines to finish three runes from Freya's Aett: Uruz, to bind the wraith to the body; Raidho, journey, to send the wraith to the Land of the Dead; and Thurisaz, the Gateway, to lock it behind the Gate where it belonged. Bert screamed, vocal chords breaking, as Aether swept through the runes to purge his body of the evil within.

Before she could complete the ritual, something hard slammed into her ribs. She screamed and fell, catching herself in a roll away from the unseen danger. Four more aptrgangr had snuck up behind her. Four! Ianna had said two, and Grace had never seen more than three in one place. Just her luck.

The bodies were young males, but the wraiths inside were older, more powerful. Coordinated limbs and a cocky hitch in their step. It would be easy to mistake them for humans—just another biker gang out to shake her for lunch money—except Bear was hissing, fangs out. His thick fur stood straight up in all directions like a fluffy porcupine.

Four on one. Even if she were fully healed and rested, her chances were much better for flight than fighting. She wasn't too proud to back down from a fight—death wasn't worth it, especially death without paying off the blood debt, forcing her to be an enslaved ghost, stuck on this side of the Gate. They blocked the mouth of the alley. Debris clogged the other end. Looking around, she didn't see any fire escapes she could flee up.

The ringleader slapped a large piece of broken rebar against his right palm. She'd bet her bone knife the imprint of that bar was right now decorating her ribs.

"Get out of here, Bear," she ordered.

He scrambled. Smart feline.

For a moment her rough-and-tumble facade grated off like the thin veneer it was, leaving just Grace, a scared girl with no one but a cat for company. For a moment, the shadows of this flesh-and-blood alley beneath her palms flickered into that other alley, on a not-so-different night, in a not-so-different part of town, where the truth of her vulnerability hit home in the smash and blood-soaked feast of those first undead. Casting off her human blinders.

Shattering her childhood innocence and leaving her horribly, dreadfully alone.

She wiped the dust out of her eyes. The gold slave bands heated, tempting her to use them. Their invisible tether worked both ways; the Regent to force her to his will, her to call him to her aid. Unlike him, she couldn't use it to trace his whereabouts. Unlike her, he didn't have to come when called.

She refused to go back to the way things were before the Unraveling. Asgard was a new master, but she wasn't that girl anymore. She was so tired. Her injuries hurt. New ones. Old ones. Over six months of bruises and scrapes and torn muscles. The scars she'd earned in the earthquake of the Unraveling and the burns from the fires afterward still decorated her skin. She'd never gone this long without a healing.

But she was determined to go it alone. Norgard hadn't been the golden savior she'd first thought him to be. She'd never make that mistake again.

The ringleader towered over her crouched position. He wore beige trousers and a white dress shirt, crisp and unmarked save for the constant fine ash that covered everything. His sandy brown hair was combed neatly to the side. The rebar smacked against his palm.

Muscling up her courage, she crooked her finger at him. "Didn't anyone ever tell you it wasn't polite to sneak up on a lady? Why don't you come over here and try that again."

"You smell good," the aptrgangr said. His even-toned voice echoed slightly, as if it came out of a cavern instead of a very human voice box. His eyes rolled in the back of his head.

She was in deep shit.

Leif tapped his cane along the bars of the barbaric bone fence of the House of Ishtar. Ianna, the High Priestess, had a flair for the dramatic. He needed to feed. It had been far too long, making him weak and dangerously unpredictable. He was a liability in this state. Every human with even half a soul looked good.

Tiamat help him before he killed someone.

The girl from the council trial, the blood slave with almond eyes and the scent of rose petals, had stuck in his head all day. All blood slaves were connected to the malachite ring, causing it to heat when one came near. But she had been different somehow. He felt the pull in more than the ring, and he wanted to know why.

Or maybe he was just avoiding what was really bothering him. Sven's iron crown smothered him. Every day revealed more sick machinations of his brother's design. Every day he realized a bit more how little he had known Sven at all. A twisted, power-mad individual. A man who in his depravity had engineered the collapse of civilization, all so he could free a demigod from hell. Leif wanted to hole up with his experiments and never emerge. But he couldn't. He had to set things right.

Worst of all, he missed Sven. Was it wrong to miss someone so obviously deranged? Madness came for all Drekar eventually. Watching the world change while he didn't. Watching everyone close to him die, again and again, a thousand lifetimes of pain and loss until he became immune to it all.

Leif wondered if Sven had known he had passed the point of sanity. Leif wondered if he would recognize it when it came for him.

The brick fronts of the buildings here in Pioneer Square were quiet, the street empty. The curfew bells had rung at six; the smart hid in their warded shelters and awaited the saving dawn. But there were few things that would mess with a man who turned into a twenty-foot-tall dragon.

The House of Ishtar inhabited an old Victorian mansion.

A warm glow poured out the leaded glass windows into the murky dusk. The plucky sounds of a harp and the grate of laughter filled the quiet night. Inside, young women in corsets and lace served the Babylonian goddess of sex and fertility. They ministered to the men who came to worship. Flesh. Blood. Skin. Sweat. Benediction could be found in the slick slap of skin on skin. Salvation waited in the hot press of lips and the slow slide inside a woman.

But not for him. He needed a higher calling than base lust. The Houses of Ishtar provided a safe, steady source of food for the Drekar. Admiral Jameson was right to fear his kind: without the restraint of civilization they could succumb to the soul hunger and wipe out mankind.

Leif paused to inspect the magic work of the fence. Norse runes marked the ivory surface. He knew few Drekar who still dabbled in the ancient runic magic and fewer humans who could wield it. Birgitta would know. He would ask when she came back from checking on her family in Oregon.

The marks drew Aether through them, but the spell was unfinished. The House of Ishtar, with its merry glow and enticing music, stood unprotected.

Leif turned away from the beckoning warmth and followed the tainted pull toward the mouth of a dark alley. He heard a harsh smack and the sick thud of a body hitting the pavement. Instinctively he knew what he would find.

He hurried. His skin grew taut over his human form. He felt his eyes slit with his dragon sight, the world narrowing to shades of blue and green, and a trickle of smoke escaped his nose. His hands Turned to claws, shredding his black leather gloves. He turned the corner into the mouth of the alley and stopped. Aptrgangr: those who walk after death.

They had the Walker surrounded, her back to the brick wall. Leif couldn't take his eyes off her. The long, blue-black hair obscured her expression. Four undead moved in around her. A thin man with a rope. A well-muscled assailant wielding a broken piece of rebar. Two more with wide shoulders and beefy fists. He couldn't stop the fear that gripped his chest at the sight of a woman under attack.

She held up a knife, but her arm jerked. The muscled man raised his rebar to strike.

Leif shook himself out of his stupor and roared. It didn't matter that he wanted nothing to do with the blood slaves. They were his. No one touched what belonged to him. He didn't know what this little human meant to him, but he intended to find out.

A roar shook the alley. The brick behind Grace trembled. Caught off guard, the aptrgangr loosened their hold on her limbs and she twisted free. A monstrous dragon tried to squeeze into the alley from the street outside. It was three times the size of a man and covered in rust-colored scales tipped in green that sparkled even in the dim light. It snapped its massive jaws at the aptrgangr, showing three rows of jagged white teeth. Smoke curled from the end of a long snout, filling the narrow passage with the scent of cinnamon and smoked meat. The green eyes—slit like a cat—glowed.

Grace's stomach dropped out the bottom of her feet. She took advantage of the aptrgangr's distraction and ran in the opposite direction. The wavy edges of her vision turned black. Her side burned—her rib good as broken—as if the dragon behind her had already set fire to her ailing body. All in a day's work.

Fleeing screams and the crunch of bones, she jumped over Bert's inert body and scrambled over a Dumpster at the end of the alley, only to be stopped by a crumble of bricks and trees. The street beneath her feet opened to expose the

Underground. She couldn't jump down there, not without canvassing an exit first.

No way out.

Grace squeezed herself between the Dumpster and the crumbled wall. Not hiding, *resting*, she told herself. But the blood beat in her ears, and the slow scrape of scales and claws on brick followed her down the alley. The knife in her hand trembled. She could barely raise her arm.

The dragon found her hiding spot no problem. He nosed away the Dumpster. Metal screeched across the pavement. An ancient being blocked the sky. His eyes focused on her: intelligent, powerful, curious. Scales rippled down a sinuous body. Strangely and terribly beautiful, like the sharp edge between pleasure and pain. It hurt her eyes to look at him. She wanted to stroke her hand across that long muzzle. She wanted to put her hand in the beast's mouth.

Freya's madness, she tempted fate. Again and again. One of these days some monster would bite her hand clean off. But that adrenaline rush drew her, lit her up like a tree at Christmas. When a girl was death's handmaiden, sometimes all she craved was to feel shockingly alive.

She squeezed her eyes shut against the temptation. The dragon mewed and drew nearer, butting her side like some great, demonic puppy. Pain shot through her rib, and she cried out. The dragon hissed. Cinnamon filled the air. His sharp teeth snatched her by the leg and pulled her out.

"What the hell do you think you're doing?" she yelled. "Let me go! Let me—*oof!*"

The dragon set her down gently, and she leaned her cheek against the cold brick ground, breathing heavily and waiting for the world to stop spinning. She was going to have a fucking headache when she woke up. Heat and light flickered behind her closed eyelids. She braced herself. She could imagine the Turn, because she'd seen it before; the scales shattering into sprinkles of light; the giant limbs shrinking to human form; the godlike naked physique bathed in a golden glow. Curse and thank the gods.

Norgard had always waited a beat, glorifying in his nudity, aware that it made Grace uncomfortable. She couldn't say the exact moment when her excitement and hero worship had given way to anxiety. He had known her dark secret. Her shame. She couldn't hide her fascination with the dragon's wicked beauty.

Most people thought the Drekar's monster form was most dangerous, but they were wrong. When faced with a twenty-foot-tall fire-breathing dragon, survival mode kicked in. A sane person didn't try to fight a dragon. A sane person ran and lived to fight another day.

The human Drekar form, on the other hand, was much more subtle. It specialized in cunning and deception. It was just as dangerous to her, but her primal instincts didn't get her feet moving first thing. The Drekar's looks made the sun stop in its orbit to get a good look. The ardor-inducing pheromones made a person want to rub up against it. It destroyed all reason.

They were gods among men; she didn't know how anyone mistook them for humans. Beautiful, terrible, erotic. She'd been sucked in when she was just a naïve sixteen-year-old, and she hated to admit, but they still had the power to turn her knees to jelly.

"It's a trick," she reminded herself.

Leif Asgard was no different. She kept her eyes averted. She would not let him affect her.

"What in Tiamat's name do you think you're doing?" he asked, voice deep with smoke and Aether.

Irritation flittered through her brain—she didn't want help—but reality came back as her left side throbbed around her busted rib. Steeling her face, she scrambled to a sitting position. The brick wall at her back steadied her.

He cast her a cursory glance and then bent over the fallen

aptrgangr, Bert, with his angry red runes burned into his flesh. Asgard's eyebrows lifted as he studied her marks. "Who taught you this?"

"Who do you think?"

"You need to burn the body, or it could come back."

"Thank you, Captain Obvious."

His glance cut through her. His eyes were emerald green. So mesmerizing, she could lose herself inside them, if the pupils weren't currently slit in anger. It popped the illusion that he was human.

Norgard would have punished her for failing a mission like this. Not immediately. He would wait, letting the tension curl in her gut until she wanted to beg him to do it already. The wait was worse than the punishment. Nothing so simple as a beating. Psychological games were his specialty.

Asgard ticked his fingers against his thigh. A curl of smoke drifted from his nostrils. She could think of a hundred reactions he might be contemplating, but—like his brother—not one flickered across his inhumanly beautiful face.

She wanted to push him. To make him snap that perfect composure.

With a nod, he decided. He turned to the aptrgangr body. His jaw dropped—unhinged farther than any human jaw could—and breathed the magic of his kind. A burst of flame lit the alley, controlled yet chaotic, shot through with gold and amber. Her shaking limbs curled toward the heat. She hadn't realized she was cold.

The body sizzled and the scent of burning meat filled the air. It bloomed and died in seconds. Even the bones melted, leaving a man-sized print charred into the brick.

The fire left starbursts in her eyes, and when they cleared, the Drekar Regent was leaning over her. His green eyes swept her body, cataloging her injuries, memorizing her weaknesses.

"I'm fine." She struggled to rise, pushing against the wall

behind her so that it took her weight. Somehow she found herself on the ground again. Crap.

A muscle twitched in his jaw. "I can see that."

"Just . . . resting."

He reached out, and she winced. His hand froze an inch from her cheek. His eyebrows rose a fraction. Damn, damn, damn. She usually had a better grip on herself. Never show weakness.

Slowly, he traced the outline of an old bruise along her jaw. His fingers trailed heat along her sensitive skin.

She couldn't stop the shiver that took her. "Cold," she explained.

"Hmm," he hummed, noncommittal. His hand dropped. "Those are old bruises. You seem intelligent. How did you get in this situation?" He caught her as she made a nosedive.

Grace started to panic at his large hands on her arm and waist. Her breath clogged in the cotton of her throat. Her pulse pounded. Sweat broke along her palms. This was nothing she hadn't survived before. She fought for calm.

"How long have you gone unhealed?" Propping her against the wall again, he crouched in front of her. He was naked. A new shiver wracked her, but not from the cold. Smooth, golden skin covered his muscled forearm. He smelled of cinnamon and something darker, like hot mulled brandy. Before she realized what she was doing, she found herself leaning into that scent.

No, no, no. His musk was messing with her head. She would not be an easy target. "Won't sleep with you."

Even Norgard wouldn't heal her in an alley. He had standards.

Asgard blinked. His shoulders shook. "Darling, I'm not desperate enough that roadkill looks remotely appealing. I doubt you've got enough life left in you for a good kiss, let alone a good shagging."

"Doesn't work if you don't," she mumbled. "Blood's not enough."

He was silent for a long moment. "You need to be healed." He Turned one finger to claw and sliced the vein in his right elbow. She felt his strong hands pulling her from the wall.

It was so easy to fall away from the cold brick into his warm embrace, but she fought it anyway. Her lips closed on his skin, and she couldn't help the moan that escaped her when her tongue found his hot rush of blood.

Her eyelids were too heavy to keep open. She let them close. She was going to have a killer heartache when she woke up.

Chapter 3

Leif cradled the semiconscious woman in his arms and forced blood into her mouth. Tiamat damn Sven to the bottom circle of hell. He watched her bruises fade as his healing blood did its magic. First the old ones disappeared. Then the new bruises turned purple, then black, then faded back into her clear olive skin. Beneath his fingers, her rib cage knit back together.

She was a tiny thing. What did she think she was doing, fighting those who walked after death? Was she suicidal? He didn't know the specifics of the blood debt, but he didn't think death was a way out. She had obviously been trained to fight. He'd seen that much in the alley before he'd Turned. Trained to fight and carve runes and who knew what else. Sent out to do battle with the damned and then? What then had Sven demanded of her? Did he heal his little aptrgangr killer so that she could work again?

No. His brother had worked her over so that she believed his blood wouldn't heal her if she didn't give him her body and soul too. A handy lie that would kill her a little at a time as surely as a cancer.

What wouldn't Sven stoop to?

Leif let out a long breath and wiped the smear of blood

from the girl's lips with the back of his hand. She couldn't be much more than twenty, but her eyes were hard. She hated him. He was unused to that look from a human woman. Usually they laughed, flirted, and tried desperately to find a way into his pants.

He ran his hands over her lithe body, trying to be impersonal. He had no doubt that his blood would heal her, but as a scientist he knew the importance of double-checking his experiments. Ah, the lies he told himself! He gave a rueful smile.

She was surprisingly muscular for someone so small. He could easily crush her small bones in his claws. Her features displayed a mixed lineage. Korean, perhaps, and Italian. Her blue-black hair hung loose, matted now with dirt and blood. The long hair was impractical, given that everything else had been chosen for stealth. Her faded black jeans clung to her skinny waist. They were ripped and slashed, but not for fashion, and worn almost threadbare. A sturdy leather corset protected her torso. Material that had once been alive provided the best protection in the post-Unraveling world. It held an Aether residue of its life.

Her black hooded jacket over the top added concealment, but it wasn't warm enough for fall. He would have to fix that. Her heavy black boots had steel toes. A sheaf for her knife hung from her leather belt and leather braces protected her wrists. In her pockets he found Thor's hammer, needles, and a running iron. Curious.

Aether swirled around her, almost like she was drawing it to her. When he pulled back the jacket, he found a line of runes poking out of her corset top. That could explain the strangeness. Leif had never taken much stock in the old runes, but this Walker believed—her skin was a mass of blue and red ink.

He reached to undo the corset and see more, but a large

black and white monster jumped out of the shadows and scratched him across the hand.

"Bloody hell!" But it was just a cat. He laughed at himself.

The thing glared at him, obviously ready to defend its mistress again.

"I was looking in the name of science," he told it.

The cat was not impressed. It twitched its mustache. Leif gathered the girl into his arms and stood. Sven had left this strange, tattooed blood slave in his care. Sven was mad. What terrible plot did she fit into? He had to keep a close eye on her until he figured it out.

"After you," he told the cat. At the mouth of the alley he turned back and breathed fire through the narrow lane. Rubbish caught. Branches and fallen boards snapped and popped. Brick heated as the fire grew. Flame took the bodies, one by one, setting them free. He said a small prayer for whatever gods they worshipped to look after their spirits on their way through the Gate.

The smell of burning meat followed him out.

Kingu swept through the street in Pioneer Square on the back of a harsh north wind, his wraith body ethereal but vast. Tendrils of his power snaked down the narrow brick alleys, searching for his quarry. It had been here recently. He could feel the dark, thrumming essence, the ancient, rich power beating to the rhythm of the earth's core. It called to him, but he was too late. This time.

After an eternity of captivity in the Land of the Dead, where he'd been caged since the usurper Marduk had slain his army, stolen his Tablets, and cast him out of Babylon, Kingu should be more patient. His diversion back to Babylon had been a mistake. He'd lost precious time rejuvenating himself in the salt waters, and when he'd finally arrived, nothing remained of the old empire but sun and sand.

His dreams brought him back to the place of his escape. His quarry was here, waiting for him, trapped like he had been. He caught flashes of it now and then. *Patience, patience, my love.*

He blew through the smoldering alley and out the other side, into the merry glow of the torches. A small temple to Ishtar, built of flimsy wood, not like the great stone gardens that the goddess was used to, stood gaudily in pinks and reds. The Aether flowed around it, beckoning him. Silly little bells thought to keep him out. He laughed and knocked them down, a sudden gust of wind and ill will. His wraiths followed in his coattails. They clattered the bones of the fence and pulled the shutters off the windows. Their war song screeched through the dark.

Inside the Priestesses trembled, their bare flesh nipping in the sudden chill, their eyes wide, mouths thin and trembling. Not one of them drew her spear.

Kingu peered in the windows, and ice climbed over the windowpane. He didn't see any weapons at all. Men, coats off, trousers down. Women, lace-covered, fingers plucking harps and flutes, soft and round and rosy-cheeked.

Sacred Courtesans, all of them. Where were the warrior maidens? These humans sought to worship only one side of Ishtar.

Kingu laughed, and the iced window cracked, shattering the room with broken glass. Crying out, the humans drew back.

Still, not one of them went for their weapons. Some of the menfolk tried to protect the shivering harlots. It should have been the other way around. Ishtar, if she still walked the mortal world, would be enraged, and when Ishtar was enraged, the underworld and all its denizens broke loose.

Feeling generous, Kingu decided to teach them a lesson on her behalf. He led his wraiths through the house, shattering the silly china baubles and delicate fripperies that had no place in a temple of Ishtar. Silken drapes and velvet curtains ripped from their moorings. Cabinets and poster beds crashed against ceilings like so much kindling. Shrieks filled the house, an eager melody to the percussion of his destruction.

He left the humans alive. Swooping out the now-empty door frame, he led his wraiths into the darkness. He was hungry. On another street, three human soldiers patrolled. Nothing else moved, but the wind and the ash and the sharp waves splashing against the seawall. He paused, studying their build and swagger. One laughed. The other grinned. Unaware of their surroundings. The third lifted his barreled weapon to sweep the shadows. Young and vital, wary but not weathered. No grit, no stamina, no cruelty. None had the warrior spirit he needed. The humans of this strange new world were made of river-bottom mud. He needed hard mountain rock and the unflinching drive of the desert sand.

Tiamat would send him what he needed. Until then, he would collect for his army.

Calling his wraiths to follow, he swooped down to the three humans in the street. Sensing, but not seeing him, they scattered, not realizing that he inhabited the air all around, cocooning them in his dark embrace. The first man, sandy hair, youthful face lacking the wrinkles of maturity, the yellow skin a reminder of scurvy, searched blindly through the fog. Kingu let him see. He reared up, revealing his true form, three demonic heads snapping, three long rows of razor teeth, sharp scales glittering over heavily muscled haunches, spiked tail whipping out to shatter the iron poles of torchlights along the street.

The man froze, terror etched in every feature. His heart stuttered, tripping over itself, blood coursing in intermittent bursts until he choked on his own fear. So weak.

It was a simple thing to make him strong.

Kingu bent down and sealed his mouth over the man's lips. He breathed out, washing the man with his essence. Plucking a wraith out of the Aether, Kingu shoved it down the helpless man's throat. The battle was short. Taking over, the wraith looked out of the man's eyes with cunning and bloodthirsty vengeance. Satisfied, Kingu turned to the other two.

His army grew by three men that day. More hounds on the scent, his quarry was within his grasp. Let the trumpets blare. The hunt was on.

The nightmare took her like it always did. First the cold. The numb pain in her legs and arms. She couldn't move much, in the way of dreams, like she was trying to crawl through chest-high mud. Next came the panic. She needed to move.

And then the smell of the Underground hit. The mold. The damp. Like someone's flooded basement had been sealed shut and left to rot for a century. The pervasive iron.

In the dream, Grace Mercer was dying. She had done a lot of stupid things in her short twenty years on earth, but this last one had taken the cake. Rushing helter-skelter into a dark, abandoned building was not something she usually would have done without casing the place, or at least letting Bear sniff the perimeter for her. But she had seen the little girl disappear through that rusted door and had acted without thinking. She had to save the kid. She hadn't seen it coming. That little girl hadn't been more than six or seven, for Freya's sake. The picture of innocence. Golden curls bouncing. Striped rainbow tights under a green corduroy jumper. Saddle shoes on her feet.

And even though it had happened a long time ago, she still felt the sick foot in her gut at the memory of that child.

She'd followed the girl into that dark structure at a dead

run, only to realize—far too late—it was a trap. A beam fell, knocking her to the floor with a blow to the head. She'd called out to the little girl and watched, horror stricken, as the child turned and fixed her with those empty wraith-filled eyes. When was the last time Grace had encountered an aptrgangr child? They were innocent, bodies and souls hale and hearty, unwearied by years of heartache and misery. It was a natural defense against possession.

Something else had jumped her then, two hell-spawned creatures that stalked the night. The head injury destroyed her sense of balance. It was a miracle she'd made it out and dragged herself this far.

The rotting beams of the tunnel floor sent splinters into her grasping fingers. She just had to make it to the first trip wire.

Every inch of her body hurt. That was an understatement. A trail of blood followed her, leading any pursuers right to the Underground lair. Fuck. One more reason for Norgard to rip her a new one. She choked at that. Maybe dying would be easier. More bearable. But she couldn't die out on the street where her empty shell would be free for any old vengeful spirit to seize. She had to make it to someone who would dispose of her properly. No way in hell she was coming back as one of those monsters to terrorize the living.

She owed that much to her parents. To Moll and Oscar and Hart. To Bear, wherever he'd run off to.

Damned Bear. If he'd been there she wouldn't have been tricked.

But maybe he had been there, and she just couldn't remember, falling up and over and through the rabbit hole in the topsy-turvy web of the dream.

More tears dripped down her cheeks, filling her mouth with the salt and tang of blood. The tunnel walls spun around her in a kaleidoscope of brick, beam, and broken crockery. The refuse of a century ago collected in the gutter along the side of the wooden boardwalk. One arm in front of the other, she dragged herself forward, pushed with her unbroken leg. Every movement burned with agony. Every breath felt like a stab with a butcher knife.

She wanted to stop, just to rest here a moment. Maybe this was far enough. Surely the runners would have seen her by now and could get to her body before the wraiths did.

Hands rolled her over and lifted her. Blackness—sweet, sweet, blackness—curled over her. She wanted to let it sweep her away, to sink down into oblivion and end this terrible pain.

"For fuck sake, stay with me, Reaper!" Panic in a voice that was usually calm. Oscar's blurred face. His long, cunning fingers gripped her jaw. "What'd'ya do this time, bitch? Do I have to babysit your ass all the time?" His hazel eyes swam above her. Three of them, no, five.

She tried to speak, to tell him not to worry. It was a relief, really, to leave this weary realm.

A shadow passed over her, and Oscar's face was replaced by something far less pleasant. No, she wanted to scream. Please, no. Surely this time she was too far gone.

"Ah, my sweet." The sound of Norgard's voice cut deep inside her, twisting, corkscrewing into her vulnerable soul. There were worse things than bodily injury. "Take her to my chambers."

Suddenly she wished she had let the wraiths take her. Better to die and become a flesh-eater than to live with *this*.

Please, she wanted to beg. *Please don't let him take me.*

But in the way of dreams her tongue wouldn't heed her command. Useless. Lolling.

Oscar didn't look away, but he didn't do anything to stop it.

Coward.

No, Grace was the coward.

The giant, carved wood bed slipped into view, and she

fought harder against the cottoning fever dream. Above her, the painted ceiling swirled with color and flames—Dante's hell illustrated and expanded by some manic artist with a paintbrush and an opium pipe.

Wings unfurled across her vision—giant, scaly things, purple-grey skin stretched across the long fingering bones. The mattress sagged beneath the weight of the monster that bent over her, kneeling between her spread legs. The sound of ripping fabric. Jeans and shirt sliced from her body. The fabric stuck to her wounds, and she stifled another moan as it was roughly pulled away. Norgard's erection burned high against her naked thigh, seeking entrance.

Everything had a price.

She watched, detached, as he scraped one long claw across his throat and blue-black blood welled from the cut. A shimmering droplet fell, scalding her tongue when it landed. It rolled, thick and unbearably sweet, down her throat.

Without his blood she would die. It would only cost her soul.

Grace fixed her eyes on the painted image of the gates above her head, and surrendered all hope.

Chapter 4

Grace gasped awake and found herself in an unfamiliar alcove. Mechanic odors thickened the air: biodiesel and oil, smoke, but also honey, for some strange reason, and beneath it all lurked iron and a hint of cinnamon. Drekar.

She reached for her knife, but it wasn't at her hip. For a moment she was disoriented. She fell off the cot and landed hard on her side, knocking over a small table and shattering the glass of water that had been sitting on it. She swore and staggered to her feet.

Norgard was dead. He couldn't hurt her anymore.

But his brother could. She steeled herself. Her jacket was unzipped, her corset askew, her boots off. Not the way she'd left them. Oh, Freya. Seen one soul-sucker, seen them all. She shouldn't expect anything different.

Leif Asgard heard her banging and appeared from around the corner. His face would make angels weep: glowing skin, square jaw, tousled hair in varying shades of blond, and those green eyes that shone like jewels. He was too gorgeous to be real, and he didn't even know it. A smear of oil crossed one chiseled cheekbone. His hair stuck up at odd angles. Even messy, he was beautiful. Large brass goggles were pushed on top of his head as if he had just stepped away from an experiment. "You're up."

She tore her eyes away. It was a trick. The devil walked in fancy skin. The room, now that she examined it, was a little alcove off the larger room. It was crammed like a rat's nest with brass boilers and metal pipes, beakers and tincture jars, and shiny copper wiring. She was in the bowels of the Drekar Lair, in the mad scientist's laboratory. She'd never been here before.

"Welcome." He wiped oil off his hands with a rag and stuck one out to shake. "Let's start off on the right foot this time, shall we? Leif."

She busied herself rechecking her clothing. She zipped the hoodie up to her chin.

He cleared his throat and withdrew his hand. "I wasn't sure how long you would be out, so I brought you home. The lab took a bit of a beating in the Unraveling, but at least it didn't slide into the sea like some of the Sound-side rooms." He brushed a bit of earth off a nearby pipe. "Almost good as new."

She made him nervous. This was Asgard's sanctuary, and he'd brought her here. What did that say about him? That he trusted a blood-sworn mercenary? That he thought she wouldn't slit his throat and run at the soonest opportunity? He was an idiot. He might own her soul, but she would never make it easy for him.

Asgard shifted his weight. "Are you recovered?"

"Where's my knife?"

"A remarkable instrument," he said. "Where did you get it?"

"And what happened to my bike?"

"It was a bike? It looked like a junkyard reject—"

"It was mine!"

"Calm down." He held up his hands. "The death trap is parked outside. Your cat is safe too."

"My—don't touch my cat!" She focused on his forehead so she wouldn't have to meet his eyes. *I've seen you naked*, his eyes would say. *You weren't half bad.*

Asgard stilled. The air in the room seemed to shrink.

"You've got what you want. Now give me back my stuff."

"I got what I want," he repeated slowly. The scent of iron rose with his anger. "And what exactly did I want?"

Damned if she would spell it out for him. His brother had liked playing mind games.

"Look at me when you accuse me of being dishonorable," he demanded. "Or are you such a coward that you can't come out and say it? You don't even know me."

"I know enough."

"Is that so?" His voice dropped. His rolled shirtsleeves displayed muscular forearms and a faint dusting of coal. His hands were stained reddish brown with the distilled essence of biodiesel. Why didn't he get a slave to do his dirty work? The Drekar Regent shouldn't be filling his own smoky lamps. Shouldn't he be out trying to take over the world? Or repopulating his family of monsters? That's what his brother would have done. Norgard would have crowned himself king of all Seattle by now and set to work trying to knock up every surviving woman.

"What have I done to deserve this evil reputation?" Asgard asked.

"Regent—"

"I'm not my brother."

She met his gaze then. His eyes pierced her fragile armor. Same as his brother, he could strip her with a glance. Norgard would have stopped there, letting his eyes rove over her flesh as if she were naked and available anytime he bloody well chose.

Asgard wasn't content to fondle her curves. His eyes stripped off the shielding black and barreled on through, probing beneath skin and muscle to the heart of her.

It freaked her the fuck out.

She crossed her arms over her chest. "Prove it. Let me go."

"I'm not keeping you here—"

"No." She raised her chin and pointed to the spot beneath her jacket where the gold slave band burned her skin. "Let me go."

Asgard ran a hand through his hair. "I was afraid you'd say that. I can't—"

"Fine." He refused to free her. He was exactly like his brother. She would pay off the debt herself. "Give me back my knife and let me get back to work."

"How do you feel?"

She grimaced. What kind of question was that? She felt like a million bucks. Rested, repaired, like her ribs had never met a brick or piece of rebar in her life. Drekar blood hummed through her system like an amphetamine. She could run a marathon, fight a dozen aptrgangr. There was nothing like Drekar blood to cure what ailed you, except of course for the price of the damned stuff.

Asgard reached out to touch her, and she jerked back. He let his hand fall open. He had large hands. Working hands. Oil and grease and coal dust under his nails. He should have chapped, calloused skin, but his damned magic blood wouldn't let a single cell get busted. Immortal, Drekar had blood that regenerated every wound except one.

She'd seen a Drekar die once. A sly red-haired bastard named Vikinstrom who liked his girls young and his sex bloody. Grace didn't know what crime had been the last straw for Norgard, but she had been in the Great Hall the day Vikinstrom died. Norgard had pulled the great bone sword from the pommel of his throne and sliced the Dreki's head clean off before he could open his mouth to scream. Blood had sprayed. Oh, so much precious wasted blood. She'd waited for the head to regrow or the spinal column to reach out and reknit itself. But it had lain there in a pool of red. The eyes in the severed head had stared up at the great jeweled ceiling.

She'd never looked at Norgard the same way again. He'd given her hope; that was the moment she knew he could be killed.

But the Unraveling had stolen even that revenge from her.

Asgard cleared his throat. The green in those eyes was like the bottom of the sea. Gorgeous and otherworldly. She forced herself to imagine what they'd look like in death, staring empty and shocked, just like Vikinstrom. Yes, he could be killed, but who then would inherit the ring? Thorsson? That would be worse.

"How do you feel inside?" he asked. "Rundown? Heart heavy? Or is that your normal state of existence?"

She took a good look at her emotional state and was shocked to find herself perfectly normal. A little angry. A little scared. But none of that bone-weary fatigue or dirty sensation that usually defined her postcoital state.

It didn't mean anything. Maybe he was telling the truth. How could her body be healed if he hadn't fucked her? It would change her understanding of the way things worked. It would change her history, her justification for the last four years. She didn't want to examine it too closely.

"Fine," she snapped. "I need to get back to work."

"You had old bruises. I guess I don't have to ask why you haven't been healing them. But I have to wonder how you got them. Why have you been fighting? What could possibly possess a tiny thing like you to go hunting aptrgangr when you don't have to?"

"What should I be doing—painting my nails? Serving Ishtar?"

"Gods no—"

"Then what? You haven't sent me on any missions—"

"Exactly. You should have stayed out of trouble."

"Aptrgangr are rising faster than the Kivati can put them down. Humans are being killed. They need me."

A muscle twitched in his jaw. "So it's altruistic."

"By Freya, no. I need the money. You think this blood debt is going to pay itself?"

He studied her, his eyes raking her body. She knew what he saw: muscled from fighting, lean and a little underweight. She had never been curvy and feminine, but now her cheekbones were a little too sharp. The glint in her eye, a little too hungry. Who knew why Norgard had been drawn to her? She was sinew and bone, and he could have had anyone.

"Why did he train you as a fighter?" Asgard asked.

She crossed her arms. "I'm good."

Asgard's eyes dipped to her lips. "There's something . . . odd about you," he said, half to himself. Absently, he pulled a small brass spyglass from his pocket and put it to his eye. Humming to himself, he adjusted the gears and studied her through the glass. Nothing he'd done so far had been this impersonal.

I'm not a science experiment, she wanted to growl. "That's Hart's."

"The Deadglass?" He dropped it from his eye and turned it over in his hands. "My brother had it commissioned when he first arrived in Seattle. Do you know the story?"

She shook her head. That had been over a century ago. The Drekar and Kivati were equally out of touch with real people time.

"There was no war then." He flipped the Deadglass and his hand clenched over the brass. "The artist was a Dreki who fell in love with a Kivati girl. It might have all turned out, but . . ."

"But the Kivati hate the Drekar."

He gave a sad smile. "Even Paris couldn't call a truce between these two houses. My brother was power hungry. He used the distraction to make his move. Burned the city to the ground. This Deadglass is one of only two in existence. The only one, I guess, now that Sven took his monocle to the bottom of the sea. Do you know what it does?"

Hart, a fellow mercenary, now free, had showed it to her a couple times. "Shows ghosts."

"More than that. It sees that which cannot be seen with the naked eye."

Grace raised her chin. "And what do I look like in the glass?"

"A beautiful woman who sparkles with a thousand stars."

She balled her hands. The moment was suddenly too warm. "Where is my knife?"

He shook himself. "Fighting. Such a waste." Turning from her, he led the way into the adjoining room. Machinery filled every inch of space. The air clotted with steam and loud noises. In the center of the room, a dozen biodiesel lamps lit a long worktable. Wires snaked across a pile of castoff metal, tubes and a man-sized sheet curved like a chest plate.

On top of the chest plate, curled in a ball, lay the cat. Bear looked perfectly at home. Asgard reached for him.

"Don't! Bear doesn't like to be touched."

Asgard raised an eyebrow. "No?"

"No."

As if to test her, Asgard put his fingers on the cat's fur and stroked. Grace waited for Bear to snarl and bite him, but instead the traitor purred. Asgard didn't smirk. He turned his face to the cat. "I don't know anything about the blood bond. I've never studied the old magics. They always smacked of superstition to me."

"It's real, all right."

"I can see that. My work has always been of a scientific nature, but that won't help break a magic bond. To study the bond, I'll need to do some tests—"

"On me? Yeah, right." Bear might have drunk Asgard's

Kool-Aid, but *she* wasn't submitting to any of the mad scientist's designs. Not willingly.

Asgard stepped away from Bear, and she breathed a sigh of relief. "Not curious, are you? Not even in the name of science?"

"I need to go." She wasn't going to let him test anything. She remembered the blood binding ceremony too well. Nothing could break it but paying off the debt. She was human, and he was Drekar, and there was nothing he had that she wanted except her freedom. And her cat. "I won't say it's been fun, but, you know, things to do and all."

Asgard picked up a copper tube the size of a lipstick container. "The runes on your chest, what do they mean?"

She played with the zipper of her hoodie. He'd no reason to take off her clothes without her permission.

"Stop looking so affronted. Nothing happened. I would never force myself on an unwilling woman." His voice snapped her head around. A trickle of smoke curled from his nostrils and floated to the ceiling.

Norgard hadn't forced her. That was the rub of it. He had coerced, so she could never really claim she had told him no. It wasn't rape then, was it? She had willingly succumbed to having her soul shredded, piece by piece. First, because she thought she loved him. Then, because she needed his blood. She was too jaded to believe in love anymore, but she knew sex cost good coin. Elsie had it right. Why give it away, when you could get rich from it?

Asgard growled low in his throat and fiddled with the copper tube. Suddenly a burst of blue fire erupted from the top.

She jerked back. "Warn a girl, would ya?"

Bear jumped off the table and hid. Leif tossed the lighter to her and she caught it. The tube weighed next to nothing, but it packed a punch. She flicked the hidden button on the bottom, and fire shot out.

"Careful," Asgard said.

Freya, yeah. She could use this baby. There had to be a catch. "How does it work?"

"Curious now, are we?" He leaned against the table. His linen trousers draped artfully over long, muscled legs. The top few buttons of his white shirt were undone, revealing a sleek, rock-solid chest. Beneath the biodiesel lamps, his skin shone with the luster of a thousand tiny scales. By all rights he should be cold as a snake, but she knew if she touched him he would be hot. He was bigger, rawer than human men. His scent transmitted pure sex. He smiled lazily, and her knees wobbled.

"Turn off your fucking pheromones," she snapped. "They don't work on me."

"If they don't work, why should I turn them off?"

Gah. She threw the fire tube at him.

He snatched it out of the air. "Not good enough? I designed it to be so efficient that it should last you at least six months before you need to refuel. You can adjust the height of the flame too." He turned the base of the tube clockwise and flicked the switch again. This time the flame was short, the size of a regular lighter.

He'd made it for her? "What's it cost me?"

"What is it worth to you?"

She eyed the tube. She'd lost her lighter, and she needed fire to burn the bodies so another wraith couldn't animate them. Not to mention all the other things she could use it for—light when the torches blew out, fire to keep warm, a weapon. "Not much," she lied.

"Then the price won't be much, will it?" Asgard stood and sauntered closer. His ancient green eyes hid a hint of laughter. "Maybe we should sweeten the bargain."

Grace didn't bargain with the devil. She always ended up on the losing end.

The Dreki invaded her personal space, blocking out the

light and smoke of the lamps and the sound of the whirring machines. Leaning in, he put his face next to her ear. His hot breath on her neck sent shivers racing down her spine. It's not real, she reminded herself. It's just a Drekar trick. He'd screw anything as long as it had a soul.

"Regent—"

"Leif," he breathed.

Oh, Freya, no. She would never call him Leif. "Send me on an assignment."

He pulled back. "Why?"

"Otherwise I'm going to keep taking whatever job I can find. No matter the danger."

"Right." He unzipped half her hoodie before she could protest, slid the tube and the Deadglass into the front of her corset, and zipped her up again. He lifted her chin with one long, elegant finger. "I demand payment."

She steeled herself.

One corner of his broad mouth curled. He leaned in, cinnamon and musk curling her toes in her boots. The clock on the wall seemed to still, an eternity stretching between the threat and the reckoning.

And he feinted a hairbreadth from touching her lips. His mouth hovered by the delicate rim of her ear. "I'll collect later." Then he turned and strode away, leaving her with the Deadglass and the tube lodged heavily between her breasts like a twenty-ton IOU.

How dare he try to ensnare her further in his debt? She was going to pay that bloody thing off and stick the golden slave bands up his ass.

"What about my—"

"Weapons are on the table in the foyer," he called back. "Your sad excuse for a bicycle is on the factory porch. Your cat ran and hid; good luck finding him." The reddish-gold light wreathed his head, steam clouding the end of the laboratory like sulfur smoke. He looked more inhuman than ever. She would be smart to remember that.

For Freya's sake. Leif threw the nearest rack of beakers across the room in a satisfying crunch. Why did he have to make an ass of himself? His grandfather would have washed his mouth out with lye. He'd always fancied himself civilized. A gentleman. But Grace brought out the barbarian in him. Something primitive took hold, the dragon that had crawled out of Tiamat's primordial waters. Unrefined. Ruthless. Hungry. It took one look at that little hellion and wanted to eat her up. She called to his deepest, basest appetites. One sarcastic glance from her, and his gentleman's gloves came off. Raw-knuckled and raving, he might as well knock her over the head with a club and drag her back to his cave by her hair.

Gods, what was wrong with him? He'd baited her. It went against every chivalrous bone in his body. She'd believed he was the worst sort of lowlife. Believed he would force himself on an unconscious woman, and it made him spitting mad.

But rather than proving her wrong through his actions, he was actually living up to her poor expectations of him. Exchanging favors for the flame thrower, indeed. He had designed it especially for her after seeing her need for a dependable lighter. It was just a silly trinket, but it could make her life a little easier. What had possessed him to bargain with her for it? Maybe he was just as mad as Sven after all. He had always prided himself on his logical, scientific thinking, but she made all the blood in his brain rush south.

Freya take Sven and his blood slaves. Grace demanded a job, but he couldn't knowingly send a woman out into danger. He couldn't in good conscience refuse to let her pay off her debt either. He was in a bind.

Leif rammed his shoulder into the copper boiler next to him. It fell and cracked on the hard stone floor. The clang reverberated through the room.

Erik Thorsson, his brother's deranged right hand, burst into the room with his sword drawn. A berserker of whom legends were made, he'd never really crawled out of the primordial soup. "Regent!"

Leif straightened and ran his hand through his hair. "Ah, Thorsson."

"Who attacks?"

"No one. Nothing. I was just . . . getting out a little bit of aggression, don't you know?" Leif picked up a beaker and hurled it at the wall, where it shattered.

Thorsson gave him a blank stare, but put away his sword. Leif could breathe again. "The girl . . . bothers you? I'll take care of her."

"No! No." But a thought occurred to him. "Follow her, Thorsson."

"But—"

"Keep her safe, but don't let her see you." Normally, Leif wouldn't want a Dreki like Thorsson anywhere near a woman, but Thorsson had taken Sven's loss personally and poorly. All his considerable loyalty was now stuck squarely on Leif. Leif could use that to his advantage. The berserker wouldn't cross him.

"And Thorsson—don't touch her." He leveled his stare at the larger man, and the Dreki bowed his head.

"Understood."

She was his.

Chapter 5

Grace found Bear and stormed out of the lair. Her dinged-up bike waited for her against the porch of the weather-worn mansion that had once housed Loki's Chocolates. The Drekar had replaced the damaged mansard roof and shattered, leaded-glass windows, and painted the new wall boards cherry red. It looked almost respectable. She put Bear in the plastic daisy basket that hung from the handlebars and walked the bike down the long, brick walk toward the iron gates. Two hulking Drekar guarded the gate, weapons ready, eyes glowing in the darkness. They leered at her.

She ignored them, as she always did, because she was the Regent's property and therefore untouchable. Mounting the rusted bike, she headed down the hill and through the Drekar city of Ballard. At least Asgard had had the decency to bring her ride. Him and his stupid offended honor. What game was he playing? He didn't act like any of the Drekar she'd met. They all went out of their way to put her in her place.

Thinking of Asgard put a sour feeling in her stomach. He wanted her to trust him, but the moment she let down her guard, she knew he'd strike. The thin hint of dawn drew an outline of the Olympic Mountains across the horizon. It was just enough light to find her way onto the old Interurban highway that connected Ballard to downtown. Since the bridge over the canal had survived the Unraveling, extra effort had been made to clear the road. Now it cut through the debris like a spell-tipped blade, from the Drekar territory in the north, past the Kivati stronghold of Queen Anne, and down to the human-occupied sections in the old downtown. Sections not directly controlled by a major player were at the mercy of highwaymen. But at least the highwaymen kept their sections free of aptrgangr. If they charged a toll on the section they guarded, who could complain? It meant humans could walk safely to the shanty pubs and tent cities that had sprung up along the road.

At the foot of Queen Anne Hill, she passed through the closed-up stalls of the Needle Market. It had grown overnight like a weed between cracks in the cement. Most of the supplies were salvaged: canned goods; clothing; building materials, mostly straight nails and reusable wiring; two-by-fours that had been cut from the bones of houses no one lived in anymore. The original owners were long gone, or if they weren't, no one was around to enforce property rights. Other stalls offered magic materials of dubious origin and effectiveness. Fortune-tellers and heathwitches made a brisk business in portents and potions. For the right price you could hire a priest or shaman to exorcise the evil spirits from your house. Crystals, gris-gris, dried cat gut, pickled bat wing, powdered dragon bone, new age books dug from the rubble—anything and everything could be found at the Needle Market.

Not that those little magics worked, but the belief they did helped some people sleep at night. Grace wanted to pound stall owners for taking advantage, but who was she to take away that little bit of hope? If it helped . . . every little bit was worth it.

By the time she reached the crater that had swallowed the

land from Pike Place to Belltown in the Unraveling, the back of her neck had started to itch. It could mean nothing, but she hadn't survived this long by ignoring her instincts. Time to find company. She skirted the crater until she came to the new Butterworth's Tea Room and Opium Parlor. The original building, a former mortuary and funeral parlor, had crashed along with the rest of Pike Place Market. The new location was a bland warehouse, but inside it was almost like old times. The sentimental patrons had dug Norgard's giant carved dragon bar from the rubble and placed it center stage in the new bar overlooking the hungry sea.

She almost liked the new place better. It perched dangerously on the edge, and that's where its patrons had always been. Misfits like her and power brokers like the mayor, glitzed-up girls and Ishtar's Maidens selling their wares. Opium fiends and goth clad wannabes. University kids and ravers. They all mixed and mingled under Butterworth's red glass lights. It was the perfect place to see and be seen, or to hide away in full view, as she liked.

"I'll be back in a bit, Bear," she told the cat. He gave her a baleful look, but stayed curled up in the plastic basket. She locked the bike against a metal grate on the side of the building. So Asgard didn't like her bike, huh? Even a "death trap" like this was valuable post-Unraveling. A ride, any ride, was better than walking. The dragon emblem carved on her lock kept it relatively untouched. She wasn't too proud to use her Drekar connections when she had to.

Entering Butterworth's was a little like coming home. Doc, the bartender, kept the place hopping just like old times. Those who hadn't made it to shelter for curfew stayed all night. Even now the opium booths were packed. On the parquet floor people danced like it was the end of the world, and perhaps it was.

Grace slipped in and out of the crowd until she found Oscar.

"You should know, girlfriend, that pissed look is scaring away my mark."

"Tough. I need to talk to you."

Oscar sighed theatrically and followed her off the dance floor to the great, carved bar. They found Hart, the only one of Norgard's mercenaries to have won his freedom, already staked out on a bar stool next to his wife, Kayla. Hart was a Kivati Wolf who wore Bad like a cologne and ate Dangerous for breakfast. People saw him coming and ran the other way. Grace had seen beneath the sarcasm and big bad reputation to the gruff, but loyal, heart underneath. But he wasn't one of them anymore. He'd rejoined the Kivati, and if the bump under Kayla's striped dress was any indication, his pack would be increasing in size.

She made Oscar sit between them.

"Still sore?" Oscar whispered.

"He abandoned her."

"He went back for Kayla. She's forgiven him, why can't you?"

She cleared her throat and motioned to the portly bartender.

"Be gentle, Reaper," Oscar said. "Strength doesn't mean you know how to carry a heavy grudge."

"I can hear you, you know," Hart growled.

Stupid inhuman hearing. "I thought now that you scrape for Corbette, you'd gone soft," she yelled over the noise of the bar.

Hart growled. She could feel it in the vibration of the air, the raised hair on the back of her neck that had her instincts ready to run. The Mad Wolf looked out of his human eyes. The thin violet band around his iris flooded into the black. Grace held her breath.

But then Kayla put her hand on Hart's knee, and the tension rushed out of him like the tide fleeing the beach.

Damn, but Grace would never get used to that. Shaking her head, she pulled the Deadglass out of her shirt. "Asgard gave me your ghost finder—"

"Keep it," Hart said. "Ain't many ghosts on the Kivati's hill."

She smoothed her fingers over the brass. It could come in handy, especially if Bear was going to be picking up new friends. Her lip curled. She stuffed the Deadglass back beneath her shirt. "You're going to stay then?"

"Seems like it." He leaned in. "Corbette has us scouting outside the city. Outpost towns are being picked off one by one. Whole populations, gone. I'd rather lay low beneath his stuffiness's dark shadow than stick my neck out as bait, if you know what I mean."

"I wonder how many of those frontier people are now haunting our fair city. Aptrgangr numbers are up."

"Lose your bands, Reaper," Hart said, and the gold slave bands around her upper arms seemed to heat. "That gold won't do you no good on the other side of the Gate."

"Soon, Wolf." Not soon enough. Grace waited until Doc had filled their drink orders, then said her good-byes and motioned Oscar to follow her. She needed to get away from Mr. Big Ears. Slipping through the crush, she cradled her teacup against her chest until she found a secluded alcove. Between the exposed brick and a steel beam, she tossed down the oolongtini.

"Liquid courage?" Oscar raised his eyebrow and leaned in. "Well, well. What could be so serious that our dear Grace needs a drink?"

"Screw you." She slouched against the wall and watched the undulating mass of bodies. She wanted him to ask. She wasn't sure how to say it herself. She wasn't good at this talking thing. "You know I never ask you for favors."

He crossed one pin-striped leg over the other and twirled his teacup around his finger. "Never, darling. Asking is the hardest part."

Oscar got her. He was her best friend, and she could always count on him to understand what she didn't say. He was pretty close to paying off his own blood debt. She didn't want to imagine doing this job without him at her back. "Asgard has decided to get involved."

"Finally. I was beginning to think I'd be reduced to selling my secrets to the Kivati, and they're not worth much now that the old bastard is dead. So what job did Asgard give you? Need a friend?" Oscar leaned forward.

"No, he thinks we should be sitting on our asses, *safe*." Grace snorted.

"How boring. I don't think I've been *safe* since I was nine."

"Like anywhere is safe. In the last week alone, five people have reported seeing the shadow of a monster-sized, three-headed dragon."

"Kingu?"

"Sounds like it, but Asgard doesn't want to hear it. What's in Seattle that Kingu would come back for? That slice of the Tablet of Destiny? I don't think anyone has seen it since Rudrick used it to open the Gate. Asgard is busy playing with his machines and pretending to work with the Kivati. He doesn't want to bloody his lily-white hands."

"I see. But you're looking better." Oscar motioned to the side of her face where her bruises had disappeared.

"Yeah, about that." She shifted in her seat. "Did you ever get healed by Norgard?"

Oscar sat back. "Sure. But a right nasty business. I try to win my dragon's blood from a different source."

"Who, Zetian?" She tried to imagine Oscar sleeping with the Drekar female and failed. Zetian was like a black widow; she'd bite a man's head off.

"No. Other mercenaries. Let them pay Norgard's price. I bet them for their bottles. I never lose."

"You never bet me."

"You never have bottles."

If the Drekar blood could be drunk like a cordial, it didn't need sex magic to work. A cold sickness rolled through her belly. She'd never examined Norgard's claim too closely. Had he ever come right out and said that she needed to fuck him to heal? He had never offered her bottled blood. A Dreki couldn't lie outright, but he could suggest like crazy. She'd just assumed it wouldn't work.

They both watched the movement through Butterworth's for a long moment. Beneath her calm face, rage boiled up. That bastard. How had she survived so long being such a blind fool? She didn't want to hear this. She'd never asked the price before. They didn't talk about hard stuff like that. You didn't make friends when none of you would be around long.

So many of them went on assignment and didn't come back: Savona and Peter; Kat laid down by a Kivati bomb; Emmett, Bill, Andy. Grace had buried Molly herself on the bluff so she could always see the sun stain the sky red and pink over the mountains. Not even four months in Norgard's service; Molly came back, but she wasn't Moll anymore. A ghost had a way of disassociating with the living. It didn't belong on this side of the Gate. It warped. Festered.

I'm going to go now, she thought. But she didn't speak. She just left. Fuck Oscar. What was she supposed to do, huh? He could have said something, but would it have been worse knowing? She'd always suspected, deep down, that sex magic wasn't a necessary part of the Drekar blood's pull. But she'd wanted to believe it. It made everything easier. First she'd wanted to believe Norgard loved her. Then she'd wanted to believe it was necessary to take some of the pressure off. To make it less dirty. To take away some of the responsibility for her actions. She'd slept with Norgard only to heal. It wasn't a choice. Gods damn him.

"Wait, Reaper." Oscar followed her out of the stuffy bar into the grey light of dawn.

A raincloud of ash drizzled to the north. The waves crashed angrily against the ruined seawall a few stories below the edge of the crater. Scavengers were already hard at work. They crawled over the pile of twisted metal in front of her like coal-blackened monkeys. Kids as young as five or six edged along the top floors of the gutted tower. With the windows blown out, the sea air barreled through, whipping their thin little jackets and pulling them closer to the dazzling drop.

Where were their parents? She wanted to yell at them to get away from the edge, but she knew they needed this work. The church and Kivati had set up soup kitchens, but the lines out the door stretched for hours. Her own stomach growled in sympathy.

How could she be so caught up in her own problems when she had it good? A roof over her head. Food in her belly on most days. An occupation that could bring in the big bucks if she could only keep it for herself. She'd never liked whiners.

She turned to Oscar. "You have anything else I should know about?"

He squinted up at the scavengers. "Naw, just rumors."

"What rumors?"

"You know, in the broadsheets. Some guy calling himself the 'voice of the people' says a vigilante chick is saving people stupid enough to be caught out alone. I wouldn't want anyone to start pointing fingers."

"Don't know nothing about it," Grace grumbled. She called to Bear, who appeared from a doorway looking put out. She unlocked her bike and stowed the lock. "Only rumors. You see any more broadsheets, you rip 'em down, you hear?"

"Can't stop the news."

She helped the cat into the basket.

"Let the people fight their own demons," Oscar said. "You got enough on your own. Even the Raven Lord has closed Queen Anne to non-Kivati. No more handouts. No more hand-ups."

"These people?" She motioned to the kids high overhead. "Starving softies?"

"You'd be surprised how many find their strength when their back's against the wall. That's what the old boss was good at. He demanded more from a person than they thought they had in 'em."

"Like me?" she asked. A grieving sixteen-year-old whose soft fingers were fit for nothing but piano. She'd earned her calluses fast enough.

"Naw. Not you, Reaper. You were hard with hate the first moment I met you."

I was soft, she thought. Love had done that to her. Her parents' love. She'd expected good from people back then. She'd been infatuated with the man who had given her the tools to her revenge. It messed with a person's brain, so that she thought she was in love with Norgard. She would have done anything for him.

Soft. Weak. Naive. Easily manipulated. She let each of those hated words pound into her, and each bruise was a memory. A reminder. She needed to be iron-plated. She'd survived Norgard, survived the Unraveling, and she would survive this too. She was hard as the rock beneath her feet.

"You don't have to fight," Oscar said. "You could teach them instead. Let them fight their own battles. You'd be a good teacher."

"Hmm."

"Charge them for lessons."

"I'll think about it." She mounted the bike and took off, skirting the crater, toward Pioneer Square.

After a few blocks, the sun shot tendrils of red across the horizon. She passed men and women in heavy canvas overalls waiting for the work cart. The tech nerds who used to be petty kings had fallen on hard times. They had no usable skills in the new economy. Code and *World of Warcraft* didn't translate well to basic survival in the real world. Like the Great Depression, empty hands were put to work: scavenging debris from the broken city, laying brick along the Interurban, digging coal in the reopened Ravensdale Mine, or rebuilding the Gas Works. Grease, oil, and ash were baked into their weary faces. Backs bent, arms muscled, even from a distance they reeked of misery and gin.

She passed a huddle of sloshed guys, presumably stumbling to the coal mine after a long night at Butterworth's. Something about their stance didn't sit right, so she looped back around. The two hooded men were wrestling with something on the ground. When she stopped, another man popped from the alley mouth. He leaned drunkenly against the brick wall.

Definitely not right. Still, it wasn't her fight. Oscar's warning blared in her head. She shouldn't earn a do-gooder reputation. No one would hire her if she gave away her services for free.

The tallest hooded figure saw her. He rose from his crouch. A body lay behind him. If it was aptrgangr, she'd congratulate them and move on. She coasted a little closer. The body's face was hidden, but she noticed he wore a black armband. Kivati, Western House. Same House as Hart. Wraiths posed little threat to Kivati, but humans did. Gods, she hated bullies.

Screw Oscar's advice. She swung her leg off the bike and leaned it against the building next to her. She let her madness show in her eyes. She avoided fighting humans, but these men looked like they could use a little steam breathing down their necks. She had to work at making humans take notice. She thought about Zetian, Norgard's Dragon Lady advisor, and channeled her inner bitch. "Strange place for a conference, boys. You should move along."

The tallest man moved toward her. The Kivati on the ground didn't move. Dead? The second man rose and glanced down the alley. Someone was still down there. Someone who made him nervous. He nodded to the tall one. "Come on, Rob. Let's go."

"Why, Kyle? We just want to spread a little love. The girl is almost ready to convert."

The skinny man at the alleyway twitched. His eyes skittered away, dancing over the ghostly office towers and back to her, but never landing on one thing. He was high as a kite.

Perfect. He wouldn't be a threat. Grace rolled up her sleeves, exposing the long line of crimson runes running down her arms above her energy meridian.

Rob whistled. "Nice. You see, Kyle? She's cool. Aren't you cool, chica?" He shuffled toward her. She noticed a small blue flame tattooed at the base of his left thumb. A quick glance told her that the skinny guy sported one too. They belonged to a small militant sect of New Revelation—the Mark of Cain. "You want to see the supernatural, baby? I can take you to heaven."

"No, this one's a freak," Kyle mumbled. "Marks only wants clean girls. Let's get out of here."

So Marks was collecting young innocents for his church out at sea? Grace would love to give him a piece of her mind. But it was a lot harder to fight a human than an aptrgangr. For one, she was worried about permanently damaging a human. Killing one still counted as murder, and the New Revelation folks would avenge one of their own.

"Oh, yeah, Rob. Take me to see the light," she said and spun out in a roundhouse kick.

Alcohol didn't help Rob's reflexes, but he was trained. He snuck one fist past her, catching the edge of her eye, before she dropped him with a kick to the groin. Kyle took off running. The skinny dude panicked between following Kyle and helping Rob, but discretion won out over valor and he left Rob curled in the dirt.

Grace squatted down next to Rob. She squinted through her left eye, which throbbed with the beginning of a nasty shiner. "Is that a girl you have trapped down that alley? I'm about to go see what I can see. Am I going to like what I see, Rob?"

"We didn't do anything to her," he whined. "Marks wants 'em pure."

"I see." She stood. "Rob, you have about three minutes. When I get back, we could have another little chat, but I don't think you'd like that as much."

He pulled himself up. His face had turned a mottled red. "Don't tell me what to do, bi—"

She palmed her knife and held it up to the torchlight so that he could get a good look at the spell-tipped blade. "Come again?"

He recoiled. "Dragon whore." She let it bounce off her. She'd been called worse. The important part was he left, and he didn't look like he'd be back.

Grace glanced down the alley and found a woman in a cloak huddling against the wall. Thin shoulders, thin frame. The hood hid all but the tip of her pointed nose. "You can come out now. I'm not going to hurt you," Grace said to her as she bent to check the Kivati.

"Is he alive?" the woman asked.

"Do you want him to be?"

"Yes."

The Kivati was breathing. "You're in luck." Grace turned him faceup. She recognized him. Johnny. His eyelids fluttered.

A red welt decorated one eye. His straight, coal-black hair fell in a tangle down to his nape. He was about her age, around twenty. His totem was Crow, and he had the fine cheekbones of the bird tribes. Two thin, white scars sliced diagonally down his cheeks: the Kivati mark of dishonor. He'd handed the Kivati princess over to Rudrick, a Kivati Fox who'd had aspirations of leading a revolt. Rudrick had assaulted Princess Lucia and shed her blood in an ancient Babylonian ceremony to bring down the Gate to the Land of the Dead. The result had unleashed global earthquakes, an army of wraiths, and Kingu. Johnny might have been too stupid to know what Rudrick had planned, but in Grace's mind, that was no excuse.

Grace slapped his face. "Rise and shine, Van Winkle."

The man stirred. "Luce?"

Grace took another look at the woman. Rich, unarmed, and out of place. The fine wool of her cloak was dyed a midnight blue. The black toes of her heeled boots indicated good-quality leather. If this was the Kivati princess, she was a much kinder woman than Grace. "Are you sure you want him alive?"

"Johnny's life is forfeit to me." Lucia shrugged her frail shoulders.

"What were you doing out here?"

The princess gave a bitter laugh. She was only eighteen, but she sounded eighty. Her blood had brought down the Gate. Her innocence shattered. Her mind fragmented, if the rumors were true. "Are you going to lecture me now?"

"Not me." Grace knew what it felt like to be the subject of gossip, to have everyone know your humiliation. There was no place to hide when the shame corroded your gut. The cancerous feeling moved with you. The best she could do for Lucia was to leave her alone. She stood and turned to go.

"Wait."

"Look, I've been up all night. I gotta go."

"Can you teach me to do that? To fight?"

Grace snorted. Delicately, she drew her finger across the bruised corner of her eye. "That wasn't much of a fight."

"I want to be able to defend myself. I'll pay you."

Something about that irked. "No offense, Princess, but I just don't see you fighting. You're not a killer. Some bruiser comes at you again—hell, some skinny guy with ten pounds on you could best you. You're not going to kick his butt—you're going to run like hell."

"You don't know anything about me." Lucia fisted her hands on her hips.

Grace saw her own rage mirrored there. How many times had she wanted someone to see past her bullshit? There was the face she showed the world and then there was the woman inside. Tough, but wounded. Angry, but kind. "That isn't an insult. You're going to run, because that's your absolute best defense. I'll give you some advice: ditch the dress and get yourself some sneakers."

"What do you care? I said I'll pay you. What I do with it is my business."

"Fighting lessons make some people take stupid chances. Exhibit A." She pointed to Johnny. He opened his eyes and squinted. His hands moved to the lump on his head.

The princess lowered her hood. The rising dawn glowed off her snow-white hair. The Unraveling had sucked all the color out. "One of them threatened me, while the others attacked Johnny. He didn't defend himself." Lucia's youthful face tightened. Her eyes were two pools of ancient against her unmarked skin. "I will not be a victim again."

Grace ran a hand over her face. She could identify with that wish, more than she'd like to admit. She never let herself think the word "victim," because that didn't help her situation. "So what are you doing out here? The first part of not being a victim is not taking stupid chances." *Do as I say, not as I do*, she thought darkly. Oscar would laugh his ass off if he heard her now.

"I could ask you the same question." Lucia turned her pointed nose in the air. She could pull her high and mighty routine all she wanted; it wasn't going to work on Grace.

"You don't see me wandering about at night unless I have a damn good reason to." Grace turned to Johnny. He pushed himself off the ground. He rubbed the back of his head. She held up two fingers. He scowled at her, and she dropped them. "What did they want?"

"Off-duty Mark of Cain," Johnny said. "The New Revelation death squad."

"And Corbette allows them to wander about 'converting' girls?"

Johnny and Lucia exchanged a look. "He's . . . not himself of late—"

"He's busy."

Too busy to keep an eye on his traumatized fiancée? Or did Johnny's appearance mean that whole shindig was off? Maybe the Raven Lord didn't want a tainted bride. Grace scowled. "All right, I'll teach you a couple tricks, but it'll cost you. I tell you what I know, and you can do with it what you like."

"Luce—" Johnny warned.

Lucia cut him off. "I accept."

"If you can slip out again," Grace said, "meet me at Butterworth's. Tomorrow?"

Lucia offered a tremulous smile. "I'll be there. Thank you."

Grace waved her off. Now she had a job. She should be bouncing off the walls, so why did she feel nervous? Things were finally going her way. She'd better watch her back.

Chapter 6

The road to hell was paved with bureaucrats. The last thing Leif wanted was to become one of them, but every move he made seemed to drag him further into the cogs of the great political machine. Take, for instance, the rusted towers before him. At one time Gas Works Park had been the site of a coal gasification plant that provided power for half the nascent city. It sat on a prime piece of real estate that jutted out into Lake Union with a gorgeous view of the broken towers of downtown.

Leif tried not to stare at them. He'd liked civilization, and the constant reminder of its loss only made him morose.

Lake Union was a swamp of its former self. When the Ballard Locks had broken, half of the water had drained into Puget Sound, leaving twenty feet or so of green slimy lake bottom exposed. Rain, slime, and more rain. He might as well be back in bloody England.

He wondered if London still stood. Nothing in his research definitively pointed to its destruction, so he preferred to think of his adopted city as it existed in his memory. It was a boon that he couldn't check himself; that way lay madness. A Dreki who couldn't keep up with the damage time wrought to his world lost his will to live. There was much to find dissatisfying in this life, but he preferred it to the alternative.

What had Sven been thinking?

"I am not my brother," he reminded himself.

"What was that? I can't hear you over this infernal banging." Zetian waved her list at him. After months of badgering him to hear supplicants in the new Great Hall, she'd finally brought the fight to him.

Work crews were on site sunup to sundown, and Leif visited when he could. He had a foreman, but he liked to direct the restoration personally. Zetian had abandoned her hope of getting him on Sven's ostentatious jeweled throne. Leif had told her he'd rather dine with Ereshkigal in hell, and perhaps she'd finally taken the hint.

"I'm working, Zetian. If you want my attention, you'll have to keep up." He took off over the muddy lawn toward the south tower where the steelworkers were soldering the last seam in the spare boiler. Workmen had blasted through his latest round of instructions. At this rate the first small batch of gas could be produced at the end of the week. He couldn't wait to show Jameson just what his people could contribute to the new city. This would be a major triumph. He should never have to prove his usefulness again. Science and ingenuity would win out, no war required.

"You are impossible," Zetian said.

"So I've been told."

"You haven't even seen the coal. Corbette will never deliver."

"The first shipment is on its way as we speak. Just in time to test the equipment." He pulled out his gold pocket watch and checked the time. "I sent Thorsson this morning to check on their progress."

Zetian thinned her lips. "Should I quit then? I'm not much use as an advisor if you disregard my advice." She had urged him to stall the retrofit, or finish in secret and keep the gas for himself. He was trying to reinvent their reputation, not reinforce their image as underhanded, two-faced bastards. Couldn't she see that? But she saw every interaction as an opportunity for the Kivati to finish their dragon extermination campaign. The Kivati had killed off the local population of dragons—the Unktehila—centuries ago. Ever since Sven showed up with his Drekar followers, Corbette had been trying to finish the job. Perhaps she was right.

"You have my undivided attention until Thorsson arrives," Leif said.

"Try not to look petulant," Zetian said. She reached out and adjusted the lapels of Leif's black silk suit, glancing up at him through her lashes as she did. Leaning close enough that her breasts, encased in a tight band of red silk, barely touched his chest, she pouted her ruby lips. "Use your considerable . . . charm. Your brother may have shielded you from court politics, but even you can't have survived two centuries without developing a deft hand at it. Charm is your greatest weapon."

He gritted his teeth and watched a dark shape rise from the water, oozing lake muck, and swing its tentacle at a passing duck. The Unraveling hadn't just freed an army of wraiths. Oh, no. It had scurried things up from the dark deep. Things that should have stayed down there. The water wasn't safe for humans or Drekar anymore. The tentacle caught the poor duck and drew it down beneath the waves.

"That's better," Zetian said. "You look positively murderous." She had a line of petitioners waiting for him at the base of Kite Hill with Joramund and Grettir on security detail. The two Vikings were part of his brother's personal guard, led by Erik Thorsson. The three Drekar were Leif's opposite in every way: uncultured, unsympathetic, and immoral.

The petitioners ignored the berserkers through some feat of bravado. It was about as easy as ignoring a stampeding rhinoceros. Leif passed the line with a brief, tight smile, and followed Zetian to the crown of the hill, where a gilt chair had been placed in the center of the giant sundial. He had to give Zetian credit. The hill might be sparse, the grass brown. Nothing hinted at the Regent's nobility and power but the gold paint on the chair. But the stunning backdrop of Lake Union shot out behind him, and the ruined city spread across the horizon gave his position an air of danger. Sitting here he would look like a barbarian king resting on his knoll while the village burned.

He clapped slowly. "Bravo, Zetian. You should have been in show business. All I need is a fur cape and a bloody broadsword."

"You are too kind, my lord. Hold on to that image while you meet these demands."

"Right. So you want me to laugh then." He settled into the damned chair and called the first petitioner.

There were quite a few requests for basic necessities: food and water, help rebuilding shelters in the Drekar-controlled territory from Ballard east to the Gas Works, and arms for the merchants along Ballard Avenue to fend off looters and hungry citizens. Leif told Zetian to take care of it. He hadn't realized how many people depended on him. The citizens of Ballard still looked to the Regent for safety and leadership. Not the Drekar as much—they would happily seize power for themselves—but the very human descendants of those Scandinavian immigrants that Sven had brought with him when he had carved out his kingdom by Puget Sound.

Still, Leif didn't understand why Zetian couldn't handle these requests by herself. Finally Grettir brought up Snorri Longren, and it became apparent that Longren, a Dreki who was older than dirt, wouldn't listen to anyone but the Regent.

"Try to think like your brother," Zetian hissed low before the Dreki climbed to Leif's place on the hill. "He's hoarding resources for himself that rightfully belong to you. He flirts with madness. You must hold him to the edge, or end him. It is your duty."

Leif allowed a small shiver of recognition before he steeled his shoulders. Immortality came with a price. He had been searching for a cure to the madness that plagued them, but he hadn't found one yet. All the more reason for Zetian to rule, so that Leif could tend his experiments.

"I can't share what I don't have," Longren said. With red hair to match his infamous temper, gold rings on all his fingers, and a green suit to set off his green eyes, many people took him for an Irishman. The oldest Dreki among them, he'd pillaged the world over before Sven had convinced him to settle on the new frontier. Leif had no doubt that his knowledge was worth more than all his buried resources combined, if only madness hadn't warped the data in his brain.

Leif tuned out most of Longren's apologetic response to how he would like to use his personal resources and fortune to help rebuild the city, if only he could. Drekar couldn't lie, but they could obfuscate like crazy. Leif had better things to do with his time. He finally cut him off. "Are you telling me that you don't have two tons of fresh water tanks buried somewhere in North Bend?" Longren's eyes widened a fraction. Leif showed his teeth. He might have left politics to Sven all these years, but that didn't mean he didn't have claws of his own.

"How can I know what remains after the disaster?" Longren asked.

"You can fly out there and dig it up. Christ, man, do I have to do everything myself?"

Drekar didn't share. They didn't cooperate with Kivati. They didn't help humans out of the goodness of their own hearts. Leif wondered how his brother had built his empire. Norgard had manipulated the hell out of his people, forcing them to work together for his own ends. Surely that was an accomplishment in and of itself.

Zetian brushed her jet-black hair behind her ear in a signal to cut off this interview. He could hardly keep all her signals straight.

"Longren," Leif said, "I expect a report of your assets in, oh, three days. At that time, I will decide how best you can be of use to this operation. You will not leave the territory. You will arrive in the Great Hall to give your accounting in person to me. I will have your word on the matter."

Longren's jaw tightened. "I am old, Regent. The blackened sky is no place for these weary bones." Leif's stomach clenched. "I would ask you a question in private."

"No."

"But—"

Leif stood. "The answer is no. You will find me those resources. You will stay here where I can use you." Sven had always thought the older ones weak, but Leif knew they had a great deal to teach. How much wisdom had Longren collected in his four centuries? How much art, language, and culture could he recount to rewrite old history books that had been lost in the fire? Leif didn't want to be in charge of a dying people. He wouldn't let them choose to give up. "Go. I'm done here."

Longren left. There were still more petitioners, but Zetian saw the look on Leif's face and knew better than to push. She ordered Grettir and Joramund to dismiss them.

"You did well, my lord," she said.

"I hate this."

"But you did it anyway. That is the measure of a ruler; the willingness to do what is necessary, no matter the circumstance, no matter the pain. They do not respect love, only fear."

The Drekar had had that motto pinned before Machiavelli was a twinkle in his ancestors' eye. They tended their human flocks, provided for their meals, but always used fear to bait the hook. Now things were changing. Humans had learned of their existence and were seduced by their power. Every day some idiot landed at his doorstep begging to be made immoral in exchange for his soul. It didn't work that way, of course, but someone had been spreading rumors.

"Tell me about Sven's slaves," he said. He hadn't wanted to ask, but it occurred to him that Zetian might know more.

She rolled her task list, her long red nails scratching against the thick vellum. "He collected them since the great age," she said, speaking of the Viking Age when Sven had come into manhood. "It was tradition. I believe Fafnir taught him, or if he didn't, I don't know."

"There are more?"

"Slaves were always taken in the raids."

"But the blood slaves. Do you know the magic that binds them?"

She hesitated. A crow passed overhead—Corbette's spy. She waited for it to fly out of earshot. "Free will."

"A sacrifice?" He mused over it. There was power in sacrifice: blood, life, virginity. Free will was a new one to him, but he saw how it could be used. Giving up one's persona. Blind obedience. "And how is it such a secret?"

"He took street kids. No one noticed them missing, because they didn't exist to begin with. Scrappy fighters, the lot of them. He educated them. Gave them a home. Family. He gave them their every desire. A chance to be rich on their own. A chance for revenge."

"So how do I free them?"

She finished rolling the list and tied a red satin ribbon around it. "They earn their freedom once their promised service is fulfilled."

"And how are those terms decided?" He wondered how much Grace still owed.

"I don't know. I don't know!" Zetian threw her hands up,

sending her breasts swaying in their silk wrappings. "And I don't care. Use them, abandon them—it's all the same to me. But you're not doing them any favors by keeping them home in bubble wrap. You're only prolonging their enslavement."

"But—" He broke off when he spotted a black dragon with silver-tipped scales hurtling toward them from the east. "Thorsson."

The dragon roared.

"Something is wrong," Leif said.

As the dragon neared the Gas Works, shouts rose from the workers. Leif knew without looking that signs against the evil eye were going up. Otherwise brave men would make the sign of the cross or flash the pagan symbols tattooed on the tips of their fingers. More would clutch the gris-gris most wore beneath their shirts to ward off evil. Stupid. Irrational. But Leif shouldn't blame them; the dragon roaring toward the park was a terrible thing to behold. Even he could see it. The size alone dwarfed a man. The razor-sharp claws and three rows of jagged teeth were the stuff of nightmares. Spikes ran along the dragon's spine from his head to his tail, and steam trickled from between his jaws.

Still, it irked that they feared Drekar when they were under Leif's protection. And their silly charms wouldn't ward off a dragon, even if they were true magic, which few were. Fake shamans and counterfeit wards were more plentiful than rats along the Interurban.

The dragon tacked, dropping from the higher air current, flapping his huge membranous wings as he landed agile as a bat on the hillside. Leif was struck by the majesty of the great beast. The beauty. He would never forget the first time he'd seen a dragon flying out over the North Sea. Until Sven, Leif had only ever seen his own reflection in the lake behind his grandfather's fields. He'd agreed wholeheartedly with his newfound brother: it was a crime to hide something so beautiful away in the shadows.

Thorsson Turned. The Aether rippled over him like a sunbeam bouncing off the morning tide. A flash, and then Thorsson was on his knees, his back dripping with sweat, his chest heaving from his hurried flight.

"What happened, Thorsson?" Leif asked.

"Where is the coal?" Zetian demanded.

Thorsson raised his head. His lip curled back from his teeth. "The Thunderbird lost it. Kingu has returned."

It was late afternoon by the time Grace headed to the House of Ishtar to get paid. She hadn't gotten into a fight with the walking dead since the alley where Asgard had found her, which, considering her luck with aptrgangr, was eerie. She couldn't ignore the itch at the back of her neck. Her black eye from the human fight had turned into a real beauty. As she walked from her shop in Flesh Alley, she made a point to pull down the broadsheets that had been tacked to old electric poles through downtown. She skimmed a couple. Oscar had been right: Corbette had closed Queen Anne to outsiders. He was marshaling his troops, but no one knew his target.

She found the House of Ishtar in ruins. Overturned furniture and broken windows. Shredded drapes and smashed china. Maidens swept the floors and hammered boards over the empty windowpanes. A pile of trash in the front yard burned merrily. What on earth? Grace slipped in the back door and looked for Elsie.

Ianna, High Priestess of Ishtar, breezed into the receiving room, head high, power dripping from every jeweled finger. Not an inch of skin showed beneath her chin, but the clinging silk enumerated every curve. Her blond hair was pulled back in all manner of twists and braids, and still more jewels hung glittering in the candlelight. The sexual promise that was often in her warm voice and inviting eyes was gone.

She was all business, cracking the whip with a glance. "Ladies, please! I want this mess cleaned up, and I want it cleaned yesterday. We have not survived the mountains falling just to shut down over a little indoor windstorm." She clapped her hands, then spotted Grace. Blood rushed to her face. "You!" She pointed her ruby-encrusted finger at Grace like a revolver. "You did this."

"How could I—?"

"The fence, damn you. Your runes are lousy, good-for-nothing hocus-pocus!"

"Hey now, I didn't have a chance to finish them—"

"You let the Kivati desecrate my temple!"

"Kivati?" Why would the Kivati attack the Drekar-owned House of Ishtar? She thought they had a truce. "Even if I had finished, the runes only keep out wraiths. There isn't a keep-everything-out spell."

"What did I pay you for, you little fool?"

Grace crossed her arms. This was so not her fault. "I can't do anything against the Kivati, unless they're dead."

"Of course not! But this. This!" Ianna swept out a hand to encompass the general destruction. The china cabinets were smashed, tea sets scattered about in tiny porcelain fragments. The velvet drapes hung shredded from the dowels. The cold breeze blew through the empty leaded panes. Glass shattered. "This is all your fault. I'll ruin you."

Grace felt her stomach slip into her shoes. She had banked on finishing this job and getting a nice referral to the other houses for her work. There were all sorts of pretend shamans hiring themselves out with protection tricks, but none of them had her knowledge and expertise. This was something she could do that was constructive to buy her freedom. Not destructive. Not killing and death. "You hired me for two jobs," she said. "I did the other."

"Oh, yes." The Priestess planted her fists on her generous hips. "Protecting us from the aptrgangr hoards." Her voice rose again. "They would have been better than smashing my house!"

"I killed the aptrgangr for you," Grace said mulishly. "There were more than you said there'd be."

Ianna laughed. "You are not getting a penny from me."

Grace could feel Elsie hovering around the corner out of sight. The Maidens were all industriously ignoring the scene like she'd never helped them out of a scrape. But it was her word against Ianna, and the High Priestess owned them. Grace pulled out her last card. "I'll tell Asgard."

The Priestess dipped into an exaggerated bow. "Be my guest. I'll send him the bill for this. I hope he adds it to your debt." She straightened. "Now get the hell out of my—Erik, darling!"

Grace turned and found the Regent's insane right hand towering over her. How a man that thick could move so quietly, she had no idea. He'd always seemed more frost giant than dragon. Even in human form, his eyes were perpetually slit. He smiled, showing a mouthful of sharp, pointy teeth.

Grace tried not to back up.

"She hurt you?" He pointed to Grace's bruised eye. "I can fix it." His eyes changed, interest flickering in the inhuman depths. He let his gaze wander down.

"No, thanks." She tried not to cover herself instinctively. Thorsson knew what Norgard had made of her. To be fair, she didn't think the man's opinion of her had changed; in his primitive testosterone-laden brain, all women were objects. She'd heard the Maidens he visited were paid extra for the privilege. Norgard hadn't let him rough up the merchandise too much. He owned the Houses of Ishtar and liked his property alive and working. Norgard had leashed his crazy-ass henchman, but Norgard wasn't here anymore.

Thorsson turned to the Priestess. "What happened to the House?"

"Thunderbirds," the Priestess said, all obsequiousness. "They sent the wind."

"But you didn't see them," Grace clarified. "Did you?"

Ianna's lip pulled back from her teeth.

"Answer her questions," Thorsson ordered. Since when did Thorsson back Grace up?

"Yes," Ianna said. "Some showed up not a half hour later."

"Kivati, here?" Grace asked. "Which House? East? West?"

"Does it matter?" Ianna looked to Thorsson. "They didn't speak a word to anyone and left before I could demand answers."

"But the Kivati wouldn't attack a Drekar economic source," Grace said. "We have a truce."

"Truce." Thorsson repeated. He ran the edge of his blade across his palm. A line of blood appeared. The cut closed in the next instant. Thorsson hadn't been happy with the truce. He liked killing.

"Did you feel the air heat up?" Grace asked.

Ianna required a grunt from Thorsson before she answered the question. "No, a cold wind."

"Kivati can manipulate the Aether, but they tend to heat up the molecules of air, not cool them down," Grace said. "Ghosts are cold—"

"But what would a wraith want with the Maidens of Ishtar?" the Priestess snapped.

"Easy prey," Thorsson said. He raised the point of his sword and mimicked jacking off. Orgasm was a moment of vulnerability, when mental shields were completely down. Wraiths could manipulate the physical world, but they couldn't feel pleasure without a body, and they craved it. The patrons of the House would be in danger if the Maidens didn't keep the place free of wraiths. But the bone fence hadn't been finished.

The Priestess gave Grace a black look.

"I'm sorry, okay?" Grace said. "But it doesn't answer the question: why here, why now? There have always been wraiths."

"Not this many," Ianna said. "And not this strong."

Chapter 7

Grace tried to slip away from Thorsson, but he grabbed the back of her collar. He dangled her off the ground until her hood started to rip.

"Lemme go."

"No." He set her back on the ground and clamped his hand around her forearm, right below the gold band.

"Where are you taking me?" She hated the sweat that beaded her upper lip and armpits. Her heart pounded, and she knew he could hear it because he smiled.

"You like me? Eh, little girl?" He grinned to himself, and it was a mean look. She could easily imagine him burning and pillaging across the Baltic Sea and all the way to Moscow.

He dragged her along, his stride eating up three of hers. He was humming. She couldn't decide if she was better off pretending to be docile or self-assured. He wasn't going to be intimidated by her little knife, that was for sure.

After a few blocks she was panting for breath, and she realized something. He wasn't just humming, this brainless muscle. He was humming Sondheim. *Hello, little girl.*

She tripped on the cracked street and would have fallen if he hadn't trapped her arm. He swung her around the corner to where the Regent's black carriage waited on the high street. Crap. Asgard was going to be pissed. Thorsson rapped on the door twice, yanked the handle open, and threw her in. So much for civility. She was surprised he bothered to knock. She landed on her hands and knees on the carriage floor, shiny black boots an inch from her nose and leather, oil, and the overwhelming scent of cinnamon and iron. She turned her head and found voluminous red skirts.

"My, my." A woman's amused voice came from somewhere up above. "Pussy cat, pussy cat, where have you been? Tell me, kitten, how do you manage to get tangled in my strings so often, hmm?"

"That will be quite enough, Zetian," Asgard said. Grace winced. He pulled her off the floor and got a good look at her bruise. His nostrils flared. "Ishtar take you. What have you done now?" He touched the swelling edge of her eye, and she shied away. "My grandfather had a word for a girl like you: Trouble."

"Don't coddle the girl, Regent. Or perhaps you don't know what your brother used her for?"

"I know enough."

Grace felt her face flush with humiliation. She pulled away and sat back against the red leather seat, pushing as far into the corner as she could get. Asgard sat across from her looking elegant in his long crimson coat and sharp grey suit. He'd brushed his blond hair into a loose queue and polished his boots, but his fingers were still stained with ink and coal. He'd never be as stylish as his brother; Norgard had been beautiful as an ice sculpture, every line planned within an inch. Asgard's elegance had a rumpled air, and it made him seem more touchable. Warmer. Almost human.

Grace shook herself. To her left lounged Astrid Zetian, the only female Dreki in the territory, with her high Scandinavian forehead and Imperial dragon cat eyes. Gorgeous and smart and scheming. More deadly than even Thorsson.

There were few Imperials left, even before the Unraveling, and they never left their rugged mountains in the interior of China. Zetian had wanted more than monks and poetry. She'd come across the water during the Gold Rush, settling on Seattle for the same reason Norgard had: It held a cracked Gate.

Grace was pretty sure the ancient Dreki had been Norgard's lover. She wasn't some doe-eyed young girl who could be ensnared and entranced. Zetian was a woman empowered by her sexuality. When she came to a man's bed it would be on her own terms. She was on top. Carnal. Calculated. Passionate. The very image of a fertility goddess, Zetian would sweat and sweat beautifully.

Grace curled farther into her corner and tried to fade into the leather.

"Don't you want to know why you're along on this little adventure?" Asgard asked. His green eyes were dazzling even in the dim interior of the carriage. A few strands of blond locks framed his high cheekbones. His cravat was slightly askew. Grace could easily imagine these two beautiful creatures grappling against the headboard just seconds before she sprawled inside. She felt like a pigeon among peacocks.

She raised her eyebrows and stuck out her chin. "You can't get it up without an audience?"

His lips parted. "Excuse me?"

Zetian chuckled. "The wee babe is jealous, darling." She leaned in to Grace and her scent skyrocketed.

Grace held her breath, but Zetian waited her out. A girl needed oxygen. The pheromones were heady. The first whiff made her eyes almost water with need. She clenched her thighs together against the acute ache. Sweat beaded on her lower back. She fought the urge to touch her fever-bright skin or bite suddenly sensitive lips. She shut her eyes and pretended she felt nothing. She'd had a lot of practice.

"Come, little fighter," Zetian whispered, her breath hot on the delicate shell of Grace's ear. "You want to play rough? I will break you."

"Enough, Zetian," Asgard said. Grace opened her eyes at his sharp tone.

Zetian retreated to her side of the carriage, her mouth pulled in a satisfied smile like a cat in cream. "Just showing your little slave her place, my lord."

With a jolt, the carriage began to move. Grace braced herself between the seat and the door, her feet planted. Asgard inspected her ripped hood briefly and studied her black eye. She turned her face away. "I'm fine."

"You look it. What were you doing at the House of Ishtar?"

"What's it to you where I go?"

"The House is destroyed. It's my business to find out why."

"Right, so I went at it with a big mallet and my knife. Really wanted to give Ishtar the old one-two, you know?"

His mouth curved. "I don't doubt you could cause that much destruction, given enough time. Doesn't matter. Thorsson will tell me."

"Is he following me?" She could almost feel the steam billowing out of her ears.

"I thought I told you to stay away from fights."

"I thought I told you to give me a job or get out of my business."

Zetian laughed. "That's the problem with feeding a stray pup, darling. They never appreciate it."

"I did some work for Ianna," Grace told him, "and was picking up my fee. It sounds like wraiths did it, but she wanted to blame the Thunderbirds. Some showed up a little after the attack and checked out the house."

"A lot of people want to blame Thunderbirds this morning," he said.

"And maybe we should join them," Zetian said. "It's

unwise to side with the scapegoat." Asgard's nostrils flared. She tapped her long red nails against the leather carriage seat. "What more do you need, Asgard? A white glove slapped across your cheek? Corbette swore upon the Aether to purge us from the Earth. The Aether! There is no oath more binding. Even if he is innocent of these charges, the truce won't last. Don't let your first act as Regent be to let our people be slaughtered."

Our people? Norgard would never have risen to that bait; he didn't give a flying Freya about other Drekar. They lived so long as they were useful to him. But Asgard seemed to care. His irises narrowed to slits. "Corbette has been arrested."

"What?" Grace sat up.

"This morning at six o'clock, two teenagers entered the Church of the New Revelation with crossbows and proceeded to shoot at the worshipping congregation. They were subdued and killed before they could be questioned. The Church has declared war on all supernaturals. The teens were Kivati. Jameson believes Corbette ordered them to do it."

Grace felt her stomach drop. "But, why? Kivati are sworn to protect humans."

"Is that what they call it now?" Zetian asked. "Opening the Gate? Protecting humans?"

"Rudrick went rogue," Grace said.

"If one Fox revolted against their leader," Zetian said, "you know a hundred more are thinking it. Rudrick couldn't have pulled the Unraveling off alone. Perhaps Corbette wanted to add humans to the list of races to wipe from the playing field. Don't look at me that way, little girl. I have a vested interest in keeping humans alive, especially those pure souls of New Revelation." Zetian's forked tongue slipped out and licked her ruby red lips. Her hungry eyes bore into Grace.

Grace couldn't back up, crowded into the corner as she was. The carriage wheel bounced in a deep rut, throwing her across the carriage and into Asgard's lap. Soft grey wool covered his rock hard thighs. The lightly pin-striped vest hid washboard abs. His arms came around her, anchoring her in the rocking carriage, but it was suddenly too much. Too much heat and iron and overwhelming male body.

She was keenly aware of her own vulnerability. "Don't touch me!"

He let go, allowing her to scramble unceremoniously off his lap and back to her corner. He and Zetian watched her with cool eyes. She knew she was being ridiculous. She would never have ordered Norgard like that. He would only be more likely to do it.

Asgard gave her space. He pulled the curtain back and watched out the window. "Corbette went peacefully when Jameson's soldiers arrested him. He is at the council hall now, and I've been called to be a witness against him. I want you there, Grace, to keep your eyes open. You've had more direct contact with aptrgangr than any of the others. Consider this your first job."

"I accept," Grace said before he could take it back. She had no chance of getting another job with the temples after Ianna followed through on her threat. Besides, she didn't want to be left out of this brewing storm. Asgard was offering a chance at information, and after five years in the dark, she was starving for a taste of light. "It's Kingu," she told him. "You should have prepared for this."

Asgard studied her for a long moment as the carriage rocked. "I'm afraid you might be correct, and I'm sorry for it."

She inhaled sharply. An apology? An actual admission of wrong? She had to remember that Asgard was Drekar and a master manipulator. He might pretend to have emotions and honor, but he was younger. He still thought of himself with human contemporaries. Hadn't had the centuries to lose his connections and his grip on sanity. But deep down, they were all the same. Norgard. Zetian. Thorsson. Asgard. Monsters, every one.

Leif arrived at the council building and ushered everyone out of the carriage into the weak, late afternoon sun. They moved more readily than he did. He knew that if he entered those wide blue doors there was no going back. Corbette and Kingu and war lay in wait inside the building. But it was already too late to back out. He had one chance to diffuse tensions between the three populations. If he failed, Zetian would win, and his experiments must turn from quality of life to machines of war.

Inside, he allowed Jameson's soldiers to divest Thorsson of his broadsword even though he knew it would make the man brood. He was less amused as they stripped Grace of her weapons. Each knife took a bit of her armor, until she was only a fragile, tiny human in pitifully thin skin. Thorsson, Zetian, and he could all sprout scales, claws and fire in a blink of Aether. He didn't like it that Grace was left vulnerable, but there was nothing he could do. He watched the soldiers like a hawk; his slit pupils hurried them along, fear rank on the wind. He was pleased that they missed the knife in her boot. He was less pleased that they ran their hands up and down her body, searching with their dirty paws. A savage glance from him, and they backed off.

Zetian raised an eyebrow. She motioned for him to proceed first into the council chamber. All trace of her earlier game was gone. She was all cool business. Advisor to the king. Humans didn't understand a female's power, she said, and when they recognized it they feared it. In front of them she played a shadow of herself. Dispassionate, logical, but a little bit dull. They never knew what hit them.

"I can't go in there with you," Grace hissed.

He knew what she meant; she got by on sticking to the shadows. "Stay on the sidelines. Take notes." He bit back the need to shield Grace from all the watchful hatred he sensed in the council room. The best he could do was to disassociate himself from her, and so he let her go. Once she was out of earshot, he motioned for Thorsson to guard her.

Thorsson grimaced, but followed her.

"You coddle her," Zetian said. "She is a warrior."

"She is human."

"You will break her spirit. Norgard couldn't do it. But you will, if you keep on this path. She will curse your name."

Leif stared at her.

Zetian shrugged. "Fine. Do as you wish."

Soldiers held back the mob in the council chamber, same as they had the last time he set foot into this mockery of a court, but this time they called for Corbette's blood. He paused in the doorway, and the anger was so palpable it masked his presence.

All eyes were on Corbette, and the tide had turned. He sat in the defendant's gate like an ancient cedar tree; tall and unbending. The winds of change tore about his branches; he would crack and fall before he budged. His straight black hair fell past his collar. The dust of the road lay upon his suit. There was a careworn look about him—a shocking change from his usual fastidiousness. If that was the state of his dress, his mind must be a madhouse.

Or perhaps he was too busy planning his new war to care for his appearance. Leif clenched his jaw and tried to look calm. He remembered the endless years of war. Sven had shielded him from most of it, but he read the paper and could guess what the reporters left out. Every warehouse fire or arson investigation that had turned up empty had not been for lack of police intelligence. The gang shootouts and hijacked shipments had not been so mysterious. He didn't want to return to that time. He needed peace for his people.

He needed to find a cure for the immortal madness and a stable, nurturing environment to increase his population.

Fafnir was laughing somewhere in the world. There were too many variables for Leif to control. He thought of his mother. She would have wanted him to try.

Through the ring, he felt Grace slip into the peanut gallery and knew Thorsson would keep her safe. It was full of Kivati. If Corbette planned to take out the opposition in one swoop, this would be a perfect opportunity. The Regent and his advisor, the admiral and his cohorts. Only Marks was missing.

Leif was beginning to think like Zetian. Tiamat help them all.

At the defendant's gate, Admiral Jameson grilled Corbette about the youths and the Kivati's animalistic violence. The admiral wore a black armband and had the flags at half-mast. Surely not for the slain at New Revelation?

"Wild animals should be kept in cages with radio collars," Jameson said. "We should have warning when the man walking down the street toward us is a vicious killer. We need watch lists—"

"I am responsible for all my people," Corbette said softly, "but I can't learn anything from those boys if they're dead."

Corbette showed admirable restraint. Jameson was trigger-happy. He had soldiers and guns, and it was no secret that he wanted to expand his territory northward. He coveted the Kivati's hill, the high ground out of the infill and fallen mess of downtown. Mostly, he wanted to own the Interurban and the commerce that went with it. The trade routes were once again the path to power.

A soldier rushed forward and whispered into Jameson's ear. Announcing Leif had arrived, no doubt. The general looked up and found him. "Ah, our other supernatural representative has arrived. I call Regent Asgard to the stand."

Leif hesitated only a beat. He took the appointed place

next to Corbette, feeling very much like he joined him in the stocks. Zetian, as his advisor, sat next to him. "We need to talk," he murmured to Corbette.

Corbette stared straight ahead.

Zetian nudged Leif with her foot. A sick knot formed in his belly.

Admiral Jameson surveyed the crowd. He'd apparently learned stage presence since Leif had last seen him; he played to the audience and rode on its moods. "Lord Corbette says he doesn't know where his animals are at all times even with his magic woo-woo." Jameson paused for the crowd to boo. "And he thinks we won't defend ourselves against these terrorists? Walking into our shelters and barracks and massacring our brave soldiers and civilians?"

"Barracks?" Leif looked at Zetian, who shook her head.

"And speaking of magic," Jameson settled back into his tale, like some cowboy by the fire, spinning his audience closer, "how can this supernatural king deny knowledge of Fort Seattle? Two soldiers, undeniably human, brave men, loyal men. Lieutenant John Wallis: thirty-four years old. A husband. Father. Proud to serve the new administration to fight back our enemies and bring peace again to our cities. A loyal soldier." His voice rose with the murmur of the crowd. "And his faithful compatriot Trevor Duquette. A career military man. Bereaved husband and father. His family stolen by these supernatural folk who messed with something they had no business messing with and destroyed the world as we knew it. What do you have to say to that, *Lord* Corbette?"

"Human soldiers?" Corbette said. His voice softer and deeper than it should have been. "I have no knowledge of your people's transgressions."

"But two incidences of violence. They walked into the barracks and started shooting, just like your two boys in the

Church." Jameson tightened his hand on his gavel. "These are connected."

Beside Leif, Zetian crossed her arms. It sounded like wraiths had taken over the bodies of the two soldiers. He let out a breath he didn't realize he'd been holding. Thunderbirds attacking the House of Ishtar looked doubtful. If the Kivati hadn't breached the peace, there was still hope for him.

Leif turned to the audience chamber, following the invisible tether, and found Grace. He could have shot her blindfolded. The Aether sparkled around her, but he felt it more than saw it. She was partially hidden by the mob of humans. She grabbed a scrawny kid by the shirt. He was about eight or nine, a little thing with twig limbs and overlong, greasy hair. A newsboy cap slouched low over his eyes. No one seemed to notice. Grace must know the kid. Leif checked, but he wasn't one of his blood slaves. At least there was no leash from the hated malachite ring.

His eyes swept the audience and picked more urchins out of the mob like mice in a crowded pub. He wondered why he hadn't seen them before. They were good. Trained. Four or five of them quietly slid through legs and past stuffed back pockets, using the crush for cover. Every eye in the room was on the drama unfolding at the defense gate and not on the pickpockets collecting wallets, purses, jewelry and money clips, buttons and coins. Probably the laces from shoes if they thought they could get away with it. Times were tough; he couldn't blame them.

But it made him think of Sven, and how Grace knew the kid, and acid washed his stomach with another unpleasant suspicion.

Maybe they did belong to him. Maybe there were more out there who needed his help. Food, shelter, clothing, a fucking job.

And he'd been ignoring them for six months. They were children, Freya curse him.

He resolved to hunt down his brother's holdings after this.

Jameson slapped his hands on the banister in front of Leif. "Regent Asgard, perhaps you could enlighten us to how supernatural elements take over the minds of others. What is the connection between Kivati and those animals of the wild? They can take over crows' minds; why not a human? Speculate, if you will, how those Kivati boys might have been manipulated into their actions. Come to Lord Corbette's defense, because he isn't coming to his own. I'd be perfectly in my rights to see this as an act of war."

Leif steepled his fingers. This was it—the chance for peace rested on his shoulders like an activated bomb, and he didn't know which wires to snip. He suddenly wished for Sven's silver tongue. Jameson, in his own bid for power, thought to put Leif and Corbette at each other's throats. Divide and conquer—the truest path to domination. Leif thought about his newfound dependents and shored up his resolve. He could do better. They deserved it.

"Admiral Jameson," Leif said. "The Kivati and the Drekar are distinctly different races and in no way represent the supernatural population as a whole. But I can tell you what is generally known about Corbette's people. They manifest their power at puberty, when they go through a spiritual journey and connect with their totem animal. I believe it to be some sort of vision quest. After that time, they can transform between human and animal shape and have some other powers associated with the Aether. Only some can connect with wild animals, like crows, in order to pass along information. But I've never heard of them connecting to a human."

The blood had drained from Corbette's face. He stared straight ahead.

"And the Kivati killers?" Jameson asked.

"One might speculate the youths were on their vision quest. During such time, they open themselves to receive their totem and might be vulnerable to possession. Kivati are otherwise known to have very strong mental shields. They are naturally resistant to wraiths—ordinary wraiths, I mean, which are bad enough. But who knows what a demigod like Kingu could do? We simply have no empirical evidence to inform us, and I think it's unfortunately quite likely that he has returned. Take the unusual Aether currents of late—"

"Enough," Corbette hissed. The Aether buzzed, swarming through the room like an angry hive. Corbette's power to manipulate the Aether was legendary, but it was tied closely to his emotions. Anyone could see the man was stretched thin. The mood in the room rolled in on the Aether, a storm surge headed toward this mostly civilized assembly. The audience sucked it in and played it back, growing angrier.

Leif could do nothing to stop it. The Aether rolled over him, rubbing over his human skin as if to expose the scales. He fought the urge to Turn. His eyes slit. His vision narrowed. The colors shifted to blues and greens. His wings tore at his back, anxious to stretch into the sweet Aether storm that brewed and bubbled between the fragile wood walls.

Jameson couldn't see it, but he began to sweat. "No, tell us more about this Aether. The source of Kivati power, right? Well, we've been working together for six months, and I've still seen neither hide nor hair of sharing of this mystical woo-woo. It's time that changed. I'm getting mighty suspicious of the quality of this collaborative, you get me, Regent?" He glanced jerkily around as unseen currents whipped past him. "And what . . . and what do you have to say to that, Lord Corbette?"

The temperature in the room climbed. Leif leaned into it, welcoming the heat even as he knew the danger it posed.

"The Regent seems to be well informed," Corbette said. He stood. "My time here is wasted."

"Regent," Zetian hissed. "You must stop this." Her eyes were bright gold. A bead of sweat trickled down her temple.

Leif grimaced, but stood. He released his pheromones, thinking of Grace and feeling a tiny bit guilty. The humans began to relax as his calming scent spread. The feedback effect lessened.

Corbette shot him a killing glance, the violet rings of his pupils dilated till they blotted out the black. It suddenly didn't seem too far-fetched that Corbette might have sent his Thunderbirds to destroy the House or destroy the human's cult. With a flip of his long black coat, Corbette stormed out.

"Stop him!" Jameson yelled. "We aren't finished. You exit those doors and our treaties will be through—Corbette? Corbette!"

Leif could see the future in Jameson's hate-filled eyes—territories deteriorated into fiefdoms, civil war, no more rebuilding. The destruction of all that he had worked for. Toppling his chair, he hurried after Corbette. He had to salvage this.

Chapter 8

The Raven Lord stormed out of the council chambers with two Thunderbirds at his heels. His coat flared out behind him. The fleur-de-lis wallpaper curled from the wall in his wake, peeling down like linoleum on a hot summer day.

Leif followed him out. "Corbette, wait. We're all worse off if we don't work together. Rein in your power and think, man!" The double-paneled doors swung open with a crash. Dusk inked the sky. Crows filled the trees.

Corbette paused at the top of the wide cement stairs that led down to the broken sidewalk. "I don't need anything from you, Dreki. The policy of open cooperation has failed. Apparently I needed a reminder. It won't happen again."

"Three populations, three attacks. Kingu is a danger to all of us—"

"Kingu?" Corbette scoffed. "What will you do against your demonic kin? What can the humans do in the face of a demigod? Nothing. I am taking care of it. Alone."

"Is that what you told those poor boys' parents?"

Corbette's lip drew back from his teeth. He advanced on Leif. Corbette was shorter, thinner, but the Aether crackled out from his skin like a human conductor. It took all Leif's concentration not to back up.

Leif's unease grew. "By yourself? But the threat is against us all. The humans can't withstand an army of wraiths. They'll be decimated."

"Since when does a Dreki care for the fate of humans? The Kivati survived before they showed up and will continue to do so when they perish from the earth. They are none of our concern, if they ever were. We are not tied to them."

"Unlike us, you mean."

"I am done caring for your flock. See to your own."

"You can't be serious. We need to work together—"

"No. This incident has proven the rot of our unfortunate collaboration. I saw what happened to my father, and I won't let the same thing happen now."

"My brother was wrong—"

"You and Kingu and your demonic kind do not belong on these sacred shores." Corbette's eyes glowed violet in the dim light. There was a mad look about him, and Leif had the feeling he was finally seeing beneath the civilized mask. Danger and death stared out, like an old god. Heartless. Pitiless. Cruel.

It made him want to back away very slowly, but he knew within him lay a monster of equal power and cruelty. If he chose to use it, if he chose to embrace the heartless darkness of the dragon, he was more than a match for the feathered madman. Except that he needed Corbette alive and uninjured and sane.

Corbette didn't have the same restrictions on him.

"I thought you were a man of science and reason," Leif said, feeling the dragon crowding to the forefront of his mind. "But I can see I was wrong. I need that coal." The cold washed through him. He thought of Sven. "I will get that coal one way or another."

"Is that a threat?"

"There is a long history in Seattle of pulling down the hills to fill in the tide lands. A large crevasse recently opened at the foot of Queen Anne. It would be a pity if your hill followed suit."

Corbette tilted his head to the side and gave him a long, slow stare. "Then we understand each other."

Leif felt Grace slip through the crowd at his back. The weight of the invisible tether grew more pronounced. Side-stepping, he blocked her from the Raven Lord's sight. She'd call him high-handed for it and be rightly irked, but he didn't care.

Corbette turned his face to the sky. The Aether shimmered around him and his two Thunderbirds. Their long coats flared out in a shimmery golden glow and changed to feathered wings. Their noses lengthened to sharp beaks. Corbette's Raven was larger than a man, violet beady eyes, sharp talons. The Thunderbirds dwarfed him. They were dragon-sized, and the shadow of lightening singed the tips of their wings. Pushing off from the ground, they soared into the darkening sky. Their tailwind rocked the street with a clap of thunder, slamming shut the doors and rattling the windows. Leif shielded his face. The crows rose from the trees and followed.

"That bastard!" Grace said behind him. "Who does he think he is with his high and mighty routine? The Kivati have humans do their dirty work; they aren't all self-sufficient."

"He's hiding something," Leif said. "Or he's scared."

Grace shot him a disbelieving look.

"He's scared, and he's running. His control on his people is falling apart, so he's going to hole up in his compound and shore up his defenses. Two Kivati youths were taken. That's never happened in my memory. There've always been aptr-gangr, but no Kivati has been weak enough to be a victim."

"I thought you all had some woo-woo defenses against possession."

"You say 'you all' like all supernatural races are the same.

Say what you really mean, Walker. You think monsters can't possess monsters, is that it?"

She shrugged her shoulders and muttered something unintelligible.

Thorsson had rescued his weapons from the soldiers at the door, and he lumbered over, followed by Zetian. Her long red skirts snapped back in the gusts of wind. Her slit eyes glowed with the need to change. The Aether still sparked and crackled around the building almost like static electricity right before a lightning storm.

"With this storm, it's hard to believe the Aether won't hold an electric charge," Leif said. "If only I could run some tests . . ." But Corbette would never agree.

Zetian laughed. "Just think if you possessed the power to manipulate Aether like the Kivati, dear scientist, you might change the world."

"I've never seen a machine that could do half that—"

"Ignorant man." She closed her fingers around his left hand, and her thumb stroked the underside of his malachite ring. "Science is not the only way. But let's make a quick exit, darling. The mob follows."

He saw that she was right. Humans trickled out of the council doors. The soldiers Jameson had sent after Corbette clung to their guns and began to look around for new prey. They wouldn't want to come back empty-handed.

"You still think he plans for war?" Leif asked Zetian.

Zetian gave a tight smile. "More than ever. Don't let down your guard."

There was a power vacuum; even Leif with his inattention to political life could see that. Corbette unhinged. The humans infighting and scattered. The Drekar unwilling to cooperate with each other. It was a fertile ground for Kingu, more than Jameson, to divide and conquer. But what could he hope to win? Spreading seeds of fear through an already fearful populace seemed redundant.

Leif raised a hand to run through his hair and found it standing on end. Damn Corbette. He'd call the man theatrical, but that was more Sven's style. His brother would have left every meeting with thunder at his back if he'd had that power. He'd funded Leif's experiments to produce a device that could manipulate the Aether, but Leif had never come close. Sven would have used it for ill, and no matter what Leif refused to see about his brother, perhaps some part of him recognized the threat. He'd never melded runes and steam until recently. Until Grace.

"I'm outie," Grace said and moved toward the stairs.

He grabbed her by the back of her hooded sweatshirt. "Company." He'd been watching a group of humans waiting in the shadows beyond the torchlight. Spread out, they stood as if frozen. The whites of their eyes gleamed with reflected light. "Aptrgangr?"

Grace stilled. "Looks like it."

The aptrgangr took a step forward into the puddles of light. At least three were already dead: head wounds and rot gave them away. Pale blue skin stretched tight across blank faces. The rest appeared fresh, but freshly dead or freshly possessed remained to be seen.

"Damn Corbette," she said. "I bet his magic tantrum called them."

"We shouldn't linger," he said.

"I can't leave these people unprotected." She motioned to the growing mob.

"They would leave you in a heartbeat."

She stuck out her lower lip. "You don't know that."

"Would you stake your life on it?"

"Doesn't matter." She palmed her knife. "Let me go."

"Your willingness to martyr yourself, while touching, is stupid," Zetian said. "Your life belongs to the Regent."

Grace clamped her mouth shut.

Leif rather admired the woman for her bravery, but he

knew it was the mortal half of him that thought it. The dragon half had claimed her as his and wouldn't allow her to endanger herself for anything. Still, these humans weren't worth it. It irked him that she thought so little of herself that she'd trade her life for them. "Grace, you don't think I'm going to let you fight off fifteen undead by yourself, do you?"

"Then help me. Or better yet, hire me to do it—"

"Not this again."

"Kingu screwed my job, Regent. You're my last shot. I'm not going away until I earn my freedom."

"How about I pay you to not endanger yourself?"

She seemed to consider it.

"You can catalogue my library, or something."

"Or something." Zetian laughed.

Grace's face darkened.

"That's not what I meant." But he'd already lost her.

"Forget it. I don't need your charity." She started down the stairs.

"Thorsson," Leif ordered.

Thorsson pushed Grace aside, and she stumbled against the railing. The berserker stepped onto the cracked pavement and pointed his sword at the nearest aptrgangr, a thin woman with dirty blond hair tied back in a kerchief and the grit of a scavenger beneath her nails.

"Wait!" Grace held out a hand, but didn't touch the Viking. "I can save some of them."

Leif didn't like the thought of killing a woman. "Can she be saved?"

"Yes. Maybe. If she's not too far gone."

Leif didn't like that answer when fifteen stood against them. The setting sun gave way to a grimy dusk, blood fading over the mountains like Tiamat's life. The last of the Kivati Crows cawed overhead. Leif glanced behind him to the humans trickling out of the hall. Some meandered heedlessly down the front steps. Some saw the aptrgangr and knew what they were. From these, cries went out.

"Don't go there!"

"Stay in the light!"

"Someone get the admiral!"

But the admiral was busy nursing his bruised ego, and unless Leif was very much mistaken, Corbette had already abandoned the humans to their plight. "And now what? Would my dear brother take the easy road?"

Zetian shook her head. "And lose this chance at winning the court of public opinion? He was never one to squander resources. You should take a page from his book. Play hero of the people."

Grace scowled and hunched her shoulders. Her dislike of his brother was a palpable thing, like a rain shadow hanging over her head. Or golden manacles weighing her down. Who could blame her? Sven had been many things. A smooth political player. A strong leader. A kind, if distant, brother.

Had he ever been a hero? Maybe to an awkward young boy desperate for some male companionship from his mysterious kin. Leif's childhood was marked by a lack of knowledge of his dragon half, except in the stories of the Nameless Ones who flew in the night. Then Sven showed up, the unknown brother, and took Leif under his wing—literally—to show him the stars and introduce him to the splendid dark history of the dragons. Mystery brought to light. Sven cut a dashing figure, like a pirate king in the picture books. Leif didn't want to see beneath the shiny surface to the truth of why people made the sign of the evil eye against his brother and his kind.

But what Sven might call willful blindness, Leif wasn't afraid to name love.

"Well, Asgard?" Grace asked. "The wraiths grow stronger while you count cracks in the cement."

She was right. The storming Aether gave power to the undead before them. From the dark, more eyes gleamed. While he waited here, the Aether drew wraiths like maggots to rotting meat.

A cocky young human in a hockey tee stepped forward. A revolver stuck out of his back pocket. "Reverend Marks says the damned won't touch a true believer. We have nothing to fear," he told the people. "Let's go. Let the monsters fight each other."

"I wouldn't recommend it," Leif called out.

The man pulled the gun and swung it at Leif's chest. He aimed, steady and ready. A fool who knew how to use a gun. He thought that would be enough. "We don't need your help, demon."

Thorsson growled. Leif simply stepped aside. "So be it."

"No!" Grace shot him a look so dark it should be reserved for murderers and rapists, but then she still thought he was both. She dodged Thorsson and raced down the steps ahead of the revolver-toting human. The aptrgangr stirred at her approach. She ran straight at the thin female aptrgangr. The aptrgangr raised her arms, and Grace slid underneath and rammed a sharpened iron stake into its back. The undead faltered, but didn't fall.

"Help her!" he ordered Thorsson, but at that moment the idiotic humans decided to make a break for it and the aptrgangr attacked. There were indeed more hidden in the shadows than had first presented themselves. The aptrgangr were gifted with Thor's unnatural strength, too strong for a human to fight hand to hand, but they were allergic to iron. Grace stabbed another long railroad stake in the aptrgangr's flesh, and it crashed to its knees. Gods, she was fast. Quicker than any human he'd seen.

The humans on the other side weren't fairing as well. Their bullets hit their mark more often than not, but did no damage. The undead pressed on, the wraiths inside unstoppable with mere bullets.

The wind rose, blowing ash and dust into his eyes. He blinked, and Grace was already slashing at a second aptrgangr. He wanted to order her to stop with the full force of the slave bands, but she would be left without defense with five undead between herself and rescue. Tiamat blind him!

Grace watched the woman lose the fight with the wraith possessing her. Between one breath and the next, the twitch stopped and the gait smoothed out. It was too late to do anything. The host was good as dead. The aptrgangr looked right at her and something clicked in her blank eyes. A recognition that made no sense. Wraiths sometimes haunted the people they knew in life, but Grace didn't think this was one of those times.

She raised her bone knife and palmed the railroad stake. She pushed away the clench of sadness at the brief moment of hope. It was dangerous to pity a creature who would crush her as soon as look at her.

Thorsson neatly decapitated a second aptrgangr who had come up behind the woman. Red splattered the woman's cheek and hair. She didn't even blink. Grace braced herself and sprang forward. She heard a roar behind her. Stabbing the iron stake into the woman's neck, she sidestepped the woman's grasping arms, right into the path of two more walking dead.

She wasn't quick enough to dodge the next blow. Falling to the pavement, she twisted her ankle. *Sloppy, Grace*. Still more converged on her, and even Thorsson's swinging broadsword couldn't hold them back. What was going on?

Asgard entered the fray and pushed through the crowd to reach her.

She locked eyes with the nearest aptrgangr who rose

above her. The short, potbellied man wore suspenders and the tarnished brass star of one of Jameson's deputized vigilantes. "What do you want?" she screamed.

The aptrgangr stared straight at her. "The Heart."

She hadn't expected an answer. "What heart?"

"Tiamat's."

"Well, fuck." Tiamat. The Babylonian goddess of chaos. Mother of all dragons and the demon horde. The vengeful goddess who'd given her lover, Kingu, the Tablets of Destiny and sent him to wage war on the gods. Kingu attacking Seattle was bad enough, but he was only a slain demigod. Tiamat was the real deal.

And that was all the interrogating she had time for as he reached down to grab her shoulders and yank her to her feet. Her ankle protested beneath her weight. She stabbed him in the arm with her stake, and his hand dropped uselessly to his side.

She grabbed his other hand and tried to pry it from the crushing grip on her shoulder. "Who is running you?" she ground out. It was a stupid question, because all signs pointed to Kingu. Couldn't keep a girl from hoping that the answer this time would be different. Aptrgangr on the rise and Kingu sightings and coordinated attacks on the three races. Now aptrgangr looking for a goddess's heart—aptrgangr who rarely teamed up or fought for more than their selfish pleasures. How many clues did a girl need? Even Asgard had to see it.

One moment the potbellied man was crushing her shoulder, and the next his head was replaced with a swipe of razor-sharp claws the length of her arm. A red and green dragon curled around her, protecting her from the crush of undead. When had someone last protected her? Her parents, in that dark alley, the last time she'd seen them. Her father never hesitating to step between her and danger. Her proud mother's last order: *Run!*

She'd never let someone take the fall for her since, but she'd been in plenty of scrapes where she stood as some poor soul's last hope. Her parents' last sacrifice had been paid forward and then some.

The dragon surrounded her with those gorgeous, glistening scales. For one bright moment she felt protected. Cherished. It scared the bejesus out of her. She didn't want to lean on anyone, especially not *him*.

"You're in my way!" she shouted. But the monster only shook his terrible head and set the trees ablaze. Couldn't he see that she needed to be free? "Gods damn you, get out of my way!"

The dragon screeched and twisted. Something was turning the aptrgangr back, and the dragon spread his wings. She flattened against the ground, but he grabbed her with one of his giant claws, trapping her in a cage of his talons.

"Don't even think about—*gah!*" She screamed. The ground dropped out beneath her as the dragon picked her up and launched into the air. She hadn't realized how much she disliked heights until this moment when the street lamps shrunk from view and the dilapidated buildings turned to Tinkertoys and sailed away.

Kingu arrived just as the skirmish broke. He blew through the street and slipped in through the ear of a large, ruddy human. The man brandished one of those strange smoking guns the mortals favored. He broke in through the man's consciousness between his aim and the fire, easy to do when his attention was focused elsewhere. He took a long breath and transitioned. His green and blue vision colored in as much as the night would let it. He stretched and flexed the new muscles he controlled.

Inside the mind was a fog of smashing, sparkling images. No memories were recorded linearly or precisely. A human remembered a few, then his perception filled in the rest. But it was enough for Kingu to get an idea of who had called this Aether storm.

He flipped through the hazy images until he found three men in a chamber. His host had been in the audience. The words didn't carry, but the body language told Kingu what he needed to know. The clean-cut man in the green jacket held himself like a city leader. The blond man with the slit irises was Tiamat's blood. But it was the dark man with madness in his eyes who called the Aether to him.

Interesting.

Chapter 9

Soaring over Puget Sound, Leif's stomach threatened to revolt. He'd exposed his true form in front of humans. Even now, when the bones of his mother's father were so much dust beneath the thin English soil, he could hear the man's chiding words: "Hide yourself."

But in that crowded street full of panicking, angry mortals and a force of walking dead he'd never hoped to see, only one concern burned crystal bright: Kingu was here.

He'd smelled the demigod on the Aether wind, and his primitive reptilian brain had taken over. Not to save himself, but to save *her*. The young woman fighting and whirling around the aptrgangr was vulnerable in a way he, dragon kin, would never be. Kingu would crush her like a pebble beneath a steamroller.

Leif had turned, time and blood slipping from his face, and picked her up in his talons. He didn't look back to see if the demigod followed. He didn't look to see what Kingu searched for, or if it was even there hidden among the humans. Flight was the only thing that saved him.

He sailed above Puget Sound with the terror of Ragnarök nipping at his tail. Grace's screams only drew his heart rate higher, until he realized her fear wasn't directed at a jabberwocky-sized demonic dragon following. She was afraid of heights.

He descended through the clouds over Shilshole Bay. Sven had built the Drekar Lair directly into the cliff face beneath his Scandinavian stronghold in Ballard. The tunnels drove deep into the earth. The face looking out toward Puget Sound and the cloud-ringed Olympic Mountains had been cased in giant glass windows, which were thrown open during the high landing periods of dawn and dusk. Inside, a great hall put Odin's grand throne room to shame. Jewel-encrusted ceilings. Gold inlays. A stone fireplace big enough to roast three oxen. It was a gaudy vision of everything a dragon was rumored to want. Shiny gemstones and glittering diamonds covered every inch of space. A century of dragons flying through the windows and landing had gouged deep furrows in the river stones of the floor.

Now silent. Half crumbled into the sea. The gems exposed to the grasping gale winds. They glittered when the sun touched them, some uncovered tomb of a once great king. Leif had been to Egypt as a young man when the pyramids were first excavated. The lair felt like that now: a secret of a bygone time that should be left hidden to the ages. A sparkling landing pad, stripped of its defenses and left to the ravages of time and wind.

He felt like a trespasser, and he knew what he considered this great room to be: the resting place of his brother's grandiose persona. Sven was in death as he'd been in life: over the top, concerned with shock and awe and manipulating those around him.

Leif rarely used this entrance to his laboratory. The ghosts were too thick.

He took pains to set Grace down gently, but she still fell on the uneven stone. With a scrape like a tile saw, his claws skidded over the floor, drawing further furrows in the rock. He should have flown in circles longer. He should have disguised his trail, done something to throw off Kingu, but he was worried about the girl hanging from his feet in the cold wind. And what could he do to throw off a demigod? He wasn't Marduk with an army of Babylonian gods. Kingu was a force unto his own.

His bulk slammed up against the caved-in portion of the ceiling, and his breath left him in a hiss of smoke. Stunned only momentarily, he let his worry roll into anger and used that burst of energy to Turn.

The sky outside the shelter of the enclave roiled. Rain began to fall. Waves crashed against the cliff face. His servants kept the fire burning to signal the landing strip in the dark, and the firelight flickered over Grace's prone body. She stirred and pulled herself to her hands and knees. The rain splattered her back. Her dark hair hid her face as she moved into a crouch. Her black sweatshirt was ripped. A bit of blood smeared across her fragile wrist. How dare she put herself in danger? Had she no care for her person?

"What do they want with you?" he demanded.

She shook her head and looked up. He couldn't make out her features in the dark.

"Well?" He stalked forward. He knew his anger was unjustified, but he couldn't stop it rolling off of him to snap and crackle like the logs in the fire behind. As he drew near, she quickly rose to her feet. Always on the defensive. Always ready to fight. Didn't she know he would never hurt her?

"Who?"

"The aptrgangr. What are you to them?"

"I don't know what you're talking about."

"They seek you out."

Her head jerked back. "Maybe just a little part of them wants to move on, did you ever think of that? They need my help."

"You believe that."

She shrugged.

"How convenient for you." His deep voice reverberated

in the rocks beneath their feet. He knew she felt it travel from the souls of her boots and into her bones, stroking her from the inside. "You just happen to go hunting, and the undead show up. You just happen to make quota again and again. Just happen to save innocent civilians in the nick of time wherever you go."

"Hey, I don't like what you're suggesting—"

"Convenient for you that you—small, mean little thing that you are—manage to fend them off with a slip of a knife. I might not know all the old myths, but I know aptrgangr. Inhuman strength is their calling card. They crush their victims to death. How is it that you manage to fight them and win?"

"Fuck you. I'm good, that's all." Her chin jutted out, and the firelight played over her delicate features. She wasn't earth goddess beautiful—too boyish, with no hips to speak of and little chest—but her chin formed a delicately feminine point, and her grey eyes would lure in a drowning man. Her hair cascaded around her shoulders. He wanted to coil it about his fingers as he brought her stern mouth to aching surrender. She was all sparking fire and more prickles than a blowfish. He would strip her defenses one by one until she welcomed him.

"Oh, sweet," he said, soft and dangerous and full of promise, "I bet you are very, very good."

She gave ground. He followed. He could tell the moment she realized her mistake. The rain splattered her hair at the edge of the cliff.

He had forgotten that damn drop-off, and now he was the aggressor. Like some gothic melodrama, he had driven the shivering maiden to the rocky drop. What had come over him?

He spun on his heel, realizing belatedly that he wore no boots, and that, in fact, in his anger he had forgotten to clothe himself at all.

Wonderful.

Giving the girl his backside, he retreated into the hall. His feet left prints in the dirt from the collapsed roof and the salt from the open sea winds. He wondered idly if his nudity turned her on at all, or brought her only the unsettling memory of his brother's patronage. She wasn't some quivering virgin, not technically, but he had the impression that she'd never entertained on equal ground before.

He wouldn't have her any other way.

He heard Grace shake herself and follow, her hesitant footsteps growing bolder as her lingering fear sloughed off. He forgot what a human felt at flight: the ground dropping away, the keen thrill of hurtling through the skies, the edge of death lurking far below in the impact of the hard ground, the light-headed buoyancy as higher and higher he climbed till his lungs screamed for oxygen.

But not all humans were Dionysus, seeking divinity in the sun. Some were root bound as the great tree Yggdrasil. He suspected this was the case with Grace. She seemed the kind to form attachments deeply. The kind who had a few close friends and preferred each day settled and set, knowing who and what she'd encounter. Leif was the same way. Sven had mocked him for it, but Leif liked stability. His dragon side secretly craved the thrill of flight, but his human side wanted deep roots. He couldn't have both.

"The aptrgangr weren't after me," she said. "They came for Corbette. He called the Aether storm."

"Yes, I know."

"You were there. The dead are called to the Aether—"

"But what about the four in the alley before that? Tell me, are you used to fighting four at once, or was that just an off day?" He bent to retrieve the pile of clothes he kept at the back of the aerie. She couldn't hide her quick intake of breath, and he smiled to himself. Perhaps there was something to be said for the unsubtle attack on her senses. She couldn't ignore him when he flexed his muscles pulling on his trousers. It was ungentlemanly of him. He used a cudgel when a feather might have been gentler. He found his patience wasn't infinite as he thought. "Come now, Grace, you can't believe there's nothing more to it. Or do you accept everything at face value? You stumble across the walking dead wherever you go?"

"They're everywhere since the Unraveling. It's not me."

He turned and caught her watching him. He didn't let his pleasure show. Instead he raised his eyebrow and pulled on his shirt, knowing that firelight would show off the taut muscles in his chest and arms. Water beaded on his skin. The minuscule scales softly glowed. He hadn't lived two hundred years without knowing exactly what his body did to a woman. He hadn't appreciated it much as a weapon before, but in this he was clear: she thought him a liar and a scoundrel. Nothing he said could pierce through her thick, protective shield.

But her body and her head weren't in accord. He could make her want him until she burned with the same unfulfilled lust that ate at him. And then, when she could bear it no longer, she would come to him and let him ease that sweet torment. Perhaps that would be all it took to get this damned inconvenient feeling out of his system, but he doubted it. He was counting on rocking her world, to bind her to him with more than magic and desperation.

As his head cleared, he watched her tongue flicker out to wet her lips. It shot a thunderbolt of lust straight to his groin, so that he had to turn away from her alluring form and think mundane thoughts. Damn it. He didn't want to scare her. In his head he recited the periodic table of the elements. *Hydrogen, H. Helium, He. Lithium, Li.*

She followed him through the cleared part of the cave-in to get to the tunnel. Once, the Drekar Lair had extended four stories beneath the surface. Tunnels deep into the earth provided housing for the warriors, harem, and visiting dignitaries. Storerooms and treasure rooms. An armory. And farthest from the cliff face, his laboratory. Much had been crushed in the earthquakes, but he'd set his servants to dig out and reinforce what could be saved. They'd found stockpiles of food, cloth, tools, weapons, and other war supplies.

Sven was nothing if not prepared, and he'd planned to take over the world by freeing a demigod and his demon horde. He'd known the quality of Aether would change once the Gate fell, thanks to Leif's own experiments. He was prepared for no electricity. But they'd both been around long before the advent of the electric light, or the gaggle of technology that had consumed the world just prior to the Unraveling.

Leif pulled on his spare boots and led the way to his laboratory.

"You were in that alley too," she said, once the silence grew too heavy and her anger bubbled to the surface. "Kingu wrecked the House of Ishtar right after you'd left. And another thing, you keep getting in my way. I don't need your help. I've been hunting aptrgangr for four years. I haven't had anyone's help before, and I don't need it now. I'm fucking good at what I do—all innuendo aside—and I don't need you mucking it up with your giant tail and slash-grab routine. The wraiths just escape if you don't bind them before you kill the host. They find another victim. Let me do my job. I don't need anyone to rescue me. I don't want you—"

"Kingu was in the street just now." He glanced back over his shoulder to watch her face pale with some satisfaction. She hadn't known. She needed him, even if she wouldn't admit it. He had to push down the rage that built over the thought of Sven sending her out unprotected. A woman should not have to fight. A woman should not have to face death alone.

"And that's why you picked me up like a sack of potatoes and ran away?"

"I didn't run away. You, Walker, should appreciate the phrase 'live to fight another day.'"

"You couldn't take a demigod?"

"Though it wounds my manly pride to admit, no. I couldn't. And neither could you."

"Huh."

He climbed over a large boulder and turned to offer her his hand. She refused. Stubborn woman.

She climbed awkwardly over the rock. "Well, that's it then. The aptrgangr are following you and Corbette and Jameson—three leaders, three positions of power. You were in the alley; Kingu showed up. You were at the council hall; Kingu showed up. It makes sense. You're his heir. What else are you holding for him, besides the throne?"

"I am not Kingu's heir. The throne is Tiamat's."

"Potato, pot-ah-to. What could he be looking for that both the Kivati and Drekar have?" She paused. "What about that slice of the Tablet of Destiny used to open the Gate?"

"You mean Tiamat's Tablet of Destiny?"

"That's the one." Her mouth thinned. "You knew Norgard had a god-object and did nothing to stop him."

Leif raked his hands through his hair. "That's unfair. I didn't know my brother had it until it was too late. He didn't share his plots with me."

"Kingu used the Tablets the first time he waged war. They gave him power of some kind. Something about resetting the Destinies of the Gods, but I don't know in practice what that means."

"I don't think Sven took it to his grave. The Kivati Rudrick stole it and used it to open the Gate to the Land of the Dead. Maybe it's still down in the caverns beneath the city. We need witnesses. Who else was down there when the Gate fell?"

"Besides Rudrick? Your brother and four Kivati: Hart, the Wolf; his mate, Kayla; the Raven Lord and his fiancée, Lucia Crane."

"Corbette. He was exhibiting unusually strong Aether activity. I sound like Zetian when I say it, but maybe he's hiding the Tablet. It might explain his erratic, but powerful, new abilities. We need to talk to him."

"We?"

"You wanted a job, didn't you, Miss Mercer?"

They reached the door to his lab. Rotating the large brass dial, he picked out the five-digit combination lock, unlocked the thick steel door, and let her inside. He had the perverse desire to carry her across the threshold, but squashed it. Nonsense talking. Besides, she'd already been in his lab. The first time he'd carried her through the door, but she'd been unconscious. The gesture was lost on her.

And if that thought made him some sort of demonic Quasimodo, so be it.

Corbette landed on the flat tower roof, Changed to human form in a burst of Aether, and began snapping orders to the guards. His second in command, William Raiden, head of the Southern House, waited for him at the edge of the parapet. Like all Thunderbirds, Will was a tall, brooding mass of muscle. Unlike the others, he was too old to let his fiery nature rule his good sense. Will had been Corbette's father's advisor before him. Without Will's guidance, Corbette would never have been able to wrestle his people back from the brink. He wouldn't let a power-hungry human, a two-faced soul-sucker, or an undead demigod destroy what he'd worked so hard to create.

"Kingu is here," Corbette said. "He's not playing around the hinterlands anymore. He's brought the fight directly to the foot of the hill and slashed through the human's silly pack in one brilliant move."

"And Jameson?"

"The admiral ate it: hook, line, and sinker. He actually thought he'd arrest me."

Will laughed. He turned his blond head to the south where the ghostly towers of downtown huddled in the dark. "And the Unktehila? Kingu destroyed their whorehouse. Norgard would have jumped at the chance to blame us."

"Asgard will do the same in time. His blood is just as damned. We can't trust the humans or Drekar to do anything but get in the way. It was a Kivati who freed Kingu, to our great shame, and it will be a Kivati who sets things right. We will draw Kingu out and finish him ourselves."

"But a demigod—"

"He's no god of mine." Corbette stalked through the tower door and down the circular staircase to the main hall below. "We must continue to draw him away from the city until we find some way to defeat him."

Will followed. "Can you match him with the Aether?"

Corbette curled his fists. "No." He could barely hold on to the tenuous threads of power. He felt like a raw boy again with his first touch of Aether. He had no control then, and his adolescent emotions made him a danger to all. "If only my father had done the necessary thing, we would never be in this mess."

"Halian was wrong. You will avenge this taint on our sacred honor."

Corbette glanced back. "You've always had faith in me, Will."

"You need to rest, Emory. Find yourself a loyal woman and settle—" Will broke off as they turned the corner and almost ran over a thin young woman dressed all in black. She could be a ghost for all the noise she made, or the pallor of her skin and hair. Had she been sneaking out again?

"Lucia—" Corbette said, but she'd heard Will's unthinking remark. Her spine straightened, and she spun on her slippered foot. "Wait!"

Will put out an arm to block his way. "Let her go, Emory. She's been through a terrible ordeal. She needs peace, not a man who singes the air around him. Give her room to breathe."

Corbette stopped and watched her flee down the long mahogany paneled hallway. The biodiesel lamps flickered over her thin retreating form. Paintings of his ancestors lined the walls; the ghosts of the past watched her go. Their eyes turned to him. *You failed her.*

"The best way you can help her is to defeat Kingu and wipe his kind from the face of the planet, as you swore to do." Will dropped his arm. "Only the Lady can heal Lucia now."

Corbette concentrated and drew his emotions into himself. He felt the shimmering water retreat. It took a long moment of silence before the Raven stopped beating its wings inside him to go after her. "Have we found the Tablet of Destiny yet?"

"Kai's team has been diving for it for three days. If it's in the crater, it's only a matter of time."

"Time is something we don't have. Alert the four Houses. No one is to leave Queen Anne Hill unescorted." Especially not Lucia, but she always found a way. How could he protect her if she wouldn't stay put?

"What about the Needle Market?"

"Draw guards around it, but let it go unmolested. We can't withdraw completely."

"Why break ties with Asgard then?" Will asked. "Why not use him to draw out Kingu, and then sacrifice him to the fight? As long as he's willing to send his troops to their death, we might as well use him."

"But how do we know he won't join Kingu first chance he gets?"

"I've taught you better than that," Will said. "Asgard might be soulless, but he is still a man."

"Right. Find what he loves," Corbette murmured, staring down the now-empty hall, "and control it."

In Asgard's lab, Grace studied the corkboard covered in diagrams and illegible notes in a sprawling hand. Tacked in the corner, tin types gave way to black-and-white photographs: Asgard with friends at a pub. A white house on a bluff. A Wagnerian Brunhild in a horned helmet and a bronze bustier on stage. The actress had light-colored hair and the broad forehead of a Swede. The same large eyes as Asgard. His mother?

It was unusual for a human woman to survive the birth of a fledgling. The baby sipped from the soul of its mother in utero. She'd heard it Turned in the womb, baby claws and fangs and scales scraping soft pink flesh and delicate internal organs.

Drekar lived too long and saw too much death to be sentimental. It was always an act. She thought of the Kivati hung up on their Golden Age, heads too far up their asses to see the end of the world coming before it was too late. Stuck in the past like a great dying mastodon.

Grace might be mortal, but she knew better than to get hung up on the past. Her own pictures of her mother, of her childhood and whole extended family, had been thrown out with the trash when the house was sold. Her parents' unsolved murder and her own disappearance had left her childhood things without an owner. Her mother's piano had been sold at auction, her father's good pots and pans given to Goodwill. Her toys and books had brightened up some other kid's room.

She was left with nothing except her promise of vengeance and the cold comfort that she had nothing left to lose.

Even her memories were fuzzy, except the last—a woman drowning in a pool of her own blood, throat torn out, long black hair plastered to the reddish brick, her grey eyes unblinking.

Grace ruthlessly shoved the memory into her mental black box and dragged the iron manacles around it once again. The box shook, angry memories thudding against the lid, trying to claw their way out.

Her father might have told her that trick, but Sven had helped her perfect it. Many of the creatures now howling in the dark interior were his creation. "If you're brothers, why don't you have the same last name?"

"Half brothers." Asgard fiddled with the ring on his finger, slipping it up to his knuckle and back. "Have you ever heard the prayer, 'Save us, oh Lord, from the fury of the North men?' It was written by some of Sven's early victims. He liked it so much he adopted Norgard as his last name, which means 'north' in Norse."

Grace wrinkled her nose. She could easily see Norgard doing that. He was in love with his own importance. "And Asgard?"

"My mother named me after the palace of the Norse gods."

"She thought you were a gift from the gods, is that it?"

He shrugged. "You think me too damned for even a mother's love? Harsh, Reaper. Even for you."

She crossed her arms. "Your sire let her raise you?"

"My mother was an opera singer in London, and Fafnir was only passing through. He didn't know about me. She had me in secret and dumped me on the north shore of England with her parents. Morfor, my grandfather, was a Lutheran minister. They raised me when she returned to the stage, but I saw her every summer during the off season."

"How did a couple of humans know what to do with a fledgling dragon?"

He smiled with real fondness. "They were Swedish immigrants. My grandfather outlawed the old tales, but my great-grandmother lived with them, and she was a pagan and a heathwitch. She was a thorn in the old man's side, and he forbid her to practice. Between the four of them, they kept me alive and hidden, gave me a modern education and brought me up in a culture that valued science over superstition and fear." His smile faded. "Sven didn't have that luxury. Fafnir was all he had, and he wasn't the best role model."

She didn't want to feel sorry for Norgard, so she didn't say anything. He'd never told her anything personal about himself, only asked questions. She'd spilled her guts, thinking he cared. She'd been wrong.

Asgard turned from the picture of his mother. "I didn't meet Fafnir until I was full grown, and by then his magnetic persona had little left to impress me."

He was trying to humanize himself with these little personal vignettes. She didn't want to hear any more. "What do you know about Tiamat's Heart?"

He raised one eyebrow. "Not much. Why do you ask?"

"I asked one of the aptrgangr," she said slowly, realizing how weird it sounded. "It said it wanted Tiamat's Heart. Some spirits are more sentient than others. Like Kayla's sister. She anchored herself to the Living World so that she could tell her sister where to find the key to the Gate."

"Go on."

"Well, this aptrgangr didn't seem too smart, but it was focused."

"You think the aptrgangr have flooded the city looking for Tiamat's Heart?"

"Could be. Maybe Kingu is looking for it too."

"Strange." Asgard turned away and strode to a bookcase at the opposite edge of the room. The floor-to-ceiling dark shelves were stuffed to the gills with old, leather-bound books. She watched him walk, a smooth arrogant roll like a large cat. His boots made no sound on the slate floor. He ran his fingers over the books until he found the one he was looking for. Pulling it out, he flipped through the yellowed pages, but shook his head. "The dragon tomes only have our creation story and the myth of how the Gates came to be. It says nothing about Tiamat's Heart, except that her other limbs and organs became the sky and the sea and the land."

"You don't sound convinced."

He slid the book back with a thud. "I am a man of science. While I understand the presence of the gods is real, it's hard to reconcile what I see in the world with the old myths. Our earth is made out of the body of a goddess? What were they standing on before she was slain? I've always thought it more allegory than fact."

"But you've seen Kingu—"

"And he is the first demigod I've come across. Where are the gods, I ask you? Sleeping at the bottom of the sea until our darkest hour, as some say? Where were they when the Gates fell and the world forever blackened?" His fists clenched at his sides. "The old tales of the gods paint a picture of avaricious, vain, and at best indifferent creatures. They were not all powerful; they engaged in petty, selfish squabbles no better than human kings, with no care to the damage their games wrought. And when Kingu first rampaged across the earth, was it the head gods who rose up to stop the slaughter?"

"No."

"No, it was a human: Marduk. A warrior who might have been exemplary, but mortal. Because it is only mortals who care enough, who are invested in their communities and the outcome of their short life threads. There is the irony; only mortals, who have such short sweet passages upon this earth, are willing to sacrifice it all for their fellow men. Immortals—vainglorious, self-centered bastards all—

care only for prolonging their miserable existence." His green eyes looked haunted.

He cared, she realized with a shock. Vainglorious immortal or no.

"But Marduk became a god once he won," she said.

"And he became just as much of a selfish ass as the rest of them. His human progeny were enslaved so that the gods could be at leisure. The stories were rewritten to give him divine parentage and wipe out his shameful beginnings."

"Norgard believed—"

"Sven believed in whatever would get him farthest. He was his own god. Or how else do you explain his plan to unleash Kingu? Sven would've had to be greater than a demigod to control Kingu and his horde. The cult of Sven." Asgard shook his head, and she read real sorrow in his eyes. "He must have finally believed his own bullshit, and that has always been the undoing of powerful men."

"You weren't helping him?"

"Gods, no." She watched him warily. She noticed lines of strain around his eyes for the first time. "Sven was secretive, even if I was willfully blind. I didn't know about your . . . situation. I'm sorry."

An apology.

She felt some of her defenses crumble. Her stark hatred of all things Drekar couldn't stand up to this new picture. Asgard was different. Younger. Brought up by religious humans, of all things. What in Freya's name was she supposed to do with this information? It shook her picture of the world, and she'd already had her world shaken enough, thank you. Since the Unraveling, there were only one or two things that had stayed constant: Drekar were the spawn of Satan, and she wanted all of them dead.

But now she couldn't say that with the same force.

Ye gods damn it.

"Well, they may be absent," she said, "but I wouldn't

want the old gods around anyways. And if Kingu is really looking for Tiamat's Heart—the heart of the goddess of chaos—then I don't think anybody, mortal or immortal, wants to be around when he finds it." She paced back down the aisle. She had new scrapes and bruises, and she'd twisted her foot in the fight. She tried to hide it, but she stepped wrong.

Asgard was there in an instant, steadying her elbow, keeping her from falling on her face. She didn't need anyone to catch her, but for one moment of weakness she wanted to lean into that embrace, to rest against him like a tree curls against the mountain in a thunderstorm, to let his heat trickle into her weary bones.

"You're injured." His voice was low with carefully leashed anger.

She set her jaw. "'S'all right."

But he didn't let go. He picked her up and turned her to face him. "Spitting nails will only prolong your torment." He kept those green eyes set on her face, daring her to look away. She didn't blink from sheer mulishness. A little smile played at the corner of his mouth. He raised his wrist to his mouth, and his teeth flashed in the dim light. Sharp. Feral. And then blood welled from a small cut on his wrist. The droplets beaded, taunting her. To refuse now would only play into his hands. It would only prove what he thought of her: she was contrary and stubborn and reckless.

She wasn't reckless; she was brave. She wasn't stubborn; she stood firm to her ideals.

Slowly, he lowered his wrist, stopping an inch before her mouth, forcing her to move, to accept his healing blood. To ingest his essence of her own free will.

What's it gonna cost me? she wanted to ask, but she knew that the question would only make her look weak. She stared him down as she moved that extra inch. It felt more like a long mile to executioner's row. The challenge was plain.

The tip of her tongue darted out to taste those ruby droplets before her lips pressed—oh, so softly—against the firm skin of his wrist. His pupils dilated and slit to an inhuman cat-eye. A golden sheen spread over the emerald of his iris. She licked his wound, drawing his essence into her.

Bold. Brazen.

Shockingly intimate.

Closing her lips over the cut, she sucked and watched his Adam's apple bob as he swallowed hard. The shock of cinnamon traveled like liquid fire up her tongue and down the back of her mouth, warming her from the inside, knitting together her torn and bruised places, smoothing the soreness and easing the pain. She squeezed her thighs together. His nostrils flared. The cords stood out in his neck. His lips parted, skin glowed, body practically vibrating with energy. All her fear dissipated, because she knew he would hold himself back if Armageddon erupted and they were the only two people left on this bloody hunk of earth.

In this battle of wills, they were at an impasse. She wouldn't back down. He wouldn't let his baser instincts overrule his honor and prove her right.

He thought she was scared, but she would kick fear in the teeth when she saw it.

The gods help them both.

Healed, renewed, senses overwhelmed with the same hunger that showed on his face, she tempted fate just to prove she could. Her lips left his skin with one last kiss.

Chapter 10

Snow had started falling across Leif's vision, interspersed with little electric bolts that didn't exist. He was quite sure of that. The snow, not as much. His vision must be malfunctioning, because Grace Mercer had just willingly kissed him in a shockingly intimate manner of her own volition.

A man had reason to hope. He would be the first to admit that his coldly rational brain lacked the proper imagination to conjure the sheer pleasure of her tongue rolling over his skin and her usually stern lips soft and caressing.

Sucking his essence. Ye gods.

His body vibrated with unspent need. It was all he could do not to jump the woman like a dying man in the desert.

It had been a long drought. And he was sorely in need of an oasis.

He suspected they both were, Unraveling and demigods aside; their personal demons thundered through their minds even in this quiet solitude behind the warded doors. Maybe this could be a chance for both to find some small respite.

But he knew deep in his dragon bones that once he had Grace he would not give her up. Not for Kingu. Not for his kingdom. And not for the haunted ghost of his dead and thrice-damned brother.

Leif wasn't any good at politics, but this was one thin sheet of ice that he had a vested interest in crossing over. Every time he thought he had her figured out and stuffed into a properly shaped cube, she turned into a dodecahedron. The Unexpected heated a fire in his blood, and she was unexpected.

He wouldn't push her to do something she truly didn't want, but damned if he would sit back and let her walk away simply because she was afraid to seize it. He'd had his doubts, but after that little display, she couldn't hide that she wanted him. She might hate herself for it. But he wasn't his brother. He wasn't a monster. And he would prove it to her if Tiamat herself rose up from the depths and laid carnage for his weakness.

Some of his feeling must have slipped into his eyes, because she backed up, raised her pert nose into the air and turned away like she hadn't just made love to his wrist.

"How do you feel?" His voice churned out like he'd swallowed the whiskey rocks.

She looked around, anywhere but at him. "Fine."

He had to give her just enough space not to scare her off, but he wouldn't let her out of his sight. Even if he didn't want to explore this thing between them, the aptrgangr were after her. She might be a fighter, but she was his to protect.

"So you don't know anything about the Heart?" she asked.

"Longren is the oldest among us. He would know if anyone does."

Her lips thinned.

"He will do you no harm."

She snorted. "I can take care of myself."

Mount Si rose cragged from the small mountain range known as the Issaquah Alps. Pre-Unraveling, it had been popular with hikers. The entrance to Longren's lair hid on the leeward side of Haystack Rock, the bald outcropping at the mountain's peak. Unlike Sven's civilized eco-dwelling, with its proper roof and elegant seaward windows, Longren lived in a primitive hole in the ground. Leif almost expected ox bones at the foot of the cliff and a burnt path leading directly to the cave mouth, but there were no clues that the mountain housed anything but dirt, except a few talon marks on rock, broken trees at tail height, and blackened branches. The clouds covered the mountain so often that even the smoke from Longren's chimneys blended into the grey sky.

Longren met them himself. He wore a green smoking jacket, no shirt, and snakeskin pants.

Landing in a wide clearing, Leif bowed so that Grace could climb off his back. She jumped down and stretched her legs. She'd wanted to ride a horse. A three-day ride on an ill-tempered beast just so she wouldn't have to acknowledge the beauty of the dragon's flight. Riding on his back by choice crossed a line; she couldn't pretend he was either man or monster anymore. He was both and neither, something otherworldly and majestic. Determined to show her, he had swooped low over Lake Washington and dragged his tail in the midnight waters. She hadn't been able to hide her whoop of excitement. Flying beneath the starry sky was the closest to heaven his kind could get.

He'd never shared it with a human before.

Leif Turned and the leather harness fell to the ground.

"Clothe yourself, fledgling, before the lady faints." Longren stared fixedly at the sky. He sighed. "I don't suppose you've changed your mind?"

"No." Leif pulled his clothes out of the leather satchel attached to the harness and dressed. "We need information."

Highly territorial, Drekar didn't let other Drekar into their space unless coerced. Sven's brilliance had been in uniting the Drekar from the western United States and up into

Canada beneath his rule. He dangled economic and political promises in front of them like candy, and if they didn't fall in line he killed them. His rule had lasted more than a century—the longest-running Drekar fiefdom of its size in the Western world. In his absence, Drekar had moved to reclaim their small, personal territories. Leif had been content to let them do so, except now the threat of a ruler worse than Sven challenged them all. Kingu wouldn't bother dangling economic partnerships. It would be all blood, all the time. No peace for Leif's experiments. No peace for any of them.

Longren paused at the cave entrance, but he couldn't refuse a visit from the Regent. Leading them through the dark mouth of the cave, he strolled down the tunnel deeper into the belly of the mountain. The rough dirt walls gave way to an arched ceiling lined with purple velvet. Pop art hung on the walls between the flaring torches—soup cans and splatter paint and more than a few pictures of Marilyn Monroe. Leif suspected if he looked closer he might find a couple velvet Elvises.

"So what is it, Regent?" Longren asked. "Have need of a lost Athenian tragedy? An abandoned work by the Marquis de Sade? Want to know who really pulled the strings when Paris went to war, hmm? What artifact of history draws you to my doorstep?"

"What do you know about Tiamat's Heart?"

Longren flashed a startled look back at him. The torchlight cast shadows over half his face. The hollows of his cheeks were stark. "Ever wondered why Drekar have no souls?"

Leif shook his head. "I've never had much interest in the tall tales behind the science." Aether, like oxygen or hydrogen, had the same properties no matter what one believed about it. When Einstein and other midcentury human scientists decided the Aether was no longer needed to explain waves of light, Aether didn't cease to exist. It still quietly wove the fabric of the universe. Myths were cultural relics; they changed like the tide. Leif held little stock in them.

"And you," Longren asked Grace, "do you find solace in fairy stories?"

Grace walked a step behind Leif. Her boots tripped to keep up with the two Drekar's long strides. "I know Tiamat was butchered for parts. I know Marduk split the worlds and set up the Gates. His city, Babylon, was the original Gateway to the Gods. If a myth doesn't relate to the Gates and sending wraiths across them, I'm out of tricks."

Because Sven had trained her, and Sven had never believed in giving people more information than he wanted them to have. Longren was probably the same way. Leif didn't have time to wheedle every last scrap of evidence out of the Dreki. Threatening Longren would be the first step on that long slope down into dictatorship, but Leif would do it, if he had to. Being the Regent had its perks.

"It's not a well-known story," Longren admitted. "And I could never find the original material. I found an extended epilogue to the Tiamat legend in an antiquities market. It was a copy of a copy of a copy. Hardly worth noting, but it explained so much of our origins."

"And it mentions Tiamat's Heart?" Leif asked.

"And so much more, dear boy." Longren led them out of the tunnel and into a wide cavern. Two glass panels divided the room into three sections: In the middle, young men—human, muscled, and model pretty—worked shirtless in the heat of a forge. Sweat dripped down their chests, but the glass protected the other two sections from the heat and humidity. The men pounded steel into swords and shields. On the far side sat three industrial sewing machines. Bolts of sequined fabric leaned against the wall.

The section closest to the tunnel mouth held velvet couches and a wet bar. A thick shag carpet in red, orange and yellow covered the floor, and a fieldstone fireplace heated the room. Floor-to-ceiling bookcases covered each wall. Candelabras reflected off a disco ball, sending light sparkling across the lounge. Cats occupied every horizontal inch of furniture.

"It's a pity you didn't inherit any of your mother's dramatic talent," Longren said. "The world was a dimmer place when we lost her star." He poured himself a drink from the bar. "Help yourself to a drink, and sit. Don't mind the puddles of fur."

Leif poured himself and Grace each a finger of brandy and shooed a tortoiseshell cat off one of the velvet couches. As soon as he sat down, two more cats mobbed his lap. He scratched one under the chin. It purred happily. Grace curled up with her drink in the thick shag carpet by the fire. Strands of wet hair plastered to her cheeks. She watched the forgers through the glass; the cats watched her.

"So Tiamat's Heart. Let me start at the beginning." Longren moved to stand on the opposite side of the fireplace and set his glass on the mantel. He cleared his throat. "In the beginning"—his voice boomed theatrically off the glass panels—"there were the primordial waters: Tiamat, the salt water, and Apsu, the fresh. Yin and yang. Two halves of the whole. And all was as it should be." He took a sip from his glass for dramatic pause. "But then they had children, the original pantheon of Babylonian gods. Dratted, ungrateful little beasts. Their children grew jealous of their parents' perfect love. One of them slew Apsu, and Tiamat, crazed with grief, swore revenge. She birthed the world's monsters"—he laid a modest hand on his chest to indicate himself and his dragon brethren—"and gave them to her lover Kingu to lead in battle against the gods."

"Along with the Tablets of Destiny," Leif added. Grace's attention had been caught by Longren's overly dramatic recitation. He was certainly a character. One edge of her stern mouth kicked up. What would it be like to make that mouth curve all the way? To make her let go enough to laugh when she wanted? He narrowed in on the idea. His mind set about plotting.

"Correct, but for this tale it suffices to say she trusted Kingu with her monstrous children, her magical Tablets, her divine body, but not her Heart. Her Heart belonged to Apsu. She was love-stricken, and cared for nothing but revenge against the gods who had taken her husband from her. She risked her babes and her lover in battle, and lost everything. Marduk defeated Kingu and his demon horde. They were condemned for eternity and trapped behind the Gate to the Land of the Dead."

"I didn't take you for a romantic, Longren," Leif said.

"I have hidden depths," Longren said. "True power resides not in brains or brawn, but in the heart. Because Tiamat failed to give Kingu hers, he didn't have enough power to overthrow the gods. He was thwarted in love, thwarted in power, and thwarted in victory. He has an ax to grind, and an eternity to plot his revenge."

"And then Marduk slew Tiamat and butchered her for parts," Grace said. "Her various pieces became parts of the night sky, the rivers, mountains, and so on. But her Heart? What did that become?"

"This is where the missing piece I found fits in. Because Tiamat launched her war in the name of love, the gods devised a special punishment for her. She must never be reunited with her husband Apsu. They cursed her Heart to roam the world alone, outcast, and forever parted from her mate."

"But you said her Heart contained her powers," Grace said.

Longren pointed one long finger at her. "A point to the girl, professor."

"So Kingu is searching for the Heart of Tiamat, and if he finds it he inherits all of Tiamat's powers?" Leif felt the responsibility crash over his shoulders like a tidal wave. Bad enough that Sven had unleashed a demigod bent on revenge. But with Tiamat's powers, Kingu would become a full-fledged god. "He's planning to wage war on the gods again if he finds it, isn't he? Bloody hell."

"Marduk became the supreme god in Babylon, but his progeny are humans," Grace said. "If Kingu wants revenge, he's coming after everyone. The gods who cursed him, the monsters who failed him, the children of Marduk, the human who defeated him. No one will be safe."

"I'm not too worried." Longren waved his hand airily.

"So how do we find the Heart first?" Grace asked.

Ye gods, she was magnificent. She assumed the problems of the world like a queen. No bellyaching. No thought for herself. Leif stared at her. The firelight played over her glossy black hair. The three cats preened beneath her hand. Her brows furrowed in worry, her shoulders tensed. She was only a small human woman, but he read determination in her silver eyes. She was going to find that Heart or die trying.

Leif felt suddenly ashamed of his refusal to bear the Regent's crown. While he'd been safely ensconced in his lab, she'd been out on the streets fighting for survival. Not her own survival, but that of strangers. She would claim it was just a job, but he could read the broadsheets as well as anyone. She fought when she didn't have to. She fought when she didn't want to. Beneath her prickly shields hid a generous, selfless spirit. And now she would take on a vengeful god without the slightest hesitation.

He could learn so much from her. She deserved a braver, equally generous soul.

Longren's smile was resigned. "If Kingu is prowling around Seattle, there is a good chance he has tracked it to somewhere nearby, but hasn't found it yet. The Heart could be moving."

"Are we looking for an actual beating heart, or something

containing the Heart?" Grace asked. "An amulet of some sort? Like the Tablet of Destiny shard that Rudrick had?"

"I hope not," Longren said. "With the Tablet, the Heart could rewrite its own destiny. Bad enough if Kingu got hold of both. All he needs to resurrect his corporal form is the Tablet, the Heart to power it, and Tiamat's essence—the salt water. Fortunately I think the Heart is trapped in a living thing. Think of it as the original wraith. It's most likely sentient and could very well have its own agenda."

Chapter 11

"Fuckin' A," Grace swore. "That's all I need: a wraith with god-powers."

Asgard stood. He paced across the floor to the glass pane and watched the forgers hammering. He came too close to her. He smelled of wet male and cinnamon. She watched the muscles shift beneath his linen shirt, coiled and graceful like a predatory panther. Next to him, the forgers looked scrawny. He could pull off intimidating when he focused like this. Power and intent wrapped in a pretty package. His blond hair hung to his shoulders, long eyelashes framed his piercing eyes. But his planted boots, thick neck, and bulging forearms said he could break her if she stepped a hair out of place.

He ran a hand across the stubble on his jaw. It was a nervous gesture that put centipedes in her belly. Norgard never doubted himself; he had been calm as a lake in winter. She'd thought all Drekar were like that. Asgard was a powerful, fire-breathing dragon. If he was nervous, there was no hope for the rest of them.

She could delude herself only so far. The real problem was the humanness of it. She wanted to stick Asgard in her mental box labeled DREKAR with the rest, but he kept popping back out like some gods-damned jack-in-the-box, surprising her with un-Drekar-like behavior.

She pried her eyes away. Everything about him screamed sex, *yes please, MORE*. And even if the outside hadn't been gorgeous god-man, his brain wasn't much to laugh about either.

Asgard turned to her and crossed those muscled arms. "Have you felt any wraiths out of the ordinary in your patrols? How would you go about searching for a particular wraith?" And there he went asking for her opinion, like he thought she had something of value to add, like he *cared*. She felt one of the rivets in her iron defenses fall out. Her breath whistled in the hole left behind.

"We need to track Kingu's movements," she said. "Make a map of rumored and confirmed sightings and all aptrgangr attacks. Track Jameson, Corbette, and your people too. See what info you can get from the Voice and send runners out for more."

"Runners?"

"You know, the street brats who spy for the Regent."

His face clouded over. "Right. And where does one find these little spies?"

"I can show you the lair, but it's been six months. If you haven't been running them, they'll have found a new game." Street kids were resourceful. They hadn't pledged themselves in Norgard's service yet, so they were free to move on when Norgard's funds dried up. She felt angry on their behalf. The Unraveling had been terrible, but they should have been able to count on food and shelter from the new Regent. They deserved better.

"I know," Asgard said, seeming to read her mind. Was her expression that obvious? "I'll make it right."

She turned her attention to the cats in her lap and let her hair fall over her face. "Whatever."

"If Kingu was behind all three attacks today," Asgard said, "it would appear that he's casting a wide net to pinpoint who might have the Heart. Maybe he wanted to see if anyone would use the Heart in defense."

"I doubt Jameson has anyone strong enough to trap or control the Heart. But maybe it's doing the controlling. Jameson is a couple marks short of a full rune. Marks is a possibility. He might swear he's against the supernatural, but he's collecting virgins for his congregation." Grace turned to study the fire. In her lap, her hands curled into the cat's fur. "There's powerful magic in a sacrificed virginity. That's how Rudrick brought down the Gate to the Land of the Dead." Poor Lucia. The Kivati girl was lucky to be alive. Grace needed to ditch Asgard by nightfall in order to make her meeting with the kid. If Lucia wanted to learn to fight to reclaim some of her personal power, who was Grace to tell her no? "And then there's Corbette. Probably our best bet for demonic possession. He's been freaky since the Unraveling. I mean, he was always intimidating, but now even his subjects are wary of his sanity." She thought of Johnny and Lucia's shared look. Maybe she could get Lucia to tell her more during their first practice. It might be useful to have a contact on the inside of the impenetrable Kivati Hall.

"Corbette already has two souls inside him. What's one more?" Asgard gave a small, bitter laugh.

Was he jealous? "Are you going to confront him about the Heart?"

"Good Tesla, no. I might lack Zetian's paranoia, but even I fear the Heart in the hands of my enemy. Corbette has no great love for Drekar or our truce. If he knew about the Heart, he wouldn't hesitate to wipe us out. It's probably the strongest case for him not possessing it, or at least not knowingly possessing it."

Outside, scattered clouds drifted across a ghostly moon. Grace loved that wet earth smell. Not the sewer of the city streets after a storm, but this clean scent of the countryside growing. Green plants and fertile dirt. She could image the rain releasing their magic, washing off the suffocating ash, restoring them, making them grow. She took a deep breath of pine and clean air.

Leif paused at the edge of the cave mouth. The moon lit the mountain crags. The shadows of the clouds chased over the rock like the Wild Hunt. Grace shivered. "Longren, you never said how dragons lost their souls."

"I didn't, did I?" Longren said. "With the Tablets of Destiny, Marduk cursed Tiamat and the losing army. Dragons, the monsters in Tiamat's own image, were shown no mercy. Marduk decreed that since Tiamat's crime had been an act of love, no dragon should ever have reason to give similar offense. Dragons were doomed to walk the earth for eternity, forever alone, forever without the solace of knowing their heart and soul.

"But Ishtar, the goddess of love, was moved by Tiamat's passion for her husband. She felt sorry for the dragons, and after Marduk had laid his curse, she worked one of her own. A small sliver of grace into a grim sentence. If a dragon can convince a mortal woman to love him, she can choose to bind her soul to his forever. The dragon will no longer need to feed from the souls of others, for he will share in his love's life force. Together, they will be one body, one soul, just as Tiamat and Apsu were. They will break the curse. Lovely tale, isn't it?"

Longing speared Asgard's face. "But what if his soul mate is human? What about his immortality?"

"That's the clincher. He gives up his immortal life for a mortal soul. He will pass from this world into the next when she does. Together. Whole. Love is true immortality."

Grace squirmed. This talk made her very uncomfortable. Longren and Asgard sounded wistful, damn it, like they weren't evil, selfish creatures but lonely, heartsick men.

Poor, cursed dragons? She almost felt sorry for them, and if she did that all her protective hatred would crumble like dust in the wind.

"Forever is a long time to search for one's soul mate," Longren said. The ghost of a smile chased across his mouth, mirroring the clouds overhead. "I would ask you again, Regent. The darkness calls. Let me find peace—"

"No." Asgard cut him off.

Grace felt like an intruder on a private conversation. What did Longren want? To die?

The moon emerged, casting Longren's face in sharp relief. His eyes were two pits of black against bone-white flesh. "You deny me twice."

"I need you. You're old, wise, and more powerful than you let on. You can hold off the madness a while longer."

"Don't make an enemy of me, boy. I'll take what hurts you." His eyes flashed to Grace.

She pulled in on herself. *Leave me out of it*, she wanted to scream. *There is nothing between us.*

But Asgard moved to stand in front of her. "Remember who you speak to." The thunder of command rumbled in his voice. Feet planted, shoulders back, his aura seemed to grow. Grace felt her breath hitch and her heart pick up speed. She had never seen him look so menacing, or so in charge. Maybe she'd been wrong about him. Asgard had it in him to be a fearsome king. He just had to want it.

Kingu floated on the tide, riding the whitecapped waves as they tumbled over each other to crash upon the seawall. The salt water revived him. He could almost taste Tiamat's tears. In the water below he sensed blacker spirits hovering in the deep. He needed to dive down and see if they had what he sought, but for now he left them alone. They saw him but left him alone too, for which he breathed a sigh of relief. He wasn't the most powerful being beneath the sea. Not yet.

Rising from the salt water, he slithered over the seawall and perched on the crumbling cement wall. A crow watched him crawl out, and he took great joy in seizing the little creature's mind. Slipping inside the bird's body, the world sharpened. A moment of disorientation, then he flapped his little black wings and took off. He jerked sideways as he got his air legs and learned to steer.

Along the seawall he flew. The crow's mate followed him, crying. His army was combing the city. He'd searched elsewhere, but kept coming back here. The Heart was somewhere close. He could only feel it when it woke from slumber.

Kingu drifted on a current of air until he spotted two people in the rubble below. He descended to watch them. They had been young, soft things, he guessed, but the strain of the world picked them slowly apart. Careworn. But they had that glow he had such fascination with. They were locked together in an amorous embrace. He was at turns fascinated and ragingly jealous. Once he had known that, hadn't he? It was so long ago. So many millennia locked behind the Gate, cursed to be parted from his love forever.

Soon he would be reunited, and their glow would put this paltry human light to shame.

He left the crow in a burst of power, letting the tiny body fall to the hard concrete below. Its mate screamed and flew to it. The pitiful cries fueled his building rage. Why did these fragile creatures get to burn with such brilliance, when his own kind was cursed from knowing their soul's other half? Why did mortals deserve to know that warm embrace, when he, Kingu, destroyer of worlds, was always an outsider?

Tiamat had never given him her Heart. Her body, her Tablets, her army, but never her Heart. That had belonged to her husband, Apsu, and when he died, she'd torn the fabric of the worlds in agony.

Kingu had savaged the earth for her. He'd given everything, and still he'd never owned her as fully as these two sad little humans whose lives were less than a pinprick on the tablets of history owned each other. They were wrapped together, lost in their embrace, ignorant of the crust of dirt, of the rat two paces away, of the decaying bones buried far beneath their feet, of the dark water spirits and even him, Kingu the Great, nearby.

Ignored.

Tiamat might not have given him her whole Heart, but now he would take it for himself. They would be united together, as they should have always been. Their light would set the world on fire. Together they would mold the earth in their own image.

No one could stop them.

The humans broke for air, and as they did he slipped inside the breath they took. Their eyes widened, and in their last moment they clung more fiercely together. It enraged him. He squeezed their hearts until they burst.

The sound of the grieving crow was a blink to stop too, and he soared from that blighted spot, leaving behind four broken bodies. He felt the Aether gathering some distance away and soared off to investigate. Perhaps his love woke once more. He would be ready this time.

Grace woke up to a face full of fish breath and big, soulful yellow-green eyes. A heavy weight compressed her chest. For a moment she didn't know where she was, and then a cat paw landed in her mouth, and she knew she was home in the little shop that housed her tattoo parlor. The familiar lime-green ceiling beams stared down at her. Across the room, a potbellied stove whistled softly as it powered a few seismograph and Aether readers. A spring in the corduroy couch dug into her back. She'd crashed after Asgard dropped her at Thor's Hammer, a converted carriage house squished in a dark, Aether-twisted alley near Pioneer Square.

Alone. Just the way she liked it. The cat didn't count; he didn't talk much.

Bear meowed.

"All right, I'm awake." She pulled herself off the couch and fed him from the dwindling supply of cans she had stockpiled after the Unraveling. She'd fought off Black Friday crowds to raid pet stores just like everyone else. "Soon you'll have to get your own food," she warned. He blinked at her. "Just a heads-up."

He had left her a hairball in the middle of her chalk circle. "Thanks," she said. "Best birthday present ever."

If her parents had still been alive, she would have woken up to the smell of hot batter and maple syrup. A party hat would have been waiting at her bedroom door. Her mom would play "Happy Birthday" on the piano as Grace slid down the stairs in her Tigger pajamas. Her dad would join in, singing from his place at the waffle maker in the kitchen. It would be the same celebration were she six or sixty. And now, at twenty-one, she missed their presence something fierce.

Today, October beat down the door in grey, isolating sheets of water. Brown leaves scattered against the door. The nude branches of the trees scraped against the outside wall.

Today there would be no waffles, but if she got to Butterworth's before curfew, Hart or Oscar might buy her a drink. Drinking gave the memories teeth, and noise and people chased them away. She couldn't sit around and nurse her self-pity. She had to start canvassing for Kingu rumors.

Today was also the anniversary of her pledge. The golden bands on her arms tingled. She hadn't seen her naked biceps in four years. She wanted to curl up in a dark corner and forget, but Asgard wanted her report in the morning.

She made a mental to-do list: One demigod—check. One

wraith Heart containing god-powers—check. One Tablet to rewrite destiny—damn and triple check. It was going to be a long day.

Selecting the cleanest black shirt and jeans from her remaining three outfits, she examined herself in the square mirror over her sink. What did Asgard see? Her face was symmetrical with big serious eyes and too thin lips. She hadn't had a haircut in five years. The ragged edges brushed her lower back. Maybe she should put a little extra effort in for her birthday. She combed out her hair with her fingers and rebraided it.

Bear finished his dinner and came over to wrap around her legs.

"I like you, Bear. We understand each other." She petted his head. He sniffed her fingers and walked away.

Outside, iron and glass lanterns lit the storefronts of Flesh Alley. Early afternoon signaled the start of the day in this small patch of abnormal. The apothecary and occult bookseller had already hung their shingles in the rain. Next door, a patron huddled beneath the striped awning of the Ishtar Maidens while he waited to be let in.

In front of her stood a large, pink beach umbrella. The rain scattered like rice across the top. Sheltered beneath, out of the rain, stood a shiny new silver bicycle with a large pink bow. The front tire was twice the size of the back. Both were thick enough to off-road or ride over street debris. A customized plastic windshield and rain splatter shields made it dorky, but practical. A large metal box was welded to the back pannier rack.

Grace pulled on her worn rain jacket and headed into the downpour. She examined the metal box. On the backside was a door, and inside she found a thick red pillow sheltered from the elements. Velvet covered the walls. Someone had painted PRINCESS in pink across the top.

She found a card sitting in the box addressed to "Miss

Mercer." Someone had left her a new bike. On her birthday. Someone had gone to considerable trouble to dig up her past and find the right date. The card was good cotton with the Drekar emblem embossed on the cover. Inside, large loopy handwriting read, *I've removed the death trap.*

Romantic. She could hear Asgard's pompous tone now. She couldn't accept the bike; she might as well add a million dollars to that IOU.

The metal of the bike was such shiny silver. She reached out to stroke the smooth lines. Bikes cost a premium. This one looked sturdy, but fast. The frame was light enough to be titanium, but he'd reinforced parts of it with something stronger.

"We can't accept this, Bear." Pulling it out from beneath the pink umbrella, she swung one leg over. The fit was perfect. She put one foot on the pedal. It had twelve speeds and a glow light. Pushing off, she rode it through the rain and across the street. She looped back around. Even in the rain, the bike was a dream to ride. The traction tires didn't slip on the slick brick. She stopped in front of Thor's Hammer. Bear watched her from the dry doorway. "We can't."

Braving the rain, he jumped into the cat carrier on the back, turned around twice and settled down. He wasn't budging.

Crap.

Leif found Grace at Butterworth's fighting with Maidens of Ishtar in an alley that reeked of fish and salt and the tang of unwashed bodies. He watched her, because he could. She pulled her punches and moved slow, not like the last time he'd seen her with the aptrgangr. This time there was no danger, so he could take pleasure in the simple act of watching her move. She danced over the asphalt and brick, spun on her worn heel, and planted a fist in the blond woman's belly. With a grunt, the blond crumpled to the ground.

"Ishtar take you, Elsie," Grace said, kneeling by the woman. "You're supposed to block. Keep your middle and your head protected. Your limbs are expendable, but one good stab at those internal organs and you'll bleed out."

"I thought they'd crush us to death," said a shorter, freckled girl in a bright pink pantsuit.

"Yeah, so don't let them get a good lock on your head or belly."

The blond woman, Elsie, moaned. Grace patted her shoulder.

On the opposite side of the alley, a thin woman in a long blue cape watched from the shadows. A man with a black armband stood behind her. Kivati. Leif felt his irises narrow, and his world descended into dusky blues.

"That's enough for today, I think," Grace said. "You gotta practice."

"We'll keep an eye out, Reaper." Elsie pulled herself off the ground. Her voice was a little breathless. "But if Ianna had an object of power, she wouldn't have hired you. No offense."

Grace nodded. "I want any mention of aptrgangr or supernatural activity. Your clients so much as sneeze at an aptrgangr, I want to know about it." She caught sight of Leif. "Class dismissed. Thanks, ladies."

The Maidens slipped past him through the mouth of the alley, each pausing to curtsy on their way out. They had changed from their confining silk gowns and geisha wraps to wide silk pajama pants in fuchsia and saffron and lime green. Lace-up boots with pointed toes, black gloves, and small pie bonnets completed the look. He wondered if Ianna knew what they were up to. The new styles were hot enough to please Ishtar, but better suited to fight.

Grace examined the brick wall next to her.

"Taking that civilian army idea into your own hands?" he asked. The dusk swirled around her black ensemble and black hair, seducing her into the shadows and the night. She didn't move like any human he'd ever met. She walked apart, alone, on the edge of this world and the next. He needed to take her to Birgitta. The heathwitch might make some sense of her. "Walk with me."

He led her out of the alley and along the narrow edge of the crater that had swallowed half of downtown when the Gate broke. Deep in an underground cavern, a crevasse had opened up, allowing a twister of souls to escape and break through the ceiling, sucking in dirt and detriment and the roots of the buildings above. The earthquakes had finished the job. The piers had been the first to go. The steep hills on soft mud infill slid down next.

He waited for her to say something. Behind them, music, light, and smoke from the biodiesel lamps spilled from Butterworth's open windows. Bells jingled constantly as patrons pushed through the door, sounding like street corners at Christmas.

"Did you like the bike?" he finally asked.

"Bear is a boy."

"Ah." He'd guessed wrong. He would have to repaint the PRINCESS sign on the box for her. "Who was that girl with the bodyguard?"

"Lucia Crane."

He stilled. "Corbette's fiancée? Trying for an interspecies incident, are you?"

"Hey, you wanted intel. She owed me a favor."

"You think like Zetian."

Grace thinned her lips. Prickly woman.

"It was a compliment. I don't like using minors—"

"She's eighteen."

"—but we have few options. What did she tell you?"

"I asked her about the Tablet of Destiny. She remembers

it." Grace hesitated. "Rudrick used it as a knife to cut her veins to open the Gate."

Leif watched as Grace's hackles rose. Her shoulders tensed, the muscles in her jaw flexed, and her eyes flashed silver. If Rudrick were still alive, she would gut him on a sharpened stick and hang him on the edge of the crater as a warning: *This is what happens when you mess with the Reaper's friends*.

It excited him, her aggression. She would never be cowed by the dragon. She was Joan of Arc and Boudicca and Fu Hao all in one.

"Does Lucia know where it is now?" he asked.

"Corbette had Kivati digging in the crater for months. All his water tribes—Salmon and Whale and even Turtle—dove in the flooded tunnels. They had a few incidents with some of the less friendly deep water creatures. One of his Thunderbird generals was in charge. He found the Tablet along with Rudrick's crushed body. Corbette let him keep it. He wears it around his wrist as a memento of what the Unraveling took from him."

"Which Thunderbird?"

"Lord Kai Raiden."

"Ah. Same one who was in charge of guarding my coal shipment." Leif cleared his throat and looked over the edge. The black water crashed against the foot of the cliff. "Sven killed his twin brother."

"So he's not going to let you have it." She followed his gaze over the side. Concrete and steel stuck out along the sharp drop-off. The sea churned in the crater bowl, hungrily nibbling at the land beneath their feet, undercutting the buildings and streets. It was only a matter of time before the whole place slid into the sea.

But what city wouldn't? Time stretched out before him; civilizations rose to thumb their nose at Mother Nature, but she took them all back to her bosom in the end. Longren was right: the mountains and the continents would vanish until only he and his immortal kin remained. Alone with the chilling darkness.

"I bet Kingu is looking for the piece of the Tablet too. He used it to attack the gods. Marduk fought him with a web of light, thunderbolts, and fire, but he didn't win until he took the Tablets away. I bet Kingu needs the Tablet to restart his war. Could explain why he's stalking Kivati, if Kai Raiden has the Tablet. Maybe they don't have the Heart at all."

"But it doesn't explain Corbette's strange Aether storm or his behavior. His loss of self-control. His abandonment of the humans and his responsibilities to the council."

"You haven't shown much interest in the council either."

As an accusation, it stung. So he'd been busy. So he'd assumed the people tangled in Sven's strings would be happy not to have a ruler breathing down their necks. "But that's a continuation of my behavior. Not a marked personality change. Something is wrong with Corbette. We have to assume the Heart is also calling to Kingu, and Kingu is following Corbette."

They walked back to Butterworth's. Grace had brought the new bike and chained it to a steel grate across the street. Leif allowed himself a small, private smile. "And the aptrgangr haven't mentioned anything else besides the Heart?"

"What, do you think we sit around chatting?"

Chapter 12

Lucia lunged. A fine mist fell on the veranda of Kivati Hall, slicking her divided gown and plastering her hair to her face, but even a blizzard would be better than staying inside. Corbette's emotions rolled through the building like their own personal indoor weather system. The Great Hall flashed hot then cold. Inside, ladies sweated in their corsets and petticoats, and the next moment froze beneath their thin shawls.

She slammed her knee into an invisible opponent like the Reaper had shown her. Crotch, eyes, throat. After this, she would practice running around the grounds. The Raven Lord hadn't forbidden her that yet. Thank the Lady.

Lucia was afraid to sleep at night. Sometimes the nightmares were enough to keep her walking the dark hallways at midnight, but lately the real threat of fire kept her sleeping with a fire extinguisher next to her bed. Her memories of the Unraveling were etched on her soul. She remembered the earthquakes and the flames that raged through the city. She remembered the cyclone of souls that broke through the Gate to the Land of the Dead all too well.

And she knew that if Corbette's control on the Aether continued to unravel and his anger sparked the tinder of this wooden palace, she would die in the flames. Her ability to manipulate the Aether, always weak, always shaky, was almost nonexistent now. She couldn't call a rain cloud to smother the fire. She couldn't force water from the air to dampen her skirts and keep her from becoming a living torch. Sometimes she wished she'd never read those history books on Victorian life, because she knew exactly how terrible it would be to have her skirts catch fire and her petticoats go up in flame. It would be a slow, agonizing death.

Sometimes she fantasized about the next world. But the hellfire she'd witnessed during the Unraveling kept her very sure she wanted to stay on this side of the Gate to the Land of the Dead. Nothing could make her go back down in that crater, and there was no other path through the Gate.

Lucia lunged again and this time slipped on the wet planks. Her slippers shot out from under her and she fell, hard. "Ye gods damn it!"

"Language, Lady Lucia." She was startled to see Lord Kai watching her from the doorway. He looked disreputable as ever with his long, curling mane of black hair and his open shirt. Leather pants, not wool. Black motorcycle jacket and a bandoleer. He must have just come back from patrol. He shook his head in that slow, mocking way of his. "You've picked up some filth from your midnight strolls."

"How did you—?"

"It's my business to know what goes on in the Western House." He took her gloved hand and pulled her off the deck. She glanced to his wrist. The leather thong peeked out from beneath his sleeve, showing just the edge of the jade Tablet. She swallowed and looked away. Being this close made her nauseated. "Don't worry." He pulled her near. "It'll be our little secret."

She extricated her hand from his.

"I hear congratulations are in order."

She blinked at him.

"The Raven Lord's sister is coming to visit. Does this mean the happy nuptials approach?"

Lucia felt like she'd taken a punch to the gut. Corbette still wanted her? He barely talked to her! Her parents would be ecstatic. She wasn't ready. "He has a sister?"

Kai hooked a thumb in his bandoleer. "One big loving family. Lady Alice, the black sheep."

Her lungs squeezed like she'd already run a mile. She didn't know *anything* about Corbette. She'd tried so hard to become the perfect Kivati Lady since the Unraveling, but the effort was suffocating her. Be good. Be demure. Be proper. But she'd always had the heart of a rebel. She had more in common with Kai than she did with the straight-laced Corbette. At least until recently. Corbette's control was slipping; it made him more real, but also infinitely more dangerous. *Be careful what you wish for*, she thought.

"You're shivering," Kai said. He shrugged out of his thick jacket and wrapped it around her thin shoulders. "Come inside out of the cold."

She allowed him to steer her into the Hall. But Corbette met them, and she knew what he saw: his fiancée wrapped in another man's coat, his trusted general with his arm around his china doll. A wave of heat bowled through the long hallway. Sweat trickled between her breasts.

Corbette's eyes flashed violet. His head tilted. "Good morning."

She wriggled out from under Kai's arm and his coat. The Thunderbird knew what was good for him. He took a step back. "Good morning, my lord." He took off like the gentleman he wasn't, leaving her alone to face the demon.

Corbette scowled with his great black brows, looking down his great hooked nose at her like she was an ant to be crushed. Forcing her hands into her skirts to hide their shake, she gave a pretty curtsy. "I hear your sister is visiting."

She waited for him to tell her about his sister, that the

wedding was still on, that he still wanted her after everything that had happened. She watched his shoes. They didn't betray his anger by tapping. They stayed perfectly still. Might have been carved from a frozen river. People said the Raven Lord didn't have feelings, and he certainly pretended not to. But anyone who could feel so much anger had to have passion of the opposite sort. Once he found his mate, he would move the world for her.

Frankly, that ferocity of passion terrified the socks off her.

"Alice and her . . . husband will be joining us," he said finally. "But don't worry, we will have warriors guarding you. You don't have to fear him."

Her head jerked up. "Guards inside Kivati Hall?" She couldn't even roam her pretty prison alone anymore? "Who is he?"

His lip curled. "Drekar. I will protect you." *This time* hung in the air between them. "Nothing to fear as long as you stay here." As usual he seemed to strip away her skin to the tender, hidden part of her.

How could he see so much and still be so blind? "Like Rapunzel locked in her tower. Safe from the wolves who bayed outside?"

His gaze slid off her like falling ice at the edge of a glacier. He turned to the open French doors. "Rapunzel was safe until she left."

"But not from the witch."

"No." He took a step back into the hallway. "Not from the witch. But the witch wouldn't hurt her. Never." The illusion of feathers rippled over his skin.

He scared her. Not that he would hurt her deliberately; he would die first. But his stranglehold on himself and his ideals stifled her. She was not perfect. She had never been perfect. And he demanded perfection. From his people, from his generals, from himself most of all. The woman who would be his queen and rule beside him needed to be perfect too. No one, not even Lucia, would want any less for their leader. He had protected the Kivati way and kept their people from dying out after his father had almost lost the territory to the Drekar. He was the linchpin of their world. His mate had to be his match in everything, or she wouldn't be able to compete with his true love, the Kivati.

Lucia would never be that woman. The crown of the Crane Wife had ground her down until she shattered like bones in the flames. She'd never been allowed to discover herself. Even now, when she couldn't bear his scrutiny, when nightmares kept her screaming awake and she had no Aether magic to speak of, he wouldn't let her go. To let her go would be to admit defeat.

Worse, to admit he had been wrong about her, and the Raven Lord was never wrong.

She thought of the Reaper. Grace managed to wield personal power even enslaved to the Drekar. Lucia wanted to be more like her. Tough as nails. To get the Tablet, Grace needed access to Kai. This was Lucia's chance to make a difference. She believed in Grace's quest, but she knew Corbette would never hand it over if he thought the Drekar wanted it. Lucia needed to get Kai and the Tablet far away from Kivati Hall, and give Grace the opportunity to snatch it.

"Grant me an engagement gift," Lucia blurted.

"Anything."

"I want to see the city lit up again. I miss it. Make the Drekar Regent finish the Gas Works. Build gaslights across the Interurban to protect travelers."

"So Lord Kai wants to redeem himself."

"It's not about Kai, but you should give him the chance. He lost the first coal shipment. His dishonor reflects poorly on us."

Appealing to the Kivati honor worked as she had hoped. He gave her a sharp smile.

"Consider it done."

The chimes above the door to Thor's Hammer jingled. Grace ignored them, but it was harder to ignore the sudden alertness in Elsie's body, spread naked beneath her needles and ink.

"Stop moving," Grace ordered. All her concentration was on the copper hammer as she inked the rune into the skin above the last vertebra. Complete focus was essential. She felt the Aether humming through the needle, saturating the ink of the tattoo. She couldn't lose her focus or the protection rune would be worthless.

"But hello, handsome," Elsie purred.

"I said don't move." Grace blocked everything out. She didn't smell cinnamon and iron. She didn't feel an electric presence sneaking up behind her. She didn't . . .

"Freya take you." Her fingers slipped and the thread of Aether snapped. She threw her tools on her worktable and spun around. The bone knife slipped into her hand without conscious thought. Asgard stood there like a brilliant, blond sun god. "Can't you read? It says DO NOT ENTER. What is unclear about that?"

He towered over her. The point of her knife pressed into the silk of his cravat, but he ignored it. His eyes pierced into her, daring her to push farther. He could break her like a twig. Tension snapped the air between them. Tension, and something hotter.

She would tell him what he could do with his interest.

Elsie broke it. "Do introduce us, Grace." She sat up, milky white skin glowing in the light of the biodiesel lamp. Long blond curls artfully fluttered around the rosy tips of her nipples. Pink lips pursed, inviting.

Grace dropped her knife and gave him her back. Next to Elsie, she was invisible. Short. Plain. Temper like a bear cub. She liked it that way. "Regent Asgard, may I present Elsie, Maiden of Ishtar. Elsie, the Regent."

She stuck her hands in the bucket of water on her worktable and scrubbed at the red and black ink on her fingers. Behind her, Elsie cooed, something artful and witty and well rehearsed. Grace didn't envy Elsie her profession, but sometimes she wished for Elsie's training. The ease with which she turned men's minds. The power she maintained, even flat on her back.

"I live next door with a few other Maidens, but you may usually find me at the House in the square." Elsie's tone danced like the light of a flickering candle, so different from how she spoke to Grace.

"Mmm," Asgard said. "Where Ianna's High Priestess."

"Oh, you know it! I can't believe I missed your visit. We must have been ships passing in the night. I serve there four nights a week and high holidays."

Grace couldn't help sneaking a peek and found him staring at her. The beautiful, naked blonde beneath his nose might have been a fly for all the notice he paid Elsie. A hint of laughter danced at the corner of his elegant mouth.

She grabbed a towel and scrubbed her hands.

"It would be an honor to have you worship with us," Elsie said. The invitation lingered in the air like incense from a night-blooming flower. A sensual promise.

Grace busied herself cleaning up the remains of the ritual. She crammed the lid back on the ink bottle and tucked her needles into her leather holder. Better that he turn his attentions elsewhere, where they were wanted. It was always a relief when Norgard had sought more fertile pastures. Well, not always. At first it had hurt. She'd been naive, but what sixteen-year-old wasn't? Once the scabs on her heart had toughened up, she'd realized what a fool she'd been. No one would ever have the power to hurt her again.

Norgard was dead, but if Asgard thought he could pick up where his brother left off, he had another think coming. He might own her slave bond. He might demand her body. But he would never touch her heart. That was hers, and hers alone.

"Elsie, come back tomorrow," she snapped. "We have to start all over again." Elsie started at her tone. "And you." Grace turned to Asgard. "What do you want?"

One blond eyebrow rose. "I wasn't aware I needed an invitation to my own business."

He had a point. She had forgotten that he had inherited all of Norgard's possessions, Thor's Hammer included. She was too used to calling this shop her own. Her black drapes covered the thin windows. Her silver-threaded couch—found after hours of combing secondhand stores—provided a safe place to crash after long nights. Her bottles of herbs and potions lined the walls. Her chalk circles and painted wards decorated the floor and door frame.

But Asgard owned the building. And these hands that had fashioned the drapes, that had spent long hours in the vats of slime to make those potions, that had drawn those wards, he owned them too. She would have to remember. She owned nothing.

Elsie slipped her sheer chemise over her head, letting the silk flow softly and slowly over her curves. Grace gave her a flat look. The Maiden usually tugged her clothes on like any normal person. This seductive act was all for Asgard.

It pissed her off.

"A moment." Asgard reached out to halt the flow of silk down Elsie's back. He examined the unfinished mark over the last bone in her spine. His large fingers traced the delicate skin above Elsie's perky, rounded ass.

Elsie gave a breathy little moan, and Grace tried not to roll her eyes.

"An interesting design," he said. "What does it mean?"

"Ishtar's wrath," Elsie said. "Most Maidens get the symbol for her sacred courtesans or her sexual power. But she was the goddess of war too."

"So you're channeling her anger." He gently pulled the under gown over Elsie's rump and turned to Grace. "Is that what's tattooed all over your back too?"

"Oh, no," Elsie said. "Grace doesn't need any help with aggression."

Asgard smiled.

Very funny.

"Ishtar led an army of the dead, did you know that?" Elsie slipped on her corset over the chemise and motioned for Grace to help lace it up. Grace obliged. She felt Asgard watching her. His presence radiated outward, like a rip in the Aether, impossible to ignore. "The High Priestess won't talk about it, but Grace and I have been researching."

"Tell me," he said. He turned that movie-star smile on Elsie, and she preened like a flower turning to the sun.

Grace bungled the laces. Elsie knew she didn't know how to do this girly crap.

"Allow me." Asgard took the laces from her. Grace snatched her hands away and backed up. Another little smile played along his lips. So much for not letting him see how he affected her. She had to do better.

Elsie was oblivious to the power struggle tainting the air behind her. "Ishtar knew how to stand up for herself. She took what she wanted. Grace, find that passage, will you?"

Grace was only too happy for another task that didn't involve corsets or men or sex. An army of the dead? That was more her style. She picked up the book she'd stolen from the House of Ishtar, flipped to the page on the *Epic of Gilgamesh*, and cleared her throat. "The oldest mention of aptrgangr anywhere in the world is found on Ishtar's tablets. She was a petty and vengeful goddess, and when she didn't get her way she threatened to raise the dead. When Gilgamesh spurns her advances, she says, 'I'll wreak havoc of my own right down to Hell. I'll loose the goddamn devil. I'll rain corpses. I'll make zombies eat infants and there will be more dead souls than living ones!'" She flipped a couple pages. "And here again when Ishtar goes into the underworld she threatens, 'I will knock down the Gates of the Netherworld. I will smash the doorposts and leave the doors flat down, and will let the dead go up to eat the living. And the dead will outnumber the living.'"

"She sounds downright bloodthirsty," Asgard said.

"Most old myths paint powerful women in a negative light, but this is pretty explicit. She commanded an army of the dead to do her bidding. I think Kingu is leading her army. He's raising aptrgangr to do his searching for him."

Asgard helped Elsie slip on her gown. He certainly knew his way around a Maiden's clothing. "So Ishtar, in her pity, gave Tiamat's children three gifts: her sacred courtesans to feed our soul hunger, her army of the dead to extract vengeance, and a soul mate to end our curse."

There it was again: that intense longing that cracked the calm beauty of Asgard's face. Only an instant, and it was gone. But Grace had seen it twice now. How could he believe that soul mate crap? It was a death sentence. What immortal would give up forever just to be with one woman? What idiot would chain her soul to a Dreki for eternity?

"That is so romantic!" Elsie said. "Grace was telling me about your soul mate. You poor dear."

"Els, I'm sure the Regent has business to talk about. I'll see you tonight. Same time?"

"You can't leave bruises this time. I have to work."

"Keep your fist up then." Grace shooed her out the door

and Elsie left with a little wave, mouthing, *Lucky*, behind Asgard's back.

Grace shut the door against the chilling October wind and turned back to find Asgard taking up her space. The room was immediately shabbier without Elsie to draw the eye away from the threadbare chairs and cracked walls. Asgard with his crimson coat and golden hair had too much class to slum it on Flesh Alley. Sitting on her couch, he leaned back and made himself right at home. Bear climbed into his lap.

Traitor.

She and Asgard had become entirely too comfortable together since the trip to Mount Si. It gave her an itchy feeling between her shoulder blades. She needed air. Changing her mind about the cold, she opened the top half of the Dutch door. Outside, leaves crunched beneath shoppers' boots. A pack of feral hounds rolled a garbage can in the alley. The scent of sugar and brewing applejack drifted from the apothecary across the street.

Inside lounged Asgard. On her *bed*. So it was technically a couch, but she slept there. Even with the long, narrow room between them, she wanted to back up.

"What happened to your forehead?" he asked.

She reached up to touch the bruise across her brow. She'd almost forgotten about it. "I fell."

He crossed his heel over his left knee.

"Really. I was searching the House's library for more info on Kingu and the Heart. Ianna almost caught me. I had to climb out a window."

"You should have free access to the library. I'll talk to her."

"Don't. She's still mad about the fence and Kingu's attack. She hasn't even found out yet that I'm teaching some of her girls self-defense. You'll just make it worse."

His jaw set. She felt the gulf drop away between them again. Distance was safer. She moved toward him.

"As much as it pains me to send a woman into danger," he said, "I need your skills. I have a job for you."

"Really?"

"Corbette has been persuaded to reopen the coal-gas-works project." Asgard rose from the couch and strolled across the room to examine her bottles of ink. He found the rune books and flipped through one. "The Thunderbird who holds the Tablet shard will be guarding this second shipment. As part of the negotiation, I will be sending a few of my own to accompany the wagons and make sure there is no foul play."

"I can do that."

"Don't make a stupid play for the Tablet. Kai Raiden is a well-trained Aether mage with two hundred pounds on you. But if the opportunity arises—"

"I'm on it."

He studied the book. There was something he wasn't telling her. He closed the cover and replaced it on the shelf. "At best it will be a long, slow trudge in the mud, and you gain us some valuable intel and the means of defeating Kingu. At worst, Kingu tries for it again, though I don't know why he would. His latest attacks have been on Corbette, not Lord Kai. I think he's following the Heart, not the necklace."

She felt a rush of anticipation. There was something twisted about her. She liked that adrenaline high too much, that dance with death on the edge of the abyss. It called to some morbid part of her. Everyone fell eventually, but every time she escaped by the skin of her teeth was another chance to thumb her nose at Freya and Ishtar and any other incarnation that wanted a piece of her soul.

She negotiated bringing Oscar as her backup and Hart, if the Kivati would let him go, and made Asgard sign one of her new contracts for the two-hundred-dollar fee. After the

High Priestess had robbed her, she was determined to lay things out legally. Not that anyone would come to her aid if Asgard left her high and dry. The Regent was judge, jury, and executioner.

He studied her. "Just when I think I have you pegged, you surprise me."

"That's me—more tricks than a two-bit whore."

"Don't. Don't cheapen yourself. Sarcasm is your shield, but it cuts both ways."

"I don't know what you're talking about." She felt him approach. She imagined some giant reptile creeping up on its prey. *I am not prey*, she reminded herself. His presence gave her a tingling feeling along her skin, like static electricity in a thunderstorm. Pre-Unraveling, of course. There was no such thing anymore. Except she felt it when he drew close. It shouldn't be possible. Her pulse sped up in excitement or fear, she couldn't tell which. And sometimes weren't they the same thing?

But she didn't want to go there, not this time. She'd been burned once. She knew better than to stick her fingers in the socket again.

He brushed her hair off her neck. His fingers traced the brand on her skin, reconsecrating it with his own heat. "This looks purposeful, this raised mark. Who did this to you?"

She tensed, and he lifted his hand. The delicate skin on her neck still tingled from the heat of his fingers. Telling him about her first brand felt like a running iron had poked through her skin and burned along the muscle beneath it. "Your brother."

"Tell me."

"My parents died when I was sixteen. We had driven to Seattle Center to see the ballet. We walked back to the car through an alley. I remember I had the flu, but I didn't want to stay in bed on my birthday. I was being stubborn."

"Who, you? I can't imagine it."

She crossed her arms. "I think I fainted for a moment, and then two strange guys were blocking the alley. I know now they were aptrgangr, but I thought then they were just drugged-out. My mother was screaming at me to run. I ran. My parents died."

"You did the right thing," Asgard said. "Don't cheapen their sacrifice. It was their right. They loved you."

She rolled her shoulders. Now she would have fought, but back then she hadn't known the first thing about self-defense. Running was always a good option.

"So how did you get the mark?" he asked.

"I woke up with it." She'd woken up to Norgard's smiling face. She'd thought he had saved her. By the time she'd realized her mistake, it had been too late. She'd already pledged herself to follow him to the ends of the earth. "He brought in this old Norwegian lady to ink me."

"A heathwitch."

Grace shrugged. "Norgard never told me anything about her. I called her Tunta. She didn't speak English. Her teeth were yellow from the snoose she never stopped chewing, and her eyes were the bluest blue I've ever seen. She showed me the little magic I know and inked the next runes down my spine and on the insides of my wrists." She held out her hands so that Asgard could see the crisp blue ink over each pulse point. "He told me it was to make me stronger. Those first two years were hell."

"What did he do?" Asgard's voice dropped low, almost a mimic of Norgard, arctic and base.

"He threw me right in the ring without training gloves. Not against aptrgangr, but against his best mercenaries. Hart broke my jaw during my first fight. He's never forgiven himself for it."

She could practically hear Asgard's teeth grinding. "Let me guess, my kind brother healed you right up and sent you back to the ring."

"But it did make me stronger. Tunta lived on a pallet in my room until I had all the runes memorized. Gods, the smell of chewing tobacco still sends me back. Then Norgard tested me until I got the results he wanted. I wanted to please him. I've never studied so hard. On my seventeenth birthday, I fought my first aptrgangr, and Tunta disappeared. By then I was champing at the bit to get my revenge and make my *master* proud." She choked on the word, but it was nothing but the truth. "I had marks down my arms and legs. I've filled it in more since then. Every time I feel weak or out of control I put another rune on myself."

"You? Out of control?" He laughed softly. "I'd like to see that."

Grace forced herself to breathe through her mouth. The heat in his voice drew her in. The faint whiff of cinnamon lured her to relax. She was tired of fighting it. She closed her eyes. Iron control was all she had holding her together. "Want me to lose it like Corbette?"

"I can't see you throwing a magical temper tantrum."

"No." She understood the Raven Lord more than she wanted to, but perfectionism and zealotry drove him up bat creek. Her self-control steered her down a different path. Shit needed to get done—she did it. No bellyaching. No pity party.

If she lost it, she would crumple in a puddle of bones and tears. Shit would cease to get done. People depended on her, and there was no one to step into her shoes. She was the last line of defense.

Asgard slid his finger down the side of her cheek to raise her chin. She opened her eyes. His emerald-green gaze anchored her to the floor. "I want to see you spiral out of control. I want to watch you lose every tightly wound spring." He wrapped a strand of her hair slowly around his hand until it pulled her head up sharply. He held her motionless.

She could kick him, if she wanted to. She could break his hold on her. He dipped his head. Her lips parted.

"I want to wring every bit of steel from your spine."

"Why?" She breathed the word. His mouth hovered an inch above hers, whispering mean, mad things like they were candy. She braced herself for him to close that distance. The tension in her body vibrated like the strings on a violin. One pluck, and her body would sing.

"Because once all of those iron spikes you call grit shatter like blown glass, only then will you see the true strength inside you. It's not hate, and it's not anger, and it's not the ability to destroy. There is a goddess inside every woman, and she is a creator of worlds."

Grace slapped him. Her hand came up all on its own and hit his cheek with the force of an anvil.

His head jerked to the side. His body didn't move an inch. His mouth stretched in a tight smile. "I suppose I deserved that." Releasing her hair, he slowly rubbed his jaw.

"You want to do me a favor, do you?" she asked. "You can get the Freya out of my shop."

Chapter 13

Ravensdale lay three hours from Seattle as the crow flew. The four Kivati guardsmen might have flown there in that time, but they couldn't carry the coal back. The journey would take five days if all went smoothly: two to get there, three to return with ten wagons full of freshly minted coal. Grace had five days to see if she could steal the Tablet of Destiny shard from around Lord Kai's wrist.

It started ominously. The ten Kivati warriors who were supposed to guard the shipment turned into four due to some last-minute emergency. The four who came were in a sullen temper. The real action was happening back at Kivati Hall, and none of them wanted to be here picking up rocks. No one would tell her the details, but she could guess: another Kingu attack on Kivati soil. She needed to pump Lucia for answers. Did Corbette have the Heart? Was Kingu following its Aether trail? How did one defeat a demigod anyway?

For the first time she itched to be back in Seattle, not out on a job. The House of Ishtar's extensive library waited, its secrets hidden between the leather and vellum pages.

"Keep up, Mercer. If you and pretty boy here fall behind, we aren't going back for you." Kai Raiden had the look of a desperado with the tailoring of a Kivati Thunderbird general, like they thought a lot of fine wool and linen could contain all that wildness. His black mane of curls softened the harshness of his features. He held himself like a Roman centurion of old, but his eyes were more Spartacus than Caesar; bleak desolation carved into those black depths, the thick circle of violet said he rode the edge of the Change. She could imagine him galloping across the fields of Sparta with sword and shield, his path of destruction rending the very blood from the earth.

She raised her chin and patted her knife at her hip. Never show an animal fear. "Must have been tough, General, losing that shipment the first time. How'd the Raven Lord take it?"

The violet in his eyes flared. He could make the mud beneath her open up and swallow her whole if he chose to—his ability to manipulate the Aether should be that good if he were one of Corbette's chosen four. He wanted to; she could see it in the way his fingers twitched. But after abandoning the first shipment he had something to prove. He held himself back. "Saddle up."

Compared to the Thunderbird, the three Crow guards were lean. Runner's builds, but top-heavy. They exuded power. Part of it was the tangible self-confidence—they thought they were better than everyone else. Part of it was the Aether that ran through their blood. Hard to seem weak when you could manipulate the fabric of the universe to do your bidding. Must be nice.

All four wore the black armband of the Western House. Of the four Kivati Houses, the Western House was where they sent the troublemakers and hotheads. It had earned a reputation, and it was said Corbette sent them in whenever he had business that couldn't be won on the straight and narrow. Like blowing up Drekar holdings, which meant they were the ones Grace had most often tangled with as Norgard's mercenary.

They didn't want her there. They didn't like her, rough around the edges, not dolled up in restrictive skirts like their women. They didn't trust her, Grace Mercer, Drekar spy. They didn't think she could do anything but get in the way if there was trouble. Well, fuck 'em.

She sauntered over to the pony they'd brought her and caught sight of the sidesaddle. "You've got to be kidding me." She shot General Haughtiness a dark look.

He stared back, unperturbed.

Johnny handed her the reins. The handsome Crow was young, brash, and even less enthusiastic about being here than she was. Unlike her, he didn't have a choice. She'd asked for Hart. Johnny had come instead, and the two weren't exactly on speaking terms. She wondered if Lucia had sent her whipping boy to keep an eye on her. "It's not the saddle you need to worry about," he warned.

The mottled grey horse turned its head around and snickered.

Great.

The Thunderbird rode at the front of the wagon train. Rafe and Elias scouted overhead in Crow form. Every two wagons were hitched together, each with a human driver. Johnny, Oscar, and she took up the rear. She got the impression Johnny had been forbidden from taking his Totem form—the worst sort of punishment for his kind. The usual murder of crows followed them too. It was weird to be on the receiving end of the bird's information, not the one being spied on. Crows swooped over the road searching for traps. They lined the trees as the wagon train passed through and painted the air silver with their grating laughter.

"Everyone from here to hell will know we're coming," Grace complained.

"Then we're safe as long as they've seen Hitchcock,"

Oscar said, looking up at the black-bedecked trees with a shudder.

The road skirted Lake Washington, then veered southeast along the old Maple Valley Highway to Ravensdale. Subdivisions lined the route like the tan tombstones of giants. If the suburbs had been soulless before, they weren't now; the ticky-tacky boxes teemed with ghosts.

The horse, a glue factory reject named Bambi, only tried to kill her a few times. On the third try, it reared on a stick-thin trail at the side of a steep ravine. She got off and had a come-to-Jesus chat with the creature.

"Something is spooking it," Oscar said. His Kivati-issued mount had been scraped from the bottom of the barrel too, but it had a better appreciation for continuing its flea-bitten existence.

She watched the patch of forest lining the road behind them. "Besides the crows?"

"They're Kivati horses. They should be used to crows."

Johnny turned his horse toward them. "Aptrgangr?"

"I can't tell," Oscar said, and she couldn't either.

Whatever it was, it didn't bother them on the journey to Ravensdale. They rode into town at noon on Friday. Ravensdale wasn't much more than a hitching post with a main street and a couple of patched-up stores. A forest of green, army-issued canvas tents sprouted up from the hillside where the miners lived. It could have been Deadwood or any gold rush boomtown.

Her dad would have loved this place. He always had a half-finished Louis L'Amour novel close at hand. By the time she was ten, they'd seen every John Wayne movie together. He was such a dork. But as she rode into town at the back of a real posse, with a real gun strapped to her hip, she felt less like the Duke and more like a little girl playing dress-up.

She missed him. While her mom had been all sharp edges, the tiger driven to see her daughter succeed, her dad had been the playful one. He was silly and softhearted, big on forgiveness and second chances. Especially for her. She wondered what he would think about Asgard. The lighter, the bike, the talk of honor. Asgard wasn't a prankster like her dad, but he had that same quiet strength.

Workers toiled late into the night loading coal into the wagons. That night she dreamed of long, scaly claws and slitted green eyes. She woke in a sweat, though the early frost crept over her blanket. She couldn't figure Asgard out. She would have fallen for him like a skyscraper in the Unraveling, shaken to her core till her bones liquefied and she was nothing but a puddle of *want*.

If she hadn't met his brother first.

If she didn't know better, and she did know better.

But still . . . still, there was a part of her that wanted even though she knew he was the worst sort of bad for her. The insistent, wicked little part that still wanted to dance with the devil in the scorching light of a Beltane fire. Before she burned, she wanted to hurt so good.

What was the point if you didn't pack every inch of living with joy and sadness, with the highest high and the deepest despair? She knew, better than most, that there were no Technicolor sensations in the life after this. To be a ghost was to be a grey shadow of yourself. It meant an eternity of eating cardboard and shivering in a damp, colorless world. Rage was their only option, and it turned them to wraith. She'd put down enough aptrgangr to recognize it for fact.

Loaded down with coal, the wagons made slower progress back along the highway. The Thunderbird never let down his guard. She couldn't get close enough to see if he had the Tablet around his wrist, let alone to steal it.

The first night they camped at Seward Park, at the south end of the lake. Mist seeped off the water, covering the ripples and splashes of the creatures within. It was dangerous to stay so close to the lake, but more dangerous to camp farther in the ruined suburbs. No one had cleared the houses this far from the main city. The bodies of the fallen—or what was left of them after six months of decay, wild animals, and bugs had at them—still populated the neighborhoods. So many dead for wraiths to pilot. The smell of rot and mildew couldn't be pushed back by the breeze off the lake. The park was the safest campground; it provided a large cleared space where you could see what was coming at you. The humans were nervous, even worse than the horses. Even the Kivati were on edge. They didn't like sleeping away from their wards and cozy creature comforts.

Once the wagons were circled with the humans inside, the four Kivati, Oscar, and Grace drew straws for first watch. They would take the shift in twos. She drew the midnight shift with Rafe, a Crow with auburn streaks in his hair and a thin scar at the corner of his mouth. He moved like a pretentious ass, slow and careful-like, but his eyes were quick. Between his fingers, he flipped an unlit cheroot.

The embers of the fire had died under Johnny's watch, and she toed the remaining logs together with her boot. Oscar helped her collect more wood beneath the nearby trees in the park. The cold wove its way through the thin cotton of her black hoodie. She blew on her exposed fingers to try to chase the numbness out of them. At least the rain held off. Kneeling by the pile of wood, she took out Asgard's flamethrower and set it blazing.

Next to her, Oscar whistled. "Where can I get me one of those?"

She turned the lighter over in her hand, remembering the look in Asgard's eye when he tossed it to her and the IOU he'd left. She could still feel his heavy promise lodged between her breasts. "Asgard."

"That's some present."

"It's not a present!"

"Sure, sure." Oscar watched the flames crackle as the wood caught fire. "So what else did he give you?"

"What makes you think there's anything else?"

Rafe sat on a rock a foot to her left, not helping. He stuck the cheroot between his teeth and grinned. "Pretty lil' thing like you? 'Course there's more."

"Tools of the trade aren't *gifts*. They're practical. Doesn't Corbette provide your weapons? Your armor?"

"So what was it?" Oscar asked.

She turned her back to the fire. The nearest house squatted a couple hundred feet away, on the other side of a pile of downed trees. Curtains blew out of the missing windows, beckoning. There was something out there, watching them. Something large and intent. She tried to ignore it, while keeping her spidey senses on alert. Either it would attack or it wouldn't. "Hart's Deadglass and a bike."

"A bike," Oscar said. "You're not exactly a diamonds and roses sort of gal, dearie. Maybe he's on to something."

"Go to bed, Oscar. Your shift starts in four."

"Did I ever tell you about Roxanne?"

She pulled the Deadglass out from beneath her shirt and adjusted the gears to clear her vision. "I thought we didn't stroll down that particular dark lane."

"You're right. We don't." Oscar took a swig from the small silver flask he always kept in his vest pocket. "But Roxie was something else. Bosoms out to here, blond hair down to there. She could turn a man's head was he eight or eighty. She was the bartender at Butterworth's before Doc. A real ballbuster. Had the whole place jumping. One of Norgard's own, you know? He said she was the spitting image of Wicked Nell."

"His first madam out in Seattle?"

"That's the one." Oscar took another drink. A loud splash, followed by the screech of some small mammal, marred the silence. "I would have given my front teeth for one dance with Roxie."

"But you never told her?"

"I kept telling myself I'd do it tomorrow."

"Wrong business to be in if that's your strategy." For Norgard's pawns, tomorrow had a bad habit of standing a person up.

"Tomorrow's finally here. Doc's got a new girl at the bar that promised me a dance when we get back."

She lowered the Deadglass. "What do you mean?"

"This is my last job, Reaper."

She blinked. "Why didn't you say something?"

"Didn't want to jinx it, you know how it is. But we'll be home tomorrow night. Give me an hour and I'll be drunk as two fools in love. I'm feeling nostalgic. I've worked for the Regent since I turned eleven. That's a good chunk of time runnin' and spying and conning. This is my last night on the road."

"Congrats. That's really . . . great. Big plans?"

"Just that dance. Then, who knows? Probably find myself a rich sugar mama and retire. Don't look so sad, Reaper. I'm not leaving, just changing jobs."

She turned back to the tree line. First Hart, then Oscar. Soon she'd be the last grizzled veteran in the dog pack. "I'm pretty close myself."

"Good to hear it. What will you do once you're free?"

Asgard had asked her the same question. *Avenge my parents*, sat on her tongue. Maybe she wanted something more for her life. Her parents certainly had. In their minds her future had involved taking state in the piano competition, getting into a top university, maybe a doctorate from Cambridge, eventually a smart husband they picked out for her and, of course, grandbabies. Above all they had wanted her to be happy.

Was she happy? She survived. Maybe that wasn't good enough anymore.

"I'm still thinking about it," she told Oscar.

"Something grand, I'm sure," he said. He rose and clapped her affectionately on the shoulder. Suddenly the distance she'd always kept between them seemed silly. He'd become her best friend, despite her attempts to keep him at arm's length. Trying to protect her heart from getting hurt again hadn't worked out if the thought of him leaving, even just leaving the mercenary corps, hurt so much.

She turned beneath his hand and wrapped her arms around his skinny waist. "I'm glad for you."

"Be careful, Reaper," Oscar said. He gave her a squeeze and slipped off to his bedroll on the other side of the wagon circle.

Careful? Ha. She'd been too careful with her heart and too reckless with her body. Where was the middle ground? She had maneuvered herself into a corner. How could she let go of all this anger? It had been her closest companion for five years. It propped her up when she couldn't stand, propelled her forward when her feet ached too much to take another step. If she let her anger go, what would hide the well of fear that hid in the heart of her?

Rafe slipped next to her in the cold fog. "Lighter?"

She dug in her pocket and handed him the toy. He flipped it over his fingers as he examined the small gears, the letter G carved into the brass. Lighting his cheroot between his teeth, he puffed out a breath and handed the lighter back. He followed her gaze out into the abandoned houses that ran along the edge of the park. Most had collapsed. Some from the earthquakes. Some from the mobs afterward. Ransacked, tagged with signs against the evil eye, anarchy and devil symbols, and indiscriminate biblical passages, the buildings held testament to the passing of the modern age. The time when technology was king. When brains triumphed over brawn. When television, cheap food, and armchair jobs gave rise to medical epidemics that only plagued rich, slothful nations.

God, she missed those times. What she wouldn't do for a potato chip. Just one. Greasy, salty goodness. Her stomach rumbled.

The Crow chuckled.

"Shove off," she told him.

"Here." He took a piece of jerky out of his pocket and offered it to her. "There's nothing wrong with it. See?" He tore off a piece and popped it in his mouth. She watched him chew, swallow. Waited to see if he would suddenly gag. He looked okay. Her stomach rumbled again. He grinned, a bit feral. "You aren't afraid of a little food, are you? I thought the Reaper was big, bad news. Or is this the way to ask you on a date?"

She took the proffered meat just so she wouldn't have to answer. The smoky flavor hid the meat well. She didn't want to ask what kind of meat it was, but with the Kivati it was probably legitimate.

"I thought so." He watched the thick darkness and sniffed the air. They waited in companionable silence.

The creature watching them shifted; the faint creak of wood and ghostly breath slithered between the trees. Was that cinnamon? She didn't get a malicious vibe from it, but that didn't mean much. It seemed . . . *hungry*.

Maybe she was projecting.

"So," Rafe said and took a long draw on the cheroot. His eyes left his watch to meander along her body. "Asgard sent his best little lady to see what a real man's all about, huh?"

"What?" she deadpanned. "No, I've already met Oscar."

"That pretty boy? Sweetheart, you come around Queen Anne anytime and ask for me." He took another draw, flexing his bicep as he did. The smoke smelled of cloves. It had absolutely no effect on her. "I'll show you my weapons, if you show me yours."

"Tempting."

"A real man protects his lady friends. He doesn't send them out into the swamp after a couple walking corpses."

"Protects his lady friends, you mean like Lucia?"

Rafe's spine straightened as if an electrical wire had been jammed into his tailbone. "Don't speak of her."

"All the more reason a woman should be able to fight her own battles."

"You don't know nothing, slut."

"What? A dirty Drekar whore like me shouldn't taint the sainted name of Lady Lucia?"

Rafe grabbed the front of her shirt and yanked her off the ground.

The house in front of them exploded.

The Crow was a dead man. Leif burst through the rotting timbers of the house and let his rage fuel the Aether change. The man had put his hands on Grace. Leif's vision, always green and blue in dragon form, burned red. Smoke poured from his long snout. His rage fused the pistons of his reasoning so that he couldn't move forward from this one driving thought: destroy his enemy.

"No, Regent!" Zetian moved to stop him. "You'll ruin everything."

He heard her, but the words didn't penetrate. He stretched his cramped wings and shrieked, the primeval roar that was more pterodactyl than lion.

His prey heard. The cheroot fell from between the man's lips. He dropped Grace, and she landed on her butt in the dirt. He raised his crossbow just as Leif pulled completely free from the house. His aim didn't waver, tracking Leif's dragon heart even as he pushed into the air.

Grace tackled the man around the knees, pushing him off his feet and into the mud. The arrow flew wide.

She protected him.

It was all he needed to break the rage and bring his control back in line. She'd seen an arrow pointed at his breast and lunged, instinctively, to save his life. A single arrow wouldn't slow him down, but all that mattered was her intent. Protecting the monster now, was she?

Grace would never admit it.

He could never forget it. He pulled that memory to him and curled it like a burning coal in the deep hollow of his heart.

Redirecting his flight, he soared up into the thin stream of moonlight. It slipped from between the clouds like a ripple of honey. Lake Washington spread black as an oil slick to the north. In his memory, the electric haze of a million city lights twinkled from around the lake. A blink, this civilization. Carved out from the forest depths in a flash of inspiration, only to crumble like sand castles beneath the ocean waves.

Zetian hadn't followed him from the house.

Unease crept up his spine. He followed the trail of moonlight back down to the field of brown grass to find the first lurching soldiers of Ishtar's army. Grace stood at the ready. The moonlight glinted off the blade in her hand. On her left hunched her thin friend, Oscar, with a rifle at his shoulder. She stood elbow to elbow on her right with the man who would be dead. The Kivati warriors spread out the line, crossbows ready. The humans waited between the coal wagons as a second line of defense. Not much of one, not if the aptrgangr got past the trained fighters.

Damn it. Zetian had argued Kingu would be too busy

stalking Corbette to worry about the Tablet of Destiny. Why search for a silly bit of rock when one could have all the powers of a goddess? But Lord Kai had the Tablet shard, and now the aptrgangr were here. Zetian wanted to draw Kingu out. She convinced Leif they would simply observe and rule out the Tablet should nothing happen. Narrow down the field. It had seemed like a good idea. No civilians would be hurt this far out of the city. It felt better to do *something*, anything but wait around impotently while Kingu stoked fear across Seattle.

And then there was Grace. Was it Grace or the Tablet that drew the aptrgangr? It didn't matter. He had let his wishes interfere with his expected outcome, and now she faced a field of adversaries with very little backup.

He'd screwed up.

With a long breath of fire, he took out the first five aptrgangr. The Kivati started firing and took down more. Wraiths fled once the bodies were disabled. They stirred the Aether, hot and angry, twisted with malice and hate. The wind around him shrieked. Wraiths attacked in their insubstantial form. Their passion was strong enough that he could feel their claws. He shook his long snout, trying to fling them out of his face.

Trust me to do my job, Grace kept telling him, but damn him if he ever sent a soldier into danger without a care.

Leif took another pass over the field. His dragon eyesight worked best at night, and he easily picked out Grace slashing and turning next to her thin friend. She wouldn't blink at the thought of a demigod barreling down on her. She would run headfirst into a fight, not just because she was crazy, but because she had some mad white-knight complex.

Aptrgangr were one thing, but facing Kingu was not something she was prepared for. Leif was bigger, stronger, and harder to kill. He'd gotten her into this mess, and he had to get her out. He used this thought to brace himself. How did one defeat a demigod? Sheer power wouldn't be enough.

He thought of the last time he'd fought. The last time he'd seen his brother. The last time he'd sunk his jaws into his brother's tail and tried to pull him from the skies.

Leif had lost that battle. It was an inconvenient memory at a time like this. His brother had disappeared into the caverns beneath Seattle and never been seen again. Leif hadn't had time to say good-bye.

Grace fought beneath him. He could pinpoint her location among the mass of bodies through the invisible tether. He hadn't had time to tell her all the half-formed thoughts hiding on his tongue. Delicate thoughts. But that didn't make them any less true.

He had wanted to untangle his feelings for himself first. She drove him half mad, forced him to examine unpleasant truths about himself, and skewered his lofty ideals to the wall like a butterfly in a specimen case. He couldn't escape her barbed tongue because some of what she said was true.

But if he was truly the monster she believed, he would not be here now risking his neck for a handful of Kivati and some lumps of black rock. He was not impartial where she was concerned.

The air vibrated. Fog sculpted the ruined suburbs. It crept between the houses, a river of sick, wet Aether, condensing as it came, long tendrils twining together to form a phantom shape. Three long necks began to grow out of the creature's trunk. Kingu was slow to materialize.

Leif didn't wait for the fog to form three long jaws of teeth and fire. He didn't give himself time to think. He launched forward and took the fog creature at the base of those necks.

Pain dug beneath his scales. Hot ash obscured his vision He staggered at the sudden shock and fought to keep aloft.

The reptilian part of his brain took over, driving all thought from his head except to flee. He staggered while his skin burned, not knowing up from down, until he stumbled out of the fog.

He shot halfway over Lake Washington before he regained control of his senses.

Chapter 14

Grace wiped the sweat from her eyes and moved to avoid an aptrgangr fist. The Kivati at her right beheaded the dead man with his machete. She wiped the spray of blood from her cheek.

The attack had spilled out from the line of houses, the twitchiest bodies first, rank with the newly dead. She didn't have time to get good and mad about Asgard's sudden entrance. Dead bodies didn't last long under a wraith's tender care. They preferred live ones with tarnished souls; the sick, the oppressed, the downtrodden. Easy souls to push aside and take over. But they could animate dead bodies in a pinch. It was easy to pour inside the empty shell when no one was home. Weak wraiths were usually the culprits; they were also the easiest to kill. The more powerful the wraith, the easier the possession.

The Kivati weren't thrilled to take her advice, but after the first line of bodies got back up with feathered arrows still protruding between their eyes, Rafe and his posse listened.

"Burn the puppet to ash so no one can pull the strings," she told them. Rafe curled his lip, but dropped his aim. His next bolt cut the aptrgangr off at the ankle. It toppled and started dragging itself forward by its hands.

After that came the live ones, not so smelly, not so jolting. Harder to kill.

They'd run out of bullets and arrows in the first ten minutes. She'd never been so grateful for Asgard's flame-thrower. For Freya's sake, if she didn't have that puppy they would have all died before the first tendrils of fog stretched their way across the field.

Asgard, in dragon form, streaked through the air. He was freaking terrifying. She'd never fought with a dragon before, but by Freya's good luck he was on her side.

As the aptrgangr approached she didn't have time for fear. She entered the kill zone. Her feet and hands moved of their own accord. She danced the steps she knew by heart with more drive than a New York ballerina. Aptrgangr stepped into her dance and time slowed to a two-step. Nothing existed but her and Death.

The Aether rushed through the runes in her bone knife until she felt it bond to her hand and the great river roared through them both, from her body out through her knife and into the waiting penitent. One slice severed soul from body, returning balance to the world.

Aether pounded through her like a psychedelic drug. It was damn addictive. The rush of power. The urge for more. She let pieces of herself go in the raging river, let it sweep her forward until she caught sight of the shadowed fog. It stopped her in midswing.

Run! her mind screamed. *Run!* Her body tensed for speed.

But in that fog lay a glimmer of Aether and the wild, addicted part of her said, *Mine.*

Leif's body rebelled at the thought of returning to that fog. But Grace stood mere feet from it. He turned in the air and came at it from above. Dropping his jaw, he exhaled a long string of fire. The flame illuminated the fog from within, and he saw a shape that sent fear seizing through his wings.

Three times the size of a Dreki, Kingu had three heads, each snapping three rows of jagged shark teeth. His necks fused at a powerful trunk. He had long legs, too long to hold up such a powerful body, but muscled and deadly in their own right. He radiated a promise of pain and a grim, violent ending. Death coated the edges of his claws and razored scales.

Kingu hadn't solidified yet. The white fog offered only a shadow of things to come.

Leif glanced down to the battlefield and saw two of the wagons burning. Most of the humans had fled. Aptrgangr flooded the field. Like the beaches at Normandy; their numbers would wipe out any who stood in their path.

Oscar and a Kivati flanked the Thunderbird general as he began to Change. In that brief moment Lord Kai was vulnerable. Grace moved in front of him to shield. She had a small but growing pile of bodies in front of her. Blood matted her hair. She moved like a dragonfly. If he didn't have preternatural senses, he might not have seen her arms whirring about as she fought. Faster even than the Kivati.

Zetian still hid. If he survived this, he would give her a piece of his mind. But if he didn't, she needed to stay alive to take the reins.

Leif took one last look at Grace and dropped into the burning fog. The pain began in his temples and radiated out to pierce his eardrums. His hearing dissolved into static. The fog squeezed his lungs like blown glass forced between the tongs. His scales turned to granules of sand, only to melt again in the furnace of the demigod's shadow.

This time he couldn't shake the white-hot ash that clouded his vision. His eyes watered. Soaring straight up was the only option. He rose, shaking his long snout like a wet dog. The world shifted, devoid of sight or sound. His balance faltered as the ground and sky traded places. He crashed into a building and tried to right himself, scraping his wing against the ground. He'd been on a Tilt-A-Whirl once at a county fair. This was far worse. He was a danger to himself and others. He could take out Grace with one wrong turn.

His grandfather had always told him he was, by his very nature, a danger. A danger to society. To his family. A blasphemy to the god his minister grandfather feared.

Leif had proven the old man wrong time and again. He fought his nature and never let the selfish, greedy part of him take root. He'd done his best to make the family proud, to invent tools that would improve society, to make his mark not one long black smear but an illuminated letter in the pages of history. After all these years, he had convinced himself that his nature was quite civilized.

But one tussle with Kingu and the old man's voice came blazing to his mind with all the fire and brimstone of a doomsday sermon. Worse, it rung with truth: Kingu was Drekar to the very core, no trappings of civilization, no manners or ethics. These were like gossamer webs and moonshine to the mountain. Irrelevant. Inexplicable.

Every Dreki eventually succumbed to the darkness. Cold, cruel, and heartless. Every last strip of humanity crumbling away. Unable to imagine, create, or feel anything but the rapacious shadows.

Kingu was that darkness. It was as if the part Leif feared in himself had come snaking out of his subconscious in those long tendrils of fog. He knew he could face it, but he wouldn't win. Every pass would rip away another layer of his hard-won civility like a nail torn from its bed, until nothing remained of his honor and empathy. There would be nothing left of Leif the Man, only Leif the Monster.

Even now the rage boiled in his engines. It smoldered his

reason and ate through his compassion. It made him want to lash out, damn the casualties. He could do it. It would be so easy. And the worst part was the seductive voice hissing in his ear, *You know you want to.*

And he did.

He clamped his teeth against the urge to set the city blazing.

Tiamat be damned.

Asgard the dragon careened out of the fog and made a beeline toward Grace. He flew as if a drunken monkey were in charge of the tiller, and she had to dive to the ground to avoid being taken out by his tail. Spinning, he shot into the air. His jaws fell open. He bellowed. Pain laced his thundering voice.

That damned fog had hurt him.

"Hey, dragon!" she called, but he didn't make any sign that he heard her. He flew in a tight loop-the-loop, sometimes diving sharply, sometimes climbing, like he had no sense of direction.

A second dragon shot out from the ruined house: Zetian. About half the size of Asgard, with silver scales and red wings, it had three small horns and golden featherlike whiskers. The small dragon flew to the larger one, but Asgard still flailed in the air. He couldn't see or smell her. Zetian couldn't fix him.

Asgard needed to get back online and fast. The shape building from the fog twisted up like a demonic bonsai tree, and it didn't look good.

"Oscar, cover me." Grace stepped between Oscar and a coal wagon to give her a moment's break. She'd never used the slave bond, but knew the gist of how to do it. She dropped to her knees and tore off her jacket to expose the golden bands. Crossing her arms, she grasped the bands over her biceps.

She closed her eyes. The slave bond glowed blue across her eyelids. Once she'd recognized Norgard for the lying sack of dung he was, she'd done her best to rip the bond apart, but all she'd earned was a slow, mocking smile. No budge from the bond. She'd learned to ignore it, and kept it tightly hidden away in that black box with the other poison-barbed creepy-crawlies that skittered across her subconscious in the night.

She'd never met a fight that scared her more than the things locked behind her iron walls, but the white fog came close. She couldn't fight shadows.

Taking a deep breath, she grabbed the blue wire with her conscious mind. A bolt of energy sizzled through her skin, shooting her hair out in a long, sparking mass. Could Asgard hear her through the bond? Or was it enough to know her general direction?

Here, she thought. *Find me. Find the ground.*

The dragon spasmed in midair and dropped like an oil tanker straight into the lake. The splash hit the wagons on the water side.

Oscar swore. "Nice job, Xena."

Grace didn't have time to panic. Jumping from her crouch, she spun into the two aptrgangr barreling down on Oscar. For a few seconds there was nothing but the whir of the fight. Her attention danced to Asgard and back. *She'd dropped her boss into the bottom of the lake.* The aptrgangr knocked her across the ribs. She stumbled.

Oscar put the creature out of its misery.

"We need to retreat," she yelled. "Asgard is in the lake."

"So?" Rafe said. "General, sir?" The Thunderbird was dive-bombing the dead from the air. He let out an ear-piercing shriek. Rafe and his fellow warriors began to shimmer.

"You can't leave him!" Grace held her knife to Rafe's throat, but her arm shook. This was supposed to be her ally.

He smirked. Didn't bother to knock it away. She'd never killed a human who wasn't possessed, and he knew it. She choked. Light spilled over his face and down his arms like a blanket unrolling. When he reemerged he was Crow, and he shot into the air with the other jerks she'd been fighting with. The sting of betrayal hit low like a blade across the backs of her knees. Even Norgard's mercenaries—the selfish, untrustworthy lot of them—held to the barest code of honor among thieves. At least while they worked together on a job. You didn't abandon your teammates, because the Regent would come down on you like a rockslide.

At that moment there was a cry behind her. She turned to see Oscar's body stiffen. A wet stain spread across his stomach. He faced an aptrgangr. They hadn't stopped coming just because her back was turned.

Her feet carried her forward. She slammed an iron spike into the aptrgangr's throat. The wraith fled, and the body collapsed. Her ears buzzed.

"Get up, Oscar." She shot her torch at the aptrgangr. They cringed back from the fire. "Oscar, I need your help. Get up."

He coughed. A wet, hacking sound.

She blinked furiously to keep her vision clear. "Damn it, Oscar, I said get up!" Slipping in the mud of the field, she turned and knelt beside her friend. A mass of dark liquid spilled down the front of his shirt. A sharpened stick protruded from his belly.

"You know what to do, sweet." Oscar's eyes wouldn't focus on her.

"No."

His smile flickered over his face. Ye gods, what would she do without that smile? He grasped her hand and tucked something sharp into her palm. It was a crescent-shaped piece of jade about the length of her hand with a knife-sharp inner curve. Both points were bound with a thin chord of leather. A rusty smear covered the writing etched across its surface. The Tablet of Destiny shard. She could hear whispering from it, like the spirits knocking at the Gate. Oscar had risked his life to steal it during the fight.

"No." She dropped it. "Tell me where you keep your Drekar blood." Frantically, she searched his coat pockets.

His hand moved to stop her. "Don't have any."

"You have to. You always have blood. Tell me where it is. Tell me—"

"Do it, Grace." Oscar took her hand and brought her fingers to his wound. His blood stained her fingers hot red. He tried to lift her hand to his forehead to draw the mark. He didn't make it. His arm dropped and he slumped against her. "Please—"

"No, Oscar. No! Don't give up on me. You're so close to freedom. . . ." But the breath left him, and there was nothing else to do but set his soul free. Asgard better count this as a job finished. She wouldn't let Oscar's spirit stay locked in the blood bond. Her vision blurred. Shock made her movements almost automatic. With her bloody fingers, she drew the four lines of Raidho across his forehead to bless him on his journey. The red smear in the shape of an R shimmered briefly as Aether poured through it, and then Oscar was gone.

"Freya have mercy on you," she whispered. "And let the Stone Giants welcome you through the Gate." The shining water carried him home. A rock of ice sunk in her belly. She'd been preparing herself for this since the day she met him. Inevitable, irrevocable. Just like her parents. Just like Molly and the others. But it didn't make it any easier. All her posturing hadn't prevented a lick of hurt.

Why did everyone keep dying on her? Why couldn't they live for her instead?

She carefully laid Oscar's body on the ground and closed his eyes. The pain was a live wire snaking through her chest. This was not a safe place to let herself go. The fire blurred across her watery vision. She wiped the blood off her fingers and riffled through Oscar's pockets again. She found his weapons and flask. He didn't need them anymore, so she tucked them in her own pockets.

She didn't find any vials of Drekar blood.

The Tablet lay on the blood-soaked grass, a jagged edge of rock with the taint of death. It was a black spot. Gods and men had killed for it, seeking the power to write their own destinies. As far as Grace could tell, all it brought was the power to speed up that single destiny that all shared, man, monster and gods: death.

She tucked the sharp shard into her pocket next to her golden acorn. Hopefully Thor's talisman for longevity would deflect some of the Tablet's malice. Marduk had used the Tablets of Destiny to kill Kingu. Now she wielded it; she had a date with Kingu and the sharp blade of the Tablet's edge. She might even enjoy ripping it into the demigod who'd caused this destruction. He had it coming.

To her right the aptrgangr fought. Fire spread across the wagons at her back. The terrified horses screamed. Shrieks and feathers rained from the sky. She looked up to find Zetian and Kai in their animal forms grappling hundreds of feet above the earth. It seemed like Zetian didn't agree with Kai's abandonment of the coal shipment, but what was she doing here in the first place? Had she suspected the Kivati would run at the first sign of trouble? It was absurd for the Kivati only to send four men, but maybe they never planned to deliver the coal. Maybe their only plan was to lure Kingu away from the city with the Tablet of Destiny as bait.

It would have been a good idea if it didn't mean leaving Grace to the aptrgangr.

Asgard lay injured at the bottom of the lake. She didn't

know if he could drown, but she was pretty sure he wouldn't stay dead. She imagined him drowning repeatedly, only to have his magic blood restore him so he could drown again.

Johnny appeared in front of her. Sweat dripped from his forehead. Blood matted his shirt. He thrust the reins of a horse into her hand. "This is for helping me with the Mark of Cain and Lucia, but now we're even. Get out of here. The horse will bolt once I let go of its mind. You better hold on. You're on your own."

Grace's numb fingers didn't want to grip the saddle, but somehow she mounted the horse. The torch came in handy one last time to send Oscar's body beyond the reach of the wraiths. The horse screamed. The landscape jolted past. She wrapped her fingers in the horse's mane and let it carry her from the wreckage.

Chapter 15

The terrified horse bolted north along the lake. Grace lost track of the silver dragon and the Thunderbird, and only vaguely wondered who had won. The Thunderbird was larger, but the silver dragon was vicious. The night slowed down the horse, and eventually she lost her panicked edge. Time slipped past in the ghosts of houses and snatches of urban forest along the lakefront. Wisps of stars peeked out from a cloud-strewn sky.

A few miles up, she found Asgard draped across the road fast asleep. A large puddle of water had pooled around him. Figured. And she'd actually been worried for his sorry ass.

Dawn split the horizon. Dismounting, she tied the horse to the bumper of an abandoned car, putting a bit of distance between it and the dragon. The flamethrower on low provided enough light to see by. She approached the sleeping dragon. In the dark, he appeared like a mountain of crimson shells with the kiss of moss along their edge. The scales ran from the elegant curled tail and up along his serpentine neck. The deadly, ancient eyes were shut. In his sleep he looked almost peaceful.

Why couldn't they have met somewhere else? In a parallel universe where she'd never met Norgard and her family still lived. In some strange land where it was normal to take a dragon home to meet your parents.

Choose how to play the hand you're dealt, her dad had always said.

Stuff some aces up your sleeve, her mom would retort while she slipped Grace some cards under the table.

Grace reached up and drew her fingers along the side of the dragon's neck. Her hand smoothed over the textured scales. Such gorgeous armor. The dragon stirred.

"Wake up, Sleeping Beauty," she whispered.

Those feral eyes slid open. Emerald green and so vibrant they appeared to glow in the dim light. His focus speared her like a harpoon. She could see why the legends would say that dragons could hypnotize with their eyes. There was something in that gaze that made her want to obey. It promised treasure at the end of its long claws. It promised pleasure that bordered on pain.

Use me. The traitorous thought whispered through her brain. *Tear me down and make me like it.*

The dragon smiled.

He had teeth like a barracuda. A few weeks ago she would have taken a hasty step back from those teeth. Now she held her ground.

Bite me. She wanted to beg. She shouldn't have twisted thoughts like this. But hate shared an apartment wall with lust, and she'd been banging on it for a while now. Might as well throw open the door and meet the neighbors.

Leif woke to the greens and blues of the dragon. Darkness was his kingdom, and a beautiful maiden had been deposited on his doorstep like the sacrifices of old. In his dreams the maidens never cowered. No shrinking violets in gothic nightgowns for him. He dreamed of Valkyries, heads high, spears sharp. Like this one. Her lips parted just enough to slip his finger between. Her hair was a river of blue-black. Tears in those silver eyes, and beneath that, embers, a mirror of the lust that burned through him. He saw raw need there and the bitter longing of a want too long denied.

His head slowly cleared. Grace. His Grace.

Grief creased her features. Passion burned in her eyes—emotion so intense it drew tears. One part lust, one part pain. By now he could recognize her old scars, the white feathers of the albatross that hung around her neck. These emotional scars were new, this pain borne of some recent trauma. The old scars ripped when the new ones formed, so that they bled together, raw and throbbing and bitter.

Aether flowed through him, and he Turned. She didn't retreat. He needed to hold her. He needed to comfort her. He took her in his arms, and she welcomed him. Her lips rose up to meet his. The touch ignited, flint sparking that long chord of lust. Fire met fire in the rush of lips and tongues and teeth. He squeezed her shoulders and ran his palms down the tattered edge of her sleeves. Her hands fisted by her sides. He coaxed her fingers open, just as he slipped his tongue between her lips. She opened for him like a night-blooming flower. Her scent, rose petals and sweat, drowned out the stronger smells, the horse, the mud of the battlefield, and the blood.

He caught her hips and drew them to meet his. Her body was slender as a whip, muscled like a dancer. He wanted to feel all of it. Here, alone in the dark, they met as equals. There were no witnesses but the ghosts who haunted their dreams, and the adrenaline drowned out even those.

She wrapped her arms around his waist and raked her fingers over the muscles in his back. A fast, desperate grab on both their parts. Their bodies too long a hands-off zone, but the dark released the forbidden.

Grace must feel it too. The past slid away. This moment existed for only them, and they existed for this moment.

Leif feasted on her lips. She met his tongue stroke for stroke. Sensation spiraled through him. The heat of her greedy hands and the press of her heated body. The tangle of mouths. Her curves beneath his questing fingers, her solid hips, her firm derriere.

Cupping his hands beneath her ass, he lifted her so that she fit tightly against his iron cock. Her legs clamped around him, pressing close. Ishtar, be merciful. He might have come right there.

She never stopped moving. Her nails scraped his skin, driving him wild. He was trying to be a gentleman, but she didn't want gentle. She said as much with her body snaking around his. She wanted to go so fast she couldn't think, to cast out the demons that drove her.

He could do this for her. He could make her forget. He could run her ragged until she didn't remember her own name, squeeze every last drop of passion and pain from her body, leave her languid as sea kelp washed upon the shore.

He wanted to.

He wanted to be the white knight that swept her off her capable feet, the man she turned to when the storm thundered.

She ground herself against him. Her hands tangled in his hair. Her teeth clamped down on his lip hard enough to draw blood. It would heal her, and she took it as her right. The darkness raged up inside him, all semblance of control thrown over for a moment as his primitive self demanded he take what was offered and drive himself into her sweet bliss.

She sucked his tongue into her mouth. He saw stars.

But his civilized part heard the sorrow behind her moans. And his civilized part felt the shaking of her limbs and tasted the desperation in her kiss. No man was a saint, him least of all, but civilization depended on man controlling his instincts. Without that fierce self-restraint he was no better than Kingu.

Leif waited a beat for his blood to heal her wounds, and then he softly disengaged. He pressed his forehead to hers. Her heavy breathing bordered on sobs. His forearms supported her weight, while his fingers swept small, soothing circles across her back.

"It will be okay," he whispered.

The tension slid out of her like a body giving up the ghost. She slipped her legs from around his hips to touch the ground. She fell into his embrace, and he rested his cheek on the top of her head. He held her as she cried.

Chapter 16

Leif felt the moment she shut down. Her body tensed as she slammed home the door to her inner self. Her iron mask hid that raw emotion from the world. Too late. She couldn't hide it from him. Now he knew. She could fool herself, but he'd seen the truth.

She pushed her spines out like a porcupine and untangled herself from his embrace. Reluctantly, he let her go. Anger covered her vulnerability. He could see passion radiating there, and he wanted some of it. She was so vibrant. Alive. Pulsing with a hungry glow that he would never share.

"I got the Tablet," she said. She pulled the broken stone from her pocket and held it out.

He didn't take it.

She stuffed it back in her pocket. "Oscar is dead." Her voice broke.

"I'm sorry."

"After all this death, I keep thinking it'll get easier—"

"It never does. The day you cease to care is the day you succumb to the darkness."

She turned her back on him. "What would you know?" she sneered. "You can't die."

"No," he growled, "but I've watched everyone I care

about pass on, and I can tell you this: Time does not heal all wounds. It just dulls the pain."

"You don't understand. My parents, Oscar, everyone leaves. Who do you miss—Norgard?" She laughed. "He was a psychopath. You don't know anything about family."

"My mother had other children, and they had children. I've watched hundreds of them pass through this world—"

"Like you care about humans."

He grabbed her shoulder and turned her to him. "I'm immortal, but I'm not made of stone. You haven't said good-bye to Oscar or your parents. You'll see them again. I won't. When I say good-bye, it's forever. You know what's worse than watching them die? Watching them throw their lives away and wasting such a precious gift. Drinking themselves into early graves. Fighting just to prop up their egos. The sins of the father carried on down the family line. It sickens me. You have this soul that shines brighter than a sunburst. If you could only see it as I do. You live in a blink, but you love in a solar storm."

Her eyebrows drew up. Her beautiful lip curled. She didn't believe him. "Jealous?"

"Yes, damn it, I'm jealous. Jealous of a mortal. Sven used to laugh at me." Leif flexed his arm. "Who wouldn't want to be Drekar? Power, charisma, sex appeal. My body will never age, never wrinkle, never suffer such indignity as a bruise or scrape. But I'm jealous of you who will grow old and die only to be reunited with your loved ones in the afterlife." He wouldn't. Year after year, the world turned around him, and the fires that lit those little mortal lives flared and died. He felt the cold leech into his bones, never to feel that warmth no matter how close he drew to its source. And the shadows and the darkness inside his breast grew heavy, jealousy encased in ice.

Who could blame Sven for wanting to douse that fire?

Her face softened. He didn't want her pity.

"You know what Sven would tell me?" Leif asked. "'You still care too much,' he'd say. 'Don't worry; it will fade with time.' That's what I've always been afraid of. The moment I stop caring about one more pitiful, mortal life will be the moment the darkness has won. I will become the monster Sven was. The monster you believe me to be."

"I don't think—"

"Don't lie to me. There is too much between us for that."

Asgard's retinue rescued them. Must be nice being so all important, Grace thought. They brought fresh clothes and food and too much wine. Someone had designed and sewed a new outfit for Grace, which a petite blond woman in an apron dress delivered to replace the shredded, blood-and-mud-stained threads Grace had been wearing. In it, she felt like Catwoman. The black leather pants hugged her backside. The new corset top extended over her chest and down to kiss her hips. Movable, breathable, wearable. The thick wool jacket demanded that she cuddle up inside it. Warm and light and, best of all, waterproof.

Freya save her. Asgard was slowly stripping everything from her: her tools, her bike, her clothes, her guards.

In the carriage, Grace picked at the bread and cheese. The wine, she drank. Sitting across from Asgard with the charged air clogging her lungs dragged on for an eternity. If he felt as uncomfortable as she did, he hid it well.

For Freya's sake, the man had seen her *cry*. She'd let down her guard, and he'd taken advantage. Tried to convince her he didn't have a heart of ice. As if they had anything in common. She pressed her spine against the cushioned seat back and held her hands against the black leather pants.

Oscar would have liked the new getup. He'd always complained about her lack of fashion sense. He would have been proud to die in battle and join the glorious dead at Freya's table. She wasn't sure what the afterlife looked like, but if the Norse were right, those who died in their sleep were resigned to a dreary existence far away from the golden halls of the gods. Oscar wouldn't suffer that fate.

She bit her lip to keep the tears from falling. She wouldn't cry in front of Asgard. Never again.

When they finally arrived in Ballard, she let herself breathe. Bicycles pulled hitch wagons down Market Street. Steam from the horses' mouths sparkled in the midmorning sun. The bells on their bridles jingled, chasing away the dead.

The carriage pulled in front of a squat building with a fake A-frame rush roof. It looked like a Norwegian mountain cottage. The rounded front door had been painted dark brown. Rosemaling flourishes and red tulips decorated the dark wood grain. Bunches of plastic roses cheerily popped from the window boxes.

"You think this witch will help?" she asked.

"Birgitta is Heiðr, a Norse heathwitch. Your Tunta was probably in her coven. She's mortal and human, but she knows small spells and charms. Heathwitch magic is associated with the hearth and home. They were midwives in the old days, and are starting to return to those roots now that the Unraveling has taken out modern medicine. She knows more Norse legends than I do. We'll ask her about the Shadow Walkers." Asgard straightened his long crimson coat. He must have a closetful of them. "You can't fight Kingu if you don't know your own strength."

A troll big as her shoulder guarded the door. It had long brown nails and snaggleteeth the length if its chin. A tangle of greying hair fell like moss down its back. The squinting eyes fixed on her. Creepy little thing. It had a rune carved into its forehead: Dagaz, the awakening.

Grace pushed the door open and ducked beneath the hanging charms that kept out the dead. Iron and silver bells hung from brightly festive red ribbons. Inside, the store continued the Scandinavian kitsch. Henbane and mistletoe hung from the rafters. On the shelves, Dala horses and Lucia candles squeezed next to plastic Viking helmets and golden acorns for longevity. Aprons proclaimed, KISS ME, I'M SWEDISH, and signs read, PARKING FOR VIKINGS ONLY, with a picture of a longboat. Finnish joke books and gummy candies, gingersnaps and pepparkakor cookies shared a shelf with dried animal livers and a green bottle of newt eyes. In the back stood a large loom strung with red, black, and white yarn. The place smelled like pickled herring and hot apple cider. Cozy, and yet subtly unpleasant.

A little white-haired woman welcomed them with a wide smile. She wore a bright red apron with a white flounce trim. Across her chest HOT GRANDMA was embroidered. She had a rolling gait even though she wasn't plump. "Regent, my dear boy, so you finally came to visit your old granny."

"Birgitta." Asgard's face softened in genuine warmth. He hugged the old woman. "I'm glad you made it home safe from Oregon. Ballard wasn't the same without you. Let me introduce you to Grace—"

"Hi." Grace stuck out her hand. "Granny?"

"Birgitta is my many great's niece," he said.

"Ja. But I look old enough to be his grandma. Youngin'." Birgitta gave Grace a careful examination from head to toe and then yanked her into a quick hug. "Finally, he brings a woman to meet me."

Grace waited for Asgard to tell her it wasn't like that. To tell her they weren't *together*. That she wasn't his woman.

"How was your trip to Portland?" he asked.

"Terrible." Birgitta put a hand over her heart. "The earthquakes ravaged it. But my sweet Sigrid and her family made it through. I told her to move home. She is packing."

"Good," Asgard said.

"What brings you, älskling?" Birgitta rolled back behind

the counter. A long blue cape with fur trim—just like the one Tunta had worn—and an elm staff hung against the wall. A small Bunsen burner warmed a miniature caldron full of dark ruby liquid. "Your lady's eyes are red. I have just the thing for tears. Glögg?" she offered. "It is much too early for Yule, but who knows when the spices will run out?" She lit a match and touched the top of the wine-brandy drink. The alcohol caught, sending up a blue flame. She quickly smothered it with the lid.

"We need your help," Asgard said. "How would you trap and kill a demigod?"

Birgitta laughed. "It is too early in the morning for hard questions." She poured the glögg into three white handblown shot glasses. "Skål."

Grace and Asgard each took a glass and raised it in toast. Some of the alcohol might have burned off, but there was still enough to strip paint from the walls. Grace coughed. Birgitta drained her glass and poured more. "That does it right. Now, be serious. How can I help?"

Asgard leaned forward. "Tell her about the Shadow Walkers."

"Ja. Wait, wait." Shaking her head, Birgitta went outside. Leif watched her through the open door. Muttering something, she sprinkled a handful of herbs on the troll's head and pressed her finger to the mark between its eyes. The Troll shuddered like a teakettle whistling steam; then one of its carved feet split from the block of wood and stepped onto the pavement. It climbed off the stump and blocked the door. The club it rested across its palms, ready for action.

Grace gave a soft whistle.

"The heathwitch's focus is small, household magics," he told her. "But Birgitta is unusual."

Shutting the door, Birgitta returned to the counter, pulled

out two rush-backed chairs, and motioned them to sit. She poured more glögg. Examining Grace, she pulled down the younger woman's lower lid and checked her eyes. "Do they flash silver?"

"Yes."

Birgitta sat in her own chair and took a sip of the strong drink. "Teaching the runes to a human not in the service of the gods is forbidden, you know this?"

Grace shook her head. "I was taught by an old lady with a cloak like yours. She only spoke Norwegian. Had blue eyes. Chewed snoose. Know her?"

"Ja, but you describe many old-timers. There are few heathwitches of my age. I've been training a fresh crop since the Unraveling."

"Tunta?"

Birgitta shrugged. "Means 'aunt.' Ja, but I know a woman it could have been." She spit over her shoulder. "Not a good heathwitch, if she taught you to cast without knowledge."

"She showed me how to draw the runes and named them," Grace said. She held out her wrists to show the runes that marked her pulse points. "And she marked me."

Birgitta took her hands and ran her thumbs over the marks. She shook her head and muttered a small prayer under her breath. "Heathwitch magic is the magic of life. Birthing and planting and green growing things. These are marks of binding over your life veins. No true Heiðr would do such a thing."

Leif watched Grace's face tighten. She took her hands back and studied the runes. "This is how I was taught to do it. What's wrong with them?"

Birgitta clucked her tongue. "We don't bind people, only objects. Tampering with human souls upsets the natural order of things and hastens Ragnarök, the doom of the gods. When Odin found the runes, the beginning of written language, beneath the world tree where the dragon serpent

Nidhog was hoarding them, he saw how powerful they could be in the wrong hands. With a written language, man could spread ideas like wildfire. Odin cast the runes and divined what the humans could do with them—more creative and powerful than any god could think of—and he saw Ragnarök bearing down on him. Give humans a little power, and they will rise up against their oppressors. So he forbade the knowledge of how to use them from being written down and entrusted the truth only to a select few who were pledged in the gods' service. The runes have been passed down in secret by word of mouth."

"Tunta barely spoke," Grace said. "She showed me how to make the runes and how to draw my will into them to make them work. I have a natural affinity."

"Norgard was a great admirer of Loki, the trickster god who disobeyed Odin at every turn." Birgitta reached across the counter and took a small red box with blue flowers in rosemaling across the top. She lifted the lid and offered it to them. Elegant truffles snuggled together, tops decorated with golden dots or drizzled in white chocolate.

Grace recoiled.

Leif shook his head and waved them off. His stomach sank. He put aside his glögg. He had attempted to create a serum that would approximate the feeling of love for Drekar, because a soul in love was the highest high his kind could get. His potion had mirrored the love chemical, oxytocin, but he thought it would be used for Drekar sick with the madness.

He had been wrong. He gave the serum to Sven, and Sven twisted everything around. Sven had filled the chocolates in his factory with an untested, unsafe dose and given them to women he intended to seduce. Leif's experiments had been used for malicious purposes. His work turned evil. "I shouldn't have to tell you again not to eat those."

"Ja. Why not? What is an old woman to do with her time?" Birgitta popped one in her mouth.

"Sven wouldn't care that teaching the runes and binding mortals was forbidden. He liked thumbing his nose at the gods," Leif said. "He never liked being told what to do."

"Now who does that sound like?" Birgitta asked. "Once humans had the runes, they used them to craft their own narratives, ones in which humans outwit the gods. They started to think for themselves."

"The horror," Grace said.

"Few use them anymore. Now they are an oddity sold by silly old women in tacky occult shops." Birgitta grinned. She ate another chocolate. "Not all of these are drugged, you know. Only Persephone's Delight."

Leif just shook his head.

"And the Shadow Walkers?" Grace asked.

"A few humans can work the magic of the runes if they are trained. Those few are not constrained to this plane. The magic of the runes gives them the power that Odin once feared. A godlike power to cross the realms, to sift away shadow, and walk in the footsteps of the gods."

"I don't have godlike powers," Grace protested.

"But you can banish spirits across the Gate between worlds," Leif said. "Power over death is the prerogative of the gods."

Grace held out her wrists again to study them. "Tunta had the same runes on her pulse points. Was she a Shadow Walker?"

Leif took a sip of his glögg to calm the anger building inside him. *Sven, what did you do?* "You said Tunta stank," Leif said. "Are you sure she was alive?"

"Of course, she . . ." Grace wrinkled her nose.

"Would you have known then what an old, well-situated aptrgangr looked like?"

"I don't know." Grace's voice was flat.

Birgitta rose. She waddled around an aisle stall filled with Yule tomte dolls. "Indulge an old woman," she called. "I've never met a Shadow Walker before. I want to see the runes work their magic."

Grace's fingers tapped on the counter.

"You don't have to if it makes you uncomfortable," Leif told her. He wanted to see her work in person. He wanted to study her: magic, power, mind, body and all. If he took her apart and put her back together again like clockwork, would he break some intangible gear that made her tick? Machines were easier to understand than humans. Even Einstein venerated the inexplicable power behind nature, behind the life that threaded the universe together. Leif disliked a mystery until he solved it himself, but he knew better than to mess with a human's fragile workings. In all his research into the soul, he had never come across a simple explanation that would allow him to duplicate its brilliance.

"Of course she does," Birgitta said, returning with a small velvet bag and a square white cloth that she put on the table. She handed the bag to Grace. "She must satisfy my curiosity. What do you think I told you that tale for?"

Grace pulled out a square plastic tile from the bag. One side was engraved with a Norse rune. The other side was blank. "So let's say I have this power. Could I use it to banish a demigod back across the Gate?"

Birgitta clucked her tongue. "Big plans, big plans. That is why Odin feared the runes. We humans are never content with a little knowledge. We get greedy and start looking up. I can't tell you if you wield enough power. Why don't you ask the gods? Come now, Lady Shadow, draw us the future."

Leif had seen the runes cast before, but he'd never been so intrigued. It had always seemed like a silly superstition. In most people's hands it was. Did the gods actually talk through the runes? He doubted it. But some inexplicable force allowed Grace to do her work, and it was high time he got down off his high horse and studied it. Science could only explain so much. Grace made him want to believe. If there was hope for him and his kind, he would find it. He didn't care if the cure was magic, not really, not if in the end it saved his soulless self.

She closed her eyes, pulled a handful of tiles from the bag, and cast them on the white cloth. Birgitta hummed. Grace opened her eyes and studied the pattern of the marked squares. "Yeah, I got nothing."

"You've never divined the future before?" Birgitta asked.

"I just know how to use the runes on the skin for protection, banishing wraiths, and increasing fertility, though that last one I never thought worked."

Birgitta laughed. "Well of course not, not if you didn't believe in it."

Grace shot her a sour look. "Why would I want little Norgards running around? It's a death sentence for a woman anyway. I'm not going to help with that."

"My mother survived," Leif said mildly.

"Ja, and a Shadow Walker would not have any trouble bringing a fledgling to term," Birgitta said. "The line between the living and the dead isn't firm for you. Freya will protect you." She patted Grace's hand.

Grace snatched her hand back.

Leif shifted uncomfortably. He thought of Grace pregnant with his brother's child, and a reddish-black rage rose up inside him.

Grace stood up, putting some distance between herself and memory. Leif watched her pace. Her body moved like a dancer, light on her toes, sinuous in her turns. Her hair fell in a curtain down her back.

"Using Norse runes against a Babylonian demigod seems illogical," he said.

"Not really," Grace said. "The Norse gods are just another

incarnation of the gods who came before. Whatever name you call them, whatever story you tell, they're the same deity."

"If there are different stories, how can we learn anything of the truth? Where is the comparable allegory to Odin finding the runes in Babylonian myth?"

Birgitta patted his knee. "You think too hard, child. You must learn to use your heart instead of your head."

Give up logic for emotion-driven outbursts? Never. His mother had been like that. An opera star, she thrived on the attention. Her dramatic mood swings had thrown everyone into service placating her, until she left again for London and the household could return to calm. In those days men had treated actresses little better than whores. His grandfather had shielded him from that truth, until he'd come of age and seen for himself how it had wrecked his mother's self-esteem. She would be elated one moment and dashed the next. Her beaus had come and gone with the turn of the season.

He had never treated a woman like a summer coat, and he wouldn't now. Grace was in his employ. She deserved his highest regard and nothing more. To put her in an uncompromising position would make him no better than his mother's suitors. And he couldn't forget that Grace was grieving her friend. He wouldn't take advantage of her vulnerability.

His resolution didn't mollify his driving need to possess Grace. But if he listened to anything other than his head, he would dishonor the moral fiber that his grandfather had fought so hard to instill in him.

Leif and his brother might have had the same base urges and immortal detachment, but how they chose to act on those impulses would draw the line between them. Leif could do this. He was a better man than Sven. He would prove it to her.

Even if it killed him.

"Kingu is manifesting as a wraith," Grace said. "No one has seen his physical form except as an outline in the fog. His ability to affect the physical world is limited, but he packs a bigger punch than any wraith I've met. The problem is I can't banish a wraith unless it's trapped in a human body. I have to draw the rune on something; wraiths have no substance."

"So we must wait for him to possess someone?" Leif didn't like the sound of that. What damage could he do as a human? Who might he haunt that could wreak the most terror? "If you banish all his followers he won't be able to search for the Heart."

"Yeah, but again they have to be aptrgangr."

"Could you trap Kingu in an inanimate object?" Leif asked.

"Like a genie in a bottle?" Grace asked. "'Cosmic power, itty-bitty living space'—any truth to that?"

Birgitta shook her head. "Don't know. Not my line of work."

"Can't a heathwitch summon a spirit?" Leif asked.

Birgitta laughed. "Only an idiot would summon a demigod. The old Regent took the crazy cake back to the underworld with him."

Grace picked up a Christmas decoration. Four candles made a circle around a tall wood stick. On the top twirled four chubby angels powered by the rising air from the flame. "What about a spirit circle?"

"Have you ever summoned a spirit?" Leif asked.

"No, but I've used circles as extra power to draw some runes. Norgard made me learn when none of my pendants with Freya's fertile mark worked. He thought I needed more power. He actually lasered off a few of my tattoos to see if they were blocking my abilities."

Leif tried not to grind his teeth. "Birgitta, don't your witches use spirits as guides? You must trap them somehow."

"Ja, but little ones. Elementals and a simple ghost every now and then. Heathwitch magic is not strong enough to capture a demigod. We are only visitors to the border between this world and the next. Our magic celebrates life."

"If you had a big enough circle, like Stonehenge, I bet you could do it," Grace said. "Or enough witches."

"Enough magic users working together. Maybe the Kivati could do it. They can manipulate the Aether. Corbette has enough power to summon a spirit." The Kivati were overly blessed in the soul category. He could admit he was jealous. Slice off Leif's head and he ceased to exist. But the Kivati possessed their own soul plus that of their totem, formed mate bonds easily, and procreated with great success. What would it be like to bathe in the golden glow of so many brightly burning souls? To share in that divinity, the source of all light, connected to the very Aether of the universe?

Leif would never know, unless Ishtar's blessing turned out to be true. Longren's soul mate tale smacked too much of beauty and the beast, of a fairy story. Impossible. Illogical. In it there was no predestined love, just choice. The choice to risk his heart and forsake his immortality for the love of a human woman. A fickle, dangerous thing.

He watched Grace flip her hair over her shoulder. Her grey eyes slid over him like he didn't exist. She was afraid of him. Back up, claws out, ready to take on the world. She hadn't cried again. Her friend's blood still stained her fingers. Was this the shock or the denial? She didn't take time to grieve; she just charged forward like a steam engine putting miles of track behind her.

Maybe that was enough for her, but it wasn't good enough for him. Even a strong woman deserved a break. "You're tired," he told her.

"Kingu's out there. We've got the Tablet, but we don't know how to use it. Kingu does. The clock's ticking before he finds us."

"You need to rest."

"I'll rest when I'm dead." That would be too soon if she didn't take care of herself. Dark circles ringed her eyes. Her cheekbones grew sharper the longer she knew him. She weaved on her feet.

Leif stood. "Thank you, Birgitta. Put some thought into a summoning circle. Buy what you need. Send me the bill."

Grace started to protest. "But we haven't talked about—"

"Enough for now. You're running on empty. You didn't eat anything in the carriage." Skirting the troll, he ushered her out into the morning sun, and she shielded her eyes. Her skin was too pale.

When the door closed behind them, she slammed a hand against his chest. "Don't tell me what to do. I'm a grown-up—"

"Yes, so start acting like one. You need to take care of yourself." Bossing women around; what wouldn't he stoop to? Sven's silver tongue looked pretty good about now. "We're going back to the lair. We can make plans tomorrow."

"I have my own place, thanks." She settled her feet in her fighting stance. "Sorry about the coal; you can tack it on to my debt." She spun on her heel and took off down the street.

He caught her arm. "Forget the coal—"

"Forget it? This is my life you're talking about. My freedom you're trying to take away. My livelihood. You think I'm slugging through the mud for kicks and giggles? I'm working my ass off so that I can get away from *you*!" A sob welled in her throat. She shoved him, and he saw new tears in her eyes. He released her. She stormed away. "Don't worry, I'll have your money by the end of the week."

Ye gods, she made him angry. Smoke trickled from his nose, fogging the air around him. The sun blinded his narrowed dragon vision. "You think I can let you march off alone like that? You think you're in any shape to earn more cash? Haven't you seen enough blood for today?"

Turning, she marched back to him. The beauty of Grace in a temper smacked him again. Her hair streamed out behind her. Pink flushed her cheeks. Her silver eyes sparked. "It's none of your business what I do or don't do. I survived just fine before you showed up. I don't need a fucking babysitter!"

"That's where you're wrong. If you won't listen to reason, you leave me no choice." He leaned into her until they were nose to nose. Her lips compressed, unwelcoming, hard as steel, but even then he wanted to kiss her. He twisted the ring on his finger and poured his intent into it across the damned slave bond. "I forbid you from fighting."

Chapter 17

Elsie met Grace at the side door. "You sure about this?"

Grace slid her hands deeper into her pockets. No, she didn't want to be here. She wanted to pick a fight and vent this anger with her fists. Asgard had taken that away from her. Just when she'd thought he was different, he'd proved her wrong. "Ishtar was the goddess of war. You have to have an answer in your moldering library. How do I fight a demigod? How did Marduk defeat Kingu?"

"You won't make it out the window a second time if Ianna catches you."

"There's always the chimney."

"She might put you to work."

And wouldn't that serve Asgard right? He would be horrified that he'd reduced her to paying off her debt on her back. She could see the blood drain from his face now. She felt the weight of Elsie's appraisal, even in her shiny new threads: skinny hips, hair coming undone from her braid, flat chest that no amount of water could make win a wet T-shirt contest. The Priestess would have a hard time finding anything useful about her that didn't involve her quick hands or sharp tools. "Whatever." She shrugged.

Elsie took her to the library. The *Kama Sutra* and books

like it took up only half the bookshelves. The other half were reserved for the history of the Ishtar Maidens: the Houses around the world and exploits of their most famous courtesans, the kings and businessmen who had fallen beneath Ishtar's spell, the warriors who had found their Achilles' heel was a woman. The Maidens took their duty as handmaidens of Ishtar seriously. They worshipped the goddess with their bodies, bestowed Ishtar's favors to whatever poor soul was in need of mercy.

House patrons had always been dragons, and it was rumored that this particular House had been the first thing Norgard imported when he set about settling his base in the young city of Seattle. The first Priestess had been famous for her wheeling and dealing. She hadn't just run whores; she'd facilitated political deals, back-room business mergers, gambling, and opium. As a result, the House had gold paneling, silk-draped beds, and the biggest erotica library this side of the Mississippi.

The library was still in disarray after Kingu's visit. Elsie helped her sort through the wreckage. "Is it wrong that I sort of hope Kingu finds his lost love?"

"Yes, very."

"Oh, come on, Grace. Even you can't be that coldhearted. I think it's sweet."

"Sweet that a psychotic wraith is turning the city upside down looking for his dead lover's heart? Yes. Love, sweet love."

"Who doesn't want that kind of devotion? He's waited millennia for her." Elsie flounced onto a golden settee raising a small cloud of dust. She sneezed. Her voluptuous chest threatened to pop out of her low-cut gown.

"Remind me why I'm friends with you?"

"Because I'm horribly good-looking?"

Grace smiled and threw a throw pillow at her. It was odd that someone with a bad history of sex could be friends with someone who oozed sex appeal, whose every move and thought were designed to seduce. Grace wasn't a prude by any means, but she wasn't comfortable with her body in the way Elsie was. To her, it was a weapon, plain and simple. She fed it, clothed it, toned it to be a killing machine. She wore practical clothes she could move in. They gave her a shapeless, boy silhouette, as Elsie had told her on numerous occasions.

Asgard—the overbearing ass—didn't seem to mind her shape. Even in ragged, bloodstained cotton, he looked at her like she wore velvet and silk. What would he say if she showed up in one of Elsie's dresses? She imagined herself in the light blue gown with the silver trim, her chest pushed up, her hair curled. She imagined Asgard in his crimson coat, and warmth curled in her belly. She banished the image. She should hate him, but instead she wanted to jump his bones. It wasn't fair.

The leather-bound volume on her lap contained nothing but kinky pictures from the eighteenth century. It didn't help the daydream in her head—the blue gown unlaced itself and slipped down to pool at her feet. She didn't have to imagine Asgard naked; she remembered that display quite clearly.

She needed to concentrate. She was so mad at him she could breathe fire. Her daydreams should involve ways to flay him, not seduce him. "How do you mute the Drekar pheromones?"

Elsie laughed. "Mute them? Why would I? They hardly need to use them for Maidens when what we're offering is freely available. It'd be a pleasure to get a Dreki who was actually set on seducing me. Hot as sin, they are. The whole race of them." She sighed dreamily. Grace rolled her eyes. Elsie leaned forward. "What's this about, love? The New Regent putting your panties in a twist?"

"I don't know what you're talking about. Did you check those blue books in the corner?"

"Oh, no. You listen to all my stories, but you never tell me one of your own. I want to hear all about this reclusive brother. Mad scientist, some say. He designed a vibrating hairbrush for Rochelle." Elsie's eyes took on a wicked glint. "Said scalp massage got healthy blood flowing beneath the skin, but you know that's not where she's getting her blood a-flowin'."

Grace hummed noncommittally. She ran her finger down the page in front of her, searching for any mention of Tiamat, Kingu, or Marduk. The words danced on the page. Damned if she needed to hear more stories about Asgard's thoughtful inventions, or gifts he gave other women, or his involvement with Maidens. Her teeth ground together. She didn't care what he did.

"Here's the thing, Grace. Norgard always turned his pheromones on, because he wanted the world eating out of the palm of his hand. He took what he wanted, and the more resistant the victim or twisted the demand, the more he got off on his success. But his brother is different. A real gentleman, from what the girls say. He wouldn't seduce a girl that didn't want to be seduced. If his control is slipping enough around you that you're hungry for cinnamon rolls at all hours, that means you, sugar, have made an impact that many an Ishtar Maiden has dreamed of making."

"Eff that."

"No, really. Making a man lose control is our specialty, and no one's made Asgard snap unless he good and wanted to."

Grace slammed the book shut and got up. She paced to the window. Outside, the grey drizzle scattered across the glass Clouds rolled low above the colorless city. "You're talking about the man who owns my slave bond. He's not nice."

"Maybe you just need to own a piece of his soul in return."

Easy for Elsie to say. But even if Grace had Elsie's heart-breaking powers, she wouldn't want to own another person

Not ever. She would never do to another what had been done to her. A person had a right to make his own choices. She would never take that away from someone, not even a soul-sucker.

Leif shifted through the stack of broadsheets from the past few months to make sure he had marked every last clue. A map of the city and its surrounds was spread out on a table in front of him. Small white-headed pins marked reported wraith attacks. Black pins marked Kingu sightings. Purple marked Corbette's known movements. So far there was only a weak correlation, but he lacked sufficient data. String outlined territory: purple for Kivati, red for Drekar, yellow for humans. The uncontrolled areas might as well have been labeled black for Kingu and his wraiths. Daily the line encroached upon the safe land. The safe paths through the city narrowed until they disappeared.

"This is good," Thorsson said, looming at his right with an almost proud look on his face.

"What is?" Leif searched the pins for a pattern for the hundredth time, but found nothing.

Thorsson pointed to Leif and to the map with his mead cup. "This. You. Battle strategy, just like good old days with Sven. The Regent should be a warlord. We strike first."

Leif set the sheets down and resisted the urge to rub his temple.

"He's right, you know," Zetian said. "We may make a king of you yet."

I don't want to. But the refrain grew weak. His intense dislike of the idea had fizzled somewhere between Corbette's breakdown and a pair of silver eyes. He couldn't abandon the field to a power-mad admiral, a mad, powerful shape-shifter, or his own two crooked advisors. Grace expected more of him. He expected more of himself.

It wasn't a comfortable thought. He wanted peace. He wanted uninterrupted time to create. But lately as he worked through the night on Jameson's suits of armor, his lab felt empty. The cavernous ceiling rang with the same bells and whistles as always, but it seemed more vast and cold than before. It wouldn't be the same without a certain small, fiery-tempered woman in it.

Between Zetian's political strategy and Thorsson's bloodlust, they might have a shot of winning a battle if it came to that. He still hoped it wouldn't. He was not, and never would be, a warlord. He used his intellect to create, not destroy. There had been too much blood and death when the Gates fell. But Zetian was right; someone needed to fill the power vacuum. The spirit of cooperation that allowed enemies to work together for the common good had disintegrated. There was no going back. The lines of communication had failed.

Leif had told Jameson about the Heart. The admiral had given him the strangest slow smile. He thanked Leif for his assistance, ordered his troops to start combing the streets, and disbanded the council citing an "assassination attempt by supernatural forces," by which he meant Corbette's Aether storm. His soldiers fanned into the city. Their official orders were to detain suspicious persons, and they forcibly brought in for questioning anyone who resisted arrest. In practice, every supernatural caught alone was in deep shit. Jameson had drawn the battle lines, and if one wasn't human, one was on the wrong side.

Work on the Gas Works was on permanent hold. With wraith attacks on the rise, they needed light more than ever, but Jameson's madness made it impossible to continue without fear of arrest.

Corbette was unreachable. With aptrgangr on one side and Jameson's thugs on the other, the Kivati were trapped on Queen Anne like an ant colony in winter. Leif could expect no help from that corner.

Butterworth's had been attacked less than an hour ago. A hundred people had died in the stampede.

"Where the Newton is Grace?" he demanded. He needed to know she was okay. He'd forbidden her from fighting. Even now the memory shamed him. He'd stripped her of her right to defend herself. Even in peacetime that would be abhorrent, but now when the threat of violence was a red glow on the horizon, it was tantamount to murder. What was he thinking? He hadn't been. She made him lose all reason. Reduced to ordering her about like a petty tyrant, he'd reacted with gut instinct, taken the prerogative of a male to keep his female safe.

But she wasn't his to protect in that way.

Instead, she'd seen him take the rights of a master protecting his property, and she was right to be pissed. Even if he didn't see her that way, he could never convince her of that. The balance of power was unequal. They had no future if he couldn't find a way to break this damned blood binding.

"If you want the girl, simply take her." Zetian leaned back against the gilt sun chair, but her long, tapping nails gave her away. Her goal was to mold Leif in his brother's image, a ruthless Regent fit to conquer the post-Unraveling era. She wanted someone unassailable to all but her own influence, and she saw his tie to Grace as a definite weakness.

If she wanted a strong king to lead by the nose, she'd picked the wrong man. It was time he showed her his iron spine.

He stood up. "Advisor Zetian, please share this map with the Kivati. If you can't find Corbette, find one of his Thunderbird generals. Get their coordinates. I'm sure they have information we do not."

"But—"

He dropped the full force of his gaze on her, every kilowatt of deadly dragon, every meter of force of his right to rule. She shut her mouth. "Good. Thorsson, I expect you to visit our surviving people and relay this message: Kingu is here, Kingu is deadly, and anyone who gives him aid will meet with the full force of my wrath. Do not share the details of Tiamat's Heart. But, please, tell them of Ishtar's counter-curse."

Thorsson laughed. "That pile of bull—"

With lightning speed, Leif pinned him to the wall. His claws broke through his fingertips straight into the bigger man's throat. The plaster cracked around the indent of his body. Leif smiled politely. "What will you tell them?"

Thorsson tried to swallow. Even as his blood trickled down his beefy neck, the wounds knit around Leif's claws. "Mortal. Weak—"

"A cure to the immortal madness," Leif said. "Tell them there is a cure."

"You don't really believe that ridiculous legend, do you?" Zetian asked. A curl of smoke trickled from her nostril. "Even if it were true, who would give up immortality?"

"Tell them to have hope," Leif said. "And tell them to start searching the city. Kingu is looking for a treasure that all Drekar are tied to. I would think one of us would feel it if it were close."

"And what if a Dreki does find the Heart?" Zetian asked. "You think they'll hand over that much power?"

Leif released Thorsson from the wall. The berserker sagged for a moment, then righted himself. He cracked his neck and showed a mouthful of sharp pointed teeth. "Ja. Good." He thumped Leif on the shoulder. "We find this Heart, then we fight."

"We will find the Heart and destroy it." Leif held up a hand when Zetian balked. "No one should have that much power. Not even me. Anyone who has an issue is free to meet me on the green at dawn. I am Tiamat's heir. I surrender the throne to no one."

"As you wish." Zetian moved to copy the map for the Kivati. "When did you feed last?"

"I'll take care of it." Hunger was a constant vibration in his chest. The sucking darkness made the edges of his vision flicker. He hadn't fed since he'd met Grace. After his lecture to her yesterday, that made him the lowest hypocrite. If he couldn't care for his own basic needs, he couldn't be trusted to keep her safe either. The white pins on the map danced across his vision. The aptrgangr patterns bothered him. He needed to find Grace, make sure she was safe, and get her input. She would see what he was missing.

Damn him, but he needed to find her and apologize. He'd taken away her ability to defend herself with his thoughtless order.

Leif took his carriage over the Interurban and through the Needle Market. His crest on the door opened barriers and stopped the highwaymen who preyed on travelers. It was slower, but he didn't trust himself in dragon form at the moment. When he arrived at the House of Ishtar in Pioneer Square, the afternoon rain pattered on the newly installed cut glass windows. The evening rush hadn't yet started. Piles of chestnut and sienna leaves crushed up against the bone fence. As he strode beneath the hanging bells of the gate, he paused to trace his fingers over a few freshly carved runes that lacked the crispness of Grace's work. Raidho, he thought, but the lines met at an odd angle. Sloppy. Ianna had hired some sham shaman to finish her protection spells, leaving her people in danger and Grace without work. Why did the second bother him as much as the first? It shouldn't, but through his own arrogance he'd stripped her of mercenary work. If Grace hadn't been hired to carve her runes, there were few options left for a woman hell-bent on making money.

The High Priestess greeted him at the door with a glint in her eye that he didn't quite trust. "Regent, how good of you to visit our humble temple." She waved at the Maidens lined up for his perusal. The girls preened and pouted. Some stank of avarice, others fear.

He found himself searching for a short, black-haired Maiden and shook his head. It wouldn't be fair to take this unfulfilled lust out on another woman. He had never been a user.

"None please you?" Ianna asked. She dropped her voice. "We satisfy all desires here. There is no secret longing you have that Ishtar cannot fulfill. The Goddess sees all your pleasure. Tell me what you seek. Ishtar herself is listening."

"Nothing. Just a bit of soul." He swallowed around the last word. It was a part of himself that he hated, this need. Sven had taught him to revel in it, but it was not a lesson he took to. There was too much of his grandfather in him. Too much emphasis on his lack of the divine. Too much reminder of his own damnation. The old anger curdled in his gut. "Anyone will do."

"Nonsense. The dragon knows a fake from a true diamond. If you don't seek your truth, you will never be satisfied. Perhaps something out of the ordinary for you, Regent." The Priestess motioned for him to follow her up the stairs. Two Maidens followed with honey mead and a silk robe embroidered with dragons. A thick red carpet covered the mahogany steps. They'd repaired the banister with pine, and it didn't quite match. Ianna led the way to the top floor.

He'd never been up to the third level. Ianna had refashioned the old servants' quarters into the Maidens' private rooms. The wallpaper was still a sensual red brocade, but the rest of the decor was plain compared to the lavish public rooms downstairs. He found its simplicity more seductive. In the secretive upstairs he had the chance to see behind the artifice to the women behind Ishtar's many veils. But who could Ianna be hiding up here worth taking him out of her carefully staged parlors and entertaining rooms downstairs? He waved away the robe when the Maidens offered it, but took the jar of mead. He wanted a few moments to forget the weight bearing down on his shoulders.

The Priestess pointed to a plain blue door set with a brass knob. She took a key from around her neck and unlocked the dead bolt.

"You have a Maiden locked up here?"

"Just for you, Regent. My little gift."

With a curl of foreboding in his belly, he entered the room, and the door clicked shut behind him.

The sparse room held a rickety brass bed and a small nightstand. An oval window with leaded glass in a spider-web pattern let in the only light. Standing in front of the bed, a woman waited, hands curled into fists, blue-black hair streaming down over her pale shoulders to frame her chest. She wore a black corset and tight black pants. The corset pushed her breasts high, and he was suddenly famished. When she saw him, she gave a small start and dropped her fists. Her coral lips parted, succulent and sweet.

Grace.

Hunger roared through him, and riding on its tailcoat, anger. She was working in the House of Ishtar as a Maiden. How many men would pay to put the notorious Reaper on her back? "You wanted a job," he said. Was that his voice? It had never been so low, or so hoarse. "And here you are."

She straightened. "You ordered me not to fight."

"I left you no choice." He took a step toward her.

She looked at her hands like she couldn't imagine what they would be used for now that he'd stolen her weapons. Her fingers curled uselessly. Her knife was gone. She couldn't even defend herself, and Ianna wouldn't come running if she heard screams. Maidens of Ishtar might be more like geisha than streetwalkers, but they catered to all pleasures.

"You needed a job," he said. "A job to earn back your freedom." She was such a liar.

Her eyes darted to the door, but she raised her chin. "There is no shame in serving Ishtar."

"No," he agreed. "There is no shame in desire." He took another step toward her, and she retreated. The bed hit the back of her legs. There was nowhere to run. "There is no shame in embracing the Goddess's gifts." He truly believed that. He respected the Maidens' devotion to Ishtar. But after five minutes in Grace's company, he could tell she wasn't that type of girl. "But can you spread your legs for multiple men? Can you share Ishtar's pleasure with no strings attached?"

She swallowed hard. A shaft of light slanted through the spiderweb window onto her glossy hair. He reached out and took a long strand of light and midnight. Her hair was silky smooth. He twisted the long strand around his hand until he reached her cheek, and she turned her head into his palm, the barest touch of her skin, her breath hot on his wrist. "Yes," she whispered. The heat of her cheek connected the space between them. At the edge of her jaw, her pulse raced.

"Yes, you can exchange one man for another, worshipping pleasure for pleasure itself?"

"It's just a job," she said, but her voice cracked.

Freya help him. She wanted to play it that way, did she? His vision clouded in blue and green. He wanted to tug on that strand of hair and pull her to him. To breach that distance and take her at her word. Ishtar knew what he needed and here Grace was. He wet his lips. The musk of her scent overpowered the dust motes of the room, the old jasmine incense lingering in the bed linens, the iron of his own arousal.

"Just a job," he repeated. But he knew she was bluffing. He'd taken away her power when he forbade her to fight, and this was her perfectly orchestrated revenge. It would be so easy to fall for her seductive bait—Freya knew he wanted to—but if he did this, he would never win back her fledging trust. All his honorable intentions had landed them in this angry mess. It would have been simpler if he'd let them succumb to lust. Now it was too late. Emotions were involved, tangled as a kite string in a hurricane.

In this moment he couldn't separate anger from lust. He wanted to rage at her. He wanted to show her the monster she made of him. Whatever game she was playing, she'd misjudged him. He was not a saint. The darkness swirled in his breast. The immortal madness clung to the edges of his mind like cobwebs. How easy it would be to push her down into the thick mattress and take what he needed. To lose himself in her welcoming heat. To find himself in her silken touch.

He was greedy with wanting, weak with hunger, and he was done denying himself anything.

The tension rose. Fire in the walls. Fire in her skin. Sweat dripped between her breasts, and he hadn't even touched her yet. Grace was sure hell had a special place for thoughts like these. Asgard's irises were slit, demonic, but even then she wanted him.

"So what are you waiting for?" she asked, full of bravado. Ianna had tricked her into this situation, but Grace couldn't back down now. Asgard claimed he was honorable? She'd show him how much hot air his words were. He was no better than the rest of the Drekar. Still, if he didn't get it over with soon, she would lose her nerve.

Her hair still wrapped around his palm, he leaned down to whisper in her ear. He let his body brush against hers, and an electric thrill raced across her skin. "I ask myself that same question. You, me, a bed, alone. Privacy even if you change your mind—"

She narrowed her eyes and tried to move her head back, but he held on.

"This is the perfect opportunity to finish what we started. You're a grown woman who knows her own mind, and you said, 'Yes.' I heard you quite clearly. But we have a problem, Mademoiselle Grace." He put his nose to her hair and took a deep breath. The scent of cinnamon skyrocketed. "I see you. What you say, what you don't say. I could take you here, now, and make you love it—"

"Aren't we a little overconfident?"

He fit his body to hers and let her feel the full press of his hot, hard, and ego-worthy erection.

Alarm bells rang through every nerve. "Ianna found me snooping in the library and locked me up here," she blabbered.

He shook his head and let out an angry breath. "You think I don't know that? Christ!" Releasing her hair, he took a hasty step back and paced to the door. When he got there, he spun back to look at her. His nostrils flared. "By Freya, I can smell you."

Stomach clenching, she stood up again and planted her feet. This time she had pushed him too far. She couldn't explain this compulsion to needle him and get under his skin. To bait the monster in his lair. He was too fucking composed. Why couldn't he stoop to her level for once?

Her body craved him, scales and all.

Asgard stalked back to her and didn't stop when she hit the bed. A swirling heat shot down to her core. Like a tornado, he bowled her right over into the pillowy mattress. *Finally*. His weight settled over her, all two hundred plus pounds of toned man pressing her down, making the ancient bed protest, and those extra inches where it counted settled hot and heavy between her thighs.

Ishtar be merciful.

He seized her hands and pinned them over her head. His aggression sent a thrill through her. She tried to move her hips ever so slightly. Friction. She needed friction. But he wouldn't budge. "Is this what you want, Grace? A little brimstone to scorch the sheets?" His hold tightened.

Her breathing hitched. *Yes. No. Maybe.* This was it. In about five minutes, she wouldn't have to play this game ever again. They could scratch this thing out, and then she would be free.

"I know you're thinking of my brother," he growled, breath hot against her crown. "But I'm not him."

She hadn't been thinking of anyone other than the gorgeous, angry man on top of her. He smelled so good.

"The thing is, Grace, you don't hate me. You want me—"

She could say no, but they both knew that would be a lie. Her nipples hardened.

"—and you hate yourself for it."

She hated the needy way he made her feel. He slid her defenses right out from under her. She was happy being alone, independent, until he came along and ruined it all. He made her want dreamy, impossible things. He made her start believing in fairy tales again, and *they didn't fucking exist*. Not for her. Not for anyone.

Dragons existed. Monsters existed. But true love and happily ever after? Like her parents had? Like Kayla and Hart?

It hurt too much to believe in.

She was always strong except when it mattered. Weak for those gorgeous, lying, bastard Drekar. Manipulated.

Suddenly she was sixteen again and Norgard was whispering sweet nothings in her ear, and she couldn't take it anymore. “Get off!” She pushed at his chest. Asgard didn’t budge. His hard body pressed her down into the soft comforter until all she could see was him.

“I am not my brother.” His voice held power. It reverberated through his chest, sending waves of desire down her breasts to the crux of her thighs. “You don’t have the courage to take what you want, and I won’t take it by force. Not even if you asked me to.”

“I don’t want—”

“Either you tell me you want it as badly as your body does, or nothing. There will be no half-truths. A part of you wants me to hold you down, just so you can say it wasn’t you. I am not that man.”

“Asgard—”

His body left her abruptly, leaving a chill in its place. His anger drove him across the room. The ache between her thighs intensified. *Don’t go.*

When he reached the door, he turned to look at her over his shoulder. A thin shaft of light from the window illuminated his gorgeous hair. It was a fiery halo around a face carved from stone. She’d never seen him so focused. “You will come to me willingly or not at all. I won’t wait forever. My name is Leif. Use it.”

He slammed the door on the way out. A crack broke in the door frame and ran up the wall and across the ceiling. Pieces of plaster rained down.

Grace couldn’t move. There was so much want, but she clung to the shreds of her hatred. Why? It wasn’t like her to deny herself. She knew life was short. She had to face it: she was afraid. Her hatred protected her, and Leif wanted to strip her bare. What would be left of her once he’d uncovered her vulnerable core? What if she wasn’t strong enough on her own to hold herself up?

He’d slipped out of the iron box she tried to stuff him and her feelings into, and he refused to go back in.

"Leif," she tried the name out. So personal. So exposed.

The gold bands on her upper arms burned. They could never meet as equals as long as he owned her soul. She would always be his blood slave and he, her master.

She had already been through the relationship wringer. She had built up her daydreams and offered over her fragile teenage heart on a platter. Norgard had crushed it, after he'd sucked all the life out of it. She didn't believe in love anymore. Two people could never meet as equals.

What if Leif did the same thing? If, after she submitted to him willingly, he laughed in her face? She didn't want to stop hating him, because deep down she suspected he was everything she'd ever dreamed in her silly little girl fantasies.

Leif was hotter than Thor, smart, and honorable.

Norgard had never been able to break her, but Leif was different. If she let herself fall for him, she was done for.

Chapter 18

After swinging past Thor's Hammer to pick up Bear and her bike, Grace went home. It wasn't home to her anymore, of course. It hadn't been for a long time. But when things got bad and she needed to think, she always came back here, to the little yellow house overlooking Lake Washington, where on a clear day she used to watch the Mountain stretching into the sky.

She would climb into the apple tree when no one was home and imagine the bulbs her mom always planted pushing their way out of the rich dark soil between the roots of the old tree. The branches creaked in the wind, and she remembered her father tying a swing onto the strongest limb, her mother scolding the whole time about how he was going to fall to his death. But the smile he gave when he finished and they both watched Grace swing for the first time made the whole effort worthwhile.

She liked to remember them that way, her father's arm encircling her mother's plump waist, her mother in her black slacks and no-nonsense square-rimmed glasses letting herself lean into his embrace.

Not how they were at the end. If their ghosts hadn't

passed on to whatever afterlife they believed in, she knew they would be here, where their happiest moments had been.

The house stood vacant. One wall had collapsed in the Unraveling. The family who'd moved in after the bank had seized the house had disappeared. The paint peeled in places, showing the dull brown undercoat that her mother had hated.

Grace sat in the swing and listened to the comforting creak of the branch overhead. She turned her back on the house, letting it brighten in her memory. The wall built itself back up. The yellow filled in like a paint-by-number picture. Wooden slats grew over the gaping holes. Glass filled the windows once again. White lace curtains blew through the open casement in her upstairs bedroom. She could almost hear the grand piano as her mother plucked out Beethoven and transitioned into a Mozart sonata. Her father would be in the kitchen making gnocchi and cracking Godfather jokes. A phantom sun shone on the scene behind her, warming her back. At her feet pansies, lavender, and zinnias twined up from the ashen ground.

The cat rubbed himself against her legs. "You would have liked Mom's music," she told him. A dark front blew in from the south, sending whitecaps across the surface of the lake. Ash snowed softly across her vision, and she blinked away the moisture in her eye.

"She didn't like pets, but she would have liked you. You're both a little prickly." Bear rested and licked his paw, seeming to say he didn't care for the comparison. "She liked people too, but pretended not to." Her mother liked to complain about crowds and entertaining, but she basked in the glow of an audience. Her music would light her up, some hidden ingredient making her fingers fly over the keys.

The wind whistled through holes in the empty shells of neighboring houses. Grace pretended it was the sound of her mother practicing scales. How many times had she sat out here and listened? The appetizing smell of sizzling tomatoes and garlic wafting out from the kitchen. The laughter of neighborhood children playing in the yards. The everyday ordinariness of it all. She'd thought it would never change.

"I wanted something bigger than this," she whispered. "But only because I didn't know how good I had it. I wanted to be a Somebody." She laughed softly to herself. "Important, you know? And now look at me." She was the Reaper. Not something her mother would have bragged to her bridge club about. She could imagine her mother tucking a strand of straight grey hair behind her ear and asking why she hadn't found a nice man yet.

"You took the last one, Mom," she whispered.

In her imagination, her mother clucked her tongue. *You haven't been looking hard enough.*

"I've been a little busy."

Her mother only raised her eyebrow in that look she had. A successful surgeon, virtuoso pianist, mother and wife. Gardener, bridge player. The only thing her mother hadn't done was cook, and that was a godsend. She was a tiger mother, and Grace had never had a chance of keeping up.

Her mother had talked to the dead, too. Her dead grandmother, to be exact. The two had had extensive arguments, and as a kid Grace had always thought her mom a little crazy.

"Grandma is dead," she used to say.

"That doesn't mean she can't still nag me," her mother would reply. And maybe she'd had it right.

Hindsight, and all that.

Bear stared at her.

"So I met this guy," Grace started. She could see her mom's ears perk up. Her fingers paused on the keys, only a breath before she transitioned into a soft waltz.

And? Mom would ask.

"You wouldn't like him," she admitted, but had to stop

Maybe, maybe not. They wouldn't have liked Norgard, for certain, but Leif was different. He seemed . . . honorable, as hard as it was to admit it. Her parents were very big on honor.

And does he treat you well? her dad asked.

"He drives me crazy. Orders me around. Tries to wrap me up in cotton. I can't breathe!"

Her mom nodded. *He's a good one then.*

"Dad never coddled you."

He knew what was good for him. This boy will too, you just have to tell him.

Use your words, her dad said. *You Kim women never say what's on your mind. You expect a guy to use telepathy.*

Humph, her mother said.

Grace agreed.

Bear passed her again, rubbing around her legs. She reached down and scratched his head. The wind picked up, cold fingers from the north scattering the ghosts from the overgrown yard and across the deserted street.

"It's easier to talk to dead people," she told Bear. "Or you. You don't talk back."

The cat gave her a flat look.

"But I guess I can still understand you." She pushed up from the swing and turned back to the decaying house. It was always a shock. She tried not to look at it straight on, because the memories didn't squeeze her chest quite as hard. "Good-bye."

Grace pulled herself together before stepping through the brass doors of Asgard's laboratory. She had to do it quickly. Her chickenshit feet wanted to turn and run in the other direction. There was no turning back from this. The point of no return wasn't this act of stepping across the threshold; it had been crossed long ago. She couldn't pinpoint it exactly. When Asgard had first kissed her? When he'd ridden in on his white horse that first day in the alley with the aptrgangr? Or maybe in the council chamber, when she'd seen him sitting calmly in the hot seat while an angry mob called for his blood. He'd seemed so proud and aloof then. Like he thought he was better than the rest of them. A god among men. Gorgeous. Haughty. Cold and collected.

She had wanted to take him down at the knees just for spite.

He had worn her down with his kindness. Chipped away at her defenses with his honesty and openness. Shamed her with his generosity when she'd closed her heart to others. He wasn't what she had expected.

Leif had added ten tables with metal suits of armor since she'd been in his lab. He bent over one of them, goggles on, a smudge across his forehead. Wielding a blowtorch, he burned a large rune in the center of the suit's chest. He heard her enter, but pointedly didn't look up.

She didn't know what to say. "I'm sorry" seemed less honest, somehow, because she was still angry. But her anger was directed inward. The tangle of lust and irritation itched inside her.

She let her curiosity carry her forward. That current had always been too strong to swim against. She leaned next to him against the worktable. His scent was musk and fire. The muscles in his back and arms flexed as he directed the heavy torch.

Leif finished the rune and pulled the goggles off his head. He studied the etchings, a furrow in his brow.

"You're doing it wrong."

He glanced up then. "Can I help you with something?"

Ye gods, he was going to make this hard for her. Maybe he didn't feel the same heat she did. Maybe he really was ice inside. She was surprised her heat didn't turn him into a puddle. "Raidho, but it's right side up. You want it reversed."

"What do you want, Grace?" His voice was tired. He put down the torch.

She turned to face him. Great sky gods, he towered over her looking like one of Lucifer's angels. Muscle and sweat and deliciously tousled hair. *Take me*, she thought. But still he didn't touch her. Did she have to throw herself at him? "What do I want? What do you want? You're always telling me what to do: Take command. Make up my mind. Then when I finally do, you act obtuse!"

"Are you coming on to me?" One eyebrow rose. "A soulless lizard with all the emotional depth of a rock? We wouldn't want that."

"I never said—"

In an instant, his icy calm dissolved. Lightning heat flared in his eyes. He lunged forward, pinning her between the mechanical suit and his hard, hot body. Her ass hit the edge of the table. His muscled legs pressed between her thighs, spreading her. Cold metal against her back. Burning man against her front. Her breathing ratcheted up. "Is this what you want? Tell me. For Freya's sake, tell me yes now or run."

"Yes."

"Gods." Her affirmation loosed a wild thing. He kissed her. Hot, wet, and out of control. He claimed her mouth like he would devour her. Ravenous, insatiable. Sensation rippled across her body. She couldn't think with his tongue down her throat and his body consuming every spare inch of her flesh. His mouth found her neck, sending shivers down her spine.

She moaned. *Freya, yes.* This was what she'd been waiting for. This was what she needed. Why had she held out for so long when all this heat waited to banish every last dark thought from her mind? She could drown in him.

His hands skimmed beneath her black sweatshirt and found her corset. "Damn it, Grace. I'm going to have to liberate you from these confining gender roles." Overwhelmed with the feel of his teeth and lips against the sensitive hollow beneath her ear, she almost didn't notice when he ripped her corset down the front.

"Hey!" Her nipples peaked in the sudden chill. Her breasts sprang free from the binding fabric. He had uncovered her runes. They twisted across her skin like a circus freak.

He didn't seem to mind. If anything they turned him on. He kissed each one as he explored her chest and shoulders. "I'll buy you new clothes. A hundred. In silks and lace and leather, if you want. Gods, I've wanted to touch you like this." His hot hands covered her breasts. His clever thumbs circled her areolas, narrowing in on her raised peaks. She was one spark away from a lit fuse. Her core clenched and unclenched, wet and desperate with need. She clasped her thighs around his solid legs, grinding herself into him.

"You are so beautiful," he rasped. His graceful fingers plucked her nipples, while his mouth did wicked things to the delicate skin where her head met her neck.

"A little less talk, Asgard—"

That brought him up short. His hands froze, and she wanted to cry from the sudden deprivation. He raised his head. "I don't think so. I told you; I won't be a nameless fuck."

"Leif."

His slow grin brought to mind a tiger. A feral, hungry edge that made her basest instincts say *Run*, and her womanly instincts pant in heat. "Leif, what?"

"Leif . . . *please*."

He slid one hand down her belly to the inseam of her pants. But there he paused.

She wanted friction. She tried to wiggle closer to those clever fingers, just an inch away from easing this aching need. His legs held her at a distinct disadvantage. A slave to his mercy, she had no leverage. "Damn it! Move your hand!"

"Say my name."

"I already did!"

"Again. I want to make sure I didn't imagine it."

"Leif! Leif! Move your damn—*ughnn!*" His fingers pressed through her pants to the ball of electrified nerves at her crux. *Yes. Here. Finally. Move.*

His hand slipped away again. "Not like this."

"This is fine. Don't stop—"

But he seemed to have gotten over giving her control. She'd finally stuck her hand in the dragon's maw, and now she was in the jaws of a master. He had the power to do what he wanted with her.

Picking her up, he set her on the table so that she leaned back between the brass legs of the suit of armor. Her breasts hung free. A welcome breeze from the open air ducts high in the ceiling cooled her heated skin. He hooked her knees over the machine's legs, one on each side, spreading her for him. The position left her open as wide as she could go, uncomfortably tight, splayed to his mercy.

He drank her in, and the hungry look in his eyes stopped her from protesting the neglect of her more sensitive areas. His look was a touch all of its own. The lust-soaked wonder in his eyes brought something small and fragile skipping to life in her breast. She didn't want this vulnerability. This was just about sex. Nothing more.

The look on his face said he might not agree. No one had ever looked at her with such wonder.

It scared the bejesus out of her.

She tried to rekindle that fire of a moment before, but her emotions were all tangled up inside her breast. Sex and need and unrequited lust and blood and sacrifice and slavery and friendship. She didn't know where one stopped and another began. Could she have sex without giving up her sense of self? Would she still like herself in the morning? Her brain automatically tried to extract all emotion out of the act. To protect her. To break this down moment by moment until it could be dissected and dismissed as easily as taking a piss.

"I've lost you," Leif said. "Come back to me." He stood back and ran a hand through his hair.

She didn't want him to go. "We can still do this." But it sounded weak even to her ears.

"Damn right we can." He began to unbutton his shirt. Inch by golden inch, his chest came into view, his long fingers working magic on those buttons like Michelangelo's chisel called David forth from marble. His chest gleamed, pecs defined and stomach hard, a sleek body with a panther's grace. He unrolled his shirtsleeves and pushed the shirt off his shoulders.

She watched the white linen flutter to the ground, a flag of surrender to this lust that charged the air between them. Swallowing, she looked back at his godlike body.

He unbuckled his belt.

She was still nervous she'd freeze up again, but the heat had returned. She fought the urge to clamp her legs together against the ache. Instead she lounged back against the machine, trying to look cool, open, and willing.

Please don't be a gentleman, she thought at him as he dropped his clinging trousers.

Un-freaking-believable. She'd seen his naked body before when he'd Turned, but this was the first time she'd allowed herself a good, long look in the smoky lights of the biodiesel lamps. A commando Norse god in the flesh. Gorgeous and powerful and sexy as hell. Her tongue stuck to the roof of her mouth taking it all in.

With slow, lazy grace, he turned in a circle, giving her a good, long look at his every angle. A wicked smile played across his face. It promised naughty, naughty things to come.

But he still maintained his distance. The challenge in his eyes said, *Come and get it.*

Her hands fisted against her pants. This was her moment: wallow in the past, ruminate on her own insecurities or seize the day.

Grace jumped off the table. "Move that hot ass over here." He humored her and lowered himself to the position she had just vacated at the foot of the brass machine. He lounged back on the table, weight on his elbows, thighs parted. His eyes trailed her hungrily. All that masculinity and power coiled and waiting for her touch. "Are those tiny scales sparkling in the lamplight?"

"Why don't you find out?"

She trailed her fingertips over the carved abs, pointedly ignoring the organ most clambering for her attention. "Nope, velvet smooth."

"Grace." Leif's voice was ragged. Need turned his green eyes to catlike slits. For the first time, the inhuman eyes actually turned her on. A dragon might lurk beneath his skin, but right now he was all man, and she wanted that man with whatever twin creature hid inside him. What other immortal tricks could he do?

"Grace," he said again, more serious this time. Tension bound every muscle in his body. He surged forward and grasped her arms just under the gold armbands. "Please."

An order of such vulnerability and need. She couldn't turn away from that. She felt the same down to her all-too-human soul. "Lie back," she ordered. Taking charge, she slid her hands down his thighs and brought her mouth to the base of his cock. Leif gave a choked moan. His muscles shook.

"Don't hold back," she said. "I'm not as delicate as you think." She was tough, and she was mean, and she was enough woman to match him any day.

With one slow lick from base to tip, she drew a guttural cry from him. She'd never realized how empowering sex could be. She'd reduced the great beast to absolute *putty*.

"Grace, you're killing me." The third time her name left his lips. Too aware, still. She would drive every thought out of his pretty little head. The salty tang of him slid over her lips. In and out, slow and sleek. She took her time driving him to the edge. But the power pulled both ways, because as she took his pleasure, her own need grew.

The sweet perfume of his musk filled the air as his passion rose. It stoked her desire. Smell, taste, touch. His arousal strained against her tongue. A sheen of sweat beaded his beautiful body. His muscles bunched, holding back. An assault on her senses, driving her wild before he even touched her core. She held on as long as she could. Clenching her thighs together could only do so much to ease her ache.

Grace wanted to make him beg, but she broke first. With one last lick, she released him, panting. Eyes wild, he reached out to caress her breasts. "I want to see you," he growled and tore the button from her pants.

"I needed those," she said as she shimmied out of them.

"You don't need clothes. You will be gloriously naked chained to my bed from this day forward."

She thought about how easy it would be to keep him here prone on the table to do with as she pleased. She needed some spelled handcuffs. Later.

Pulling herself up, she climbed on top and straddled his thighs.

"On second thought—"

"I don't want you thinking at all," she said.

"Isn't that supposed to be my line?"

She shook her head.

He crooked his finger at her and licked his lips. "Come closer, let me—" She didn't let him finish. With a deep breath, she impaled herself on his shaft. Pain shocked her. It had been a while, and he was so thick.

"Ishtar save me." He grabbed her hips to steady her. She blinked against the uncomfortable fullness and tried to will her inner muscles to relax. "You are so tight." His fingers slipped over her clit and circled. Shock and pleasure washed over her, and suddenly the tightness eased to deep fullness. She slid down another inch. Leif sucked air between his teeth. "Ah, gods, she already has. You feel so good, so right. You'd put even the goddess to shame, and that isn't a blasphemy, only truth."

She basked in the sensory overload and tightened her inner muscles, making Leif squirm beneath her. But soon her nerves called out for friction, and she moved, leveraging herself up and sliding down again. Leif's eyes rolled in his head. He was her victim, helpless to move from her feminine wiles. Was this what Ishtar's Maidens felt? This power they wielded over men. This heady control. Bringing men to their knees.

She'd never come to sex as an equal before. Leif wasn't the only one affected. Far from it. Her legs shook with the effort to push up, and only his strong hands on her waist kept her from falling over in a quivery pool of jelly, especially as her pace increased and his circling thumbs drove her to higher pleasure. She felt raw and exposed in a freeing, mind-numbing way that she wanted to go on forever.

And then the friction increased, and she knew if it didn't stop she would fly apart in a billion glittering pieces to float away on the Aether, an explosion of energy and light.

Leif twined his fingers through hers and let her push into his vitality and strength.

Did all Drekar need to suck a piece of her soul to finish? She fumbled her rhythm.

"Grace, don't stop. I'm losing you." Stopping her, he sat up and scooted them both off the table, holding on to her the entire time. Her legs were still wrapped around his waist. Her arms circled his neck. He didn't bat an eye at the extra weight.

She licked her lips. "Do you need to feed—?"

His eyes took on a hard edge. "No." Gently, he untangled her legs and arms and set her belly down across the worktable, ass in the air, chill metal on her peaked nipples. "Keep your pretty little mouth away from me." He took a moment to lay kisses down her spine to the tip of her tailbone.

"What are you—?"

"Relax, Grace. I've got you. Trust me on this." He put her hands on the suit of armor and squeezed them as if he expected her to hang on. She felt the command in his body. The tables were turned: her on her stomach in the vulnerable position, him with the power and control. Except that this new position was safe; he couldn't reach her mouth to sip from her soul. She didn't have time to be anxious, because he spread her legs again and entered her with a single thrust.

"You are mine," he said as he speared her to the core, even deeper than she thought he could go. She couldn't move, pinned to the table beneath his weight and his pounding, demanding presence. His hands shaped her ass possessively. Her cheek pressed against the table, and she held on for dear life. He was going to shatter her. "When I am inside you, you will think of no one but me. Nothing but how good I feel and how hard I'm going to fuck you. When you come, you will come screaming my name."

Her moan echoed through the cavernous room, wanton, free with all the sexual power of a goddess in full lust. She couldn't believe it came from her lips. She couldn't deny it. He thrust deeper. His stomach slapped against her ass. He had the control, but his voice rasped with the same need she felt. Neither one of them was cold and calculating. They were equals as his thrusts built this fire to a raging peak. She didn't know where he ended and she began, only that he filled an emptiness inside her she hadn't known she possessed. She thought she would break apart. Each moan, each powerful thrust sent waves of passion building inside her. Aether poured over her sweat-slicked skin, tingling her sensitive nerves, until all she felt was the wild, untamed tide washing over her.

She screamed, "Leif!"

A moment later he followed her over the edge into the abyss. Shivers racked his body. As he leaned over her, his skin was hot and wet against hers, fire where he laid his cheek against her back, cool where he touched his lips, ever so gently, along her spine. The romantic gesture disturbed her bubbly post-orgasm haze. While her mind floated back to earth, the part of her brain she'd been ignoring started shouting into the empty space: *This one could break you.*

All the more reason to fear him, because it was true. He could seduce her body. Charm her mind. But he would kill her with kindness. If he cared about her at all, he would leave her her heart.

Chapter 19

Leif kissed the bumps along Grace's spine, his lips saying everything he couldn't put into words. The gods had never designed so wicked a temptation as Grace's skin. She might dislike his drugging scent, but she didn't know how her natural human rose musk blurred his mind and made a fool of him. Her taste, her moans, the feel of her slick folds welcoming his cock. He would stay here forever in her drugging embrace. Civilization could go to the dogs; all he wanted was right here. To languish in selfish indulgence making love to this fierce little woman. To make her laugh until she forgot her past, every wraith, aptrgangr, and Dreki that had bled her strong heart. As the warm glow of lovemaking called him off to sleep, he pulled his little fighter into his arms and carried her to the alcove where he kept his lab cot.

"It's not the Savoy, but it's better than that metal table." What kind of lowlife made love to a woman on a metal table anyway? He wanted to kick himself. She deserved better than that. He didn't realize she'd come to him so soon. He'd issued an ultimatum, but he didn't realize how strong her resolve was. She'd overcome her numerous reservations with his nature and her past to come to his bed. Ishtar's own strength. Freya's good luck. He knew their attraction burned deep, but he'd never dreamed it could be so good.

She seemed strangely reluctant to meet his eyes now.

"Regretting it so soon?" A wry note crept into his voice.

"No."

But he could tell she was lying. Damn the gods. He sighed. Wrapping her in his arms, he stretched down on the cot. He didn't want to let her go. She was his now. But if she struggled to get up, he knew he would have to let her. "Do you want to talk about it?"

"No."

He held her and luxuriated in the feel of her in his arms at last. The gold slave bands pressed against his side. They hung between them like lead weights. Unequal—master to slave. *Take me as I am*, he thought. A king, a captor. He might own her soul, technically, but what was a measly soul when she was in possession of his all-too-breakable heart?

"I didn't go to the temple to work," she said.

"Good." He felt her bristle.

"But I could have. I can do what I want—"

"Yes."

"And you took away my—"

"Power. I know. I'm sorry." Closing his eyes, he tapped into the slave bond between them. "You have the power to fight as you see fit. There are no restrictions on your person." The bond crackled with his order.

After a beat, she settled again against his chest. "I went back to search the library. Marduk had a scepter, a ring, thunderbolts, a magic web, and fire, few of which we have. Our only saving grace is that Kingu isn't a full-fledged demigod—he's a wraith. To seize the Tablet of Destiny, he needs to possess someone so he has hands. He can't hold it as a wraith. I don't know if the same is true for the Heart, but if we catch him possessing a human, I can banish him. There's gotta be something about defeating Kingu in the

House's books. I found one that looked promising before Ianna found me."

"I'd offer to ship her to Antarctica, but I'm feeling rather fond of her at the moment. You're here in my arms. It worked out."

"She's not worth the trouble." Grace rolled off him and padded away to find her pants. The sudden loss chilled him, but the sight of her walking away warmed him right back up. She wore nothing but her black boots. Compact muscle toned her lithe body. Runes ran up her spine and spider-webbed out to her shoulder blades. Two long lines of ink trailed over her ass and down the backs of her legs to disappear into her boots.

It was the hottest thing he'd ever seen.

"Ianna is good to her Maidens. She's a bit like Ishtar in that way. She can be benevolent or she can be a bitch, the goddess of love or the goddess of war. No one is all good or evil; it's our actions that make the difference." Her eyes flickered to him and away, and Leif felt pierced through his nonexistent soul.

The admission had cost her—proud, stubborn woman that she was. She didn't think he was all evil, even though he was Drekar. The knot of worry released in his gut. She hadn't slept with him to prove her courage or a point or whatever angry, twisted reason she might have come up with.

Pulling the book from her bag, she walked back, flipping through the pages as she did. Hot damn, the front view of her body was even better than the back. Blue-black runes spiraled out over her womb and across her heart. She was not unselfconscious in her nudity; there was an erectness of her carriage, a defiant lift of her chin that said she was hyperaware of her lack of clothes.

She was beautiful. Her skin glowed beneath the lamplight. With each step her long hair swayed like a curtain of spider silk down her back. In her determined stride he saw

Ishtar conquering the battlefield. Why couldn't she see how magnificent she was? No wonder Sven had tried to ensnare her, but he hadn't been able to tame her fire. Grace was a force unto herself.

"What do the runes mean?" he asked. "And why do you have so many?"

"Most are for protection, like Thurisaz, which means 'thorn.' It can be used for defense or destruction." She pointed to a stick with a triangle coming off it like a flag over her heart. There were many more creeping over her ribs in chains of blue-black ink.

The Aether sparked between them. She burned brighter than other humans. Power greased her movement. The spiderweb of runes seemed to throb with a magic all of their own.

It reminded him of a magic cage he'd once seen far in the northern tundra of Lapland. The local shaman had trapped an ice elemental in a cage of reindeer bones carved with ancient runes. The bones were still bloody—the death of the animal had fueled the spell that kept the enraged elemental at bay.

Grace pointed to another rune over her solar plexus. "Algiz helps focus my will to perform the banishing spell."

She stopped just short of him, but he bridged that gap by reaching out and tugging her closer. He liked having her here in his arms far too much. He knew anything that smacked of possessiveness made her nervous, but the need to hold her was too great. Not to trap her, just to bask in the warmth of her soul light.

He could feel the anxiety rippling beneath her skin. They'd taken a giant step in their relationship, and she was confused as hell as to what that made them. He valued commitment. She valued freedom. He had to prove to her that the two weren't incompatible.

Grace flipped through the book. "I don't know about the

scepter and the ring, but we can re-create Marduk's other three weapons. A net—"

"My suits of armor shoot nets and fire."

"Great. The Kivati Thunderbirds can draw thunderbolts, and your Drekar can breathe fire too. What we need to do is draw Kingu into the open and trap him with thunderbolts and fire. I've been looking for a book on how Marduk used the Tablet of Destiny, but so far no luck."

"Rudrick used it as a knife during the ceremony to bring down the Gate."

"Yeah, but what would I do, carve a rune? I doubt I have enough oomph to draw the Aether through such a powerful object."

He was beginning to suspect that she had more power inside her than she realized. She was faster, stronger, and more Aether-conductive than any human he'd ever met.

"I bet the Heart sleeps most of the time," Grace said. "Otherwise Kingu would know exactly where it was."

"The aptrgangr—" He paused to weigh his words. "They would be attracted to the Heart, wouldn't they?"

"Definitely."

"The Heart might even be calling them. Wouldn't Tiamat want to be found and resurrected? And it's inside a living thing, Longren said. Moving about the city."

"It would have to be a freaking powerful host."

"Or someone magically enhanced. Maybe someone who doesn't even realize what's inside them. Someone who just happens to find aptrgangr everywhere they go. Who happens to be strong enough to fight them even though she's only human."

Her head came up. "What are you trying to say?"

"I think Tiamat's Heart is inside you."

* * *

Grace's stomach dropped out of the soles of her feet. She pulled out of his arms. "I'm not a fucking zombie!" How could he even suggest something so stupid? So insulting? That she drew aptrgangr to her like some freaking magnet? That she was responsible for the destruction Kingu caused?

She saved people, damn it. She didn't endanger them.

"Calm down." Leif raised both hands. "It's all right—"

"It isn't all right! I am not possessed."

"Possession implies that the Heart is in control—"

"Screw you." A glint in his eye took her expletive and sent it somewhere she didn't want to go. Beneath the biodiesel light, his pale skin glowed, delicious and otherworldly. He wasn't human. He didn't understand. And she'd let him in. She'd *trusted* him. Pain was a vise around her chest. She'd just made the biggest mistake of her life. "I am not aptrgangr."

"You have a very strong spirit."

"There is nothing controlling me but you! You know what? I don't need this." She grabbed her clothes and bag and headed for the door. "I'm not controlling aptrgangr or anyone else. I don't own anyone. I don't force anyone to do anything!"

"Calm down," Leif said. He rose slowly. She couldn't see past the haze of red. "Not by choice. I'm not saying you mean to, but the evidence—"

"Fuck that! You wouldn't know the nose in front of your face. Did you know when you demand I do something that I have to do it? You're so caught up in your own importance that you don't realize how high and mighty you act. Do this! Don't do that!" Her hands fisted at her sides. She wanted to lash out. He was a liar! "You are just like Norgard!"

It was the meanest thing she could think of to say, and the barb hit home like a tomahawk missile. She saw it fling through the air and hit him squarely in the chest. His head snapped back. He blinked and dropped his gaze to the floor.

Slamming through the door, Grace ran into the dark hallway, pulling on her clothes as she went. Leif's shirt was a dress on her and it reeked of cinnamon, but he'd ripped her clothes. She had nothing else. She didn't care what he thought about her. He was wrong. She would prove it.

Her feet carried her through the tunnels to the caved-in aerie. Far below, waves crashed against the cliff base, wrathful hands of a Mother Nature that hadn't quite finished the job. The clouds rolled across the sky, not raining yet, but getting ready to unleash their next attack.

She punched her fist at them. Damn the sky gods. Damn the Kivati's dark Lady and the Drekar's pantheon of dead deities. Who had come when the Gate crashed down? Who had woke in their hour of need to save the world from the final apocalypse? Who had shown mercy when her parents died or after? No one. She made her own luck. She was her own strength.

It was weak to depend on power mad spirits and immortal warriors alike. When your back was against the wall, there was no one to count on but your own two fists. She might be tied to that hated malachite ring, but she'd be damned if she was responsible for anyone else. She ruled her own mind. Her body, no. But her mind was her own. Her heart was definitely not some dead goddess's.

What would it mean if she didn't have her own emotions all this time? Would Tiamat, the mother of all dragons, feel love for her soulless children? Had her teenage crush on Norgard been just a reflection of Tiamat's feelings?

Had her feelings for Leif been real or completely fabricated? A lie, like everything else.

And Leif's strange attraction to her, was it her, or the slave bond, or the pull of like to like, dragon to dragon, his subconscious recognition of his goddess within her?

She stumbled up the stairs along the edge of the cliff and let her anger sweep her around the ruins of the factory. The brick gothic building perched there like a mausoleum. The spiderweb windows watched her. The screen door laughed. Grabbing her bike off the fence, she rode past the Drekar guard and headed south. White-tipped waves chopped up Lake Union. Trees full of crows cackled at her as she rode over the foot of Queen Anne. The Needle Market slowed her down.

Move it! she thought furiously, but if she had any god-powers inside her, they didn't work on living creatures. The crowds did not magically part in a red sea of fury.

Of course they didn't. She did not have the Heart of Tiamat inside her. She was not possessed!

Once amid the steel bones of downtown, the wreckage of civilization slapped her in the face again. There were no gods. No compassionate ones, at any rate. She could well believe in primordial chaos, for it looked like someone had tried to drag civilization back there. Forces of destruction, pain, vengeance. These were alive and well in the world. She passed the brothel and the secluded opium dens in the haunted alleys of Pioneer Square. People would try anything to pull the wool over their eyes. She had never run from the truth. Her mind was her own.

She turned the corner and ran into a pack of aptrgangr. How easy it was. Wherever she went, there they were. She wanted a fight, they came to dance. It never occurred to her that others might not find it the same. Did she call them to her? Did she somehow draw them near with this magic woo-woo, the zombie queen gathering her army?

If she wasn't the Reaper, her whole identity was lost. Grace Mercer, pied piper of the dead.

She jumped off her bike. It fell against a nearby grate with a clang. The aptrgangr didn't jump. They circled with their too-blue skin and their too-white eyes and their grave-dirt nails just waiting to claw her veins out of her skin. Too many. Where did they all come from? Had she really called them here with her need for a fight?.

"I'm not your mommy," she said. She raised her bone knife and slipped an iron needle free from her brace. "But you'll do what I say, because I'm a badass motherfucker."

The aptrgangr approached.

She waded in. The iron burned in her fist until she plowed it into a body. The bone knife cut through the crowd like a scythe. She didn't think. Kick. Swipe. Stab. Rinse. Repeat. Moving until her muscles burned and her back pressed up against the cold brick wall and still they came. So many. More than she'd ever faced before. Stupid. Suicidal.

Unless she really did have Tiamat's Heart inside her.

Maybe her subconscious was trying to tell her in the only way she would understand. Here, back against the wall, unbeatable odds, she was faced with a choice: find her inner goddess or die trying.

Her mother would be ashamed of her. *Think*, she would say. *Use your head. What a waste.* And she'd cluck her tongue.

You Kim women are too stubborn to give up, her father would say. *Tiger women.*

Grace let the bone knife fall from her fingers and clatter to the ground. She was dimly aware of bruising and bleeding and pain leeching through her poor body. She closed her eyes as the undead swayed toward her. She took a deep breath, calmed her mind, and listened. An aptrgangr wrapped its arms around her chest. Her breath whooshed out of her lungs as the monster squeezed. In that moment, she looked inward beneath the skin and muscle and bone to the metaphysical plane, where she found the mechanical bulwark caging her heart. The iron plates were riveted shut against pain and sorrow. She was impenetrable. A fortress against the dark. Nothing went in. . . . Nothing got out.

Her head started to spin from lack of air as the aptrgangr tightened its hold around her ribs. Quickly, she threw her will into popping the rivets and throwing open the iron plates. A burst of divine blue fire shot out, searing along her nerve endings to the tips of her toes and fingers, and in its wake burned rage. The aptrgangr who crushed her chest burned immediately to ash.

Power, ye gods, the power. She could evaporate oceans with it. Crumble mountains. Seize empires. Slay gods.

Vengeance, the Heart screamed in her mind. The malevolent presence was something wholly foreign to Grace's being, yet sickeningly familiar. She could feel its call for retribution like it was her own. That pulsing drive that had carried her through five years in Norgard's service, that had given her a reason to live and fight, that had driven her on when all hope seemed lost, crystal clear as a pealing church bell, here it lay. A thousand times stronger. How long had Tiamat's Heart been trapped inside her? How long had she relied on Tiamat's hate to propel her forward? Were any of her emotions her own?

Pain poured through her as fire roared out. She couldn't hold it. With Tiamat's eyes, she saw the world in a different light. Narrowed blues and greens, like a dragon. The aptrgangr horde swayed back from the force. In her eyes, they sparkled with the Aether of their wraith souls.

"Get back!" Grace screamed, and to her amazement, they did. And still the fire raged. Ye gods, it hurt every poor mortal cell in her poor mortal body. Tears leaked out of her eyes. She couldn't contain it. Couldn't stop it. Her body was a beacon for an otherworldly flame that threatened to turn her to charcoal.

She could feel the Heart trying to take over her mind. Slippery as an eel, it sent shadowy tentacles across her body. The images of a hundred aptrgangr she'd fought flashed through her head. All this time they were called not by her skill with the knife, but by her unholy possession. Tiamat inside her. The zombie queen.

Never. No wraith is going to take me over while I still live.

Her revulsion gave her an edge. With her last remaining strength, she reached out to the runes inked across her skin and pulled the Aether through them. Tiamat's Heart shrieked in one last blast of blue flame, and the surrounding aptrgangr disintegrated in a cloud of black ash. The burst of power—bright light against Tiamat's dark presence—gave Grace just enough juice to slam shut her iron defenses again.

And then it was gone, and she was done. And somehow, miraculously, she was still alive. She shook so hard her teeth rattled in her head. Her knees gave way, and she slumped down the wall to hit the dirty ground. Her bones chattered. Her vision was blurred, but it had returned to her normal, human color palate. Grey, charred brick. The grey of the cloud-strewn Seattle sky. Grey and grey and grey.

And suddenly green.

Vibrant green eyes peered into her own with an intensity that anchored her. Blond locks above and a crimson coat below, but those eyes were all she needed. Leif. His hands rubbed her arms. He crooned something. She couldn't hear for the roaring in her ears. She couldn't talk; her throat had been burned raw.

Slowly, so slowly, feeling came back, hearing came back. She clung to those green eyes as the world shifted around her—a new world she didn't understand. Truths she didn't want to know, but not knowing didn't make them any less true.

"It's okay. You're okay," he crooned. "Let's get out of this rain."

She hadn't noticed the water falling from the sky. Her hair dripped into her eyes. She still wore his linen shirt, now torn and bloodstained, and it clung to her chest as he lifted her. The torchlight of the nearby shop cast his face in sharp relief. He seemed otherworldly and a little fierce. If there were still aptrgangr in the area after Tiamat's blue fire, they wouldn't stand a chance against him.

She hated him seeing her vulnerable, shocked to her core. It was easier to be weak when she was pouring blood out a head wound. But this injury was inside her. She would give anything to get it out. Leif said nothing as he carried her through the empty, waterlogged streets. Letting herself rest against his chest, she listened to his heart's steady beat. One heart, one pulse. He hummed a deep, soothing melody that she didn't recognize.

She'd survived the fire of the gods. The goddess of all wraiths curled around her heart like a shadowy leech, but it had failed to take over Grace's mind. She'd won, but at what price? How long had she been ignorant to the monster inside her? She felt soul-stained. It was worse than any beating she'd ever encountered. Worse even than that terrible night when she'd fought Norgard's strongest mercenary and pledged her soul to Norgard's use.

Fuck Norgard. Had he known then what lived inside her? Had all these runes he'd inked across her skin been nothing more than an elaborate magic trap? Not to keep the wraiths out, as she'd thought, but to keep the chaotic force of Tiamat's Heart *in*.

Why hadn't she ever noticed her irregularity? Shouldn't she have known if she was possessed?

Possessed.

And there was Thor's Hammer right in front of her with its blue Dutch door and its wards carved in the frame that kept out the dead and damned.

"I can't go in there!" Panic and bile rose in her throat. She was barred from her home. What if even the cat hissed at her now? She couldn't bear it. "Let me go!" She struggled against Leif's hold, and he set her down gently on the broken sidewalk. She stumbled to the gutter and dry-heaved. "Get it out! Get this thing out of me! I'm not possessed. I'm not—"

She reached for her knife, and Leif caught her up. "None of that."

"Get it out." The plea slipped out of her bloodless lips. More like a sob than a proper sentence. She rubbed her mouth with the back of her sleeve. She felt dirty. Bruised and bloody and ash-covered she could live with. But this was a thousand times worse than Norgard's soul-sucking. She was *possessed*. There was a demonic entity inside her. Controlling her. She hadn't thought her situation could get any worse, but she was wrong.

"You have survived this long with the Heart in you. A little longer won't hurt. You are stronger than you know." Leif helped her stand and hobble to the door of Thor's Hammer. "You have not changed. Those wards are yours They didn't keep you out before, and they won't now. They are keyed to you—"

"And the Heart."

"Yes." He unlocked the front door with a skeleton key and guided her through.

Bear met them. He sat and watched her with those big soulful eyes. Grace's lower lip trembled. She reached for him, and he bolted out the front door. She burst into tears.

"Calm down," Leif said. "It will be okay."

She turned on him and drew her knife.

Chapter 20

Leif stared at Grace. Even angry and frightened, she was breathtaking. Eyes shooting sparks, passion in their depths. Strong and determined not to give an inch, but the knife in her hand shook the slightest bit. He wanted her soft and pliable, breathy and waiting under him. Wanted to dominate her, because a spirit so vibrant and strong couldn't be chained. The challenge of it called to his ancient, hungry bones.

"Don't tell me what to do," she spat. "Don't patronize me. Don't—"

"Shh," he said.

"Don't tell me to shush!" Her cheeks stained red. Her small chest drew shaky breath after shaky breath. "You have no idea what it's like to have a soul inside you."

His lips twisted in a wry smile. "No. But that is another issue entirely."

The knife dropped from her hand. "There is no proof the Heart is inside me." He could see the lie in her eyes. A battle for the truth warred inside her small, tough body. She fumbled with the pocket of her pants and pulled out the Deadglass on a long brass chain. Hands shaking, she pushed it toward him. "Take it. Just . . . look at me, damn it. Tell me what you see."

"I've already looked at you through the glass once—"

"Look again," she snapped. "Please."

Accepting the Deadglass from her cold fingers, he put it to his eye and adjusted the gears. "I see a beautiful woman. Your soul sparkles with a thousand tiny stars. The runes on your skin glow white as the Aether flows through them, creating a web around your body that the Deadglass can't penetrate." He lowered the glass. "I'm sorry. There is no giant flag waving the Heart's location in your chest. If there were, my brother would have noted it long before now. He never tried to tap into Tiamat's powers. He risked your life sending you out to do battle with his adversaries. All signs indicate that he never realized the true nature of your curse." Leif couldn't take the distance between them anymore. Grace stood stiff as marble. He put his hands on her shoulders and rubbed the shocked, frozen muscles. She couldn't withstand her inner battle and him at the same time. He circled around her—kneading, petting, gentling her like a hissing cat—and felt pleased when she let him. Her body trusted him, even if her mind fought him off.

It wasn't him she raged at. Let her use him as an easy target. She needed someone to pin this on, and he didn't mind if it was him, as long as he was useful. As long as he could be helpful to her. He had so much to make up for.

"Norgard wore the Deadglass monocle," she whispered. "He should have seen it."

"He saw something dark inside you, because you said he drew the first rune. But your natural shields must have trapped the Heart first. You beat her all on your own."

He pressed her back to his front and held her hands in each of his, not enclosing like a jail, but pressed together like a wall she could lean against. He let her work her way around the matter. There was no other way. Sometimes he got like this when there was a particularly difficult problem that needed an elegant solution, too elegant, too terrifying to come at straight on. He needed to sidle around to it, let the answer slowly dawn on him like a warm sunrise. The truth was light. Even a fire, terrifying and dangerous, could be a weapon or a cure in the right hands.

"I'm not stronger than a goddess," Grace whispered.

"You're a survivor, Grace. Nothing has changed about you. Every bit of knowledge gives you power, not Tiamat." Leif held her shaking and folded her into his embrace. Like a flower that bloomed in the ashen, cracked ground, she would adapt. She would grow. Still, he wished he could take this terrible burden from her. He hummed deep in this throat.

"You're doing it again," she said.

"Am I?"

"Hmmm. I wouldn't feel like this without your dragon drugs."

"Of course not." He waited a beat. "How do you feel?"

"Like my knees are jelly."

He held all her weight against him and pressed his nose into her silky hair. She smelled of smoke and herbal shampoo. "You are a rock."

"Jelly all the way up to my fingertips," Grace said. "Jelly and quivering and . . . what are you doing?"

He nibbled behind her delicate shell of an ear. "Hmm? This?"

"It tickles. I don't need you to hold me up."

"Nope, you don't." He still held her, and she let him. He worked around to her side and slid his arm down to swipe her legs out from under her. Gently, gently. Picked her up with a little "oof!" and kept her distracted the whole time. His lips brushed her cheeks and kissed the corners of her lovely wide eyes. He worked his lips over her eyebrows and around to the other ear, skipping down to her chin, feathering kisses along her swanlike neck. He could feel her succumbing. Could feel her leave the battle of her soul and slide into that heated place where touch and taste were the only truths.

"I'm going to regret this," she said.

"Say no then. It is in your power. Regret is such a wasted emotion."

"No."

Leif stopped moving with her and stood still, only holding her to him, letting her body warm the frozen draft through his empty shell. His muscles tensed with the need for release. His cock throbbed. He ignored it. It was enough to hold her to him. Enough to touch her without her flinching away. She accepted his embrace, and he sensed no fear.

He could also smell her wet heat, her growing frustration. He grinned into her hair. Grace wiggled in his arms, trying to move closer.

Still Leif waited. "I'll outlast you in this," he said, his voice gravelly. "I might go mad with wanting you, but I will wait. Patiently, feverishly, letting the anticipation build. When I have you I will have all of you. Not just your body or soul. I want your mind, your spirit, your passion. Your very breath. I want your heart, Grace. It will be all or nothing. I can't accept anything less."

She let out a frustrated breath and pushed at his chest. He set her down.

"My heart? You bastard!" She shoved him, and the force of her anger took him back a step. Her touch packed a jolt of power. Some of her hold on Tiamat's Heart must have loosened. "Whose heart do you want? Mine? Tiamat's? Do you just want to own me to use this thing inside me? There is a fucking dead god inside me, controlling me. You can't have my body or my whatever. There is nothing left of me. Gods." She wrapped her arms around herself.

"Grace. Do you hear yourself? No one has ever been able to control you. Point out one time—"

"Fuck you. You've done it. You forced me to talk at the hearing. You ordered me to stop fighting—"

"By the blood magic of that bond, yes. I'm sorry. I didn't mean to. But the underlying contract in that magic is your will. Yours. Not mine, not Sven's, not Tiamat's. You handed your will over to the ring's use."

"Don't remind me!"

"No, listen. You're so bloody strong, you trapped a Babylonian goddess. Do you think my brother's little ring could keep you trapped if you really put your mind to breaking it?"

Her face blanched.

"Don't misunderstand me. I'm not saying you could have freed yourself at any point in the past. You've come a long way from that shattered young girl. My brother—" He took a deep breath, hating Sven all the more. "My brother used sex and runes to keep you bound and emotionally ensnared, because it was the only way he could control you. He must never have realized the true nature of what is inside you, but he recognized your potential for power. He bound you and waited for you to come into your own. You are the strongest woman I've ever met."

She stared furiously at the floor. A deep gash in her arm slowly leaked blood. He ached to hold her, but she needed to know she could stand on her own two feet. She needed to believe in herself. If she saw the gorgeous, powerful woman that he saw, she could seize her own destiny. It was the only way to save her.

"Every woman has a goddess inside her. You just need to believe in the power of your own awesomeness." He caught her as she sagged to the ground. "Grace, Grace."

Tears trickled down her cheeks. She was too upset to wipe them away. "Oh, so now the mad scientist thinks he understands magic? You don't know anything."

"Of course not. But I understand there is more to the world than I see with my own eyes."

"I can't—"

He kissed her, stopping that protestation at her lips. Warmth flooded him. She might be strong, but he was weak. Weak for her kisses. Needy of her touch. Addicted to her energy and presence. To her prickly, pugnacious, generous, giving spirit. He could feel the struggle in her own mind for a beat before she succumbed to his invasion. She needed this comfort as much as he did.

You don't have to be a one-woman army. Let me hold you. Let me help you. Asking for help does not make you weak, he thought at her, trying to tell her with his tongue and lips all that he couldn't speak.

He sank down with her onto the threadbare couch. The springs complained beneath his weight, but held. Smoothing his hands over her tight shoulders and back, he soothed her. Slow circles across her lower back. Long caresses up her spine. He felt her give way like a trestle bridge in a windstorm. First the bridge swayed, then buckled; then the ropes began to snap, one by one, until the whole thing plunged into the deep blue water of the maelstrom below. He tunneled his hands beneath her shirt. He was greedy. He wanted skin-to-skin contact. Running his tongue along the sensitive inner edge of her lower lip, he distracted her while he removed her shirt and pants.

Her moan escaped, and he knew he had her. She ripped his shirt down the front, popping the buttons and scattering them to the hideous couch cushions. Her tongue wrestled with his. A fight. A dance. A duel for supremacy. In this he wouldn't yield. He would conquer her reserves until he unleashed every bit of her passion. Until he freed every inch of the beautiful goddess he saw within her. Not Tiamat. Grace. She might not believe his words, but he would show her with his body how amazing he found her.

He rolled her to her back. "You're injured. Let me heal you."

Wrapping her arm around his neck, she dragged him back down, sucked his tongue into her mouth, and bit him.

The shock was followed by arousal. Christ, how she tied him in knots. He groaned. His cock turned to iron, pain and pleasure melded into one, and he ground it between her thighs. He wanted to take her from every angle until the last black memory was burned from her subconscious.

But he forced himself to take it slow; he had this one shot to break down years of Sven's conditioning. He needed to tear away every chain of self-doubt and sweep away the cobwebs of her soul. She could do the rest. She just had to believe.

He kissed a path down the runes on her chest. He swirled his tongue out and over them. Finding Algiz, he traced its shape. "This one focuses your will?"

"That's the idea—"

"Good. Focus your will on this. Feel the power of the rune as I touch you. There is magic in sex."

"Sex magic? Coming over to the dark side, Mr. Scientist?"

"When the experiment calls for it." Algiz curled across her breasts. He followed the path and kissed each one. "Sex can be used to control another person, but it can also be used to heal. And modern scientific studies have shown that it is impossible to feel fear and anxiety at the moment of orgasm. I want you to let go. Let us conduct our own study, shall we?"

Turning her to her stomach uncovered the trail of runes along her rib cage and to her spine. Her hands curled at her sides, so he took them and placed them on the armrest of the couch. "Hold on."

"Why?"

"Concentrate on how you feel as I touch you." *And not on the anger, betrayal, and shame that kept you prisoner.* At her lower back, Algiz danced with another rune. Over the last bone of her spine—the apex of her power—he kneaded the muscles. He kissed each dimple in her lower back, then slid his hands over the curve of her ass. The skin here was pale as the stars. Coaxing apart her thighs, he slipped his fingers between her silky folds.

"What are you—?"

"Concentrate!" he ordered, and the invisible tether snapped like a whip. If she needed her anger to take back her will, he knew exactly how to piss her off. Tilting her pelvis up off the couch, he replaced his fingers with his tongue. Ishtar be praised. Her taste sent flares through him. Cinnamon and iron scented the room as his arousal grew. He traced the lips of her femininity to the tight nest of nerves at the crux.

Moaning, she writhed beneath him, her body tightened like a winch. He cranked her higher until the wave broke through her with a long scream. Without giving her time to come down, he pulled himself up and slid into her. A second orgasm shook her on the heels of the first. Her knuckles were white where they gripped the couch.

"Leif," she breathed.

His name on her lips threw him over. The world narrowed to green and blue. Stars danced across his vision, and he touched heaven.

Grace thought her world had exploded in a blaze of flashing lights. Quakes rocked her body from her core outward to her fingertips and toes. She was pinioned; Leif, huge and hard, speared through her center. The rough fabric of the couch abraded her nipples. Two hundred pounds of hot muscle pushed her down, like a butterfly in a scientist's observation glass.

She couldn't imagine moving, but Leif pulled out and turned her over.

"Good thing about dragon's blood," he said conversationally as if sweat didn't drip from his brow and his chest didn't heave, "it heals a man up right quick." His wicked grin flashed, and in that moment she saw the mad under the scientist facade. He wasn't as staid as he pretended. Now that he'd turned his attention to dissecting her from the inside out, there was a crazed gleam in his eye.

Good Freya, he excited her. She should be afraid as he peeled away her defenses like the thin membrane beneath the eggshell, but all she could think as she looked up into his slit dragon eyes was, *Yes, again, more, please.*

He brought a finger to tap his jaw. "You know what? I'm not sure you've found your focus yet."

"You might need to repeat the experiment, Doctor."

"Right you are. See if we draw the same conclusion."

"I'll just lie here and let you get back to work, okay?"

His grin sprang back. It was fucking unfair that a man could be so beautiful, and inside he was loyal, kind, and smart as a whip. There was nothing keeping her from falling headfirst in love with him, and that scared the shit out of her.

"I see you thinking," he said. "You're tensing up. You're supposed to be concentrating. Work with me here, Grace. Algiz is tattooed all over your body. One hundred and three times, to be exact—"

"You counted?"

"I want you to feel every single one of them as I fuck you. And as you find that transcendental place beyond all fear and self-doubt, beyond all the conditioning of my damned brother, you will find your moment of power. Use it. Trust me."

"I trust you."

His smile was radiant. "I've never heard three sweeter words."

She scowled. She'd take them back, but the words had slipped out too quickly. He could smell a lie. "So you'll turn my body to a pile of molten nerves, and then the bond will magically snap, is that it?"

"No." He kissed her, and she sank deeper into the cushions of the couch. Gods, she made it too easy for him. "Trust your body to me, take whatever power you can from me, and then you'll be free to seize the slave bond and break it yourself. There is magic when two people come together. You lose a little piece of your soul every time, but it's an exchange. In that moment of vulnerability there lies the power of the universe. Use it. Fry the blasted ring. Concentrate your will through the Algiz runes. Use the Aether. Use me. Damn it, use the Heart if you have to—"

Fear washed through her. She tried to sit up, but his large hands pushed her back into the couch. "You're crazy—"

"No. These other symbols? They're helping you hold her, but you don't need them. Not really. Not if your indomitable will trapped her in there when you were nothing but a scared sixteen-year-old with not a mark on you. I believe in you."

Leif climbed off the couch. He swung her legs to the edge and knelt between her spread thighs. They were face-to-face. His hands burned on her skin. The cool air made her nipples peak. He believed she was strong enough to tap into Tiamat and keep her from taking over. Swallowing, she put her hands on his shoulders to ground their connection. She wanted to know that she wasn't alone. This was worse than facing a pack of aptrgangr. She had to face down the zombie queen herself and let the goddess's power fill her soul.

Grace took a deep breath and felt out the invisible tether. It sparked. She found the iron box and grabbed hold of the rivets with her mind. "I'm ready."

Determination was etched in the grim line of Leif's

mouth. He took a firm grip on her hips and slowly, so slowly, began the long glide into her. Every millimeter sparked a thousand nerve endings. Ripples ran along her flesh. Her inner muscles clenched around empty air, waiting, waiting, for that hot shaft to pierce her through. She wanted to impale herself on it, but his hands kept her still.

"There is power in giving up all control," he ground out. The tendons stood out on his neck. "I will wring every conscious thought from your body." He slid in another inch.

"Is"—she inhaled sharply at the sensation of his cock inside her—"that a threat?"

"It's a promise."

Her fingernails dug into his skin. Desperate need consumed her, stoking the deep ache in her womb. Painful, this absence, this need to be filled. Her inner walls gave in another slow millimeter to his intrusion. How could she be so tight, so needy, when they'd just done this not five minutes ago? But it was like the first time and a hundred times more sensitive than the last time. He kneaded her ass and slid in farther. Her eyes crossed in her head.

"Concentrate," he ordered. The whip of the slave bond brought her back to consciousness. His voice was the scrape of claws on rock. His eyes glowed. His ripped body—so strong, so beautiful—trembled like a feather.

She did this to him. She, Grace. She held the power to bring the Drekar Regent to his knees. She held the power inside her to slay aptrgangr and banish wraiths. Who cared what had been done to her or what evil power fueled her strength? She had been beaten and she'd gotten back up. She had been broken and she'd put herself back together. She had not let the evil inside her tarnish her soul. The strength to fight, to win, had been inside her all along.

Through the maelstrom of sensation racking her body, she pulled her mind inward to the iron box protecting her heart. Her body sparked with sexual energy. She drew on that power and released the first rivet.

A blast of blue flame shot out from the box. It was like an atom bomb going off inside her: her spine snapped straight and her hair stood on end. Energy burned along every nerve out through the tips of her fingers. A silent scream ripped from her throat, and in a flash, panic. The Heart would escape; she wasn't strong enough.

But Leif sensed her inner battle and drove himself home. "Grace!" he breathed. "Sweet, Grace."

The shock to her core broke the Heart's hold on her. The iron lid slammed back into place, and she drove the rivets in to lock it. Sweat dripped from her hairline. Her limbs shook. "I can't do it," she sobbed. "It's too powerful."

"You can. You are stronger than you know."

Grace took a deep breath of his calming scent. Leaning forward, she kissed him, drawing in his strength. He was solid and steady, wading into the battle with her.

"You aren't alone. Lean on me," he begged. "Let me bring you higher."

With her hips she urged him into a faster rhythm. She concentrated on the feel of him inside her, stoking her. Of the smooth slide of his cock. Of the shivers of need he sent rippling through her body.

She rallied in her mind and seized on that sexual energy zinging through her. With each thrust, she felt her body string higher. The Heart was no match for her. She would fry it with the immense power rippling up from her womb.

This time she pulled out the rivets with the full force of her will behind her. The Heart's blue flame shot out. Instead of fighting that terrible power, she rode it like a leaf on Niagara Falls. The Heart threatened to consume her, but she focused on her mind, on her own heart, on her inner muscles clenching around Leif's penetration.

The slave bond was a weak glow next to the Heart. Sh

seized it. "I take my will back!" she shouted. "Hear me now. You will do as I command." The invisible tether writhed in her hold, but she forced it through the blue flame of Tiamat's Heart. She belonged to herself. She took her will back. The slave bond was no match for the Heart. It caught fire and broke. Flame singed down its length, straight back to the ring on Leif's hand. Leif inhaled in pain as the malachite cracked and the smoking ring fell to the carpet. His finger was burnt black.

The Heart's anger shot out, and Grace tapped into it.

Pure unadulterated power. Hotter than the hottest fire, it burned out of her, a beacon of energy and malevolence. Ye gods, what power! It filled her mind with seductive images she could have if she handed over control. It found her deepest fears hidden in that iron box and projected them in Technicolor across the backs of her eyelids: Her parents' deaths. The aptrgangr who'd killed them in that dark alley. The memory loss and fear she'd felt as she woke up covered in blood. The survivor's guilt.

She saw it again from the Heart's point of view. It had slipped into her like it had done billions of times to billions of people before her. It drew the aptrgangr to it. She saw her parents throw themselves in front of her and tell her to run. She ran, blinded by the fire of the Heart, stumbling down the dark alley. A glance behind showed her parents' last stand, and the shock of their violent deaths slammed up her natural shields as her mind tried to protect her from that terrible pain. The Heart had been trapped. It was enraged.

The Heart flipped the visions forward in time to Norgard. It played every humiliating detail, dredged up every shameful secret from that chapter of her life. Hate filled her chest. May hellfire damn him.

You were cheated of your vengeance, the Heart hissed inside her mind. *You were denied your right to flay the scaled skin from his bones and raise his severed head on a pike.* The Heart showed an image of her as Saint George with Norgard's dragon skin hanging from her lance.

Together, the Heart crooned, *we can retrieve him from the Gate and slice him and cut him and—*

"No!" she shouted. She wrapped her arms around Leif to ground her to reality. The image was tempting. The Heart knew how to lure her in, but she would never give up her will to another again. Besides, the image of her as Saint George was just ridiculous enough to bring her back to reason.

Join me, the Heart tried again. It sent images of her stomping over everyone who had ever wronged her. But every image splashed another coat of hatred across her gut, and she felt sick. This cold, enraged presence wasn't her. There was more to her than hate and revenge.

Grace dug her fingers into Leif's shoulders and locked eyes with him. The Heart warped her vision: it slowly stripped away his flesh to reveal the dragon within. It tried to fuel her hatred, but it was wrong. Leif in dragon form didn't scare her anymore. He was a rock through and through. He was *her* rock. She kissed him on his beautiful red and green snout. She felt his lips beneath hers and seized on the truth to strip away the false vision the Heart was feeding her.

"Fuck me," Grace ordered.

Leif pressed her down into the creaky springs and drove her higher. She fed on those electric strokes, riding the power generated by their bodies to free herself from the Heart's hold. She angled her hips to take him deeper, and held on as a wave of power and wet, hot lust rose inside her. Every inch of skin was slick with sweat. Her pulse raced in her wrists against his back, in her throat, in her womb where he stoked her until the wave crested and broke.

Her mind blanked. Past all anxiety. Past all fear. She rode on a river of liquid light. No pain. No heartbreak. No chains for the Heart to grab hold of and trick her mind. She existed in light and breath and peace. Her iron shields slammed back down and trapped the Heart. It no longer spoke in her mind. It was powerless to tempt her or take control. Still, she reinforced every crack in her shields. The Heart would not be her master.

The manacles melted from her upper arms and slid off her skin like liquid gold. They fell to the floor and solidified once more. She touched her bare arms in wonder. She was free.

In the next instant the windows of her apartment shattered, sending glass shards into the room. Outside the black sky pounded on the old brick and tore the limbs from trees. A malevolent wind struck at the apartment. It would have swept through the broken windows, but the wards held. Light flickered. The building shook.

"What the hell?" she asked.

Leif took the Deadglass from his pocket and fitted it to his eye. He adjusted the gears and swore. "Kingu has arrived."

Chapter 21

Using his body as a shield, Leif protected Grace from the
flying glass. In the Deadglass, he watched Kingu swirl out
side the window and batter the empty window frames as he
tried to force past Grace's wards. The demigod appeared as
a monstrous three-headed dragon in the glass. He twisted in
the air, a creature more suited to sea than land, and hi
wraith claws had no trouble stripping the paint from the
building. He was more powerful than any wraith had a right
to be, even without a body to possess. If Kingu managed to
get the Tablet of Destiny and the Heart, he could craft him
self a new body and seize all of Tiamat's god-powers. There
would be no stopping him.

"You still have the Tablet, right, Grace?"

"Yeah, why?"

"Because you've got what he wants, and I'm not going to
let him have you. We have to run." He scooped her up. Sh
wrapped her arms around his neck. "Is there a back en
trance?"

"Yes. That door leads straight into the building behind
it. It's an apartment building."

Grabbing her backpack, he ran for the door and slamme

it open with his shoulder. The window frames shattered behind them. The racing of his heart was a steam whistle in his chest. He carried Grace into the adjacent building and found the stairwell. *Please let the building be empty.* He didn't want to lead Kingu directly to civilians, but he had to risk it. If Kingu got to Grace, millions of innocents would die.

Thankfully the building seemed abandoned. Running up the stairs to the second floor, he broke into an apartment that faced the street behind Flesh Alley. "I'm going to fly us out of here," he told Grace.

"We have to tell Corbette," Grace said. "And the humans."

"Yes."

"He'll want to kill me."

"Corbette will have to get through me first."

Her eyes were still silver. He hoped that didn't mean the Heart was awake. He couldn't feel her through the invisible tether anymore. He hadn't realized how much he had come to rely on that bond. It was like a part of him had been sliced cleanly through, and the wound wouldn't regenerate. It bled freely, a hurt he hadn't known he had. A vulnerability that his dragon blood couldn't protect. He was glad for Grace that she was free, but damn it, he wanted to feel her again. He touched her with his fingertips just to reassure himself that she was okay.

"If they kill me," she said, seeming not to have heard his vow, "I don't think that would stop the Heart. It would just free it to roam again. Kingu could capture it easy."

"Yes. But he knows you have it."

"There is nowhere I could run or hide—"

"We'll figure it out. Together." He forced her to meet his eyes. "Don't you get any desperado ideas. You aren't going to be all noble and try to draw Kingu away." *Don't leave me.* "We're in this together."

She set her jaw.

"Say, 'Yes, Regent.'"

"Yes, Regent," she parroted. He couldn't force her to do what he wanted ever again; she had to trust him.

Calling the Aether to him, he Turned just as the brick walls started to shake. His wings squished awkwardly in the small space. With a quick apology to the former inhabitants, he used his massive tail to knock out part of the wall, picked Grace up in his claws, and lifted into the black sky.

"Hurry!" she shouted, but he didn't need her warning. His honed dragon vision picked up a score of blue-tinged aptrgangr on the street below. He faced into the angry wind and flew north.

Ishtar have mercy on us, he thought. Perhaps the goddess of love would pity his lost heart. He struggled to feel Grace in his claws. He wanted to sense her feelings, like he had through that dratted ring. Ishtar seemed a sucker for tragic love stories, but this one wouldn't be star-crossed. He would keep Grace safe and protect his people. He had inherited Sven's crown for a reason, and he intended to put it to good use.

The malevolent wind pursued him north, and he led Kingu straight to Queen Anne Hill. The Kivati guards at the gates saw him coming and began to Change. *Sorry, Corbette*, he thought as he slipped past the startled guards and dove low over Kivati Hall. A black cloud of crows rose, screeching, from the surrounding trees. Leif shook them off. Before the Changed warriors—mostly Crow and a Thunderbird—could attack, Kingu was on them. They turned away from Leif to battle the new threat. The clap of thunder reverberated in the air behind him. He glanced back once to see the thunderbolt sear blue through Kingu's wraith form. The demigod and his wind shrieked and fell back.

Grace was right: Thunderbolts were effective weapons against Kingu. Now they just needed Corbette to join their cause. Leif hightailed it past the Kivati's hill and over the

Ship Canal to the Ballard bluff. Rain streaked the sky. Crows followed him over the canal and thunder rumbled far behind.

But his luck ran out at the Drekar Lair. The chocolate factory was smashed. The remaining ceiling of the Great Hall had collapsed, taking part of the land above his lab with it. Admiral Jameson's battle wagons were parked nearby, and he could see soldiers winching something large out of the hole.

Leif landed on the lawn, deposited Grace softly on the ground, and Turned.

"You led Kingu right to the Kivati," Grace said.

"I know. I should feel worse, but I don't. They abandoned my coal shipment and my woman on the field at Seward Park. Payback, Zetian would say, is a bitch."

"Look at you, heartless ruler," Grace teased. It was good to see her with color back in her cheeks. If she was making sarcastic quips, she must be feeling better.

"I've learned. There's fair play, and then there's protecting what's mine. I will use any means necessary to keep you safe."

She looked away. Retrieving her backpack, she dug out a change of clothes and put them on. "Looks like Kingu was here before he hit up Thor's Hammer."

"Did the Heart wake briefly when we made love?"

"I don't know. I was . . . distracted. I'm sorry about your lab. What's Admiral Jameson doing?"

"He appears to be picking up the suits early. He better have a good reason." Leif spotted Thorsson and his two guards coming toward him. "Casualties?"

"Ja. Two in the cave-in," Thorsson said. "Humans."

Leif ran a hand over his face. It was a relief so few had lived in the lair since the Unraveling. Only his lab, storerooms, a kitchen, and a few living rooms were occupied. Thorsson handed him a bag with a change of clothes, and he dressed. "And the admiral?"

"Arrived on Kingu's tail." Thorsson hefted his sword. "Your orders?"

"Let's see what they want."

Leif descended into the rubble of his lab and found everything trashed. His equipment was ruined. The boilers he'd so painstakingly crafted were dented like cars at a junkyard. The beakers were a garden of glass pricking up from the rocky ground. A crack ran along his worktable and cut it right in two. He had made love to Grace on that table. It hadn't survived the force of Kingu's wrath. But the suits had, which meant they worked even when not powered up and inhabited by a conscious soul. At least the runes held them together, the same runes that ran along Grace's skin and kept the Heart trapped. He hoped they would also work to keep Kingu out.

In the middle of the trashed room, Jameson supervised his soldiers taking the finished suits of armor out through the hole in the roof. He stood still as a brass statue, hands on his hips and an eager look in his eye.

"What is the meaning of this?" Leif demanded.

The human soldiers stopped winching and pulled out their guns. Slowly, Jameson turned on his booted heel. Confusion hazed his eyes for a moment, then cleared. "Regent."

"What are you doing here? This is a violation of our treaties." Leif damned himself for not paying closer attention to those treaties when Zetian was drawing them up. He shouldn't have been so laissez-faire about ruling. People were depending on him. Grace was depending on him.

Jameson didn't blink at Leif's anger. "I came to collect my armor."

"How did you know I'd finished?"

"There aren't enough suits for all my men. I'm disappointed in you, Regent."

"I used all the resources I could—"

"You don't really want humans to be protected, do you? I'll be watching you."

Grace stepped forward. "You idiot. Kingu is here. He's leading a zombie army through the city. There isn't time for this. You need to marshal your troops and order your people to the barracks."

Jameson ran his eyes down Grace's body. His lips pulled out in a flat smile. "And you are?"

"This is General Mercer," Leif said.

"What happened to Thorsson?"

"He reports to her."

In an abrupt shift, Jameson strolled off. Strange. He paused beneath the last suit of armor that was being winched through the hole in the ceiling and stared up at it. "Keep moving! Regent, when were you going to deliver these contraptions? How can I know they work?"

A wisp of smoke drifted from Leif's nostril. "They work. They will work best if you put strong men in them. Not physically. Emotionally."

"But if they need to be emotionally strong, what's the point of the armor?"

Leif ran his hands through his hair. "The suits work." His voice rang in the cavernous room. "And we will need them to defeat the demigod. They can shoot fire and nets, both which Marduk had to hunt Kingu. Humans, Kivati, and Drekar must work together. If we don't, if we let our prejudices and past hatred keep us at each other's throats, Kingu wins."

"No one wants that," Jameson said. The feet of the last suit disappeared through the roof. The lab felt deserted without it. His last great experiment sent out into the world. All that was left was ruin.

It surprised him that he didn't feel more sorrow. He had Grace. Every experiment he'd ever created could go to bloody hell.

Jameson ordered his soldiers to go.

"What about this mess?" Grace asked.

"Not my problem," Jameson said. "We found it like this. You should really keep better care of your things."

Grace scowled.

"So where is this demon now," Jameson asked, "and what is he after? Where is he going? I need details, man. My troops will be at the front of the line to battle the supernatural forces that threaten humans. You have my word. But we can't act on rumor. I need a report. What is your battle plan?"

In the end Leif secured Jameson's promise: he would provide support to the fight against Kingu. Human soldiers and weapons were his for the battle. Leif had twenty-four hours to rally Marks, the Kivati, and the Drekar too. The future of the world depended on it.

Leif called the Althing, an assembly of all his subjects. All factions except the Kivati had come to his summons. Birgitta's heathwitches and the occult businesses from Grace's street mixed with ministers from the Church of the New Revelation and the Mark of Cain. Regular citizens and Maidens of Ishtar huddled beneath thick wool wraps. Drekar lurked at the edges with their human followers.

Leif sat in the jeweled throne in front of the damaged chocolate factory and watched the crowd. The iron crown fit at his brow like he'd grown an extra set of horns. A raging bonfire crackled in the center of the gathering. Behind him, the thin autumn sun sparkled off the snow-topped Olympic Mountains. In front of him stood the hardened survivors who now looked to him to lead them to victory. He hadn't wanted to leave Grace, but it wasn't safe to have her in the center of the crowd with the Heart and the Tablet of Destiny. She had to hide from Kingu. He trusted her to keep the Heart quiet. Kingu couldn't track it unless it woke. Grace's temper was a liability, but now that she knew her weaknesses, she could be on guard. His whole being ached with their separation. Without the bond, he didn't know where she was. He couldn't feel her. He couldn't track her. He wouldn't know if she were in danger until it was too late.

His protective instincts urged him to find her, now.

But his place was here.

Zetian struck an imposing figure in red silk next to the bonfire. She threw some powder into the hearth and blue flames shot up. The Althing had started.

Standing, he accepted the dramatics, the hush, and the reverence as his due. He told them the story of Tiamat and Apsu's lost love, of Kingu's war, and Marduk's victory. He told them of Kingu's escape during the Unraveling, and the new war against the gods Kingu would launch if he found Tiamat's Heart.

Lastly he told of their secret weapon: the Tablet of Destiny, which they would use to defeat Kingu a second time. He left out the details, because it might come down to quick thinking and luck. He appealed to their honor and their love for their homeland, and he laid out the battle to come.

The Althing, by law, was an open forum where anyone could ask anything without fear of retaliation from their ruler. One by one, men approached the bonfire to ask a question, and he answered each honestly.

If he was to lead these people to their deaths, he would do it with courage. He would be the ruler they needed him to be. They needed something to believe in. They needed a new Marduk to lead them against the gods. He could arm them with swords, he could shield them with armor, but they would still fail if he didn't give them hope.

Grace concentrated on her breathing. She focused on the rush of air through her nostrils. She was calm, cool, and collected. She was a quiet mountain lake. There was no reason to panic. There were no aptrgangr searching the street where she hid.

"Can't you do something, Grace?" Elsie whispered. Her eyes were like saucers.

"No. If I fight, the Heart wakes."

"But you can't . . . I can't—"

"You can. You, Cindy and Frannie are ready. Consider this your first test."

Cindy's freckles stood out against her paper-pale face. Her fingers clenched the iron railroad spike Grace had slipped into her hand. "I'm ready."

"Good." So much for not letting other people fight her battles for her. Grace clenched her teeth and let the three Maidens rise from their crouch. She gave them a tight smile. This might be the hardest thing she'd ever done. "I believe in you."

Longest fight in the history of fights, she was sure of it but they did her proud. She watched the fear give way to adrenaline and the self-doubt shed off like a second skin. She crawled out from behind the Dumpster just as Elsie disabled the last walking dead.

"We did it," Elsie said. An angry gash marred her long neck. Finger marks pressed red against her throat. Those would bruise.

"You did it," Grace said. She knelt by the two downed aptrgangr and lit the tip of her running iron. She drew the banishing rune on each forehead. She imposed her will on the marks. The Heart stayed quiet, locked in its iron prison. "If the Kivati let him through, Leif should be pleading our case to Corbette right about now."

"What do we do?" Cindy asked.

"We go to see the Wolf."

Chapter 22

Every male in Kivati Hall wanted to kill him. Standing in the Raven Lord's grand receiving chambers, Leif wished he hadn't worn his crimson coat; it stood out like a matador's cape, the red a reminder of every shed drop of blood between their people. The chamber was packed with enraged, distrustful Kivati. He knew every person there was remembering an aunt, brother, friend, or child who'd died in Sven's century of war.

If he could convince them to set aside the past and join him, he would be better than a messiah. Still, he had to try. His hands hung open at his sides. He pleaded with Corbette as if there wasn't anyone else in the room. No posturing. No pride. He laid out the threat facing them and, hat in hand, asked for help. "Tiamat's Heart will give Kingu all her god-powers," he finished. "Please help us."

"Your goddess, your affair," said a hawkish young Thunderbird.

"After all your brother did to our people? Never!" shouted another man.

A woman in a paisley gown spat on his boots.

Lord Kai stepped forward. "I've fought Kingu. He is more wraith than monster, but he's still formidable. My brother Jace would have said this is a cause worth fighting for. The demigod is an abomination on this side of the Gate, and he's a danger to us all—"

"But the soul-suckers killed your brother!" someone shouted.

Kai held up his hands. "And so you know I wouldn't easily side with our enemies. But Jace believed in sacred honor before personal glory. For him alone we should join this effort, except we can't trust this man." He pointed to Leif.

How would Zetian spin this? Leif wondered. "We've had our differences in the past—"

"I wore a bracelet around my wrist to remind me of my brother's sacrifice," Kai said. "But your mercenaries stole it last time we 'teamed up.' Where is the Tablet of Destiny now?"

Leif met Kai's eyes. "It's the only tool to defeat Kingu."

"And so you stole it from me? Now you ask us to trust you? To join you in this battle now that you've taken the best weapon?"

The Kivati started yelling. A few booed. The few voices raised in favor of joining the Drekar-human pact were quickly drowned out.

Leif looked to Corbette to step in, but the Raven Lord's violet eyes cut through him as if he weren't even there. His advisor, the Thunderbird general William Raiden, stood guard at his side. His hand twitched, ready to call a thunderbolt from the air and destroy Leif.

Corbette let the people's objections fill the room; then he raised one hand. Immediately, there was silence. "You say your brother's sins are not your own. You say we can expect honest dealings from you. Very well. Tell me, Regent, in the six months since the Unraveling, what have you done to hunt down Kingu?

"I didn't—"

"And in that time, what steps did you take to locate and

secure the object of power that was used to orchestrate the destruction of civilization?"

"I didn't know for certain—"

"You knew Kingu could use the Tablet of Destiny to wage the same war across the world that he did the first time, and you knew both Kingu and the Tablet were somewhere near Seattle. Yet, you sat back and did nothing."

Leif closed his mouth. The room narrowed to blues and greens. How could he explain that he had been trying to right Sven's wrongs by not becoming the ruler everyone feared? He knew, now, that he didn't have to lead like his father and brother, but it seemed his acceptance of the crown had come too late. Because of his inaction, he had sins to repent for. "I'm sorry. I should have hunted Kingu, but he didn't seem the immediate threat. There were no signs of him, but there were plenty of starving, shivering people who needed direct assistance. I directed my efforts there. Give me another chance. We can be allies. We must if we are to defeat Kingu."

Corbette stood. "Your promises are as insubstantial as starlight. While you were hiding away, we, the Kivati, found the object Kingu desired beneath the treacherous rubble of the Unraveling. We risked the lives of good warriors to draw Kingu away from the civilians in the city by sending the Tablet out on wild-goose chases. We helped direct Marks's and Jameson's efforts where they would be least detrimental to the safety of the entire city. And what have you done? Shown up in council only to interfere with our negotiations. Ignored the excesses of your own people who hoarded resources—"

"I thought we were working together to bring light to the city!" Leif said, steam trickling out his nose. Gods, but Corbette twisted the truth. "Light to keep the aptrgangr at bay. Light to make the streets safe from thugs and bring warmth before winter set in. If you hadn't been working against me all this time we might have a fully functioning core of buildings right now!"

"Yes, the coal." Corbette stroked the head of his silver-tipped walking stick, the raven with its spread wings. "A useful endeavor to draw Kingu away from the city, until your mercenaries stole the Tablet and brought it right back here, endangering countless lives. Trust you? You led Kingu right to our hill and ran away while our warriors fought him—"

"Thunderbolts—the blue fire of the gods—can stop him. Your Thunderbirds drove him away. Proof that you are essential to the coming battle—"

"And now you've found the Heart of Tiamat and refuse to share its location," Corbette continued without a pause. "Why should I trust you? Why should I believe that we are all safe with you, direct descendant of the Mother of all Dragons, in possession of such great power?"

"You can trust me," Leif said, "for the same reason you lambast me for my inaction. I have no thirst for power. I rule because I must and because there isn't anyone else I'd trust with the job. I will keep my small territory and people safe, but I have no interest in world domination. I pledge you this: unless you attack us, the Heart possesses no threat to the Kivati while it's under my control. I can't promise that Kingu will give you such assurance. If you don't help us fight him, we stand little chance of winning." Leif looked to the Kivati surrounding him, but no one would meet his eyes. None spoke against him now. They were listening, at least. The small victories mattered.

In the crowd he found the Kivati princess, Lucia, with her porcelain features and the lightest lines of grief shadowed on her face. After the Tablet had been used to cut her veins and bring down the Gate, she had more reason than any of them to fear the power of the Tablet, but she didn't cower now. She raised her pointed nose and held his gaze. Maybe she could convince Corbette where he could not. He appealed directly to her. "Please. My brother might have found the key, but a Kivati man was responsible for turning it in the lock to release Kingu into the world. Do it for your sacred honor, if not for your neighbors. You don't want Tiamat to reawaken. It will be much, much worse than the Unraveling."

Lucia's face turned white as her hair, but she lifted her chin a notch. She reminded him a little of Grace, bruised but not defeated. She would make a good queen. "And what is your plan, if you rely so much on our Thunderbirds' weapons?"

Thank Freya, she listened to him! "When Marduk defeated Kingu the first time, he had a host of warriors, thunderbolts, nets, and the Scepter of Death. I can provide manpower to distract him, and the suits of armor I built for Admiral Jameson's men can shoot nets and fire."

"And the scepter?"

"We don't have the scepter, but we believe if we can trap Kingu, we can use the Tablet of Destiny and the Heart to bind him and send him back through the Gate. Kingu was a full demigod in the first battle, but he is only a very powerful wraith now. Hopefully that will be to our advantage. The Tablet can be used to rewrite his destiny. The Heart will fuel it." Gods, he hoped. Even to his ears, the plan sounded flimsy as a newborn calf. But they had nothing else.

Corbette stirred. "And afterward what happens to the Heart?"

"It must be destroyed," said Kai. "I'll do it. Give me back my Tablet and tell me where it is."

"It's not that simple," Leif said.

"This is your idea of working together?" Kai sneered.

Corbette tilted his head, an inquisitive gesture so like his totem. "You're hiding something."

Leif set his jaw. They couldn't learn about Grace. "Trust me." The audience laughed. "I haven't earned your hatred. My brother's ways are not my ways."

"We will give you time," Corbette said. "You will give us the Heart."

"No."

"No." Aether swirled out from the Raven Lord and licked up the walls. The fire in the hearth roared. "Then you'll forgive me if I turn the tables. Go to your battlefield. Ready your troops. But I'll give you no immediate answer. You'll simply have to trust us to do the right thing."

Leif swallowed. His life dedicated to science and fact and now this. The fate of the world required an act of faith.

"Lucia, wait."

Lucia turned. The Raven Lord stood, face black as a thundercloud, and pinned her with eyes given over to a dangerous violet. Kivati streamed past them on either side. A siege of Queen Anne Hill seemed imminent. "Yes, my lord?"

"I've given the order for the most vulnerable to be evacuated and assigned Lord Kai to be your personal bodyguard. He will escort you to Canada and keep you safe until the demigod is defeated."

She stared at him for a moment. With his black hair and silver hoops, he had always seemed a figure inked from dreams. His movements flowed with the Raven's grace, and his presence in a room licked up the walls like a sentient fog. As a rebellious teenager, she'd often cast him as a dark angel in her secret fantasies, but in the daylight he was nothing but properly polite.

After the Unraveling, he'd saved her. He had barely spoken to her since. He'd avoided her like an embarrassing, broken thing, and she'd let him. She'd tried to squash her rebellious urges and become the perfect Kivati lady that he could be proud of, but the more passive and pretty she became, the easier it was for him to ignore her. Now he wanted to send her away with the infants and elderly.

She was angry, she realized, and it felt much better than being depressed. Raising her chin like Grace had taught her, she let her deference fall away like wisps of thin lace. "And are you sending the other women away? My sister Delia? Violet? Lady Damnable?"

"No. If Kingu attacks the hill, Lady Damnable might singlehandedly fight him off with her parasol." The line of his mouth softened. It wasn't quite a smile, but it was a lot less frigid.

"I can fight," she said.

His jaw tightened again. "No."

"I've had a good teacher. She says I'm ready, if there is no other option. We've reached the last resort."

"No," he growled. "Kai will take you to safety, and that's final—"

"I'm physically fit and can throw a better punch than Delia, but you won't let me—"

"No." He took a step toward her. "This is not a game, Lucia."

"Don't patronize me." Her hands curled into fists. "I have every right to defend my people."

"Your people need you to be safe. The prophecy—"

"Damn the prophecy!" she shouted. The Kivati around them stopped and stared. She didn't care. "I am more than that unintelligible rambling. But fine. You want to talk about it? 'Follow the Crane to destiny, for behind her lies ruin,'" she quoted the last line of the Spider's prophecy, uttered more than a century before she was born. "Well, look around you. The city is in ruins, thanks to me. Want to follow me to destiny? I doubt destiny is hiding in a forest in Canada!"

"You are overset," Corbette said. "Kai, take her with the others."

She realized Kai was standing behind her. His hands came down on her shoulders with the weight of steel. "What about the Drekar? What about your promise to Asgard?

They need our help." Corbette closed the distance between them. His power washed over her, an untapped river o Aether that sent shivers over her skin. She was trapped be- tween two towering men. If they wanted to make her fee small and vulnerable, it was working.

"A hundred years ago my father trusted the Drekar, an they stabbed him in the back, burnt the city to the ground and massacred our people. When he died, I swore on th Aether that the Kivati would never be weak again. You ar important—" He paused.

By the Lady, how she wanted to hear him say, "to me."

"—to the Kivati," he finished. He softly touched her face The scent of cedar calmed her racing heart. Inside, the Cran curled toward him. "Please, go with Kai. Be strong for ou people. Promise me, Lucia."

She felt a sharp pain in the left side of her chest, and sh ducked her chin. "I promise."

Leif met Grace at the foot of Kivati Hill where he' parked his carriage. "How did it go?"

"Hart doesn't have a lot of faith in Corbette," Grace saic "But not everyone blindly follows the Raven Lord. Hart i calling in his favors to see who he can get to join us."

"Corbette told me to trust him to do the right thing. I hav no idea if he'll show up or not."

"We need more time."

Leif had to touch Grace. His fingers were greedy to fee her skin. The cold pinked her cheeks and the end of her nos The wind stole strands of hair from her braid. She couldn' be more beautiful. "Let's get back to the lair. Come insid I'll warm you up." He helped her into the carriage and shu the door against the outside world. "Your hands are frozen. Sitting on the leather bench next to her, he rubbed them be- tween his own. He imagined putting them warmer places.

"Did you get support at the Althing?"

"All factions are drawing troops. Zetian is coordinating. No one wants to place his men under the rule of another. It will be a disorganized mess, but better than nothing." He smoothed her hair back from her face and let his lips drift across her cheekbone. His fingers traced the shell of her ear, lightly brushed down her throat, and paused at the pulse in her neck. Blood beat through her veins. She was alive. She was whole.

In this moment, in the dim light of the carriage, they had their own secluded world. The peace before the storm. What if this was the last moment they had to be together? Even with the Kivati, defeating Kingu and his aptrgangr army was a long shot. Many people would die, and both he and Grace would be in the thick of it. He couldn't protect her from the battle. In a few short hours they would unleash the beacon of the Heart and call Kingu to the field of their choosing. He might never feel the noonday sun on his back again or listen to the waves crash against the rocky shore. He might never fly beneath the stars, his wings held aloft for sheer joy at being. He might never create, never explore, never uncover another mystery of nature or unveil that divine clockwork of the universe.

"What's wrong?" she asked. A line of silver rippled across her eyes.

He gave her a smile and pulled her against him. "Nothing. I found you. After two centuries, I'd almost given up hope."

She pushed against him. "Don't talk like we've already lost. We'll kick Kingu's ass back to the Land of the Dead and show Corbette just what we think of his pretentious bull. We've got a shard of the Tablet of Destiny; we can craft our own fate."

"Do you know how it works?"

"No."

"You'll think of something. You always do." He kissed

the top of her head and breathed in her unique scent. Forget sunshine and flight, this is what he would miss. This chance to sit with her in quiet and soak up the warmth of her soul. "I trust you."

"Do you?"

He paused at the sudden tension in her body. "Of course."

"You haven't fed."

"Ah." He sat back against the seat.

"And don't tell me you don't need to, because I know it's a lie. You've got to before the battle so you have enough strength to fight—"

"Don't worry." He stared at the opposite wall of the carriage, hating this part of himself. "I'll find a Maiden. That's what they're for—"

"Don't be an ass." She took a fortifying breath.

He could feel her vibrating with tension at his side, but he refused to look at her and see the revulsion he knew he would find. He didn't want to take that image into battle with him. "We're passing over the bridge. We'll be home soon."

Grace took his jaw and turned his head to face her with surprising strength. "Don't pretend for me. I don't want some human shadow of you. You're Drekar. You trust me? Show me everything."

A growl rumbled in his throat, and his vision changed to blue and green.

"I know what the soul kiss is—"

Twining his hands into her hair, he kissed her hard. She tasted of mint, tea, and desperation. "You saw the worst of the worst. It doesn't have to be like that," he said against her lips.

"Then show me."

Leif anchored her to him, body flush against his. The carriage swayed, and he cradled her against the back of the seat. Gently, so gently, he licked the line of her lips. He teased her mouth, little bites, little kisses that eased the tension in her shoulders, until she began to relax. He could tell the moment she became aware of another part of his anatomy clamoring for her attention. She put her hand on the seam of his pants. Letting go of her hair, he moved her to straddle him, so that the V of her thighs rode him with each bump over the brick and asphalt road. "Gods, I wish we had more time." They would be in Ballard soon, and the work couldn't wait, so he simply let himself luxuriate in touching her, smoothing his hands over her body and down to the curve of her ass.

"If you're trying to distract me—"

"Is it working?"

She laughed. "Yes."

"Good." Her eyes were shut, straight sooty lashes above wide, flat cheekbones. He traced his lips over each lid and back to her mouth. "I love you." He didn't give her time to respond. Her lips parted, and he surged in. Kissing her deeply, he felt her defenses give way, and he breathed in.

Her sparkling soul light ran like a river of Aether into his body, flooding every dark, forgotten corner, ringing his head with the peal of a spirit charm. She tasted of moonbeams and starlight. The power, the absolute glory of her being, sparkled into his empty heart. He hadn't realized how dark he had become until she chased away the shadows and lit him up like a Yule tree.

The taste of a human in love was rumored to be the finest, most satisfying drink to his kind. It was too much to hope that she returned his affection, but the small sip of her soul was definitely the best taste he'd ever had. So much so that he could believe Longren's tale. If she would have him, he could see himself being satisfied with Grace and only Grace until the end of time.

He released her, filled to the brim, and rested his forehead on hers. His breathing was labored. "Thank you."

"How do you feel?"

"Like a million bucks," he said, repeating her words from

when they'd first met. Then, he'd given her a little bit of his blood to heal. In return, she'd taken everything. His peace. His quiet. His ability to ignore the outside world while he focused on his experiments. His complacency as the Drekar struggled without his leadership. His heart. "You've changed me, Grace. I never wanted to rule. I didn't think I had it in me to take power and send men to their deaths—"

"That's not fair. There is no other option—"

"Listen. Yes, and you've shown me that true leadership isn't a thirst for power but showing up and doing what needs to be done, even when what needs to be done is the last thing I would choose to do. You make me want to be a better man. Not just a ruler who will do the least bad thing, but a king who will lead his people to victory. When I'm with you, I want to believe we can win this thing."

She bit her lower lip and looked away. Dismissive, even as he bared his heart to her. Joining forces with a Dreki, sex—these she could take. But when he brought the discussion to a higher place, feelings and promises and plans for the future, it was only too clear she had one foot out the door.

If only he had more time. He kissed her—a gentle kiss, but it still had the power to heat his blood—and brought the conversation back to solid ground. "And how is . . . it?"

Grace released a breath. "The Heart is peaceful. I think she liked that."

"Did she now?" He brought his hands down to Grace's hips and slipped his thumb between them, rubbing right where she liked it over the seam of her pants. She welcomed his touch. He wanted this to be more than about sex, but he would take what he could get. Her eyes rolled back in her head. "Mmm. Maybe you shouldn't stop."

"I like how you think."

"Kingu would never find us," she whispered.

He started to unzip her pants. Ye, gods, he loved this woman. "I—"

The door to the carriage rattled. Someone banged on the window. "Regent?" Thorsson's impatient voice.

"Damnation." He kissed Grace one last time. "Rain check?"

"You better deliver, Regent Asgard." She bit his ear lightly. "And that's a threat."

"Regent?" Thorsson asked again. "Bad luck to keep your Heiðr waiting."

If Leif was going to get another chance, they needed all the luck they could get.

The Heart lay quiet as a bomb waiting to be dropped from the Enola Gay. Not a moment went by when Grace wasn't hyperaware of it. She meticulously searched the surface of her iron bulwark for cracks. Leif's taste of her soul hadn't done a thing to weaken her defenses. Thank Freya. It was so different from Norgard. So different from the shameful wash she'd always assumed was the nature of the soul kiss.

Leif put his hands on her shoulders and squeezed. "You are stronger than the Heart. You've been holding it in for so long. Knowledge will only make you more powerful."

"You think Birgitta might know how to defeat her?"

"I don't know. I imagine those runes Sven taught you are doing the best job keeping it inside, but if we want it out—"

"Then what? What happens when Tiamat is free to roam the earth again? What happens when she takes over someone weaker? Someone vulnerable?" She'd always prided herself on being strong, but knowing it was the Heart who'd helped her all these years sent a sick jolt through her gut.

Leif rested his forehead against hers, forcing her to meet his eyes. "Grace, you haven't changed. You are still the strongest person I've ever met. You think just anyone would be able to trap a goddess inside themselves?"

"I just want it out."

"We'll do it. I promise."

Drekar couldn't lie. He really believed they could cast the Heart out of her. She wanted to believe him so bad it hurt.

The atmosphere of Market Street had taken a turn for the worst. Grim merchants stripped their shops of supplies for the battle to come. The troll in front of Birgitta's shop bared its teeth at them when they rang the bell. Birgitta met them wearing a long blue cape lined with cat fur. Her loom lay empty, and the finished weaving hung across the door.

Birgitta ordered Grace to strip. She examined the runes. "Ja. You must have been a very strong woman to start out with." She finished her study and let Grace put her clothes back on. "Those runes trap her. But you could cast her out. A spirit sending, like the Volspa do."

"I can't risk the Heart escaping. How do I kill it?"

Birgitta sat back. "How should I know? The same way you trap and kill a wraith, I guess. Bind the wraith to the body, mark it for the Gate, then kill the host. If the body dies without binding the wraith, it will escape."

"No." Leif grabbed Grace's hand. "Bind the Heart to me. Let me bear this burden."

"No."

"We'll find another way," he said. He took her jaw and forced her to meet his eyes. "Promise me you won't do anything rash. No heroics. We'll solve this together."

"I don't think we can defeat Kingu without the Heart. You need me."

"Yes. Gods, yes." He kissed her.

She let him in. Let him soothe the heartache, if only for a moment. *Live for me*, she thought as she opened to him, taking his tongue deeper. She would live on in his immortal memory. A different kind of forever.

* * *

Leif broke away. Both of them breathed like the room lacked oxygen. “You are a survivor. Don’t quit on me now. You can bind the Heart and Kingu in another body. Trap them both there and banish them.”

“But how do we choose the sacrificial lamb?”

“Let Kingu choose. He likes war. He can’t feel the heat of battle without a host. He won’t be able to resist.” He turned to Birgitta. “We need that favor now. Gather the heathwitches together to draw a summoning circle for Kingu. We need to confine him to the battlefield.”

Birgitta’s face drained of what little color it had. “What if we are trapped with him, burnt out of what little magic we have? Leave an old woman her silly pastimes.”

“Think of Sigrid—”

“Ja, ja. I know.” She waved him off. “I will stand. Let Freya’s Hall ring with the happy cackles of old women plump on wine and boar.”

Leif gripped her shoulder. He remembered her as a mewling newborn. Only yesterday he’d held her hand as she took her first steps into the wide world. He’d danced at her wedding and watched her spread her light into her own clutch of tiny humans. He couldn’t look at her and not see the shining soul that had first looked out at him with those innocent, sky-blue eyes or see the web of sparkling light she’d spun through her children and grandchildren. The wrinkles crisscrossing her face spoke of a long, laughter-filled life—the web of her love imprinted there for all to see.

He hated asking this of her. A babe to an old, old woman, she’d earned her rest.

“Come now, child.” Birgitta patted his hand on her shoulder. “I have a little strength in these old bones yet. Let me show you youngsters what we old folk are made of.”

* * *

In her bedroom in the turret of Kivati Hall, Lucia threw the last supplies into her carpetbag.

"Don't you think you should pack a nice dress too?" her mother stopped sniffing into a handkerchief long enough to ask. "What will you wear when Corbette comes to pick you up?"

Lucia closed the bag with a sharp click. Her parents had been in and out of her life for the last six months, alternating between making her feel like a newborn and a leper.

"I don't know why he doesn't guard you himself," her father said. He stood at the mantel with his pipe clenched tightly in his teeth, his brown mustache quivering. "He's been so devoted to you. How he could send you off into the wilderness with no one but that unpredictable Lord Kai as a guard, well, I don't know. Who will protect you from the Thunderbird?"

Her mother gave a little cry and buried her face in the handkerchief again. "My poor baby!"

Lucia took a deep breath. How had she survived six months of this? Her melancholy reinforced their idea of her helplessness. "Corbette needs to lead the warriors against Kingu," she told them.

Her father snorted. "Kivati will never join the Unktehila."

"Then not even Canada can save me." She stared out the window to the view of the ruined city towers so she didn't have to face her parents. They refused to see that Corbette didn't view her as a grown woman. They all had that in common. "And he hasn't been devoted—"

"He's very protective of you," her father said. "He must care for you very deeply, even after the"—her father coughed—"*incident*."

That wasn't the same thing at all, she thought darkly.

"But he should keep her close, don't you think, Milton?" her mother asked. "A queen is not just a figurehead. She is the spiritual leader of her people. Even in the darkest days, her elegance and royal bearing impart faith that everything will turn out right." She turned to Lucia. "The sky-blue gown would be perfect, dear."

Really, if her mother mentioned her outfit one more time, Lucia was going to scream. "Yes, well. I'm not the queen, and no one will see me while I'm mildewing in a forest somewhere." She picked up the bag, crossed the room, and gave them each a quick kiss on the cheek. "But you're right. A queen should be visible to her people." A plan had hatched somewhere between the Drekar Regent's visit and her parents' backhanded pep talk. She was so afraid that her father was right. Big things were happening in the world. She could let herself be bundled away to wait it out, but then she would always be a passive player in her own life. Maybe the prophesy wasn't true, but the Kivati still needed her, especially if Corbette wasn't going to put aside his oath and stand w ith the Drekar against Kingu.

It was a crazy plan. It had little hope of success, and more than one major hurdle. She was so tired of the melancholy that sucked her under, and she'd made progress in the last few weeks. The plan filled her with dread, but she was even more afraid of returning to that passive state where other people decided her fate and other people fought her battles. Afraid of the Tablet. Afraid of the wraith army. Afraid of herself, that she might have another panic attack right as Kingu attacked. If she let herself be bundled off to Canada while other people fought Kingu, she didn't think she would ever regain the little self-confidence she'd earned.

Leaving her room, she raced up the circular stairs to the very top of the tower and burst out into the open air. From here she could see the whole city. Queen Anne houses in pink and green trailed down from the hilltop; gingerbread and iron gables gave the hill a whimsical, fairy-tale air. A ten-foot wrought-iron fence surrounded the Hall and grounds. Charms guarded the gate.

The picture across the Ship Canal contrasted sharply with the view below. On the other side of Lake Union rose the new towers of the Gas Works. The Regent's troops already gathered on Kite Hill. It wouldn't be long now. She could watch the entire battle from the safety of this roof. But that would be the coward's way out. Even Corbette couldn't be that stubborn, could he? She glanced down to the lawn below and saw warriors preparing for battle. There was hope, then, that Corbette would intervene. Hope that the Kivati would win the day against Kingu and the city could finally know peace.

Crows lined the top of the tower wall. She found one she'd used before. "Here, Elwa. I have a message." The crow gave a little caw and held out its leg. She tied a small piece of paper onto it with a twist of red ribbon. "Bring this to the Drekar Regent," she told it. She hoped the Reaper was there. Lucia didn't trust the Dreki, but she knew Grace did.

The message was brief: *The Kivati will come.*

With Corbette or without him, Lucia thought as the bird launched from the tower and sailed across the Ship Canal. May the Lady have mercy on us all. She turned and raced down the stairs again, carpetbag in hand. At the bottom, warriors with the Western House's black armbands were gathering to listen to instructions from Lord Kai.

"Elinor is in charge while I'm gone," Kai said.

The Cougar nodded sharply while she finished filling her arrow sheath. "A demigod, and you're needed here," she said. "The girl is safest here too, unless you expect Kivati Hall to fall."

Kai shook out his mane of curls. "Ah, Eli, you strike to

the heart. But listen, little sister, to your elders. The Western House will represent while I'm gone, yes?"

"Yes, sir," the warriors chorused. They were a disreputable lot, but anyone could see their loyalty to each other went past House or blood. They would follow Kai through the Gate if need be.

Lucia hoped it wouldn't come to that. She cleared her throat.

Kai turned. "Princess." His mouth tightened, and he gave a half bow.

"I know you don't want to take me to Canada," she said.

Elinor snorted.

"As Corbette wills it, and the Lady," Kai said, not quite answering. "Loyalty, Lady Crane, must be earned."

His double meaning cut her. Her lip quivered, and she raised her chin. She knew she had done nothing to earn their respect. Since the Unraveling, she hadn't done anything to change their opinion of her: spoiled little rich girl, the favorite of Corbette and his blind spot. It would be easier to follow along dutifully and hide in that forest in Canada. To simply bob along in the river of Aether while it carried her where it willed. Do this, little Crane. Be that, Harbinger.

"The warriors are massing," she said. "Doesn't Corbette plan to join the Drekar? I would be safer here. I could try to persuade him—"

"What's your leverage?" Kai hefted his pack over his shoulder. "Because I'd rather fight with my men than babysit you, if it's all the same."

Just then a tall woman with ebony hair strode through the Hall's front door. She was more handsome than pretty and had the same sharp nose and air of command as Corbette. Her movements were decisive. Following her was a beautiful blond man who smelled lightly of cinnamon and could only be Drekar. Every warrior in the room reached for his weapon. Kai stepped in front of her.

The woman looked at them and snorted. She rooted he
feet in the hall like she owned the place. "Lady-be, this plac
is just as stuffy as I remember," she said. "Where is my
brother? Emory!"

"Lady Alice!" Will came running into the hall to gree
her. Lucia had never seen him look so happy to see anyone
It was a complete transformation. He stopped just short o
taking her hand. "I'm so glad to see you well."

"Well enough for the moment," she said. "But not if wha
the crows tell me is true. I hope that large army of Dreka
and humans massing across the Canal will very soon b
joined by an equally lethal army of Lady-blessed Kivati war
riors. Tell me my brother has put aside his enmity with th
Drekar. Where do we stand on Kingu?" Her mate, the Drek
Brand, came to stand next to her. He twined his fingers wit
hers and the couple stood, united in everything but blood
The sight was so strangely beautiful: two great enemy race
united in love by this one defiant couple. Lucia couldn't hel
but be moved.

But Will's face turned stony. "I don't think Emory ha
forgotten your father's murder so easily, or the rape and pil
lage of our land by those same Drekar, or the century o
Kivati blood shed for our freedom."

"I'm sorry to hear that, Will," Lady Alice said. "Fathe
was a forgiving man, but he would be ever so disappointe
if we let past mistakes sabotage the fate of the free worl
Where is the black-hearted Lord Raven? Take me to Emory.

"Hello, Alice." Corbette had been watching from the stai
and no one noticed. How could someone who seemed t
take up so much space move so quietly when he wished it
A stillness descended on the entry hall, a heaviness to th
air from the paving stones to the arched ceiling three storie
above. Tendrils of Aether swished around the walls an
climbed higher. Alice and Corbette stood staring at on

another, a lifetime of conversation spinning between them across the Aether. Only very strong Aether mages could communicate directly into each other's minds. Lucia knew Corbette could do it, but it appeared his sister was equally gifted. A pin could drop.

"I made a promise," Corbette said, face wreathed in thunder.

"A foolish promise by an emotional youth. Surely the Lady would forgive such idiocy."

"I am a man of my word." Corbette turned to Kai and his warriors. "See to your places. We protect the hill."

"But Emory—"

"No, Alice. And I will not be so easily felled as Halian was. Any man or woman who joins with a Dreki betrays our sacred honor," Corbette said. Next to Lucia, Kai flinched. Alice bared her teeth, and her husband moved to hold her back from attacking her brother. "The Dreki is not welcome to fight by our sides, but he will not be my prisoner. I am not heartless. If you mean to stay, Alice, gear up."

Lucia watched the Kivati aid disappear like morning fog over Lake Union. Lady help them all. She stood frozen for a long moment as the warriors moved to their tasks. It was now or never. Could she do it?

"Let's go, Lady Lucia," Kai said. "Our window of escape grows short."

"I have something I wish to discuss," she said.

"Can it wait?"

"No." Her stomach felt like she'd eaten glass, but she'd seen Kai flinch. She knew his secret: in one of her midnight trips to see Grace, she'd stumbled upon him and Astrid Zetian, the advisor to the Drekar Regent, up against an alley wall. Lady Alice had abandoned the Kivati with her Dreki lover, but Kai was one of Corbette's most trusted generals. There was no graver offense than consorting with their ancient enemies, and it looked like Kai, with his pants around his ankles, had been doing his damnedest to forge traitorous new bonds between their two races. If Corbette found out, he'd kill Kai himself. *Lady, please let me do the right thing.* Lucia didn't think the Lady would smile on blackmail, but it was her last hope.

Chapter 23

Grace paced nervously across the sundial on Kite Hill. Leif, Hart, Marks, and Thorsson stood to one side. The Gas Works rose from the base of the hill in brown cylindrical towers. The wide lawns had been dredged up rebuilding the plant, but the hill remained untouched.

Boatfuls of weapon-toting civilians disembarked onto the coal loading dock. Along the shore of Lake Union, humans set up camps. Canvas hospital tents dotted the far side, and Ishtar's Maidens rolled bandages and prepared stretchers. A line of Drekar hovered at the edge of the tent. They waited reluctantly to get their blood drawn and fill vials for the fight ahead. There wouldn't be enough healing blood, not in time.

More dragons landed, and the boats carrying their followers began to pull up on shore. Men with makeshift spears and armor joined the well-armed soldiers who had been in Norgard's arsenal. Humans trickled in, ready to protect their homeland and their right to survive. Last time the Unraveling had come with no warning. This time they had the chance to take a stand, and the brave ones did.

The anti-supernaturalists had refused to participate until Edmund Marks ordered his Mark of Cain to show. "Forgiveness is a virtue," he said. "Let Eden's serpent stand on the side of Good." Once the fighting arm committed, the civilians followed. They didn't want to throw in their lot with the Drekar, but it was better than rule under Kingu.

Lake Union protected the battlefield on three sides. On the fourth, a row of trees marked the boundary of Gas Works Park. Behind it stood a parking lot, bordered by the bike path, the street, and a row of squat, empty buildings. Two dragons, Grettir and Joramund, dug a deep trench around the outside of the park.

Birgitta's heathwitches set up their caldrons in a wide ring along the shore and out across the row of abandoned buildings in the back. Some of them climbed trees. Some sat on high stools. They wore blue cloaks with cat fur trim and planted their elm staffs into the dirt. A Dreki guarded each one. Getting both groups to work together had been a nightmare.

Birgitta supervised Grettir as he burned a line between each caldron, connecting them in a wide, wavy circle. The twisting line of charred earth cut through the grass and across asphalt. Birgitta followed him with a shaker of salt and a sprig of mistletoe.

The plan was to call Kingu. If he followed the pattern, he would send his army first, but he would want to take the Heart himself. The ragtag army of Drekar, humans, and Kivati would kill as many as they could until Kingu arrived. Once he crossed the summoning line into the circle, the witches would initiate their wards and trap him inside. If they were lucky, Kingu would possess a body and Grace could carve the banishing runes on the host's skin with the Tablet shard. If they weren't, Kingu would stay a wraith. The Kivati Thunderbirds would use their thunderbolts and Drekar their fire to drive Kingu, while Grace used the power of the Heart to force Kingu into a host. She'd then use the Tablet to slay the demigod.

It was a terrible plan. The Tablet hung like an anchor around her wrist. She didn't know how to use it to kill wraith. Theoretically, marking a host and banishing the wraith should work the same as it always did. Rudrick had used the Tablet as a knife during the initial ceremony to bring down the Gates. Maybe she should try that too. She could draw Aether through the cuneiform marks carved on its face just like she did with her bone knife, but she wasn't sure what would happen next.

Still, it was the best plan they had.

But whom would she sacrifice? Whose body would be the vessel for killing Kingu? Grace didn't want to send all these people into battle. It would be so much easier to run, but Kingu would never stop hunting her. Her city would be destroyed. Anyone who helped her along the way would be slaughtered. She would become the Tablet, leaving death in her wake.

Leif's Gas Works, the key to his plan to show Jameson that Drekar could be a creative force, not only destructive, stood still. Sun breaks pushed through low clouds to glint off the finished towers. Complete, shining, waiting to take the city into a new gas-powered tomorrow, ready to light the world.

But no steam curled from the massive boilers, and none ever would.

Leif was surprisingly okay with that. He had more important things to take care of.

Grace paced near him. He watched her shadow slide over the ripples in the textured concrete sundial. The glass marbles pressed into the decorated surface reminded him of children's playthings. He had ordered a few Drekar to stay behind and guard the city's children. If Kingu won, his people would see to their safe exodus south.

If Grace succeeded in defeating Kingu, he hoped he could convince her to stay with him.

"What's taking them so long?" Grace demanded. "Corbette should have been here by now. I don't see a single Kivati except Hart and his men. Corbette has to know what this means. You told him about the Heart, right?"

Leif watched the whitecaps blow away from the shore. A clear wind drove down from the north. Sven used to claim he rode that wind as he swept in to a bloody victory. Leif would have Sven's victory, but not his methods. Still, all Leif's avoidance had come down to this: an untried general on the brown plains of battle. His shirt stuck to his back. His hands didn't shake, for which he was grateful. "Corbette's not coming."

"The note promised."

"Who knows who sent it? It might be just a mind trick. He doesn't care."

"Doesn't care about Tiamat rising from the dead? Doesn't care about chaos's reign?" Her voice rose until it was a low scream. He wanted to take her in his arms and soothe her, but he was fresh out of comforting words. He didn't think he'd make it through this. As long as he could save her, it would be a fair price.

Her friend Hart, the Kivati Wolf, double-checked his rifle. He had brought five Kivati with him and set them up scouting the route Kingu's army would take. The Kivati could communicate with each other through the flocks of crows that clung to the surrounding trees like gothic Christmas ornaments. "I brought who I could, but most are too loyal to come without Corbette's order."

Leif needed Corbette to give the order. Dragon fire wasn't strong enough to herd Kingu on its own.

"You still have that Deadglass?" Hart asked Grace. "You should keep it here at the top. Best view on the field. I'll order a crow in case you need to send a message."

"Thanks." She punched Hart's arm. "Oscar would have wanted to be here."

Hart chuckled. "Yeah, he didn't like being out of the action, did he? Would have been helpful too. Maybe he coulda conned Kingu into possessing some schmuck. I don't know how you're gonna do it if he stays wraith."

"Pray to your Lady that he doesn't." She pulled out the Tablet shard and ran her fingers over the sharp edge.

Hart pulled back. "Damn, but that was Oscar's territory, wasn't it? He had the Norse fates in his pocket. Maybe he'll send us some of his luck from the other side."

"Thanks for coming, Hart. Means a lot."

"I'm not doing this for you, Reaper. No offense. This is for Kayla and the pup."

"How do you know the baby's totem will be Wolf? Maybe the Lady will bless her with wisdom and strength, like the Raven." Grace's eyes twinkled.

Hart snorted. Shaking his head, he took off down the hill to organize his small band of warriors.

"His wife is pregnant," Grace explained to Leif. She kept her face carefully neutral.

"Ah."

"She wanted to come, but he left her at Kivati Hall."

Leif approved.

"Don't you think she should be able to make her own decisions?"

Quicksand, Leif thought. "I think we protect those we love. Sometimes the action seems harsh, but the motive is love." *I will protect you with my dying breath.*

He spotted Zetian flying in from the east. The silver dragon with golden horns soared over the towers and landed on the hill. She had ancient gold eyes and delicate gold whiskers. A splash of red decorated her throat. She Turned and hit the ground running. "Ishtar's army is here."

"How? I haven't used the Heart." Grace's fingers tightened around the Tablet shard in her hand. "She's still asleep."

Leif brushed her hair away from her face. "Kingu would have to be blind to miss this much activity." He swept a hand out to the massing soldiers and civilians. "I wish I could take this burden from you."

"I wish a lot of things, but, hey. That's life."

"What do you wish?"

She looked him over. He wore a crimson military jacket with gold buttons that set off his hair brilliantly, shiny knee-high black boots, and a saber at his hip with a gold sash. Slightly piratical, but hella sexy. He made a statement, that was for sure. No one could miss who was in charge of this hoedown.

It was his face that drew her. That square jaw and high forehead; stately nose and firm, wide mouth; those green eyes seducing her like a cobra. She'd fallen under his spell.

"Time," she told him. "I want more time." She turned before she could see the regret in his face and pulled Hart's Deadglass out of her pocket. The air was alive with wraiths. They swooped and shimmered like some iridescent kaleidoscope. Waiting, she knew, to seize the fallen warriors and return them to the battlefield to fight for Kingu. She dropped the glass. "Where is Jameson? We can still do this thing."

Marks stood to one side of Kite Hill in jeans and a bowling T-shirt. A leather bracelet cuff decorated his wrist. A little hipster, a lot out of place on a battlefield. He held no weapon but his snakeskin Bible. His presence spurred his followers to action, and there were lots of them.

Grace never thought she'd be glad to have a cultish noncombatant at her side in a fight.

"Time to pray," he said. "We need a miracle."

Longren in his black and purple scales flew in late. He Turned on the hill, took what looked like an original Roman legion helmet out of his bag, and waltzed up. "What did I miss?"

Leif clasped forearms with the older Dreki. "Longren, good to see you."

"Would I miss this opportunity into Valhalla? Only the honored dead make it to Odin's hall."

Grace didn't point out he had no soul. Only the souls of the dead made it to Valhalla. Maybe he hoped the gods would have pity on him and break the rules just this once.

Leif nodded. "May we meet there together."

"Brunhilda, here I come." Longren grinned. He tossed his hair and donned the helmet. "And look, I brought more meat for the feast." He pointed to a boat with blue and yellow striped sails powering toward them. As they drew near, a roar went up from the boat. The young, hot guys wore gold-plated armor. Their matching helmets sported a red fringe.

Leif shook his head. "And here you had me convinced that you were all alone, old man."

"Just a man alone with his cats, eh? I've got a few tricks up my sleeve yet."

"Good."

Grace pointed to the line of aptrgangr in the distance. From Kite Hill, the neighborhood spread out before her. She tracked the first approach of the blue-tinged dead. "Jameson's soldiers are here, but he and the mechanical suits Leif made aren't."

"Who needs them?" Longren said. "I'm here. Let's get this party started."

Zetian came to stand next to Leif. She had changed into a blood-red suit embroidered with dragons. In her hair bobbed two long pheasant feathers. A necklace of bones protected her throat. Together they made a pretty picture: a gorgeously inhuman couple splashed red across the grey sky. Hard, cold eyes. They lit the hilltop like a beacon fire warning the countryside; the invaders had arrived.

Zetian watched the humans assembling on the water's edge. "It's time, with or without Kivati and that fool Jameson. Who'd have thought that it would be the dragons who were mankind's last hope?"

"It's all of our last hope," Grace snapped.

"No, little warrior." Zetian turned her black gaze on Grace. "But I follow our Regent, and he chooses to make this our fight. I am not afraid of death. Only the transition."

Thorsson raised his broadsword to the sky and screamed. It was a hell-raising noise, and the assembled warriors took it up until the low clouds echoed it back. Crows rose from the trees, cawing too. At least Corbette would watch this massacre. Let him live that guilt down too. He would watch his end march slowly toward him.

"Time to taunt Kingu," Leif said. "We have what he wants and aren't afraid to use it against him. Don't be afraid. You are stronger than one cut-up goddess."

Grace gave him a tight smile. The tension in her body zinged like a violin string about to snap. She had been on constant guard since learning of the Heart. Now that it came time to let it peek out and call a demigod, she was afraid.

"Don't lose hope." Leif gripped Grace's shoulder. He pulled her in for a quick, desperate kiss. Here in front of Drekar and humans and aptrgangr alike, she kissed him back. She wanted to curl up in that kiss and shut out the world. But her passion was a dangerous thing.

The Heart woke and rattled at her iron cage.

Leif knew he chanced the Heart's wrath with that kiss, but he couldn't march into death without it. Jokes with Longren aside, Leif knew there was no afterlife for him. There was no shining world beyond, no pearly gates. No gates of any kind. The Drekar could fly from this place and live many more years until Kingu's god-reign caught up with them. Who knew if it would be tomorrow or ten years from now? But he would not flee, even if this were to be his last stand. He would choose to die like a warrior on this blood-soaked earth protecting Grace. He was immortal, but not unkillable.

She wouldn't leave her people and abandon her city to Kingu's horde. Her people had become his people. He could no more flee than the beach could abandon the tide.

Who would have thought that the scientist would become the first berserker to rush the battlefield? He didn't believe in some preordained destiny, but he knew that every moment of his life had brought him to this point. He had found Grace. He wouldn't change a thing.

Thorsson's roar ended, and Leif seized that moment of silence to rally his troops. "Seattleites!" he called. The line of soldiers shouted in support. He waited a beat to be heard. "Whether you were born here or are far from your homeland, you stand here today a united front. You stand with your brothers. With your sisters. Putting aside your differences of blood or race to fight for your right to survive. To thrive. To live free from tyranny and oppression. To raise your families in peace and pursue your passions.

"Whatever gods you pray to, beseech them now. If Kingu wins, he will take everything we have struggled for and yearned for and turn it to ash. We cannot let him win. Stand with me, knowing as you do so that the glory of the gods does not lie in dying, but in squeezing every last drop of happiness from this life. We fight now for that right for our children and grandchildren. So that they may dream and thrive and create in a world free of war, free of persecution." Leif hefted his sword and welcomed the weight down through his arm. "Death comes to us all, but I would rather die in a blaze of glory fighting for my fellow man than wither beneath an unjust dictator because I was afraid to act when I had the chance. This is our chance. This is our last symphony. Join me, brothers, sisters, in taking our fight to the very gates of heaven!"

A cheer rose up from the masses.

"Rock on," Grace said.

"Ja!" Thorsson showed all his teeth. He beamed.

It looked like they might have a chance. Kingu's army tottered forward in an unordered mass.

The first round of aptrgangr hit the trench on the far side of the tree line. Leif closed his eyes for a brief moment. Oil from the Gas Works soaked the dirt at their feet. Gretti stood ready at one edge, Joramund at the other. Leif opened his eyes again and gave the signal. They blew fire into either end of the trench, and a wall of flames shot up in a ten-foot ribbon, burning the bodies of the dead who marched through. The aptrgangr screamed, but more came to replace them. Dragons flew over the field and finished off those who made it through. So far, so good.

"Where is that idiot Jameson?" Grace swore.

The soldiers behind Leif rallied as the wall of flames died down. Behind the first wave of aptrgangr stood ten giant metal suits of armor. Steam puffed from the tails and fire belched from the fingers. And in their midst stood Jameson. The gold brocade on his admiral's uniform shown like the gold of the suits. His brown hair lay perfectly combed beneath his tricorn hat. His hand rested on his ceremonial sword. He stood at attention, confidence radiating from his steel-straight shoulders, arrogance evident in his blind regard to the aptrgangr creeping up at his back. His eyes trained on the top of the hill.

A cry went up: the admiral had finally arrived with the mechanical suits. The wave of men at the base of the hill took that as a signal to attack. Jameson had already led the first charge and moved the battle line off the hill.

"He's on the wrong side," Grace said.

"Finally," Marks said. "See? A miracle, just when we needed it. Forward, people of God. Send those demons back to hell!"

"No," Grace said. "He's on the wrong side."

Leif watched the wave of soldiers reach the mechanical suits. He was too late to stop the rush toward them. Too late to raise the warning, to order them back.

The suits turned on the men.

Leif watched in horror as his inventions worked perfectly. The fingers shot flame and sleeping gas. The metal shields withstood swords, bullets and dragon fire. It was a massacre.

The line of soldiers tried to turn back. Like a wave on the beach withdrawing, it crashed back into the wave behind it. Red bled into the brown field. Fire caught the dead grass.

And more aptrgangr arrived behind his inventions and caught the men escaping on the far side.

He caught Grace's eyes. She held the Tablet in one hand and her bone knife in the other. Her blue-black hair whipped about her pale, moon face. Her teeth bit bloodless lips. She needed time. The heathwitches hadn't finished the summoning circle yet. He had given their enemies the perfect weapon. It was his duty to take them out.

"Order a retreat," he told Zetian. "All Drekar to the air to cover it. Use the Gas Works. Tear it apart. Buy us time."

He grabbed Grace's shoulders. "Thank you. I've seen eternity in your arms. You are my goddess, and if we don't win today, it won't be for lack of trying. Take my heart, love. Bring it with you to the next world." He kissed her. He poured everything he felt into that kiss. He'd lived like there were endless days stretching before him, but now there were no more seconds to think of what he might do.

Leif Turned. He launched himself from the hill. The battle spun out beneath him. Sunlight glinted off the metal suits, and fire shot from the ground and the sky. Bodies churned in the mud. Dragons soared over the field like Valkyries searching for the souls of heroes. They acknowledged his presence and bowed their long scaly heads. He motioned for them to follow him to the Gas Works, and he ripped off a metal plate. A week ago a foreman had welded it on to complete the tower. Now Leif crushed it beneath his giant claws. His vision might yet spell hope for the city, just not the way he had planned.

The five dragons followed his lead in dismantling the tower. They dragged heavy metal sheets back to the park entrance and dropped their cargo on the metal suits. Some shuddered, none fell.

Leif tore up more of his project and pelted the boilers on aptrgangr and suits alike. They smashed the aptrgangr readily enough. The wraith inside escaped to power a new dead body. The suits were harder to kill. It took concerted effort to smash one so that it couldn't rise again.

The army of the fallen rose again, against their former brothers, until the tangle of men on the battlefield resembled nothing so much as a bloodbath.

Leif caught sight of Jameson again. The man's movements were smooth, but his face held too little emotion as he stepped over the bodies of his soldiers. His gaze held fast to the top of the hill, where Grace waited for Kingu with the Heart and the Tablet.

Kingu had possessed Jameson.

It explained much: why Jameson had taken the suits from Leif's lab right after Kingu had attacked it, why Jameson was now on the wrong side of the fight. And why Jameson was fixated on Grace. She would know. She could carve the runes on his skin and banish Kingu beyond the Gate.

Finally something was going right. He roared and motioned to the other dragons to avoid Jameson. They couldn't kill him until Grace banished the wraith. Instead, he found himself protecting Kingu's host in his long march up the hill.

The battle line had retreated almost to the sundial. Jameson climbed the hill. Zetian saw him. Something dark flashed in her eyes, and then she stepped in front of Grace. Zetian Turned her hand to claws and cut out his throat.

Chapter 24

Stunned, Grace blinked away the splash of blood. Zetian stood in front of her, her hand dripping, her red battle dress shining in the partial afternoon sun. “I had him,” Grace said. The muscles in her arm ached from the effort of holding back. The Tablet shard in her hand burned with the Aether she'd drawn through it. “He was mine to kill.”

Zetian set her ruby lips in a soft pout. Her ancient eyes were cold. “Little cat, you are not strong enough to take him.”

“We had a plan—”

“This?” She laughed softly and swept her hand out to encompass the losing battle. “This is your plan? Resting on the hopes of our enemies and the weak of the flock? You have power, I'll give you that. The power to turn the Regent's mind to mush. It is my duty to protect him, and you will be his death.” She stalked forward.

Grace stepped back off the edge of the hill. The rough surface of the sundial caught on her boot heels.

Zetian shook her head. “All they see in you is the reflection of Tiamat's power. You are nothing without it. Norgard made you, but you are nothing more than a shiny plaything.”

“I trapped the Heart all by myself.”

"You? Ha. What chance does a pitiful human stand against the Great Dragon Mother? You think a scared teenage girl could have trapped anything? Norgard's brands and bonds are the only thing keeping that Heart inside you. You are a fancy magicked living cage, nothing more. You have nothing to offer the Regents except a pretty box to stick their Hearts and cocks in. You are nothing—"

"Stop it!" Grace slid down the hill a little more. Every word Zetian said struck to the heart of her insecurities. A month ago, she would have believed Zetian. But not anymore. "You're the one betraying Leif—"

"You've been a useful distraction, but no longer. Men are the face of the war, but I pull the strings. You are a danger to the Drekar. You make the Regent think he knows his own mind. His mind belongs to me. His loyalty belongs to dragon kin. Not some weak little human." Zetian let her pheromones spin out. Cinnamon and iron drenched the air, drowning out the mud and sweat and blood. "Kingu is our future."

"Let me show you exactly what this little human can do." Grace felt her eyes glow silver. The Heart thrummed inside her. She raised her knife and touched the power of the Heart. A lick of blue flame shot out of her skin and across the knife's edge.

Zetian's lips curled out in a long, slow smile. "Little sparrow, you have served your purpose. It is time to dance." She raised both arms. Instead of hands she had giant, gnarled claws. The skin at her wrists blended to small silver scales.

In her left hand, Grace gripped the Tablet shard. She was stronger than Tiamat's Heart, stronger than a goddess. She could beat this dragon harpy with the bad manicure. "You underestimate Leif," she said. "You underestimate me."

Zetian bared her teeth, flashing a row of sharp fangs. She lunged and swiped out with her claws. Grace dodged. She twirled from Zetian's reach.

"What do you think Kingu is going to do with you?" Grace asked.

"We are one of the sacred ten," Zetian said. "Tiamat's monster children. We have no fear of her rising from the deep." She circled the sundial. Her pheromones snaked out and wrapped around Grace's body. They tickled her nose, heated her core. "We will join with Kingu and raise Tiamat. The time of Dragons is now!"

Grace used the adrenaline to fuel her movements. She descended into the calm of the fight, the place where everything faded away except her and her opponent. Her concentration sharpened, every bit of her mother's teaching came into play. Grace and her knife and her dancing feet. The clash of swords and screams of soldiers died out. The blare of horns from the medical tents softened too.

Zetian lunged, and Grace sidestepped it again. She moved to catch Zetian with her blade, but the Dreki was too fast. Zetian scraped her claws across Grace's back. Three blades of fire dug furrows in her skin. She had a moment to brace herself before the pain registered in her brain, and then she cried out.

Zetian wove from side to side, taunting her. "Too weak to be consort to the dragon king. How did you ever survive his coupling?"

Grace growled. She tightened her fingers around the weapon in each hand, and pulled the Aether through the cuneiform of the Tablet and the runes of her bone knife. It was dangerous with the Heart already awake. She focused on the pain to help her maintain control.

Clouds condensed, shutting off the determined rays of sun, darkening the sky. Heavy and waterlogged. The first few drops of rain hit her cheek.

Aether sparkled at the edges of her vision.

"Baby fighter," Zetian taunted. "Plaything of the Regent. Brothers share everything, didn't you know? You were never anything more to Asgard than you were to Norgard. You are a toy. You have outlived your usefulness. I will break you, and take Tiamat's Heart myself."

Grace danced forward and tried to stab the Dreki in the gut. Zetian was faster than an aptrgangr. She spun out of the way and sliced Grace down the arm. Grace dropped the Tablet.

"Not even a good fighter," Zetian said.

Grace ran at Zetian and pulled Aether through her knife. She slashed the Dreki's claws and hit. Zetian screamed. Clutching her hand, she retreated a step. One of her knuckles had been severed. The claw dropped to the sundial and landed in a small puddle with a splash.

Leif caught sight of Zetian and Grace facing off, but Jameson's body demanded attention. His decapitated head rolled down the hill a few feet and stopped on the flat part of the path that wound around the hill. The corpse shook. White fog coalesced from the severed stump of the neck and rose into the air. It moved slowly, disoriented by Jameson's sudden demise. Kingu in wraith form would be a lot harder to put down. The Drekar had dismantled all of the suits but two. Aptrgangr converged on the park.

Without Kingu in possession of Jameson's body, Grace couldn't carve the runes. He felt the thin molecules of hope slip through his fingers like sand. Leif needed the Thunderbirds and their thunderbolts to herd the demigod. Shrieking across the hill, Leif called to his Drekar to move the fight to Kingu. Maybe if all of them turned their fire on the white fog they could cause some damage.

Grace and Zetian fought across the sundial. Rage colored his vision, but he had to trust Grace to hold her own against the Dreki female. Her betrayal would not go unpunished. Revenge was Grace's to take.

Leif rushed the fog. The first hit was as bad as he remembered. Pain lit him from the outside in. It reverberated in his head.

Kingu's voice echoed in his ears. *Join me, brother. We will write your destiny.*

The picture Kingu painted this time was drawn from the pit of Leif's subconscious desire. Sun shone through wide stained-glass windows in a new, well-stocked lab. Steam rose to a high ceiling from the shining equipment. Every piece he'd lost in the Unraveling was put back together. Completed inventions, every brilliant idea he'd ever envisioned, crowded the long room.

Three kids worked on a steam-powered bicycle together. They had blue-black hair and almond eyes. Their green irises were slit like a cat's.

Leif shook himself from the seductive vision. He breathed fire into the fog. The fog recoiled. Kingu changed the dreamscape. A cyclone broke through the stained-glass windows. The children scattered, screaming, as the machines rose into the wind and smashed against each other. Chaos turned the peaceful scene to grey-black destruction.

He couldn't save the children in his mind. The pain of it wrenched his chest. He had to fight to remember that they didn't exist. It was only a nightmare. Kingu couldn't touch his kids; they were a figment of his hoped-for future.

Leif roared and cleared his mind from the numbing fog.

His dragons charged into the fog and came out screaming. Joramund, his black scales spiked with red, shot fire blindly. Thorsson whipped his double tail and sailed straight into the ground. The impact rained dirt.

Leif couldn't let Kingu win. He needed Grace to use the Tablet to hasten Kingu's date with death.

The dragons shot fire to keep Kingu from escaping, bu they were losing the battle.

Suddenly a thunderbolt shot through their midst and hi Kingu's fog with a clap. The heavens reverberated with th sound, clouds shook. The battle paused momentarily. Sol diers chanced a glance up to see the new threat bearing down

Two Thunderbirds, an unfamiliar dragon, and a doze Crow approached over Lake Washington. An Owl and white Crane led them. Lucia and her Kivati had arrived Fewer than Corbette had promised, but enough to make difference.

Leif let the Thunderbirds take over the attack on Kingu His wings still burned, his lungs ached. His throat con stricted with smoke. Coughing, he Turned on the shore nea the medic tent and found Birgitta.

"The summoning circle is complete," she said. Blue dy rose to her elbows. The caldron in front of her bubbled. smelled of apples and the pine of juniper berries. Her whit hair stuck to her forehead. Her breathing was labored. "Th Wolf has connected with the others. We have activated th circle. Kingu should be trapped inside this perimeter as lon as we can hold it. Hurry."

"Thank you."

She handed him a sprig of mistletoe. "For your lady. living plant to ward away the dead."

He took it and returned to the top of the hill where Grac and Zetian still fought. Zetian had lost claws on her righ hand. Grace bled heavily from grooves across her back an down her arm. The Tablet lay discarded in a puddle c bloody water. They were both tiring. Zetian limped. He scarlet outfit hid the blood, but the wet silk clung to he body at her hip.

He didn't want to distract Grace from her task. The glo of the fire and the blue Thunderbolts lit her from behin He'd never seen beauty so carnal or so otherworldly. Both this earth and detached, she walked the edge of the Gate and threw her will into the bone knife in her hand. The blade flashed silver.

Zetian snarled. She clutched her injured right hand.

Grace could hardly take a breath without pain rushing through her. Tiamat's Heart thrashed in her ribs. She couldn't contain all that power. Tiamat's rage would burn through her while Zetian wore her body down. She fought for control. Her limbs shook.

"You think you can contain Tiamat's power?" Grace asked Zetian. "Why don't you try?"

Leif appeared on the crest of the hill. The storm over Lake Union and the ruined city brewed behind him. He looked like Thor, blond and brilliant, bringing his devastation down on Midgard. "Stand down, Zetian," he ordered.

He was so beautiful, Grace was struck for a long moment, just watching him. In that peace from the fight, she remembered his advice: There is power in giving up control. Power was not in holding herself closed, but in opening herself to the universe. With a long breath, she released the tense muscles in her body. She let go of her fear and stopped trying to fight the Heart.

Aether poured through her. More than she'd ever felt, more than she could imagine touching without burning to a blinding white. A river of sparkling light touched every cell in her body and shot out the tips of her fingers and toes. She was like a living conduit, open, peaceful, released, and more powerful than one human ever had a right to be. This was the goddess inside, and Tiamat in all her hate was no match for her.

Zetian's face turned as red as the silk of her suit. "You!" She tackled Grace. Grace didn't brace against the impact.

She simply let the flow of gravity call her downhill. Locked together, Zetian's teeth in her shoulder, she released the Aether in waves of blinding light. Zetian screamed in pain, but her claws were locked in Grace's back. They rolled down the steep slope toward the choppy lake. Grace didn't fight. She opened herself to the universe, and the Aether whipped around her like a funnel of water. Suddenly the blackberry bushes were on top of her, and they teetered at the edge of the lake. Her bone knife came up, and she hugged Zetian to her, knife firmly imbedded in the Dreki's back.

Zetian fell into the water, coughing blood. Grace rolled away from the edge and crawled out from the brambles. Zetian could heal, but Grace had left her knife imbedded deep. She wouldn't be a threat for a little while.

In her trancelike state, Grace could almost see the Aether sparkling all around her. Was this what Corbette saw? It was almost like looking through the Deadglass. She could see the ghosts of the fallen rising over the battlefield. In the distance, two wide arches of Aether rose up. The tattered edges wove in a phantom breeze. Through the Gates, the Land of the Dead glowed dimly.

Not yet, she told them, and turned back to find Leif running down from the crest of the hill. He held the Tablet shard in his hand. He stopped by Grace. "Gods, you're beautiful."

She raised her eyebrow. His arm came around her, and she leaned into his embrace. It felt so good to let him hold her up. So good to have someone who would always get her back in a fight. Too good, too seductive to sink into his arms and let the world fade away.

He gave Grace a hot and fast kiss. She poured everything she felt into that kiss, every word she couldn't say, every shred of emotion she shouldn't feel. Everything about the kiss said good-bye. She let her lips and her hands and her body spell out those three little words that were all she had left to give.

Please forgive me.

Resolution steeled her spine. She broke off. Kingu barreled down on them. In her trance vision, she could see his monstrous form. Behind him, the thunderbolts from the Kivati lit his three heads and giant, membranous wings. He was coming for her. She was ready.

"Leif," she said. His beautiful green eyes captured hers. Someday he would understand. Or maybe he already did. He'd been the one to call her pain what it was, survivor's guilt. She suddenly understood her parents' sacrifice in a different light. This was love. She wasn't afraid to die. She knew she'd already had more joy than most people had in a lifetime.

But she was afraid to leave him, because he couldn't follow her to the other side of the Gate. This good-bye was forever.

"I love you." She grasped his shoulders and brought his head down for one last kiss. He responded with a rough taste of good-bye, tongue and teeth, anger and hopelessness. He wouldn't give up. Taking the Tablet and the mistletoe from his hand, she pulled back.

"We just need to drive Kingu to possess another body," he said.

"Yes."

"If all the Drekar and Thunderbirds attack him at once, maybe he'll panic. He won't run away. He's too close to his goal." Leif drew his hand down the side of her cheek. She closed her eyes at his touch. "You'll be safe. The runes will keep him from getting to you."

"Go. I'll be here with the Tablet and the Heart. Let's finish this thing."

He squeezed her hand and Turned. She watched one last time as the Aether shimmered through his gorgeous body. His limbs lengthened. His skin morphed into sparkling red scales with green tips. His fingers grew and sharpened to deadly

claws. His wings drew out, elegant, ethereal membranes lik
the shadow of the moon. The dragon rose above her an
blocked out the sky. She would take this image with her to he
death. Beauty and might, but most of all, love.

His ancient slit eyes gave her one last look, then h
turned to the fog and roared. He breathed fire at it, an
the fog rose up. Thunderbolts on one side, Leif's fire on th
other, Kingu used all his strength to materialize into hi
dragon form. Three heads, three tails, three sets of jagge
teeth, black scales and burning red eyes. Mad and merciles
and heartless.

Grace took the Tablet of Destiny and grabbed hold o
the lid to the iron box inside her. Finding the peace at he
center, she released Tiamat's rage. The Heart's power sho
out in crystal-blue flame. It burned through her voca
chords and tendons, shooting out of her fingertips into th
blistered soil. Overwhelming, all-consuming pain and
mad thirst for power. Her hand crunched the mistletoe, an
the spiked leaves drew her back. Life and death, she had t
walk the balance beam. She would not let a crazed goddes
take her over.

She stopped fighting the Heart and herded it instead
shaping it, directing it, to burn through the runes on he
body. The marks caught fire and the ink vaporized. Her ski
shed color. She was free. No magic trapped the Heart in he
body, just her indomitable will.

"Kingu!" she called. "Kingu, take your Heart!"

The dragon Leif charged into the fog just as King
charged her. Kingu's wraith swept through Leif and int
Grace. The frozen cold shocked her. For a moment sh
couldn't move as Kingu consumed her mind and body.

Images flashed before her eyes. Images of her usin
the Tablet to rewrite the destinies of the universe. To rewrit
her own destiny, Leif's, Oscar's, her parents'. Kingu was sif
ing through her memories with no sense of the past c

future. Things she once had wanted drove crazily across her mind. A pink canopy bed. A sharper knife. A new ukulele. Norgard, beheaded. A cozy gingerbread house with white curtains and glowing wards over the door. Leif, chained to an iron bed. Naked.

Gasping, she tore herself from the vision and clamped down on her iron walls. "Obey me!" She harnessed the Heart's blue flame to burn Uruz, the binding, through the pulse point at each wrist. A drop of blood dripped from her nose. She sent the flame to burn Raidho into her forehead. "Journey with me."

Inside her breast, Kingu shrieked. She felt him writhing inside her, like graveyard worms, but she forced more power through the newly burnt runes.

Blue flame danced along her skin. The power of the Heart blazed from her eyes. Each word sent sparks into the air.

She squeezed the Tablet shard and carved Thurisaz, the gateway, across her chest. Blood dripped from her skin. Pain lacerated every nerve. "Be banished," she whispered, pouring every last drop of her power into that command. With a last thought for Leif, she plunged the Tablet into her own heart.

With a burst of power, Tiamat's Heart surged out of her body and into the Tablet of Destiny. The stone heated to scalding, and Grace was ripped from her body out into the rain-drenched night. Kingu shook at his cage, but the runes bound him. Aether poured through the runes and caught up his spirit in a roaring river of light. Thrashing, he sailed helplessly out of Grace's body and straight through the Gates to the Land of the Dead.

Chapter 25

Grace watched her body collapse into the blood-splattered mud. The Tablet went flying from her hand to scatter beneath the blackberries on the water's edge. The night sparkled. Her vision was twice as clear as the Deadglass now. Currents of Aether eddied over the field and flowed across the sky. She was weightless. She could join that sparkling water and be carried to the stars and through the Gate. Peace. Freedom. New adventures. Who knew what secrets the land beyond hid? Aether twirled around her spirit, soft as moonbeams and starlight, nudging her to release her feet from the ground and take flight.

"No. Grace! Please don't leave me. You are my everything. Please, Ishtar! Gods!"

She paused, one foot in the air, at the grief in the familiar deep voice. Leif cradled her bruised and broken body in one arm as he tried to feed blood into her mouth from a gash in his wrist.

"Don't you leave me, Grace! That's . . . that's an order." His voice cracked. "Please. Gods, take me with you."

Grace felt phantom tears on her phantom cheeks. He was so dear to her. Her heart shouldn't hurt this much; ghosts couldn't feel. But she felt like her heart was torn in two. *Go on and live*, she whispered to him. *I died for you.* She couldn't imagine a world without him in it. The Aether shimmered around her, calling her home through the Gate. She saw it sparkle out of the corner of her eye. It offered peace and safety after so much violence, a chance to leave her worldly cares behind, her aching body, her scarred soul. No more pain or suffering. Just peace. But she couldn't leave him here crying over her poor corpse.

"Gods damn me, Grace. Why would you give me this taste of heaven and then leave me in hell? I don't want to live without you. You are my light, my Grace." Hot tears blurred his green eyes. His hands pumped her still chest as if he could force her heart to beat again.

She drifted nearer and slid her phantom hand over his disheveled hair. Gods, she loved him. How could doing the right thing be so hard? Would the world always give her good things only to tear them away? She kissed his head and knelt to wrap her arms around him. The hair on his neck rose, but he couldn't feel her. Her arms slipped through his physical shape. *I love you*, she said. The Gate shimmered. Insistent. She felt its pull. One moment more, and then she would go.

"Don't leave me," he cried.

I want to stay.

"Take me with you. Please—"

Let me stay with him, please.

She closed her eyes against the hurt. The Aether nudged her, but she couldn't leave him in pain. She didn't want to leave him, not ever. If only she could bind her soul to his. *Take it, take all of me*, she said. *You have all my heart, my soul, now and forever. I love you.*

A bolt of light shot out of her ghostly chest. It arched straight through his, and shot down to her still body, connecting them. She felt when it took root. The light intensified. It burned to her fingertips, and she felt herself being sucked forward, pulled by that brilliant light back into her body, tie[d] with an unbreakable bond to the man next to her.

When she opened her eyes, the world spun around he[r] but all she saw were those beloved emerald eyes staring int[o] hers in wonder.

"Grace." He leaned in and kissed her. His hands checke[d] her body, smoothing every line. "Gods, Grace. You cam[e] back."

"I couldn't leave you," she said. She kissed him, touche[d] him, couldn't get enough feel of his body and mouth. "I'[ll] never leave you."

"I won't let you. I was so scared I'd lost you."

"I can feel you. Inside me, part of me."

"Always. You have always owned part of me. The bes[t] part."

"Kingu was sent back through the Gate, but I lost th[e] Heart."

"I don't care. I just want you." He paused a moment an[d] held up his hands. He turned them over as if seeing them fo[r] the first time. "Do I glow? I feel your light brilliant insid[e] me like a jack-o'-lantern. It's so warm. I thought my fire wa[s] hot, but—gods, Grace. You bound yourself to me. You kno[w] what this means. Are you sure?"

She grabbed his shirtfront and pulled him down. Sh[e] answered him with a forceful kiss. The living world was fu[ll] of uncertainty, but in this she had no doubts: Her heart be[-]longed to Leif and Leif alone until the end of time.

A roaring fire curled in his belly. For the first time i[n] Leif's long existence, the darkness held no sway. Grace['s] soul lit up every corner of his body with its brilliant divin[-]ity. Through the bond he could feel her heart beating in tim[e] with his own, and he knew that if one stopped, both woul[d]. They were bound together for eternity. She had chosen [t] bind herself again, to bind herself to *him*, and this time there would be no turning back.

"There is no blood debt to work off," he said. "No hope of freedom."

Her black jacket hung in shreds from her thin shoulders, the cotton saturated with blood. Mud caked her boots and hair. Dirt and more blood across her cheeks. But her eyes were clear. Her coral lips softened. He rocked her in one arm and ran his other hand over her body, assuring himself that she was whole.

"Loving you is freedom," she said. "I've given myself permission to have what I want, and I want you. I'm not afraid anymore."

"And how do you feel?"

"Glorious." She grabbed a handful of his hair and brought his mouth down to her. Her tongue tangled with his. Soft and wet and wanting. Finally he tasted heaven, and knew that as long as he lived, whatever his destiny held, he would never be cold again. Her soul banished the shadows inside him. Her love chased the pain from his heart.

Knowing the battle wasn't over yet, he broke the kiss. "Let's finish this."

The Kivati and the remaining Drekar had turned their attention to Ishtar's army, which still fought for meat on the hillside. The medic tent overflowed with injured humans. The towers of the Gas Works lay on their sides for some museum of history and industry to take an interest in. Forgotten, abandoned remnants of a civilized age.

Leif paid them no mind. Someday he would return to the lighting project, but he had a lot of rubbish removal to get through first. He helped run the wraiths from the field. Without their leader they deteriorated into selfish spirits again. Their organization dissolved.

Leif lost some of his fearlessness in battle. He had always been careful, but not afraid. Now he had a human soul, and the added burden that his death would put on Grace. Wherever one went, the other followed. The thought of eternity with her stretched out in a golden glowing path. He didn't fear the other side, as long as he had her.

But that didn't mean he wanted them to pass through the Gate together anytime soon.

"You're smothering me," Grace complained.

They would just have to work something out.

"And the Heart is for sure not inside you anymore? Not asleep."

"Look, I told you a hundred times already. She's gone."

"Good." He kissed her again with the Thunderbirds and Drekar looking on. "Three's a crowd."

"What about Zetian?"

"She'll be dealt with whenever she crawls out of the hole she's hiding in. Treason is the highest offense. She taught me that. We'll see how she likes some of her own punishments."

It took another hour to break up the surviving aptrgangr.

Crows descended on the battlefield. They used their talons and beaks to peck out the aptrgangr's eyes. Without sight, the aptrgangr lost their sense of direction, and they were herded into the pump house for safe removal. Many wraiths escaped. Grace found her powers diminished. It took more energy to banish the wraiths and draw Aether through the runes. She had to concentrate harder, but she could still do it. The Shadow Walker in her had had the power before Tiamat's Heart had possessed her. Her fingers slipped on the branding iron.

"Let me." Leif took it from her tired fingers and put it in his pocket. "That's enough for today."

"But the wraiths will escape—" she protested.

"They'll be back. We'll train civilians to do the banishments. It will take more than one reaper to tackle all the wraiths in Seattle even if that woman is a goddess."

"The Heart escaped."

"You are a goddess, Grace. Never forget that." He picked her up from the floor where she knelt and carried her in his arms outside. Torches lit the night sky. Men and women searched the battlefield for injured among the dead, ministering Drekar blood to those still living and collecting those already passed on for the funeral pyre. Flames from the bonfire on top of Kite Hill streaked the sky red and orange. The dead were laid to rest with a prayer to the Stone Giants to bring their souls safely across the Waters of Death, and to Ereshkigal, the Babylonian goddess of death, to welcome them home. Marks had resisted the Drekar blood. He presided over the funeral fire with his arm and head bandaged. He sat on a wooden stool from the medic tent and read passages from his snakeskin Bible. On the other side, Birgitta's witches sang of Valhalla and burned mistletoe.

He didn't care which deity they worshipped. In the end all souls passed beyond the Gate. Those wraiths that stayed would see their demise at the end of Grace's running iron. He would help her keep the city safe. Once the streets were free of aptrgangr, maybe her parents' ghosts could be laid to rest too.

Chapter 26

The new Drekar Hall rose up from the cliff edge like a bird of prey nesting on a rocky outcrop. The side facing Puget Sound was made of stone. The side facing east curled around a central courtyard where the Althing was in full swing around a large bonfire. A dragon-sized arch ran through the center of the building providing a peekaboo view of the Olympic Mountains in the distance. Below the arch, two jewel-encrusted thrones sat on a raised dais. Both were gilt over dragon bone. One had jeweled pommels with hidden swords. The other—a new artistic creation by the Drekar glass artist Brand—had iron spikes along the top and branding irons hidden in the armrests.

Dragons from all over had come to see the coronation. They lurked at the edges with their flocks in the center, each one craning his neck to see the human woman who had brought a dragon to his knees. The woman who, rumor had it, had broken his curse.

Leif watched from a window in the north tower. "I've never seen so many Drekar in one place."

"Gee, thanks." Grace ran her hands through her long blue-black hair. Her dress hugged her slim body like a sheet of liquid silver. Emerald-green jewels had been embroidered through the silk. They caught the light and sparkled like scales.

"I'm not trying to make you nervous."

"Who, me? I'm not scared of a few giant lizards. I know exactly how to make one fall." Her lips quirked up.

He turned from the window. Perhaps he didn't need to tell her that there were well over a hundred. In the months since defeating Kingu, he'd sent Drekar to scout over the Cascades and down into northern California. There were more surviving cities than he'd previously thought. Every Drekar had resisted his initial attempts to contact them. Not one had refused his invitation to see the woman who had given him a soul.

She was resplendent. The sheaf of silk accentuated her curves and pushed up her pale breasts. Two silver clips held her hair back from her face. They brought out her eyes. Fathomless eyes. Siren eyes that would sing a man to drown.

"I know that look," she said. A little frown marred her forehead. "You know I just got into this dress. We have to go down any minute."

He took a step toward her. He raised one eyebrow. "And you think they might leave if we keep them waiting?"

"Maybe." Her eyes darted to the bed, where her cat slept in the center of the maroon featherbed. The iron posts were thick enough to take even a supernatural beating. They held firm and solid as if they grew from the roots of the earth. They wouldn't break.

He'd tried.

His fingers removed his cuff links. He dropped them on the thick green carpet. The buttons of his shirt popped off one by one.

"Your steward is about to call us down," she said. She shifted her weight from foot to foot. The attention made her nervous. He knew exactly how to distract her. He knew precisely how to wind her up and calm her down.

He'd made an intensive study of it.

It was always a good idea to repeat an experiment. One never knew when the outcome might be different. If this time he put his fingers there, and his tongue over there . . .

She bit her lower lip. The silk of the dress left little to the imagination. He could see her thighs squeezing together and smell her feminine arousal growing in the small tower room. He let his own scent mingle with hers, not to trick her, not to bind her to his own desire, but simply because he couldn't help himself. Even soul bright, she brought out the truest part of him. He couldn't hide anything from her.

Her eyes slid down to the erection tenting the front of his trousers. Her lips parted. Her tongue snaked out to wet them.

"Ye gods, Grace." His voice rumbled in his throat. Pulling his shirt out of his pants, he tore it off. Her gaze stripped him like a sunburn. He wanted to bathe in it. "Let them wait. I think you've forgotten who I am. Let me remind you."

"The Regent—"

"That's right." He picked her up by her waist and threw her on the bed. She bounced. Her wicked smile urged him on. The cat complained and bolted. "Alone at last. I thought he'd never leave."

"He's only under the bed."

"As Regent, I order you to take off your dress." He watched as she slowly, too slowly, dragged the clinging silk up over her thighs. He thought his heart would stop when she paused, only for an instant, at the crux of her. "You are so beautiful. Go faster."

She moved slower. The silk protested as she slid it over her hips, tightening its hold to her luscious skin like a jealous lover. She wore no panties.

His cock hardened to stone.

"I order you to never wear panties again." He couldn't help himself. He followed her onto the bed, crouching over her with his knees between her thighs. As the silk left her breasts he replaced it with his tongue. She wore no bra either. Ishtar be praised. He licked the soft globes and drew a slow spiral around and up her peaked nipples. He pulled one into his mouth, sucking on the tip. She moaned. He replaced his mouth with his warm hand and moved to attend the other peak. "I order you to let me love you like this until you are old and grey and waiting for the Stone Giants to ferry you across the Aether into the otherworld."

A little laugh escaped her moan. "And then? What then will you order me to do? Arrogant man."

He brought the silk dress over her head and twisted it to trap her arms above her. "You have bound yourself to me for all eternity. Just like this." He kissed her mouth and let his body settle heavily over hers, sinking into her warm curves, letting his hands massage down her body to coax her thighs. "And then, when we have passed together through the Gate, some say the Aether will return us to our prime. I will start all over and love you like this again." He unbuckled his pants and released his cock. His thumb massaged her clit in small, soft circles, until he felt her body relax beneath him, and the tension begin to spiral from her core. "And again."

He thrust himself home. Wet and wanton, she called out his name. Her arms stretched against the confining silk. Better than handcuffs, stretchier, softer. Her soul shimmered inside him; he pulsed inside her, a circle unbroken, one body, one soul until the end of time.

"Again," she ordered.

He had no trouble succumbing to her demands. Kissing her mouth, he drove his tongue inside her to the rhythm of his cock. "I love you."

An hour later they finally descended to the anxious crowd. The new steward, a Dreki named Ragnar with a red beard, the stocky build of a frost giant, and glacier eyes,

announced them. "The Drekar Regent, Leif Asgard, wh
holds the throne until our Mother Tiamat awakes."

"May she never do so," Grace added under her breath.

The assembly rose and stomped their feet. "And my lady
the Queen Consort, Grace the god-killer." The assembl
roared its approval.

Grace felt some of her apprehension slide away. She tilte
her chin up and strode down the aisle on Leif's arm. He
gown shimmered in the torchlights. God-killer. She like
that. A queen sounded soft and pampered, and she'd worrie
no one would take her seriously. It didn't have the sam
defy-me-and-die ring to it as Reaper.

But god-killer was definitely a step up.

She passed Birgitta. The woman wore a traditional blac
peasant dress with red trim, and a matching vest over a long
sleeved white blouse. Embroidery along the bodice an
silver clasps completed the costume. Her white hair curle
innocently about her face. She looked like she would be a
home folk dancing in Norway. No one would suspect th
woman could summon spirits or sold poison herbs in he
shop. Birgitta winked.

Grace nodded in return. There was something to be sai
for subterfuge. She could appreciate the joke misleadin
everyone else. But it was hard to stick to the shadows whe
she stood at the Regent's elbow, and so it was easier that the
knew she meant business from the start.

At the dais, Leif turned to face her. "Grace Mercer, kill
of gods and demons, I take you to be my right hand. Ma
you be my vengeance against my enemies and my heart t
guide my decisions. I take you to be my queen. May you b
fruitful as Freya, wise as Yggdrasil, and outlast all the go
at Ragnarök." He took an iron circlet from the iron thron
next to his. The spikes would make excellent needles again
aptrgangr. "May all bear witness to your vow. Do yo
accept?" His green eyes found hers. Even though she'd sai

it repeatedly, apparently the scientist was still worried this time would be different. She would just have to show him. The Valkyries were a shadow of her indomitable will.

"Yes."

Cheers rose from the humans in the Althing. The Drekar stamped their feet until the walls rang with thunder.

Leif placed the circlet on her head. It weighed less than she'd thought it would. She took her place by his side, and together they opened the feast.

The Tablet of Destiny lay within an inch of her hand. Zetian could sense it, even though her body wouldn't obey her commands. Even though the blood still boiled through her broken body, knitting, patching, melding split cells and cracked bones. Grace's knife was still lodged in her heart. The runes had slowed her healing. She should have been in full form long before this, but every time her magic blood tried to close the rent in her heart, it pulled back from the magic blade as if stung. Zetian was forced to hide beneath the water of Lake Union, sheltered by the blackberries, like the lowest newt. She just needed a little extra power. She couldn't reach the knife handle by herself to pull it out.

It began as a low beat. Da-dum. Da-dum. A slow funeral march on a drum. Or a heartbeat, deep in the earth.

The claws that had been severed regrew. The heartbeat quickened, calling to her. The nerves in her fingers attached. She moved her new hand.

Da-dum. Da-DUM.

Come to me.

Her eyelids peeled themselves apart, and the hazy world slowly focused. Mud and green water and blackberry thorns. And there at the edge of the water, a rock. A jade rock. Only inches from her outstretched fingers. She wriggled her arm. Pain shot through her. By Tiamat, it hurt. Her head whirled, her stomach revolted, but she managed to drag her hand through the red-splattered mud and close around the shard.

Immediately the pain stopped. The stone pulsed, as if it had its own heartbeat, and the pulse seized her wrist. Fire traveled down her arm. She couldn't let go; her fingers refused to hear her. The heat washed into her chest and up her neck to burn across her skull. The blade shot out of her back.

The heartbeat thundered in her head. Like a satellite moon pulled to a larger planet, her small, weak organ lost its rhythm and began to beat in time to the drowning drum of Tiamat's Heart.

With the Tablet of Destiny still in her hand, Zetian sunk beneath Lake Union. She let the current carry her out to sea. The salt water welcomed her home.

Tiamat awoke.

Look for the next thrilling book in Kira Brady's
Deadglass series, *Hearts of Chaos*,
coming in early 2014!

And keep reading for Alice and Brand's story,
Hearts of Fire, previously available
as an eBook-only novella!

In this prequel to the Deadglass series,
one woman's desire for a forbidden man
will spark a centuries-long supernatural conflict—
and a love nothing can destroy.

She's the heiress to Seattle's most powerful shifter clan. Her destiny is as controlled and certain as moonrise. However, from the moment Alice encounters the man known as Brand, she will defy all constraint and break every rule to make this dragon-shifter hers. Brand is determined to repay the clan leader he owes his life to. But one taste of Alice's exquisite spirit will make him question his loyalty—and plunge them both into the middle of a ruthless power play. Their only chance at freedom is a gamble that could risk the future of humans and shifters alike. . . .

Look for the next thrilling book in Kira Brady's Deadglass series, *Hearts of Chaos*
coming in early 2014!

And keep reading for Alice and Brand's story,
Hearts of Fire, previously available
as an eBook-only novella.

In this prequel to the Deadglass series,
one woman's desire for a forbidden man
will spark a paranormal struggle between two clans—
and a love nothing can destroy...

She is the heir to Seattle's most powerful shifter clan, her future as controlled and certain as mountains. However [illegible] the moment Alice encounters the man known as Brand, she will defy all convention and break every rule to make this dragon-shifter hers. Brand is determined to repay the clan leader who gave his life to [illegible], but one taste of Alice [illegible] will make him question his loyalty—and plunge them both into the middle of a ruthless power play. [illegible] chance at [illegible] is a [illegible] that could [illegible] the future of humans and shifters alike.

Chapter 1

Seattle, 1889

She didn't want to like him. The stranger was too pretty, for one. Too arrogant, for another, and the last thing she needed was another arrogant man trying to manage her life. Alice watched the cocky set of his shoulders as he directed men to unload his wagon in the middle of town. Looked like a lot of useless bags of sand. Didn't he know that no amount of sand could dry out these streets? He didn't get his own hands dirty, just waved them around like some bossy Easterner. She would have moved on past and laughed as the mud splattered his boots, but the sun chose that moment to break through the ever-present clouds and illuminate his hair in golds and ambers and strawberry wheat. *Lady be. What hair!* Everything about him was golden, like the sun had Changed to human man and come down to walk among them. He wore no hat. His hair curled free to the nape of his neck. He cast their surroundings in the dull, lifeless colors they truly were. Moss green. Brown. Grey sky and grey sea and grey distant mountains. Ye gods, he lit up her world like a thunderbolt.

Hair like that should be outlawed. It could cause a person to lose all sense and fall off her horse. No wonder he'd fled here to Seattle. He'd probably caused pandemonium back East.

There was nowhere farther west to go. Seattle had been awash with new arrivals hard on their luck: gunslingers, cowpokes, gambling men driven to make it on the new frontier. They were so much worn grist for the sawmills, shingle mills, and mud-soaked pile of logs they called a city. Alice didn't mind it, because it was her town and her land and she knew the deep places beneath her feet were more than a match for these money-mad humans with their saws and hammers and constant noise. Her people had been here since time began.

She could tell this stranger was no ordinary cowboy. He wasn't the first Norseman to arrive. There were half a dozen men like him: tall, blond, and arrogant as sin. Their hardness set them apart from the other Scandinavian immigrants; they seemed chiseled from the glacier's edge. As if Vikings had walked off the pages of her history book and onto the wet Seattle streets.

Next to her, her cousin Hattie fanned herself. "Another one. I should have bought more smelling salts."

"Look at the way he moves," Alice said.

"Uh-huh. All that coiled grace. They have to be shape-changers. There's no human that can walk like that."

His eyes were turned away—Alice couldn't tell the color—and she was glad for it. Already her skin felt tight. Her stiff corset was the only thing that propped her up. *Please, let his eyes be some muddy, forgettable shade!* But she could see from his golden glowing skin and his golden glowing hair and his arrogant stance that her poor heart would be jerked again when she caught sight of those windows into his soul.

"Alice! Watch yourself, child. You're daydreaming with your new gloves in the street, and we are late." Aunt Maddie clucked her tongue and bent to pick Alice's parcels out of the road. Nathaniel, their Thunderbird guard, scowled behind her. "What could be capturing that attention of yours?"

"That's the man I'm going to marry," she said.

"What?" Hattie said. "I saw him first."

"Who?" Aunt Maddie straightened and craned her neck to catch a glimpse. "Your father will be so pleased you're finally . . . that man? You can't be serious."

"That's the one."

"He's not one of us," Aunt Maddie snapped. Nathaniel growled in agreement.

Alice turned and gave her a sympathetic smile. Her aunt's black mourning gown shadowed what had once been a welcoming soul equal to her father's. After a loss, some folk closed up and hid away their hurt, like Aunt Maddie. Some folk went the opposite direction—drinking and dancing until their feet bled as if they could fill that empty spot with noise and laughter and constant motion. Her father was one of those. Maybe that's why he welcomed the new arrivals with open arms. After her mother died, he'd been more than ready to join the wider world and the stifling noise that came with it. The economic opportunities didn't hurt either.

"A wager we can't hope to lose, Ali girl," her father had said. "Can't fight the future. We gotta hit the ground running and play this game that we were meant to play. What hope does a human have against the intellect of the Raven?" And he'd ruffle her hair like she was eight again, not eighteen and a woman grown. Halian Corbette was all big plans and overflowing optimism.

Alice knew life was precious and short. She wasn't going to waste a gift from the Lady, even if it came wrapped in an unknown package. Especially if it came with a gorgeous, golden-glowing bow on top. "And so?" she asked Aunt Maddie. "He is my destiny." As the words left her lips, she felt their truth ring deep in her bones.

"What about Will?" Maddie asked.

"What about him?" Alice focused all her attention on the Aether—that sparkling river that surrounded all matter and wove the fabric of the universe—and managed to send a small ripple of energy toward the golden stranger. It snapped and crackled through the damp summer air until it sparked against his cheek.

His head jerked around, and he saw her. His eyes were the color of the winter sky at dawn. His cheekbones cut like arrows to frame those pale blue eyes. Ancient eyes. Eyes that had seen more of the world than she, miles and miles of suffering and blood. But the world-weariness dropped away as he focused on her.

Inside her half boots, her toes curled. A little flutter like a moth took wing in her belly. It climbed until it flittered at the curl of her lips, seeking the warm glow of him.

She let her smile convey hello.

Brand tried not to stare at the ebony-haired woman in the sky-blue dress who was most improperly staring at him. He was used to looks from women everywhere—what Drek wasn't?—but this one punched him in the gut. He felt suddenly sympathetic to women everywhere who became hysterical at the first sight of him or his kind. The Drekar were gorgeous. Stunning. Not an ugly one among them. But inside was something not human. Something dark and dangerous that liked pretty, shiny things.

This girl was certainly a pretty, shiny thing, sparkling in the freshness and newness of her soul. He felt old suddenly because he didn't want to be the one to dim that spark. But he was unable to keep away. The dragon coveted.

Her companions dragged her off, evidently knowing a bad thing when they saw one. That warrior with her wasn't human. Brand would bet his entire hoard on it, which meant the quartet probably belonged to the native supernatura population that lived here: the Kivati. Norgard had warned him to steer clear for the moment. This was a chance at a new life. Brand wouldn't let the chains of his past catch him.

The West was wild. It took a fearless heart to thrive on this lawless frontier. Perhaps here he'd find a woman who didn't mind the risk involved in being with one of his kind.

He watched the retreating back of the Kivati woman and felt a lick of hope that he hadn't let himself feel in a good, long while. Another supernatural race. She was used to magic, to scales and claws. His true form wouldn't be a surprise. She might not run screaming into the night.

Ye gods, but that was a dangerous thought.

He shook himself and ran his hand over the lump in his vest pocket, where the Deadglass lay quiet and still as ten tons of lead. It wouldn't be much use out here, not where so few people had passed through the Gate to the Otherworld. The ghosts would lie quiet in a place like this. Easy graves, not like the teeming, angry wraiths in the tenements he'd left behind. Not like the bitter souls of the old world where centuries of the dead had worn the paths through the Gate into deep grooves.

He would drop the Deadglass into the bottom of the Pacific, but Norgard had insisted he bring it. So here he was. Ready to plant his stake in the new city the Drekar Regent was building. Norgard had rescued him from a black funk, and Brand was grateful. He might still be back in Sweden mired in that despair, or worse. He already felt more hopeful, and for the first time in five years he was excited to start work on a new project. He envisioned a grand chandelier made of glass icicles and lit inside by those new electric lights. A work of contradiction and contrast: ice that didn't melt, fire that didn't burn. He could already see the glass inflating at the end of his blowpipe, feel it mold to his design.

It would be good to work again.

Seattle was his chance at a new life. No more hiding.

* * *

"Skål." Brand threw back the shot of aquavit and slammed his glass down on the bar.

Sven Norgard did the same. The glass cracked beneath the force of his palm. "Feels good, doesn't it?" He took a deep breath through his nose. "Smell the endless possibility."

Brand thought it smelled like freshly cut pine, sawdust, and new varnish of the House of Ishtar, but maybe that's what Norgard meant. A new business venture. A new model of the Temple of Ishtar. An untamed paradise where Drekar could fly free and unfettered over the wide blue oceans. They could hunt in the uncut primordial forests without fear of discovery, just like the dragons of old.

"Almost like when I was a lad," Norgard said, settling back against the bar. His glacial blue eyes and white-blond hair were stark against the black of his crisp suit. The suit might have marked him a rich businessman, but the gleam in those eyes was feral. The avarice of the dragon. The conquest of the Viking. "We plundered Britain to Russia. But the world has grown small. Land is the root of a dragon's wealth. Economics is only the natural progression. This is where we'll plant our flag and watch our empire grow. It's practically uninhabited at present."

"And the local supernatural population?" Brand asked. He thought of the young woman in the marketplace. Her eyes haunted him. An unusual tawny color, ringed with a slight purple. Unnatural, though it only added to her singular beauty. But it was the certainty in those eyes that had pierced him through his dark heart. She had something planned for him, and it made him sweat.

"An old and dying race. They won't be a problem."

"How so?"

"The Kivati aren't a militant society. They lack organization and a cohesive goal. The Raven who leads them welcomes death in through his front door, and I'd be remiss to turn down his hospitality."

Brand adjusted his seat on the bar stool. "Death?"

"Don't worry about it." Norgard clapped Brand on the back and turned to the auburn-haired woman behind the bar. "Nell, any news on our friend the Raven?"

The High Priestess of Ishtar set down another glass and poured them each a shot. Her wrists jingled with gold bracelets almost to her elbows. Her looks were striking, but it was the carnal knowledge in her mature gaze that drew men in. Her thirst for power made her and Norgard two birds of a feather. "He's been in here a time or two. Likes the cards. Likes the company. Those Maidens you sent are a bunch of erudites, Regent. Not sure how you sold the girls on this dusty outpost, but they do add a touch of high class."

"Same way I sold you, dear girl." Norgard lifted his glass and fixed his charming smile on her. "More will come. The Norse won't be able to resist this opportunity."

Rumor had it Nell had been a well-respected madam out East before Norgard tapped her to set up a new temple in the fledgling town. Drekar needed souls, and the Maidens of Ishtar had been their safe source since ancient Babylon. The sacred courtesans provided ready sustenance in a setting that didn't spark riots. To be sure, Drekar still hunted humans, but feeding and flying could land a man in a lot of boiling water.

Brand should know. He'd escaped from Stockholm with the mob at his door.

The House was fairly empty at this time of morning. Erik Thorsson, Norgard's right-hand man, lounged a ways down the bar. His savage regard made the Maidens nervous. Hell, he made Brand nervous with his barely leashed violence. If madness claimed all Drekar eventually, Thorsson was over the line and then some. Only Norgard could control him, and even then it was a near thing. On the far side of the

room a couple human gamblers—a wiry logger, a hard-wor
shingle worker, and a loud potbellied fellow who was eithe
drunk or stupid or both—played cards with a strawberry
blond Maiden. The Maiden seemed to be managing them al
adequately, but the loud fellow kept stroking his pistol
Brand kept an eye on him.

A younger girl in a blood-red corset and skirt tickled th
ivories of the grand piano. The tune was a romantic ode
A little sad, a little wistful. It spoke to the homesick hear
of him.

Brand wished she'd play something else.

"Will Corbette oppose statehood?" Nell asked about th
Kivati leader, Halian Corbette.

"Doesn't matter. The territorial government is poised t
do my bidding. It's only a matter of time, and the Rave
knows it."

"He's been instituting change himself. You could mak
him your ally."

"He won't sell me the land, but he'll learn." Norgar
turned to Brand. "Do you have it with you?"

Brand pulled the Deadglass from his vest pocket. He hes
itated only a breath before handing it over.

Norgard took the small brass spyglass and raised it t
his eye. "Fascinating."

Brand shrugged. He ran his finger through a drop o
aquavit and painted swirls on the bar. He had been just
fledgling when his father had designed the Deadglass.

"What does it do?" asked Nell.

"The spirit world is all around us," Norgard said, "but w
don't see it, because the mind distorts reality based on ou
prejudices and expectations. The Deadglass strips awa
those illusions to expose the truth."

"It's a looking glass to see the dead," Brand clarified. Hi
tone didn't betray the sharp pang beneath his breastbone, b
Norgard heard it anyway.

"Your father was a brilliant artist, but weak." Norgard adjusted the focal gears. "Most artists court madness, but to lose it over a woman is such a waste of the gift."

Brand let the barb glance off him. He'd had centuries to get over it. His father had designed the Deadglass to search for his mother's ghost. He'd faded from the living world as surely as she had, even if his body was still hale and hearty. He gave no thought to the child his lover had given him. If Brand were ever so lucky, he wouldn't squander his gift. Dragon offspring were rare.

Nell leaned on the bar. "Might be a waste, but hardly unusual." Her eyes rested heavily on the loud fellow, who became increasingly vulgar as his luck dwindled. "Women. Drink. Cards. Plenty of ways to lose your head."

"And I'm sure you take advantage of it," Norgard said. "As you should. But Brand's father was a particularly brilliant glass artist. Not just anyone could design an instrument like this." The loud fellow stood up suddenly, knocking over his chair. Norgard's brows furrowed. "Let's see if it works, shall we?" He pulled the silver pistol from his side and shot the man through the ear. Blood and brains sprayed the table. The man slumped to the floor. The Maiden across from him screamed, cutting off the music. Silence fell, heavy and brooding. Brand swallowed his shock.

"Please!" Nell said. "No violence on this consecrated ground."

Norgard waved her off. "So re-consecrate it. Send me the bill." He adjusted the gears on the Deadglass and studied the body. Blood continued to ooze from the body's head and puddle on the floor.

Brand looked away. His stomach twisted. He'd seen his share of violence, but Norgard's callousness unnerved him. He needed to remember this. It was easy to think of Norgard and feel that gratitude again. But Norgard had rescued him from Stockholm for his own ends. He didn't do anything for free.

"Interesting. The spirit is peeling itself from the body. It looks . . . confused," Norgard said. "Another drink?"

"Perhaps later." Brand needed to put some space between himself and the Drekar Regent. He didn't trust Norgard's methods. He didn't like being in the dark regarding his plans. But he owed Norgard a debt, and a debt he would pay.

"You can replicate this?" Norgard asked. He handed the Deadglass back to Brand.

"Keep it. I have my father's designs. I watched him make it."

"Good." Norgard pocketed the glass. "I trust you found your new workshop to be adequate?"

Brand nodded.

"You can start work immediately then."

"I'll need your measurements." Brand would make a Deadglass monocle for Norgard as he had been hired to do, and then he would set his skills to a better use. Fire could destroy, but it could also create. This was a new land, and he intended to make a fresh start. He didn't need the ghosts of the past chaining him down.

That night he dreamed of tawny, violet-ringed eyes. He didn't need to cast runes to determine the portent of those dreams. He wouldn't sit around letting Norgard determine his future. He would seek it out, starting with a raven-haired woman.

Alice made plans. She wasn't one to wait on her heels for destiny to come to her; it wasn't the Kivati way. She dropped hints to her father until he came up with the brilliant idea to throw a welcome ball. It would be his chance to show the newcomers that Seattle wasn't some backwater town, that they had their own elegance and style that could rival any ballroom in fashionable New York.

"Someday soon, Ali girl, Seattle will knock New York off the map," her father said. "Artists will flock here for music and industry and culture. Seattle will be the place to see and be seen." He craved respectability in the eyes of the rest of the world, for he knew how they were viewed: a frontier town with nothing to recommend it, except to the poor and industrious looking to build a new life. It had its own honor about it, she thought, but her father just wanted to hear the jingle of gold in his pockets and know who pulled the strings.

Preparations for a ball gave her plenty of excuses to visit the shops in town, and if the handsome stranger happened to haunt those same shops, so much the better. She and Hattie found him at Potter's General Store one afternoon. He'd ducked inside to shelter from the rain. He had elegant hands. Perfectly manicured without a scratch, though he wore no gloves. Unblemished, they would have marked him as a useless aristocrat. But he used those hands like an artist, running his fingertips over the curve of a glass goblet, feeling the grain of the wood counter, cupping an apple in his hands as if he could taste it through his skin.

She wondered what it would be like to have those hands on her.

He opened his eyes and found her watching him.

"Is it to your satisfaction?" she asked. Behind her, Hattie gave a little gasp.

He tossed the apple in the air and caught it. His blue eyes flickered down her body and back to her face. He brought the apple to his lips. "Ja," he said. His accent was Swedish. His voice a rich tenor. The sound struck a chord low in her belly. His white teeth flashed as he took a bite.

Mrs. Potter returned to the front of the shop with her bolt

of poplin. “Here we are, miss. Latest shipment in from New York. Will this be working for you?”

Alice reached out to touch the fabric. She hardly saw the amber roses festooned with small violet leaves, perfect to match her eyes. Excitement fluttered through her breast The air in the shop tingled with unspent energy. “Yes. This will work quite well.” She heard a crunch as he took another bite. She imagined the juice of the apple wetting his firm broad lips.

“It is a lovely color,” he told the shopkeeper, motioning to the fabric.

“Thank you kindly.” Mrs. Potter preened. “I am stocking the latest styles and patterns from New York, London, and Paris. Not last year’s fashions, mind you.”

“That fast? Incredible.”

Alice stifled a laugh. Seattle might be at the uncharted edge of the map, but the Kivati hadn’t been completely secluded away. Thunderbirds, with their great strength and massive wings, had always scouted politics and culture from other parts of the globe. Kivati informants were stationed in the great cities of the world, and crows brought back the news in a semi-regular fashion.

“We have our ways,” Mrs. Potter said.

“The mysteries of fashion,” he said easily. He set a penny on the counter to pay for the apple. “And ripe apples in June what a marvelous place this is. Good day, ladies.”

When the shop bell tingled behind him, Hattie grabbed her sleeve. “A jaguar. I’m sure of it. Look at that feline grace. And did you see his eyes? When he looked at you, his pupils slit like a cat.”

“Did they?” Alice feigned indifference, while inside whoop of joy fought to escape. A shape-shifter! “I don’t think jaguars are native to Scandinavia.”

“Fair point. Maybe a lynx.” Hattie nudged her in the ribs.

Alice grinned and paid for the fabric.

The stranger had a lazy way about him, like he had all the time in the world to walk down the street and meant to take his time doing it. With those rolling hips and muscled thighs, she could watch him all day. Strolling, exactly as Hattie said, like a big çat. But his eyes were cooler than a feline, and when he caught her looking, the dark hunger in his gaze sent some primitive part of her running for safety.

A cat she could handle. He was something else.

Chapter 2

"A ball. How quaint," Norgard drawled. In his left eye, he wore the Deadglass monocle Brand had finished that morning. With one eye a smattering of gears and glass, and the other a pitiless blue, he seemed more heartless machine than man.

Brand wouldn't disagree outwardly about the ball, but he found the unbridled enthusiasm of the locals refreshing. He'd left behind the fashionable ennui. The tired positioning. The sneer at anything that smacked of true interest or affection. This backwater town overflowed with promise, and the inhabitants knew it. No one was too proud to show it. Even the local elite, with a few exceptions, seemed welcoming and legitimately honest in their affection. He didn't understand Norgard's dislike, because it was more than a distain for the provincial. Norgard seemed eager, somehow, to hoodwink the Kivati into accepting their damned kind, and more eager to banish their open ideals and stick the sordid truth to them. To jade them. To tarnish that innocent regard and make them as black and rotted as he was.

An innocent was only a cynic waiting to be discovered.

Brand refused to let Norgard's attitude detract from his night. He would see her again. All week he'd loitered in town waiting for a glimpse of her. With luck, maybe he could steal a dance.

The Kivati's new wooden palace ruled a central spot on Front Street. The wide boardwalk saved a man's boots from the thick mud of the street. The sky was almost cloudless, for once, and his spirits lifted. Perhaps Freya, the Norse goddess of love, was indeed smiling on him, because the Kivati chief himself welcomed them to the party with his beautiful daughter at his side.

He barely heard Norgard's pleasantries, or Halian Corbette's response. She was a vision, plucked from the deepest recesses of his dreams. She stood tall and strong, with wide cheekbones, a proud nose, and a lush mouth perpetually curved in a secretive smile. Her jet-black hair curled artfully around her oval face. Her tawny eyes were ringed with the slight purple edge that marked a Kivati shape-shifter. He could fall into those eyes. There was a promise there. Delight and passion and a soul unwearied by the world. Unlike his comrades. Unlike the crowded society he'd left behind. Unlike his own.

"My daughter," the Kivati leader said. "Lady Alice."

Alice. The world held its breath on that one name. It whirred around his mind like a trapped hummingbird. Wanted out. Wanted to caress his lips, but the dragon swallowed her name down to hide it and keep it for his very own. He would jealously guard that treasure.

Now he knew how the poets felt. Felled by an arrow straight from Cupid's bow. Stars aligned for this moment. A lifetime of misadventure and broken roads all leading to this single spot, this introduction, this portent. A woman. He took her hand. Such a little thing. He'd done it countless times before. He had touched bosoms and naked flesh more scandalous than a simple gloved hand. But his heart had never beat so fast. His lungs had never felt so raw. Four fingers and a thumb in soft kidskin, light as a bird's wing, and he was quivering like a boy at his first sight of a turned ankle.

Damned though he was, Freya had sent him an angel.

The little curve of her mouth said he was wrong—there was more knowledge in those deep eyes than any innocent should have—but that didn't dissuade him that some greater power was at work. The dark, frozen place where his soul should have been was lit and toasty with one smile from her divine lips.

At his side, Norgard cleared his throat. "Forgive my bumbling companion, mademoiselle. Let me introduce Brand Haldor. He is but another poor soul caught in the web of your great beauty."

She pinked slightly across her wide cheekbones. But unlike most women, who melted at Norgard's seductive words, her eyes didn't even flicker to the Regent. She held the connection between her and Brand. An entire conversation was conveyed in that look. With only a hand's touch, he felt scorched. His skin prickled. He was rooted to the floor, petrified as the Deadglass.

"Haldor," Norgard said. Sharp. A command from his Regent.

Unwillingly, Brand forced his fingers to let go. Her hand fluttered down, only to be picked up again by Norgard, who oozed charming nonsense over it, followed by the heightened scent of iron and cinnamon. The Drekar's musk relaxed the body and stimulated the erogenous core. It seduced the nose while their pleasing appearance seduced the eye, all calculated to draw in their prey.

Lady Alice would not be Norgard's prey.

Brand heard a low rumble. He looked up to see the narrowed gaze of Lady Alice's father, and knew the man was looking back at Brand's own slitted pupils.

Norgard released Lady Alice's hand and shooed him along. "Don't be a fool," Norgard hissed when they'd moved out of earshot. "They don't know what we are yet. See to it that it stays that way."

"How long can you keep that cat in the bag?" Brand asked.

"Until I have collateral," Norgard snapped. "I'm not going anywhere. I have plans here."

The Kivati had good musicians. Brand had listened to many a ballroom orchestra, but this one played with the carefree exuberance that he'd noticed in all aspects of this strange frontier town. It was as if the train that brought him to Seattle had run clear over the desperation of the prairie and into the promised land of milk and honey. He watched Lady Alice open the ball with a lanky boy on the cusp of manhood. Her brother, Brand thought. The future ruler of the Kivati. The boy had sharp features and a large hawkish nose he would hopefully grow into. The shape of his eyes and his straight black hair he shared with Alice. But his scowl was so different from her open, pixie expression that Brand could almost think they were a separate species entirely.

Alice moved like the music inhabited her bones. Brand was unfamiliar with the dance. More rhythm, more seductive swaying of her hips than he'd ever seen in a proper ballroom. It was the drums, he thought, that called to the animal inside him. She danced like she felt it too: the beat of the drums and the tap of her feet and the pulse in her veins and the beating of the great heart deep within the earth. He wanted to dance with her. He'd never been much for the bowing and scraping of polite society, but here, now, there was nothing he'd like to do more than hold her hand again and sweep her about the room.

The Kivati leader seemed to have invited the entire territory. Some were human: strong, hardened industrialists, railroad and lumber barons, newspapermen and bankers. At least half were not; they moved with animal grace and had strangely colored pupils. Brand was surprised at how many there were. And Norgard thought to plant his stake among them? When they didn't know what he was? Brand had never spent much time with another supernatural culture. Drekar were solitary by nature. They hid away in the shadowed corners of the world.

Brand was tired of hiding who and what he was.

But would Lady Alice welcome the darkness if she knew?

Then she was in front of him and he forgot the old urge to run. She was all that mattered. She looked on him with wide, sparkling eyes and a welcoming smile. She had to know what he was. She was the same, wasn't she? And here was a place ruled by nonhumans where she belonged. He could belong too.

He realized she was waiting. He cleared his throat. "May I have the pleasure of this dance?" His voice was husky. She cast him such a brilliant smile he was sure the sun had risen again in the middle of the night, and he forgot his tongue entirely. Mutely, he accepted her hand. Her hand! Ye gods, the shock of sensation even through his gloves and her own. What would happen if he actually touched her naked skin? Surely he would ignite, burned clear through to ash, leaving nothing left of the dragon who had burned countless battlefields but never known fire's painful embrace. Not till now.

The music changed to a waltz. He wasn't sure whether to thank Freya or curse her for this opportunity to draw Alice close. To put his hand on her warm waist. He could imagine it all too clearly—beneath the silk of her pink gown to her stays and chemise and down to the heat of her feminine curves—and had to look away.

Think of something else, he ordered himself. The forge he'd finished just this morning. The sand waiting for him to craft into glass. The iron and ore that would shoot through his art in red and green.

The beheading Alice's father would surely plan for him if he caught wind of the base, prurient thoughts running through Brand's head like a steam train.

This waltz was not one he knew. The drums started in after the first stanza, and the beat took hold of his legs and his arms. Faster than any proper ballroom tune. Seductive. It would be scandalous to any London ballroom packed elbow to elbow with humans, but to his animal heart it was freeing. He felt the blood beat in his veins. Imagined his wings pulsing in the wind. Heard the rapid breathing of his prey racing across the forest floor. He knew his eyes had slit. Knew the dragon showed, old and capricious and more dangerous still. His human appearance cracked, and the old fear sparked in his belly. Who had seen? Who this time would hoist their pitchforks in the night?

But he looked down and saw Alice. It was like looking into a mirror. In the drums, she heard the beating of prey beneath the dark foliage too, and was excited by it. She whirled around the dance floor to that beat. Round and round. Sweat beading on the perfect curve of her milky breasts. A rapid flutter beneath the delicate skin of her throat. Those eyes to match his own. Inhuman. Excited. Purple-edged looked into catlike slits.

"Let's get some air," she yelled up to him over the cacophony of the ballroom. She pointed toward the double French doors. He twirled her through the crush and out into the cool gaze of the starry sky.

She broke away, laughing.

"Do you find me so humorous?" Him, bumbling through a simple thing like a dance, when he'd danced with far prettier women in far more elegant ballrooms. At the moment, he couldn't name a single one.

"You look so shocked. So surprised at our little party? What did you expect to find here at the edge of the map? A cold swamp and unclothed natives?"

"Well, there is a lot of mud."

"We winged folk are not bound by the months of har travel that usually inhibit trade and culture and thought."

It was the first time she had called out her Otherness He felt quicksand beneath his boots. Was it so simple tha they could be open here? It was more than he'd hoped whe he'd set out on Norgard's mad behest.

"Wings. I'm not surprised." He'd thought her an angel o first sight.

"Devil wings, more like," she said, laughing again.

"You see right through me." It was like she had her ver own Deadglass specially for him. A Brandglass. Strippin the falsehoods and shadows, the mask from his skin, t expose the truth of what lay beneath. The dead who walke among the living. The man who suddenly felt very muc alive.

The wide cedar porch opened onto a view of Puget Soun with a garden styled after the great houses of London. Bu unlike London, the lawn's manicure wouldn't hold. Plant dipped their roots into this fertile soil and became wil things, green and lush and overgrown. Roses grew lik weeds. Weeds, like some monstrous hydra.

He wrapped his hands around the balustrade to preve himself from reaching for her.

She turned her face to the night sky and twirled, he poplin skirts spinning out. Wisps of her hair had come dow One stuck to her neck. The dance had exerted her also. H could too easily imagine the sweat on her skin from an er tirely different activity. Her flushed cheeks. Her loose hai The laughing glint in her eye and the knowledge therei knowing that he had placed it there.

Swallowing hard, he counted the growth rings in th cedar planks beneath his feet. He had a sneaking suspicio that the outcome of that entanglement would put a great knowledge in his own eyes. What would it be like to samp her glowing soul? To take a part of her inside himself to warm his black heart? She would taste like a bit of starlight, he was sure. Heaven's fire.

Salvation.

Alice couldn't believe Brand Haldor was on the terrace with her. The dance still rang in her ears, and she twirled as much for her own benefit as for his. She could dance all night if he would only dance with her. She wanted to escape the press of bodies and fly away with him, to dance with wings beneath the grinning stars over the churning sea.

Hattie had been wrong. Brand moved with feral grace, but his other form wasn't feline. The drums had shown her. In the whirl and heat she had caught a sense of Aether about him. Wings, she was almost sure of it. The phantom wings stretched over his human form. Not feathers precisely. And the eyes slit in emotion. In anger they would be enough to knock the breath out of a man and make him roll over and pray for death. But there in the ballroom, with Brand's hands on her waist and his body a hairbreadth from her own, with the heat and the musk of him saturating her underclothes and shooting straight to the secret heart of her, his inhuman irises were slit in some other fierce emotion.

Their connection thrummed with the beat of the drum and the fast riff of the fiddle. She'd needed a moment to breathe out here on the porch, but even without that touch burning hot fire, she felt their connection like a living river of Aether.

She knew she was the subject of stares and speculation back in the ballroom. How could she not be after a dance like that? And now in the night with a strange and handsome man, she was practically asking for trouble. But the rest of her kind couldn't fail to see it, this thing between them, so fast and so strong it could only be a gift from the

Lady herself. Touched by Her hand, as some things were: a perfect sunrise, safe refuge in a storm, the first laugh of a new babe. She could not ignore this. They could not judge this. Her and him beneath the stars. She wanted to launch into the sweet night and soar with him. There had never been a man she'd wanted to dance with like this.

Her father should welcome it. Bonding two supernatural races together. An unbreakable joining. The future of their race.

Even her brother couldn't refute the political good of the thing. They might not know much about this strange Other kind, but surely they were in this together. Two races fighting for their place in a rapidly changing world. Joining forces would benefit them both.

And she couldn't ignore what was in her heart, even without the coldly rational arguments. The hot, fierce part of her, her totem Owl, saw what it wanted and wouldn't wait. This. Here. Now. Damn propriety. Damn them all.

She went to Brand and stood at the balustrade. Mirrored his stance, two hands tightly clutching the unpainted rail. She felt the energy vibrating in him. Saw the strain of his muscled forearms as he clung to the wood like a drowning man. The fast rise and fall of his chest. He seemed like a man on the edge of a great precipice.

She had too much of the Trickster in her not to push him over.

"Fancy a turn about the gardens?" she asked.

"You'd tempt a monk."

"If the monk were as pleasing to the eye as certain company, I might."

"Forward."

"Brazen."

He angled toward her like an iron to the lodestone. "I'd like that."

She offered her arm. It was supposed to be the other way

around. Descending the stairs, she wished she could kick off her slippers and feel the thick wet grass curling between her toes. But some propriety must be maintained in view of the full town. Other couples mingled amid the shrubbery. They rested aching feet on the benches and took respite in the cool salt air.

The noise of the ballroom continued behind them. She knew her father would be in the gaming hall already. He'd be none the wiser for her turn outside. Drink would flow. By the end of the night, his pockets might be lighter, but he'd have fleeced the strangers for their deepest secrets. He rode a fine line between welcoming the new and preserving the old. But he was an open, guileless man. He liked a good yarn and a good drink more than he valued the old traditions.

Brand had to shorten his pace a good deal to match hers. He brought them around a bed of roses—hothouse flowers carefully gathered as seeds from England and flown here as a courting gift from her father to her mother. There was symmetry in it—a new generation courting in the same spot. She thought her mother would have approved of Brand. He was built like a warrior. He held himself with honor.

"Lady Alice," he breathed.

"Mr. Haldor."

"Brand," he corrected. "If I'm to call you by your first name, you can certainly have mine."

"What brought you here?" She'd wondered this. He wasn't a timber or railroad man, but he seemed well off.

He shifted his stance. Studied a pink rosebud and touched the thorns along the stem. "Honestly? A woman."

"You came here for a woman?"

He smiled. "A certain brazen young thing with tawny eyes. That pattern suits you, by the way." She'd made the dress from the fabric she'd purchased at Potter's.

"Thank you."

"I left Stockholm because of a woman. She made it . . . uncomfortable for me to stay. And Norgard convinced me to come here. It was a good time to cut ties with the past, to find a new inspiration for my art. Perhaps the stars willed it."

"You're telling me destiny brought you here."

"Would you believe me?"

"I might."

"You might understand." The yearning in his eyes startled her. It mattered to him deeply. "I think we are alike in some ways. A woman back home discovered who I—what I am. Too many bleak years alone, and I'm afraid I grew careless. She rallied her kinsmen to relieve me of my burdensome immortality. I was . . . indifferent at the time."

"Immortality would be a very long time to be alone." She did understand. Kivati were not immortal, but they lived considerably longer than humankind. Even a lone wolf needed a place to belong.

"Yes." He drew her hand in his. Her breath raced like butterfly wings in her breast. "I'm a glassblower, same as my father and grandfather. Norgard convinced me to escape the old land and join him. He needed artists, he said, for his new town. He promised a veritable Eden, a place to fly free."

She squeezed his hand. If he needed Eden, she would happily play Eve. "And is it everything you hoped it would be?"

"It is now." A commotion from elsewhere in the garden stopped the next question on his lips. Unease spread, jumping like fire across the desert brush. It swept through the garden and into the ballroom. Anger sparked. Voices rose. Someone screamed and then the music stopped. The great swirl of the ball turned ugly, panicked, like a demon carousel. More noise and movement but of a fearful variety.

Someone came out of the doors and called her name. "Alice? Alice, come out!"

"What is it?" she asked. They walked quickly back to the

stairs. Her brother stood above them, worry on his face. For her? It turned angry when he saw her company.

"Get away from her," Emory hissed. His eyes flashed purple. The slightly awkward boyishness was only evident in his lanky build. In his face she suddenly saw the man he would become. Older. Harder. A weight of responsibility already on his thin shoulders. She'd never seen him like this. The Aether roiled around him. Crackled from his skin. His power was suddenly obvious, but untamed. He called it unthinkingly. It was too much. There were too many innocents around him who might get hurt.

And his anger was directed toward the man at her side. She stepped in front of Brand.

"Get back," Emory snapped. "His kind is not welcome here."

"But—"

"*Unktehila*." The word snapped in the air with its own power. The soul-eaters. The Kivati's greatest enemy. Dragons.

"No." She wouldn't believe it. But she couldn't help turning to the handsome stranger for confirmation, and the tight set of his jaw said too much. Suddenly the night turned red. The stars retreated. She spun the events backward in her head. Her first sight of him. His beauty. His grace. The way women everywhere stopped in their tracks at the sight of him and his kin. Her own immediate attraction to him. To his touch and smell. Luring her in like a black widow.

Her eyes stung. She bit her lip to keep from screaming.

"Alice, I—" Brand put out his hand, but she stepped away. The commotion in the ballroom made sense. Her ancestors had killed off the native dragon population, but now dragons had returned to the Pacific Northwest. She'd been right about the wings. A soft sob built in her throat. Wings! And she'd thought to fly with him, to show him her other self. To think she'd thought him honorable! Two of a kind, she'd thought. But she had two souls twining in her breast, and he had none.

Worse, his kind stole the souls of others.

"Is that what you meant to do to me?" she asked. "Take me in the garden and harvest my soul?" Her voice shook.

"Alice, come away from him!" Emory ordered.

"No! Answer me!" She pointed a defiant finger at the man—demon—who now stared at her. She would not see the heartsickness in his expression. She would not see the way he held himself so still as if the slightest breath could break him.

"Was it Adam who asked to walk in the garden?" Brand's hoarse voice sounded scraped from the very bottom of the sea.

Emory descended the stairs and gripped her arm. Electricity charged the air around him, almost as if he were Thunderbird and not Raven. He shocked her when he touched her. What about her brother's untamed power? What if his control snapped and he laid waste to the whole hall, innocents and all? Would he be a monster simply for a curse he'd been born to?

She searched Brand's face. Even now, unmasked, he didn't attack. He was right. He hadn't asked to tour the garden with her or leave the safety of the ballroom light. She in her recklessness had done it. Her thirst to know him as he truly was. Her temptation. She, Eve.

Another scream pierced the general cacophony of the hall. Emory's grip tightened.

"What's happening in there?" she demanded.

"One of Norgard's friends attacked Rowena."

Brand's jaw tightened.

"You aren't surprised," she accused. "Did you attack that woman in Stockholm? Did you deserve to be run out of town?"

"I swear by all I hold holy that I didn't—"

"Holy?" Emory spat. "You can't trust a word he says, Alice."

"We were lovers." Brand spoke right over her brother. "But one night, she snuck into my bedchamber unannounced and caught me returning from a flight in my dragon skin. Scared the bejesus out of us both. And, yes, I hold a few things holy." His eyes pierced hers. She could see the truth in them. She could see he still believed in their connection. "The gods might have damned me to a soulless eternity, but they can't take away my hope."

"Is that so?" Emory sneered. "Well, I swear by the ghosts of my ancestors who walk these shores I will hunt you and your kind to extinction, just as they once did." The Aether crackled with the force of his vow.

"Don't, Emory," she warned, but it was too late. Dark clouds drew across the sky, and thunder rumbled as if the Sky God had heard. "No bloodshed. No more violence."

Brand put out a hand. "We can work this out—"

"You attacked first!" Emory shouted.

More commotion from the hall behind her, and then her father was there, pulling her away. The Thunderbirds drove people out into the streets as the rain came. Hard rain. Angry rain. Turning the streets to rivers of mud. She didn't see Brand again. But his beautiful, treacherous face was etched permanently on the inside of her eyelids.

The Thunderbirds urged the poor horses through the sheets of water. By the Lady, what had she done? She was so confused.

She turned her face to the sky and let the rain wash away her shameful longing.

Chapter 3

"We exterminated them once," Will said. "We can do i
again."

A temporary lull in the battle had let each side retrea
and regroup. A representative from each Animal Tribe ha
arrived for the war council. The Deer and Wolves, unusu
ally in agreement, wanted to flee north into the wilderness
The Cougars urged caution, but their claws were sharp, an
they had been spoiling for a fight since Aunt Maddie's hus
band had been shot in his Cougar skin by human hunters
Whale was indifferent; his waters weren't affected. The Crow
were happy to follow the Raven's lead. The other birds perche
firmly in the Thunderbirds' camp. They wanted to strike har
and fast and rip the very memory of dragons from the face o
the world.

Halian paced around the council fire in the great room i
Kivati Hall. "And once this batch is gone, you think that'
hold them off forever?" Curious onlookers crowded in th
doorway, and he sought to look each one in the face. "Ho
much will it cost us? The blood of our warriors. The bloo
of our children—"

"Peace is not an option," said another Thunderbird. "W
must have security."

"There are dragons in every corner of this earth," Halian said. "Our ancestors took out the native population, but at what price?"

"They are soul stealers!" Will shouted. "An abomination."

Alice curled away from the revealing light of the fire. She pressed her back against the warmed cedar wall. Inside a war raged. Brand was a soul stealer, she repeated to herself. His beauty hid a savage truth. The connection she felt burning between them, the certainty that her destiny lay with him, was a lie.

She knew it with her head, but her heart wouldn't listen.

Her father paced to his seat and threw back another shot of whiskey. He wasn't cut out to be a wartime leader. He liked to make his audience laugh, to take the seriousness of the Thunderbirds and crack it into manageable pieces. Practical jokes, spontaneity, gaiety—these were the things he valued, even more since her mother died. But then he'd started drinking and those smiles turned chilly in the wee hours of the morning.

"When you find him, Ali girl," he'd told her one bleary dawn when she'd risen for a drink of water and found him still up and unusually alone, "hold on tight. Never waste a single moment." She'd been seven, but she'd been old enough to understand his meaning. She'd promised him that when love came for her, she wouldn't ever let go.

But if Halian Corbette had seen the future and watched his daughter fall for his sworn enemy—a deathless, damned, soul-eating monster—would he still have made her promise?

She couldn't bear to attach those hateful names to Brand. And she couldn't stop thinking about his beautiful hands, about the way he sensed the world with his fingertips, about their sensual dance and the way he moved, as if the music were in his blood. How could someone without a soul create? An artist used more than his own darkness to bring beauty and meaning to his work.

“We have a sacred pact to protect the Gate,” Will said roughly. She looked up to find him towering over her. He seemed to have drawn nearer despite himself, and now his defensive stance blocked her from the anger in the room. But she wasn’t his to protect. He didn’t look at her, but each word was an arrow shot straight into her pride and loyal heart. “The damned belong on the other side in the Land of the Dead. It is our sacred duty to send them there.”

“We approach the end of an era,” Halian said. “The old ways won’t work. We can’t keep them out. Not the humans, not the other supernatural races. We must work with them. We must adapt. Embrace change. Embrace new technologies, new people, new ideas. This is the future.”

“And let them prey on our people?” A thunderbolt buzzed between Will’s fingertips. “On humans, who we are sworn to protect?”

Zeke, the Wolf representative, dug his claws into the back of his chair. “Already we must travel far to hunt. We must move north, where there is still wilderness and freedom.”

“You can run,” Halian said coldly, “but you can protect the humans better from right here.”

Emory rose. He’d listened to the argument for the last hour without comment. “Forget the humans. Who is to say they won’t come directly for our people? What is a paltry human soul when they could have the twinned souls of a Kivati and totem?” His eyes flickered to Alice. She heard him loud and clear.

Aunt Maddie rose too. “The boy is right. What have humans ever done for us? It should be Kivati for the Kivati.” A chorus of cheers greeted her pronouncement.

“Aunt Maddie raises a good point,” Emory said. “The territorial government thinks we should be part of the United States, but maybe we should kick them all out. We should found our own government.”

"Sit down, boy," Halian growled. "You're not leading this wagon yet."

"Long live Cascadia!" someone called.

Her father's shoulders fell. He poured himself another drink.

Alice had never felt so lost. She wanted her father to win, to craft a clever solution for them all to live in peace. What good was the Raven if he couldn't find a trick out of this predicament? She didn't want to hide herself away from the world or lose her uncles and brother in war. She didn't want to find her land and her people under siege. But she could see Halian being swayed by the Thunderbirds.

Shadows flickered on the wall. She watched as they snaked and moved of their own accord. They formed pictures that clarified and faded from moment to moment. She saw the war party. Claws out. Paint on. Winged serpents and Thunderbirds grappled in the sky. Seattle burned. The firelight cast a reddish hue on the thick carpet where she sat. The blood of her people stained the sacred earth.

Foresight was the Spider's gift, but Alice had always had a touch of it. She'd known this when she first saw Brand and recognized him as her destiny. She also knew the future was not set in stone; it could be altered. Even the stone of the mountain changed year to year. Wind and rain chiseled it down. Hot magma from deep within the earth pushed it high again.

Will and Nathaniel turned the discussion from if the fight should occur to how the battle lines should be drawn up. She watched her father sit down and knew he was all out of tricks. If only her mother were still alive, she could give him the strength to stand up to them. Emory was useless; he was full of teenage rebellion and a hothead besides.

The peaceful path needed a champion, and Alice was the only one left.

She wouldn't let her chance at love slip quietly through

her fingers. She wouldn't let her people fall into the darkness
of hate and war. The Lady had blessed her with this gift, despite the dragons and Kivati's great enmity. Perhaps She'd
had a bigger plan in mind when She'd tied Alice's and
Brand's heartstrings together. No argument was strong
enough to overcome the past's hatred, but love was. Love was
strong enough to overcome the darkness in their hearts, bu
only if Alice was brave enough to act.

She needed to find Brand. Together they could mak
peace between their people. There was no time to lose.

Brand tucked his wings and dove into the freezing water
of Puget Sound. He was powerful, ancient, deadly. H
should be beyond caring. He cursed himself. Cursed th
gods. Cursed capricious fate. Of course she'd run. Of cours
she'd been horrified to find him a soulless monster. Hadn'
Norgard warned him to stay away? Brand had hoped that
fellow shape-shifter wouldn't be shocked at the truth of hin
but they shared nothing but the ability to Change. He wa
damned.

The truth had never cut so cruelly as the look she'd sho
him. The blood had drained from her face. The warmth i
her tawny eyes had frozen like the icy tundra of his birth.

Again and again he dove beneath the waves. He pushe
his muscles to the burning point. Beat his wings through th
thick ocean waves until he couldn't feel them. The sting c
salt in his eyes was only an annoyance, the cold on his scale
hardly of note compared to the howling darkness in hi
breast. Why had Norgard called him here? To start anothe
war? This was supposed to be a fresh beginning.

He soared back into the air and reveled in the freedom t
breathe. Clouds covered the moon. A light rain fell. Ther
was no bright city glow to reveal him. He was free to fly ove
the Sound, the Olympics, the wide Pacific Ocean. Free

put miles and miles between him and this godforsaken town. But he couldn't outrun the despair that clung to his hide.

Even after her rejection, he wanted her.

He opened his jaws and roared into the black night. Where were the Thunderbirds? Why didn't they come and rid him of this misery? He'd relish a fight. He wanted to be rid of this intense longing, this emptiness. *Cut off my head*, he'd tell them if they would only show up. That was the only way to keep his body from regenerating. Maybe then he'd find peace, because there was nothing for him in the afterlife. There was nothing in this body to go on into the world beyond. All this rage, all this frustration would cease with his last breath.

He finally understood his father's choice.

As he released that old knot of pain, some of his rage lessened. He wove through the heavy clouds toward Queen Anne Hill, where the Kivati lived. Why couldn't their two races live together? There was plenty of room for both of them. Norgard was strong enough to keep the Drekar in check. His economic interests would be hampered by a war. Brand doubted he had anything to gain by battling the Kivati. But what did he know? Norgard was a twisted devil, and he had a secretive project that involved ghosts. Why else did he need that Deadglass monocle?

Something small and white shot out of the darkness. Brand reared back, startled. Birds usually avoided the dragon. Everything avoided the dragon. But this small snowy owl flew straight at him. He'd expected Thunderbirds—great clawing beasts that could pull fire from the air to fight his fiery breath. Instead he got one small, crazy owl pelting like a cannonball at his head. Curious, he hovered in the air. The owl circled his long serpentine neck. Its soft feathers brushed his scales.

The owl sailed past his long snout, and he caught a glimpse of tawny eyes.

Alice.

He'd know those eyes anywhere.

Brand followed her. This must be a dream. His body must be in Norgard's opium tent and his head off in Valhalla, because there was a Valkyrie if he ever saw one. She was bravery and beauty all wrapped into one. He followed the Owl east. He'd never seen such a beautiful creature. Her white feathers sported little black dots. He'd expected more rejection. Violence, even. He'd wanted a last glimpse of her to covet deep in his black dragon heart. No gold or jewels could surpass those moments dancing in her arms.

And who was he to turn away from the gods' gifts? He certainly didn't deserve it, and he half expected a trap of some kind. What had changed her mind? What god could he thank for giving him a second chance to languish near her? He wouldn't let this go. Wouldn't let her go, because, Tiamat blind him, he was a damned creature and he wanted her for his very own.

He would be happy to follow her to the ends of the earth, but she led him a merry chase through the sky and across a great unbroken forest of evergreen trees. She hid among the clouds, sending his heart dropping to the distant ground, only to pop up again at his tail, hooting with laughter. He tried to match her speed and grace, but he was too large, too muscled to have the control of the much smaller bird. The Owl and the Dragon played in the sky. And it wasn't until she started to descend that he realized his body's fatigue. A lesser man might say nerves skittered through his gut at the thought of Turning again. What could he say to her? He couldn't defend his being. It had never been enough. Some women liked the power and riches that his kind possessed, but the woman who wanted forever in his arms also wanted to possess something that he lacked.

He was determined not to let his fear show. Let the battle rage behind them. Let others fight the territory wars. He craved peace. Stability. A strong woman in his arms. Was that too much to ask?

Alice swooped through the tree canopy and landed in a clearing next to a small waterfall. Light played across her feathers as she began to Change. A million sparkling stars coalesced across her Owl body, rippling like water over her head and down her tail, and when they faded a woman stood. She was naked. Her bare toes clung to the mossy carpet of the forest floor. The Aether bathed her limbs in a milky glow. Her long, shiny hair blew back in the wind generated by his beating wings. In the cold, her creamy breasts peaked, arrows pointed at his heart. A little smile played along the curve of her lips. If this were a dream, he wanted to never wake up.

"The ancient Vikings," she called up, her tone easy, conversational, as if she weren't standing naked in a clearing with a dragon hovering above her, "were said to take what they wanted. Berserker, I think they were called. Crazed warriors without inhibitions."

She called him out and pricked his pride. He let the fire rage through him to Turn him from monster to man. Turning and landing at the same time was awkward. He stumbled as he fell on the thick moss carpet with his slippery man-shaped feet. With no claws to catch him, he landed on his knees.

When he looked up, she stood mere inches from him, her breasts at the level of his mouth. He wanted to run his tongue down the curve of her stomach to that silky patch that hid her feminine power. He wanted to kneel like this on the forest floor between her legs and worship her body.

A dragon knelt for no man. But she was more. A maiden sacrifice given to his kind since the Dark Ages. A pure, vibrant soul that might appease the hunger of his dark, insatiable heart.

He unstuck his tongue from the roof of his mouth and

cleared his throat. “Do my inhibitions offend you, my lady' I'm trying to be a gentleman.”

“I want you to be as you are,” she whispered.

His laugh was dark. He stood. Her muscles tensed, bu she didn't back down. She turned that haughty nose up a him and stared him straight in the face. “What are we doin here?” he asked. “You fled from me before. What's changed?' Another thought occurred to him, and he raised his head searching the forest. “Or do your father and brother lie i wait for me?”

“And if they did?”

He looked back down into her beautiful, wise eyes. “Le them come. It was worth it to see you fly.”

“They don't know I'm here.”

He let that knowledge settle quiet and heavy in the dark ness of the forest. He circled her. His feet made no sound o the thick cushion of pine needles. “You hear that? Nothin moves. The animals have fled.”

“They scent you.”

“Yes. Does that frighten you?”

“I am Owl. I do not fear the silence or the dark.” Sh seemed so composed, but she was not unaffected. Her puls fluttered beneath the thin skin of her wrists. Her woman scent filled his nostrils. He knew his irises were slit, inhu man. Part of him wanted to shield them from her so tha she wouldn't see the monster within. But another part of hi was tired of running. He wanted to take her at her word.

She held her ground when he stepped to her, toe to to She barely came to his chin. She was young and slender a willow reed; he could break her in two with his bare hand But her soul fire burned within, hotter and brighter than th North Star. He bent down to taste it, and her lips opened welcome beneath his demanding mouth. The taste of pir and mountain wildflower assailed his tongue. He coul drown in that kiss. He angled her delicate chin up so that he could take the kiss deeper. A soft moan escaped her throat.

And suddenly it was too much. The darker part of him wanted to seize her mouth and breathe in her soul fire for his very own, but he didn't want to take her like that. She had put all her trust in him by leading him here alone and naked. He wanted to be worthy of that trust. This couldn't be just a lark by a brazen girl. He wanted—no, *needed*—it to mean more to her.

He dragged his mouth away. "I don't know what Norgard is planning."

"He doesn't matter." Her breath came hard and fast as if she'd just flown a mile. "I thought we could make our people see reason. We could force them to cooperate by our love—"

"Love?"

"Does that shock you?"

"What is love?" He raked a hand through his hair. "Many women have spoken of love—no, hear me out. It's my face, my smell, my body. All Drekar have it. They love this human shape. But not me." He laid a hand on his chest. "Those protestations of love always shatter like thin glass in the forge."

"But I've flown with you, Brand. I've seen the dragon, and I'm still here. How many have done that?"

"None."

She smiled. "And still I speak of love."

"Yes. You would join with your enemy simply to avoid war?"

Her laughter rang in the stillness of the forest. "I'm much too selfish. The thought crossed my mind, but this is my life. I won't settle for that. This isn't for them anymore. I want you for myself." She speared him with her tawny eyes, and he felt his feet take root. He couldn't move from this ground if his life depended on it. He was like the great tree Yggdrasil, and she was the center of his world. "Do you, Brand Haldor, take me as I am?" The question rang in the quiet forest. Only the rushing water down the falls marred the silence.

The solemn tone seemed natural to this moment. He straightened his shoulders and gave his words the full weight of his vow. A dragon could not lie. "I do." He was unfamiliar with Kivati ritual, but the words rolled off his tongue, almost as if he'd walked this moment in a previous life. "Do you, Alice of the Kivati, Owl Woman, daughter of the Raven, take me as I am?"

"I do." She seized his hands in that moment. A wave of sensation rolled up his skin from his fingertips to the nape of his neck. He pressed his lips to her welcoming mouth. Gods! He tasted sunlight and summer, and he wanted to curl round her bright burning soul and never leave. He wrapped his arms around her and hugged her body to his. Skin to skin, her soft curves to his hard planes. Deepening the kiss, he lost himself. Her tongue danced with his, just like their winged dance only moments ago. First a dance of courtship across the cloud-strewn night. Now a dance of mating beneath the pine boughs and hanging moss.

"Take me," she whispered. Her demand thrilled the dragon. She wasn't cowed by the beast. He would demand all from her. More than she could dream of. But he had the feeling she could sate his inhuman appetites. He'd come searching for freedom, and found it in a woman who would take every dark and twisted part of him. He kissed her again.

Sensation rocked Alice's heated body. The fine mist couldn't cool her down. His skin abraded her sensitive nipples. His manhood thrust against the curve of her stomach. She sensed the loneliness inside him like a rent in the universe. Blacker than black. A great sucking emptiness that demanded to be filled. For a moment she was afraid.

Brand broke the kiss, breathing hard. He ran his hands over her back, gentling her, soothing her. "I won't hurt you."

Her laugh hid her nerves. "Do your worst. I am more than a match for you. The blood of the Great Goddess runs in my veins. I am more than a woman; I am Kivati. Two souls beat in my breast. The elements are my handmaidens." She summoned the Aether to her and sent it whipping through the clearing to knock needles off the trees. The earth at her toes and the wind at her back lent their strength. The ancient trees and great Sky God watched over her. The spirits of her ancestors walked these shores and sent their love through the Aether. No soulless dragon could take all of her. Her love went on and on, eternal and everlasting, stronger than the blackness inside of him aching to be filled.

"Alice," he murmured against her lips. "I don't deserve you."

"I know." She tried to communicate that love in a way he would understand in the deep primitive part of him. She relaxed into his hold, let his large masterful hands learn her shape. She'd seen him explore the world with his fingertips, and now he used them to explore every inch of her body: the hollow in her throat, the delicate ridges of her spine, the curve of her waist, the dimples low in her back.

He caressed her bottom and molded her to fit the shape of his desire. He pulled her up and against his shaft to let it tease the hot, wet pulse of her. Her feet no longer touched the mossy ground. Her legs wrapped around his body, and his thick muscled thighs supported both of them. His breathing, like her own, came heavy. He dropped to his knees with her still wrapped around him.

Lady be—she couldn't get enough of his taste and touch. Sensations washed over her. Skin to hot skin. The taste of cinnamon and smell of heated iron in the forge. The musk of

an aroused male. She planted kisses along his sculpted jaw
then moaned when he dropped his head to suckle the deli
cate skin of her neck. Her pulse raced with the beating of th
great heart of the earth, and she felt that pulse center, wil
and wanton, in the slick throb of her womb. She needed hin
to fill that empty space, even as he needed her to fill hi
empty heart.

He pulled away and took a deep shuddering breath. "Afte
three hundred years, I am made new again. Forgive me—"

"There is nothing to forgive. Let yourself go."

"Alice. Love." His arms shook. He lifted her and pulle
her down, hard and fast, on his shaft. He pierced her cente
and she almost thought she'd split in two like an oak tree h
by lightning. She kissed him to chase the brief pain away. "I
it too much?" he asked. He kissed a tear from the crease c
her eye.

"Too much." His artist hands kneaded her tense shou
ders. They worked their magic down her back, coaxing he
body to accept him. Her inner muscles relaxed. Her inside
turned to liquid need. The urge to move gripped her. Sh
pushed his shoulders trying to angle herself higher. "N
more. Lady be, can't you move faster?"

"Yes, ma'am." Laughing, he rolled them to the ground s
that she straddled him. Her knees sank into the soft moss. H
twined their fingers together, giving her support, and showe
her how to ride him. She was struck by his generosity. He
he was, an ancient, deadly being, and he gave all his pow
to her in an instant. No man had ever valued her so high
She had always been the Raven's daughter. She had alway
had to fight to be recognized on her own merit.

Brand saw her and only her. He didn't care who her fath
was, or if a Thunderbird might be competition.

"Come back to me, love." Brand ran a hand over h
cheek and drew her gaze back to his. "There now. A ma

likes to know his woman's dreaming about him at a time like this."

She raised herself slowly and settled again hard. The movement shook the laughter from his face. His lips parted.

"Better?" she asked.

"Do that again."

She did, and was rewarded with his moan. Again. And again. Until her womb quivered. Her legs barely held her up. Her limbs had turned to pudding, while his body was taut as a bowstring beneath her.

Bending, she licked the place where his neck met his shoulders. His eyes rolled in his head. "I love that I can do that to you," she said.

"You can do anything you like to me. I'm molten glass beneath your hands."

"Molten? You feel pretty hard to me."

His chuckle reverberated down to her thighs. "You haven't seen anything yet—"

"Show me." She licked the crease of his lips. "I want to fly higher."

With a groan, he rolled them again, and she found herself flat on her back, legs in the air, with two hundred pounds of well-muscled man over her. "*Min lilla gull bit*," he growled low. His powerful arms bracketed her head. His body shook from holding himself back. "You only had to ask."

The Animal in her loved this primitive display of possession. He was aggressive male, claiming his stake inside the warm heat of her body. He drove into her again and again, building the glowing embers to leaping flames. Frissons of energy snaked up her body and out to her fingertips. A wave of sensation engulfed her, and she cried out his name.

* * *

Brand watched Alice shatter as the orgasm rocked her. When she opened her eyes again, they were filled with wonder. It spooked him that a sensual act would put an innocence into her gaze, when it should have taken it out. But then a slow smile swept her, and the curl of her lip and twinkle in her eye spoke of a feminine power that he could never master. She was a goddess come down to earth. What hope did his immortal, black heart have to hold out against such power?

So he kissed her with everything in him. He tasted her lips and danced with her tongue and gave himself over to her wise, wise keeping. All the while he kept up the rhythm of their bodies together. The drums from their waltz echoed in his mind. Her soul burned like a bonfire, and he drove toward its welcoming warmth. He wanted a piece of it. Wanted one taste of heaven.

"You're holding yourself back," she murmured beneath his lips. "Be mine tonight. Let me see you, love. All of you, not just this man-shaped half."

"I don't want to hurt you—"

"You can't. I give myself to you freely. Take it. Take me."

The darkness in his breast roared. The dragon reached for her shimmering soul, brighter than gold, brighter than star fire. He felt her tighten beneath him again, and this time he seized her lips. As she trembled, a wave of energy rolled up her body. It reached his mouth and he welcomed it, a dazzling burst of light on his tongue. Her life energy connected them and rolled through his body with the roar of a tidal wave. For one brief, glorious moment, his inner darkness lit with the glow of a thousand suns.

He let himself go, and his orgasm ripped through him. His mind flashed white. And he knew peace.

* * *

Alice lay in the clearing across her lover's chest, sated and languid like a cat in cream. His beautiful hands brushed up and down her back. He paused to trace the designs that swirled up her spine.

"A tattoo?" His voice rumbled beneath her ear.

"Owl feathers. To always remind me of my totem half, even in this human skin."

"I like it."

"Thank you. The ink was applied during my totem ceremony, when I became an adult in the eyes of my people."

"Were you always able to Change into an Owl?"

"No. Not until I was thirteen. The Lady gifts us our totem Animal when we become adults."

"Any Animal? Or is it dependent on your parents?"

"Any Animal as She wills it. But She often wills it to be similar to our parents. My brother is Raven, like my father. My mother was Owl. Could you always shift to dragon?"

"Yes."

She ran her fingers over the pulse in his neck, reminding him that she was here to stay. "And?"

"I could shift in the womb. I've never spoken of it so freely before—"

"You can always speak freely with me."

He ran his clever hands down her spine to cup her bottom again. "It seems too good to be true."

"Is that so?" She raised herself on her arms over him. Her nipples peaked, and she brushed them across his chest on her way to his mouth. "I see I might have to remind you."

He swallowed as her breasts traced the edge of his lips. She straddled him. His hands clasped her thighs and moved higher. "Yes, ma'am."

Chapter 4

An hour later, still short of dawn, Alice led the way out o the tree canopy with her dragon at her tail to find a smoke filled horizon. What had happened? With a burst of speed she raced toward town. Every mile seemed like ten. Close in, she caught sight of the flames that painted the clouds dull red. Seattle burned.

Her heart dropped into her stomach. What about thei homes? Their livelihoods? The bustling city that her fathe had dreamed of?

She clawed through the choking smoke and landed in th middle of Front Street. Not caring who saw, she Changec while the wooden buildings burned around her. Men rushe to save what goods they could. Fire hoses lay abandoned i the road. The water pressure wasn't strong enough to figh the blaze. The wooden pipes burned right along with th buildings.

"By the Lady," she whispered.

Brand had Changed too, and he wrapped his arms aroun her. "I'm sorry," he said. He kissed her hair. "What can I do?

"Who caused this?" But there were scorch marks th looked suspiciously like thunderbolts on the nearby groun Deep clawed grooves raked the mud.

An earsplitting roar sounded above, and they looked up to see two Thunderbirds chasing a dragon through the smoky sky. Wide-eyed humans rushed past. Shock and disbelief warred in their faces.

"Seize him!"

Alice heard her brother's voice and spun to shield Brand. A second later a thunderbolt tore through the air. With a wild push, she threw what Aether she could influence against the force coming at them. The thunderbolt jarred a hair, smashing with a rumble and a shower of sparks into the building behind them. The wood groaned and collapsed beneath the hungry flames.

"Frost blight you!" she shouted. "What have you done? What madness is this? The town is lost!"

"Get your filthy claws off my sister," Emory ordered. She'd never heard such ice in his voice. Static zinged through the air with the force of his anger. A Thunderbird stood behind him, as if Emory were in charge. Both were covered in soot and sweat. "Come out and fight like a man."

"Stay out of this, Emory." She wrapped her arms around Brand. "You can't hurt him. He's kin now—"

"The hell he is," Emory swore.

"I won't fight you, brother." Brand held out a hand in peace.

"Just because you've turned Alice into a whore doesn't make you blood."

"Watch your tongue," Brand snapped.

"What's this about?" she asked. "What are you doing here?"

"You tell me," Emory said. "Father's men were attacked. They went to meet with the *Unktehila* and were ambushed."

"No." She didn't want to believe it. She pulled away from Brand to search his face. "Did you know?"

He shook his head. Lines of strain bracketed his mouth. "I swear I didn't—"

"Shut up!" Emory yelled. "There was no negotiation. No treaties. Nathaniel escaped to warn us, and we found you gone, Alice. And now you show up with the enemy. Ruining yourself with that soulless demon-kind. How could you?"

"I love him."

Emory's mouth curled in a sneer. Behind him, Nathaniel made a choking noise. Another Thunderbird screeched through the sky and fell, injured, into the street. He Changed and pulled himself to his feet. She recognized Will, bloody and limping.

She planted her feet, side by side with her lover, and raised her chin. "Where is Father now? What does Norgard want?"

"I don't know," Emory said.

"What are we going to do?"

Will limped closer. "Your father is dead."

"No. No, he can't be."

"He is. The Raven Lord is dead." Will raised his hand and pointed at Brand. "And now I'm going to do what we should have done from the first: exterminate every last one of these damned lizards." A thunderbolt coalesced between his fingers, and he hurled the bolt at Brand.

Alice screamed. She dove in front of Brand, but it was too late. The thunderbolt hit him in the chest. It burned a hole straight through him. Blue lightning flared out over his frozen limbs, and his beautiful golden hair shot out. He was like a terrible, fiery angel, lit from behind by the burning town, lit from within by white hot sparks. His eyes rolled into his head, and he collapsed into the dirt.

Fire burned the back of her eyelids. Her throat felt scorched. She found herself in the dirt by his side, screaming his name, running her hands over his still-warm flesh, willing the Aether to return to his unmoving chest and pump his silent heart. But her gift wasn't strong enough. No Kivati could bring back the dead. "Heal him!" she screamed at Emory. "Lady, please! Heal him!"

Emory's voice shook. "I can't, Ali. I don't know how."

"You ask the forbidden," Nathaniel said.

"I don't bloody care! Do something. Please! Oh, gods!" Her skin overheated from the burning buildings, but inside pain lanced ice shards through her soul. She wanted to go with him, wherever his kind journeyed after the long goodbye. She didn't believe he could simply cease to exist; the Lady wouldn't be so cruel. If he had no soul, she would give him one of hers. She would give him the very thing that made her Kivati: her totem, her sacred half. He could fly on Owl's wings to the great beyond and keep watch with the spirits of her ancestors until she joined him again.

There, where there was no misery, no bloodshed, no war, they would finally be free to love.

"Alice, come away from him." Will tried to pull her up.

"Get off of me!" She sent her anger through the Aether to shove him. "How could you?"

"He is an abomination—"

"I love him! There is nothing wrong with our love. You are the damned one, if even love cannot move you!"

"You're talking nonsense, Alice," Emory said. "Let's get you away from this heat—"

"No! How many must die before you are satisfied? Hattie? Will? Me? Will you throw open the Gate? Let the rivers run red with the blood of our people? What cost is your hatred?"

They had no response.

There, beneath her fingers, the hole in Brand's chest seemed to shrink. His strange blue-black blood oozed over the ragged edges of the hole, and when she wiped it away she found unbroken skin. Sweat glistened on his sculpted chest. Beads formed and slid down his front. Movement.

She felt movement. His chest shivered. It rose and fell growing stronger. Breath returned to his lungs.

"Blessed Lady," she whispered. His eyelids fluttered. She gripped his hand and held on tight. He squeezed her fingers. A moan escaped from his lips. "Brand? Love? Can you hear me?" His eardrums would have burst from the thunderbolt but if a hole in his chest could knit, then his healing was surely capable of more magic.

"Alice?" His lips barely moved. His voice was a whisper.

"I'm here."

"Don't leave me."

"Never." She swore it with the full force of her gift. The Aether reverberated with her oath. His eyes opened, and she stared into his beloved blue gaze.

The edge of his mouth quirked. "Never is a long time."

"An eternity won't be enough."

"Alice, move aside!" Will ordered. But some of the angel had left him.

She ignored him. Ignored the burning town, so many dreams floating away into the smoky night. Ignored the Thunderbirds and humans and dragons alike who fought the flames and each other. She helped Brand stand, and even though he quickly regained his strength, she kept her arm firmly wrapped around his waist.

Emory watched her with arms crossed. "I won't lose my sister to those monsters—"

"Your hatred did that. Come on, Brand. Let's leave this place."

"Stop, Ali." Emory raised his chin. "I order you to—"

"Order me? Order me? Is it such a cold day in hell?"

"Father is dead, so—"

She closed her eyes against the sharp pang. "If Father is dead, there is nothing left for me here."

Will stepped forward, one hand out. "Wait, Alice. You don't know what you're saying."

"The woman knows her own mind." Brand bent his head to hers. He kissed her, strong and full and brimming with life. "Lady Alice, the only way to kill me is to slice out my heart. I've never felt so vulnerable with my heart flying around outside of my body."

"I'll keep it safe," she whispered. "But only if you'll do the same."

"Forever," he said.

"And always."

Epilogue

Alice and Brand left Seattle and never looked back. They settled in the north, where they were free to hunt through the uncut wild forests and fly. They left a town burnt clear to the ground. Upon that foundation of ash and hatred, a new city was born. The inhabitants razed the streets and built over the bones of the past. Sven Norgard took his Deadglass and founded his city of Ballard a few leagues to the north the next year. Halian Corbette's dreams died alongside him in the battle. The Kivati scattered to the four winds. Halian's son, Emory, wrested control of what was left and, swearing to wipe the Drekar from the face of the earth, continued to fight. With an iron claw, he rebuilt the Kivati into a severe warrior caste. The war moved to the shadows, where it was hidden from the humans.

Over a century later, the blood of both sides soaked the cursed earth. The Gate between the worlds buckled beneath the onslaught of ghosts, setting the stage for a final betrayal. It will take two stubborn hearts to save this city of darkness.